"I am not pret⋯⋯⋯⋯⋯⋯⋯⋯⋯⋯⋯uth is too large! I'⋯⋯⋯⋯⋯⋯⋯⋯⋯⋯soft curves like mos⋯⋯⋯⋯⋯⋯⋯⋯⋯ice, Angela turned o⋯⋯⋯⋯⋯⋯⋯⋯⋯fire.

Suddenly she⋯⋯⋯⋯⋯⋯⋯⋯⋯pper arms as he spu⋯⋯⋯⋯⋯⋯⋯⋯get hair-brained notions like those? Your face is lovely. And too tall?" He shook his head and trailed his fingertips sensually along the line of her jaw. "Not for me. I want my woman to fit into my arms exactly like this." He gently drew her to him, circling his arms around her slender body. "No soft curves?" He ran his hands over the slight swell of her hips. "Some women don't develop too many of them until they've known the love of a man . . ."

He could see a pulse beat a sensual rhythm in the hollow of her throat as he lowered his lips to hers. "Your lips? I agree, they're just a little wide," he murmured, "but I've always heard that makes them perfect for kissing."

Angela closed her eyes as his mouth touched hers in a gentle caress. A tantalizing brush of lips. An exchange of breath. Again, and again. Then he pressed his mouth over hers, and stayed.

FEEL THE FIRE IN CAROL FINCH'S ROMANCES!

BELOVED BETRAYAL   (2346, $3.95)
Sabrina Spencer donned a gray wig and veiled hat before blackmailing rugged Ridge Tanner into guiding her to Fort Canby. But the costume soon became her prison—the beauty had fallen head over heels in love!

LOVE'S HIDDEN TREASURE   (2980, $4.50)
Shandra d'Evereux felt her heart throb beneath the stolen map she'd hidden in her bodice when Nolan Elliot swept her out onto the veranda. It was hard to concentrate on her mission with that wily rogue around!

MONTANA MOONFIRE   (3263, $4.95)
Just as debutante Victoria Flemming-Cassidy was about to marry an oh-so-suitable mate, the towering preacher, Dru Sullivan flung her over his shoulder and headed West! Suddenly, Tori realized she had been given the best present for a bride: a night of passion with a real man!

THUNDER'S TENDER TOUCH   (2809, $4.50)
Refined Piper Malone needed bounty-hunter, Vince Logan to recover her swindled inheritance. She thought she could coolly dismiss him after he did the job, but she never counted on the hot flood of desire she felt whenever he was near!

COLORADO ANGEL

JEAN HAUGHT

ZEBRA BOOKS
KENSINGTON PUBLISHING CORP.

ZEBRA BOOKS are published by

Kensington Publishing Corp.
475 Park Avenue South
New York, NY 10016

Zebra, the Z logo Reg. U.S. Pat. & TM Off. The Lovegram
logo are trademarks of Kensington Publishing Corp.

First Printing: December, 1993

Printed in the United States of America

To my very dear friend, Rosalyn Alsobrook. If everyone had a friend like her, this world would be a better place.

To Ann LaFarge and Ruth Cohen. My forever gratitude for their eternal patience.

Chapter One

Even in her sleep Angela Langford could not escape the horror.

"Why did you lie to me, Aunt Julia?" Angela asked, her voice choked with anguish. It was inconceivable that the woman who had raised her would do such a thing to her, yet the letter she clutched was proof of Julia's heartless deception. *"Why did you tell me my father was dead? All these years you have lied to me! Why did you do it? Why?"*

Julia's face twisted with anger. *"Do not use that tone of voice with me, young lady!"*

"My tone of voice?" said Angela incredulously. *"How dare you complain about my tone of voice when you've betrayed me and my father!"*

"Betrayed? You do not know the meaning of that word!" Julia drew back her hand and gave Angela a vicious slap. The sound echoed through the room. Then Julia drew herself up to her full height and spoke in a cold, caustic voice. *"Get out of my house. I never want to see you again! Do you hear? Never again!"*

* * *

"Ma'am, ma'am, wake up," the man said, shaking the young woman's shoulder.

Angela awoke with a start, her dark hair drenched with perspiration. She shuddered at the dreadful memories the nightmare had evoked.

Staring hard at her pale, drawn face, the man scratched his balding head, looking doubtful. "Are you all right?" The way she had been moaning and carrying on, he wasn't sure.

Angela glanced about the room, half expecting to see Julia towering over her. She breathed a sigh of relief when she realized she was inside the depot, and it was the ticket agent who stood over her. "No—yes, I am—fine." She placed her hand over her heart to try and slow its vigorous pounding. The nightmare had been so vivid, so real, she'd felt afraid that somehow she'd been whisked back in time to relive that terrible day again.

"Are you sure you're all right?"

"Yes, of—course I am." Angela's face flushed with embarrassment. She tried to smile, but it was a pitiful attempt. "I guess I was just having a dream. I'm sorry—I hope I didn't disturb you."

"Nope, not a bit. I was just afraid that you might fall out of the chair, that's all."

"I must have been too tired when I went to sleep." She straightened in the chair and worked the stiffness from her neck. Sleeping on a hard chair in a small railroad depot was far from comfortable.

The man nodded. "Waking you real sudden-like probably didn't help matters any. Seldom dream myself, but the wife does, 'specially after she gets upset about something. Like the time we were attacked by Injuns . . ." He grinned sheepishly and removed a pocket watch from his vest. "But you don't have time to

8

listen to my tales. The stagecoach leaves right at day-break, and that's less than an hour away. You're gonna have to hurry if you want to catch a bite of breakfast. Mother Bryan's Restaurant is right down the street. It's the best and cheapest place to eat around here. But like I said, you'd better hurry. It gets awfully crowded this time of the morning." He started to walk away, then he stopped, and turned back abruptly. "If you'd like, you are welcome to use the depot's comfort facilities to wash up."

By this time Angela had gathered her composure. She had wondered how or where she could wash, change her clothing, and make herself presentable for the remainder of the journey. She longed to soak her weary bones in a tub of steaming hot water for an hour or two. Never-theless, soap, water, and a clean dress should make her feel so much better.

She smiled gratefully. Her voice was laced with the slow, soft drawl of the south, "Why, thank you sir. I cer-tainly appreciate your kind offer and accept it gladly." She had always heard gallantry abounded in the west, but unfortunately, she had seen very little of it—until meeting this nice man. It assured her to know that com-mon courtesy had not been forgotten.

"Aww, that's all right, Ma'am. The *Denver and Rio Grande* is proud to be of service. We appreciate your business and hope you'll ride our trains again."

The ticket agent watched the young woman gather her belongings. Actually, the railroad offered no comfort facilities. This depot was the end of the line, and once passengers had left the train, they went on their way. The only "facilities" were in the room the employees used for their personal needs; passengers were not sup-posed to use it. But there was something about this young woman that made the man want to protect her. She behaved like a *lady* and he hadn't seen too many of them lately. If his wife had been able to have children, he'd like to think his daughter would behave so mannerly.

Then, remembering how she had counted and recounted her money when she purchased her stagecoach ticket—and how there had been only a few coins left—he shifted his weight and said, "You know, come to think of it, I probably didn't wake you in time to have breakfast before the stage pulls out. Tell you what, I just put on a pot of coffee to boil and since the wife packed me an extra ham sandwich, why don't you just join me for breakfast? I'd sure appreciate the company. I hate to eat alone."

Pride screamed for Angela to refuse his invitation, but the hollow, empty feeling in her stomach demanded she accept. Her voice trembled when she proudly lifted her chin and replied, "It will be my pleasure, sir."

With the coming of dawn, smoke, weighted down by the heavy frost that had fallen during the early morning, hovered over Silverlode City; a Colorado town that, like so many others, owed its existence to the discovery of silver.

This town, however, was three years old and it had progressed far beyond the mad scramble of men working at a frenzied pace in hopes of striking their bonanza. Stately hotels, mansions, and thriving businesses now lined the many streets. No more were the endless rows of dirty tents, shabby hovels, and lean-tos, except for a small settlement of ne'er-do-wells outside the town proper. Like so many others, Silverlode City was firmly entrenched in civilization—until the silver was exhausted and another strike was discovered elsewhere. Then it would probably be abandoned or left a mere shadow of its former self.

Angela shivered against the bite of winter as she left the Denver-Rio Grande depot. She paused momentarily and looked about for the stagecoach that would take her to her father. Her search for him had taken a long eight months and she thanked God it was now almost over.

The streets and wide planks of wood used for sidewalks were beginning to fill with merchants opening their shops and miners either coming from or going to work. Huge ore wagons dragged by, their drivers bundled up against the cold. Frosty puffs of air came from the draft horses' nostrils as they leaned against the harnesses, straining against their loads.

Spying the stagecoach hitched with a long team of horses, Angela switched her portmanteau from one hand to the other, and made her way down the boarded walk. Several men stood around the coach, but only two were hard at work. One stood on the ground, passing boxes and small parcels of freight up to the other man on top of the coach. When she failed to see her small trunk in either stack, Angela hurried toward the stage.

"Excuse me, sir," she said to the man she presumed to be the driver of the stagecoach. "When I arrived on the train last night, the man who works at the depot assured me—"

The man rolled his eyes in exasperation, shifted a wad of tobacco from one side of his jaw to the other. "He works for the railroad, not the stage line. What he says don't matter none to me. If you have a complaint, take it up with him."

Determined not to let the man's rudeness intimidate

her, she defiantly raised her chin and replied in a controlled voice, "Sir, I am inquiring about my luggage. When I purchased my ticket—"

"You bought your stage ticket at the railroad office?" he questioned doubtfully. He snapped his fingers. "Oh, yeah, now I recall the boss mentioning something about them agreeing to sell tickets for each other. If you ask me though, it's a pain in the . . ." Then glancing quickly at the young woman, he added meekly, "neck."

Angela paled at the driver's remark. For a moment she thought the man at the depot had taken advantage of her. Then, she was instantly ashamed for thinking that nice man would do such a thing. Being quick to jump to conclusions was a fault she owed to Julia, and it was a fault she hoped to lose before it became too deeply ingrained.

"Y-yes, I purchased my ticket after I left the train. The man assured me that he would send my trunk over here." Worry creased her brow. "But I don't see it anywhere."

The driver shrugged indifferently. "More than likely Jonesy has already loaded it in the boot. That's where we try to carry the passengers' luggage." He pointed to the rear of the stage where a compartment was covered with a heavy canvas.

"Would you mind looking?" Angela knew she was keeping him from his work, but everything she owned except for the contents of her portmanteau was in the trunk.

The man sighed and stomped off, grumbling, "Guess by God I can. Got all the time in the world to deal with a notional female worried about her frilly do-dads! Only have twenty more parcels of freight to load, more passengers to see about, and supposed to pull out of here in five more minutes." He raised the canvas and peered inside. "What color is it?" He made a mental bet with himself that the ornate trunk he'd loaded earlier was hers. It was so heavy, he'd almost broke his back hefting it into the boot.

"It's a small brown one—and it has black straps."

Raising an eyebrow at her description, he stared at her for a moment, then shoved the ornate trunk out of the way so that he could see into the compartment. In the back was a very small, shabby trunk. Gesturing toward the trunk, he asked, "Is—that yours?"

Peering around him, Angela smiled with relief. "Yes, and thank you for checking on it for me."

He instantly regretted being so crotchety. He took the small bag from her and mumbled, "Here, let me put this satchel you're carrying back here in the boot so you'll have more room in there. He approached the stage door and tugged it open. "You ought to go ahead and get on board and settled. We'll be leaving in a few minutes."

Smiling appreciatively at him, she placed her foot on the step, grasped either side of the door, and climbed inside. Not wanting to be in the way of the other passengers, she slid to the far side of the coach, then waited.

It was not long until the door was opened by a short man given to fat. He had small, piggish eyes and flabby jowls. He tossed a heavy coat onto the seat and pushed a battered, yet well-made leather case across the floor of the coach. Angela winced when it struck her foot, but she voiced no complaint.

"I keep tellin' you, you'll have more room if you'll let me put that case in the boot," the stage driver hollered from behind the man, as he passed another piece of freight to the top of the coach.

"No, sirree, my trunk can ride in the back, but this

13

case is my bread and butter and it goes where I go!" Puffing from the exertion, the man crawled into the coach. His eyes quickly fastened on Angela, and he smiled and scooted across the seat until he was directly opposite her. He pulled a handkerchief from his coat pocket, removed his derby, and patted the sweat from his face and head. Smiling, he looked at Angela again, stretched his legs so that his knees brushed against hers, then tipped his hat and said in a syrupy-sweet voice, "Good day to you, Missy. I see right now that this trip will be far more enjoyable than my last one."

Annoyance smoldered in Angela's eyes, turning them a dark gray. Although the coach was small, with its two bench-type seats facing each other, six passengers could easily fit inside without being too crowded. But evidently this man had chosen to sit directly across from her *so that he could deliberately brush his knees against hers!* Angela started to admonish him, then changed her mind. There might be another reason why he chose that particular seat. Yet, not wanting to encourage him, she merely acknowledged his greeting with a slight nod of her head, then moved her legs to avoid his touch.

"Glad to have you on board, Clint, an extra gun might come in handy," the driver's voice drifted inside. "Ain't expecting no trouble, but you can't ever tell. There always seems to be someone about who'd rather steal for a living than work. Want to ride up on the box with me and Jonesy?"

"Believe I'll pass this time, Bill. I got roped into a poker game that lasted a bit too long last night. If you can manage to keep the stage on the road this trip, I might be able to catch a little shut-eye," he replied good-naturedly.

The driver's answer was muffled when the door

opened and the third and final passenger climbed into the coach.

Angela drank in the sight of him. She had seen more handsome men before, but there was something about this man's rugged, though finely chiseled features that made her look at him more closely. He was tall; his shoulders broad. His eyes were so dark they were almost black; his cheeks were lean and muscular, and a neatly trimmed mustache framed his gently curved upper lip. Thick lashes fringed his eyes, accentuating dark, heavy brows. Though he was pleasing to look at, there was nothing ostentatious about his manner of dress. He wore brown trousers, a matching shirt, and a soft buckskin vest with a tan dress coat. His wide-brimmed, flat-crowned hat was the same color as his boots and he carried a heavy, wool-lined coat over his arm.

The thought immediately occurred to Angela that their destination might be the same. And somehow, the idea pleased her.

Aware of the young woman's close scrutiny, Clint worked himself down into the seat beside the other man and said, "Morning, Ma'am." He removed his hat and placed it on his lap. "Do you mind if I stretch my legs and prop my feet up on the seat beside you?"

"N-no, not at all. Please make yourself comfortable," she stammered, realizing he *knew* she had been staring at him far too intently.

The other man chuckled. "So, the little lady can speak. I was beginning to think you were bashful, Missy." He tipped his derby. "Hiram T. Witherspoon's my name, guns are my game," he said, patting the leather case on his lap. "Since you are a young lady traveling alone, could I interest you in a derringer?

Many women out here have started carrying them in their handbags for protection."

"No, no, thank you," she murmured softly.

Clint unbuttoned his jacket, then rolled his heavy coat and tucked it behind his head for a pillow.

As he had unbuttoned his coat, Angela saw that he wore two guns tied with leather thongs around his thighs. Men wearing guns in the west were nothing out of the ordinary, but *two guns* indicated a professional gunman for hire. She swallowed hard, recalling a conversation she'd overheard about how all gunfighters wore their guns strapped down, but that only a select few had the skill to use two. She struggled to remember all the things she'd heard about John Wesley Hardin, Billy the Kid, Sam Bass, and countless others who lived and died by the gun. She wondered how many men this man had killed, and if he was the type who killed indiscriminately.

Then Angela silently chided herself for allowing her imagination to run away with itself. The most important thing she had learned while searching for her father was not to make snap judgments. Out here in the west, looks could be deceiving. A tattered man wearing boots with worn down heels could be the richest man in town, or he could just be a prospector in hopes of finding a strike. A highly educated man might still use atrocious grammar, because most men picked up the flavor of the language spoken around them.

She felt the coach shift under the driver's weight as he climbed aboard. Her eyes widened when she heard a shrill whistle and the sharp retort of a whip. The sudden forward lurch of the coach made her reach for the handstrap and the back of the seat to keep herself upright.

Clint, amused by the startled expression on the young woman's face, lowered his head so that she could not see his smile. After a moment, he cleared his throat and asked, "Is this your first time on a stage?"

Angela, too unnerved to answer, merely nodded.

"The driver will slow down as soon as we leave town. They all like to put on a little show—I suppose for the townspeople's benefit."

"Missy, riding backwards like you are, you're liable to get motion sickness. Can't have a pretty little gal like you being uncomfortable, so I'd be happy to change seats with you," the short, fat man offered.

Angela started to accept, then she glanced at Clint who was shaking his head ever so slightly from side to side. Her brow creased into a questioning frown.

"The road to Clear Creek is awfully rough. I think you will be more comfortable right where you are." Clint shot the fat man a dark scowling look. "The stage-coaches are equipped with heavier springs on the driver's side. Guess that must have slipped your mind Witherspoon." he said coldly.

Witherspoon stammered, his face turning red, "W-why, come to think of it, y-you're right. Well, anyway, the offer is open, Missy, if you want to accept it later."

Clint settled himself more deeply into the seat and adjusted his hat so that the young woman could not see him studying her.

Even though she appeared to be taller than the average woman, she carried herself with pride and did not attempt to conceal her height by stooping her shoulders. He liked that in a woman. Her black hair was pulled back into a chignon, but the austere hairstyle did not sharpen her features, rather, it enhanced them. And, al-

17

though her light gray dress was wrinkled and showed signs of wear—almost to the point of being frayed—it was clean. She had a fresh scrubbed look about her. It was obvious she was decent and not just another one of the strumpets who flocked into mining towns, usually by the droves.

But it was the clarity of her eyes that intrigued him most. He felt that if her guard ever lowered, he might be able to see right down into the depths of her soul. Still, he had already managed to catch a fleeting glimpse of something—sadness perhaps?

Anticipation surged through him at the thought that she too was going to Clear Creek. He had seen no ring on her finger. That was the first thing he had looked for when he boarded the stage and saw her. But what business did a lady have in a wild, rough mining town? Saloon girls always arrived first, wives followed second, so where did she fit in?

The thought that she might already be engaged was strangely disturbing. As he closed his eyes, he cautioned himself not to become too interested until he found out more about her.

Chapter Two

The man named Clint had been correct, Angela thought to herself. Once she had gotten over the unfamiliar sensation of riding backwards, the seat was quite comfortable.

The gun salesman quickly attempted to engaged Angela in conversation, but his comments were too coarse and his questions so personal that she had no desire to talk to him. She removed a ball of thread and a crochet needle from her handbag and began working on a doily, merely nodding or voicing a brief reply to his comments and observations.

When Witherspoon saw that she was too preoccupied with counting stitches to talk, he pouted for a few minutes, then settled into his seat and drifted off to sleep.

A faint smile tugged at Angela's lips. Crocheting served two purposes. Not only did it discourage unwanted conversation, it helped to keep her mind and hands occupied while traveling. Little did anyone know how many times the thread had been ripped out and a new project started. There were several doilies she would have preferred to keep, but items like food and shelter were more important. New skeins of thread were a luxury she could not afford, at least not now. Maybe later when she found her father . . .

Finally, weary of her needle work, she pulled aside the canvas window covering and watched the passing countryside with awe.

This land had definitely been touched by the finger of God. As the stagecoach started a gradual ascent, Angela could see tall mountains, majestic on the horizon. The aspen with their fluttering leaves were like clusters of golden candles on the surrounding hills, with dabs of green scattered throughout as tall pines invaded their domain. The air was fresh, crisp, and clean, bearing no resemblance to the cloying sweetness that engulfed New Orleans and the humid south. There was a sense of well-being in this land, an innocence. Yet, it wasn't new. This land was as ancient as those referred to in the Bible. But, so much of it was unspoiled. But for how long would it remain this way?

Ever since silver and gold had been discovered, so-called civilization had swarmed westward, descending upon the land like a plague of locust. The towns that had sprung up so quickly had already blemished this paradise. Dust from ore pilings filled one's lungs, smelters and ore mills belched black smoke into the air, virgin forests were scarred by axes, lush green meadows had become mired with deep ruts cut by heavily loaded wagons. In some places the land was already dying.

Angela had learned that her father was still a miner and she supposed he too might be judged guilty, by future generations, of ravaging the land. But each person who claimed to know him seemed to have a great deal of respect for him. Maybe he was the sort of man who would put something back into the land in payment for what he had taken from it. At least she hoped so.

20

Angela had mixed feelings about what might happen during their first meeting. Ideally, he would greet her with open arms, but realistically, she knew that was too much to hope for. She could not help but wonder what his reaction would be when he learned the daughter he had thought dead for so many years was very much alive, and that they had been kept apart by a woman's cruel deception. Would he believe her incredible story? She could not fault him if he didn't. At times she had difficulty believing it herself. She could only hope that her mother's Bible and whatever family resemblance there was would be enough to convince him of the truth.

In her mind's eye she had conjured up a perfect man, ten feet tall and a candidate for sainthood. She would have to remember that he had faults and shortcomings the same as any other mortal and not be disappointed when he fell short of her expectations.

Sighing deeply, Angela pushed those troublesome thoughts from her mind. It was senseless to worry about future events—events that she had no control over. She would just have to wait and see what happened.

Miles passed by. And then for a long time there were only the sounds of the creaking of leather braces, the rattle of chains and harnesses, and of trotting horses. Lulled by the turning of the wheels, the rhythmical sway of the coach, Angela rested her head against the back of the seat and eventually drifted into sleep.

Clint's voice was low and deep-timbred, "Ma'am, you need to wake up now."

Angela did not know where she was; then it all came rushing back. But she no longer felt the motion of the coach. It must have come to a stop and she had slept right through the commotion. Glancing about, she felt foolish for behaving so addle-brained, it was so unlike her. But, considering that it had been four days and nights since she'd seen a bed, it was a wonder she could think at all.

Wanting to present the staid expression she reserved for strangers, she stalled for time by peering outside and noted with surprise that the narrow road was now surrounded by ancient cedars and tall pines.

Smoothing the tiny curling tendrils that had escaped from her chignon, she looked at Clint. "I'm sorry, please repeat what you said."

"The driver wants us to get out and lighten the coach. We'll have to walk until the stage reaches the top of this grade."

"Grade?" There were many western phrases she was not familiar with. "I'm not sure . . ."

"The top of this ridge. It's fairly steep and with the load we are carrying it is much easier on the horses for us to walk for awhile."

Witherspoon grumbled, "You'd think they would do something about the condition of this road. Last time I was through here we had to walk more than we rode. If you ask me, a body ought to put it in his mind to *walk* to Clear Creek and not mess with the damned stagecoach. You'd think they'd offer a cheaper fare, but no, they charge three dollars more than the regular rate!" Angrily, he flung open the door and stepped outside, not bothering to assist Angela.

Angela clucked disapprovingly, "Oh, my, he certainly speaks his mind, doesn't he?"

"That he does. I've seen him here and there, but I've never traveled with him before." Sliding across the seat, he chuckled but it was without humor. "Doubt if I will want the pleasure again."

Climbing out of the coach, Clint turned back to Angela. "Come, I'll help you."

He took her hand to steady her, then released it and grasped her around the waist.

Angela had no other choice but to place her hands on his broad shoulders for balance. Her breath caught in her throat as he lifted her. His hands were strong, yet his touch was surprisingly gentle. She could feel his powerful arm muscles ripple beneath her fingertips. For the briefest moment she felt as if she was floating in midair. The nonsensical thought occurred to her that perhaps the expression *being swept off one's feet* had originated from someone's experience such as this.

Even though the earth clock ticked only a second or two, their eyes melted together and they stood, suspended in time. Blood rushed through her veins and her heart beat an erratic rhythm. Clint's reserved expression had vanished, wiped away by astonishment. She realized he too had felt something pass between them.

Bill, the driver of the stage, called out, "Come on folks, we need to get a move on it."

The spell broken, Angela lowered her lashes and walked away, a gamut of emotions still running through her. One part of her wanted to lash out at the driver for interrupting them, yet she also felt a sense of relief. Why should a stranger's touch affect her in such a way? Even though her life thus far had been filled with loneliness, was she so hungry for affection that she would carelessly throw all caution aside? Was she making a fool out of herself just because a man behaved like a gentleman? Perhaps Julia's indifferent treatment over the years had made her vulnerable to any scrap of kindness thrown her way. Whatever the case, she cautioned herself to get a tighter rein on her emotions.

They fell in behind the coach, Angela and Clint walking in silence, Witherspoon puffing and complaining, and lagging further behind with each step he took.

Finally, Clint broke their silence by saying, "When Witherspoon told you his name, I missed the opportunity to introduce myself. My name is Clint, Clint Rutledge." He looked at her expectantly.

She could feel her face growing warm under his gaze. "My name is Angela Langford."

Amusement twinkled in his eyes. "Since I envision a Miss Langford as being a strict schoolmarm, would you object if I called you Angela—or maybe, Angie?"

During her travels few people had even asked her name and those that did had addressed her formally. She supposed that allowing him to call her by her given name would not make her less a lady. "No, I have no objections." She added a bit boldly, "None whatsoever."

"Angela! Clint! Wait up a minute! Take it easy on a short, fat man, will you?" Witherspoon shouted from behind.

Pausing, Clint shrugged his shoulders in mock resignation. "That man may have short legs, but he has exceptional hearing," he remarked dryly.

Angela stiffened visibly and rancor sharpened her usually soft tone. "Yes, but it is my opinion that he thinks he is exceptional in many other ways too."

Clint studied her thoughtfully for a moment, but said nothing in answer to her remark, yet there was a distinct hardening of his eyes.

When Witherspoon reached them, he stopped and mopped his sweaty brow with his handkerchief. After catching his breath, he muttered, "You could slow down! Nobody said a thing about us having to run!"

Bill and Jonesy were sitting atop the stage waiting for them when they finally reached the top of the incline. The driver pointed to the trees and bushes on either side of the road. "Lady, you go to the right, you gents use the trees and brush to my left." Spitting a huge wad of tobacco onto the ground, he added, "You all had better take good advantage while you can. Unless it's absolutely necessary, we won't be stopping again until we reach Meyer's ranch and put in for the night."

"You mean we will not be traveling straight through?" Angela asked. The other times she had traveled by stage, they had continued through the night.

"No, ma'am, this road is too bad for that. This time tomorrow, you'll think the ride today has been a church-social hayride. And the further we go, the worse it'll get.

"Now hurry up, folks, we need to reach Meyer's ranch before dark sets in."

Feeling slightly embarrassed for the men to *know* what she was going to do, Angela made her way into the woods. It would not have been so bad if another woman was along. But still, they were all adults and everybody had personal needs.

Clint followed Hiram deep into the brush and after he was through, he waited discreetly until Witherspoon had finished. Witherspoon adjusted his trousers and started back to the coach when Clint stopped him.

Though he spoke calmly, his voice was edged with steel. "I think you and I need to get something settled right now."

Witherspoon frowned. "What do you mean? There's

25

nothing between us that needs to be settled . . . is there?"

"Yes. Leave the lady alone."

"Wha . . .?"

"I said, leave her alone."

Witherspoon bristled with indignation over what seemed to be such an insignificant matter. "I haven't bothered her . . . besides, what I say or don't say to a woman is no concern of yours," he added sneeringly.

Clint's lips thinned with anger. "That's where you are wrong. Anytime I see someone aggravating a woman, I *make it my concern*. Your remarks fall just shy of being suggestive; I've seen her cringe from some of the things you've said. And that little game you've been playing with your knees would be down right laughable if it didn't make her so uncomfortable."

Witherspoon's mouth twisted into an ugly grimace. "So what? It's *still* my business what I do and until she complains, butt out!"

He then tried to step around Clint, but Clint grabbed a handful of his shirt and pulled the man roughly to him.

Suddenly, Witherspoon did not know what to do. He recalled the rumors he'd heard about how Rutledge once rode outside the law, and that the guns he wore were definitely not for show. Perspiration beaded on his brow and all color drained from his face. "Y-you turn me loose—or I'll report you to the driver!"

Clint tightened his grip. "Be my guest, but first, you will listen to what I have to say. You're going back to that stage and if you say *anything* out of the way, or if you so much as look like you're about to touch *Miss Langford,* I'll make you eat every gun you're carrying in that case. And by the way, don't call her by her given name again unless she gives you permission. You hear me?"

"Y-yes, sir."

Clint slowly released his grip and, smiling, he smoothed Witherspoon's shirt and painstakingly straightened his bow tie. "Now, we're not going to mention this little conversation we've had to the others, are we?"

"N-no, sir."

"And we're going to go back to the stagecoach and behave like perfect gentlemen, aren't we?"

Witherspoon bobbed his head. "Anything you say, Mr. Rutledge."

Clint followed close behind Witherspoon and as they neared the stage, Clint, with his taller height, caught a glimpse of the driver and the guard sitting with their hands raised. He immediately grabbed the back of Witherspoon's shirt and motioned for him to be quiet.

A strange voice called out, "Whoever is in those bushes, come on out with your hands up. We only want what's in the strongbox and what you have in your pockets, then we'll ride out of here. Just so you're not tempted to try something stupid, I think you should know that we've got a shotgun trained on the driver and guard, and a .44 caliber pistol is pointed underneath the lady's throat. One twitch of the finger and it'll blow the top of her pretty little head off. So, I suggest you don't do anything that's liable to make me nervous."

From Clint's vantage point, it was obvious by the pale expression on her face, Angela was frightened but wisely, she was standing perfectly still.

Clint knew he had two choices and he liked neither one. Either do as the man said and take the chance that they would be left unharmed, or try to fight their way out. If he did that though, someone was likely to be seriously injured or killed. Still, he doubted if a thief would live up to his word. While in some situations there might be honor among thieves, in his opinion there was no such thing as an honorable thief. That was just a romantic notion, mere words concocted by an easterner who *thought* that's how things should be. Personally, he never understood how a man could rob another man and still retain his honor.

"I'm not waiting all day long!" the voice called out. You've got until the count of ten." Slowly, he started counting out the numbers. "One, two . . ."

The time for indecision was over. Clint reached for his guns and motioned for Witherspoon to go on out where he could be seen by the robbers. Apparently Witherspoon considered their options and agreed with Clint, for he suddenly thrust his hands high into the air and started yelling for them not to shoot, that he was coming out. Whether he did it deliberately or by his own clumsy nature, he made enough noise coming through the bushes so that it sounded like a herd of cattle stampeding. The commotion gave Clint the opportunity to take cover behind a wide tree without being heard, where he could get a better view of the bandits.

He could only hope that the bandits did not know how many passengers were on board. If they knew there were three, he could always come on out and claim that he had been well behind Witherspoon.

"Don't shoot! Don't shoot!" Witherspoon bellowed as he approached the stage. "I'm not armed. See?" He lowered his hands just enough to spread open his coat.

"Two passengers all you're carrying?" the ringleader asked the driver.

"This time of the year we're lucky to have that many!" Bill snapped angrily.

"Shut your yap and throw down that strongbox! And if you don't want your belly full of that scattergun my partner is holding on you, you might ought to toss it down real careful like."

Clint knew Bill would not take any unnecessary chances until he made his move. Still, he had to be patient and wait until the robbers were somehow distracted. He refused to carelessly gamble with Angela's life and the lives of the others.

The man holding the pistol removed the gun from Angela's throat and shot the lock off the box. Angela flinched and her face paled even more. Then, she caught a glimpse of Clint moving from behind the tree. Giving such a negligible nod that it might have been his imagination, she moaned deeply, then slumped to the ground in a dead faint.

For the briefest moment the robbers' attention was diverted to the woman and that's all it took for Clint and Bill to get the jump on them. Clint shot the pistol from the man's hand, then burned a bullet across his shoulder, which spun him around. Bill, a master with a bullwhip, snaked the tip of his persuader around the shotgun and jerked it out of the other man's hands before he knew what had happened.

Breathing a sigh of relief, Clint hurried to the road and knelt beside Angela, leaving Witherspoon to hold the shotgun, while Jonesy and Bill tied the bandits.

"Are you all right?" he asked worriedly. He did not know if she had truly fainted or not. One could never figure how a city girl might react to such an ordeal.

She came off the ground dusting her clothes off, her eyes flashing fire. "Yes, I'm fine! But don't hold your breath waiting for my gratitude! I suppose you thought you had to make a grandiose stand at our expense! Don't you realize you could have gotten us all killed?" Having spoken her peace, she turned her back on him and stomped angrily toward the stage.

Chapter Three

The stagecoach rolled into Meyer's ranch an hour after the sun had set. A lantern with a reflector behind it had been lit and was hanging on the front porch. The passengers inside the coach were so tired, it looked like a beacon guiding them through the darkness.

Nicholas and Ralph Meyer, brothers and partners in the small but thriving ranch, came out of the barn and hurried toward the stage.

"We were beginning to worry," Nicholas said to Bill while he watched him climb down from the coach. "I've never known you to be this late before."

"Aw, we ran into a bit of trouble." He motioned with his thumb toward the top of the stage. "A couple of fellows had a notion to relieve us of the strongbox, but we changed their minds. Got 'em tied up there. That held us up a mite, then later we had to clear a rock slide from the road."

Nicholas studied the men for a moment. "Is that one hurt?"

"Naw," Bill said, working the kinks out of his muscles. "Oh, he got his shoulder burned; it's nothing but a flesh wound though. Hell, he didn't lose enough blood to fill a thimble. I can't take them with me when we leave, though, so if you can see your way to carry them into Silverlode City, the company will pay you for your trouble. I figure there might even be a reward for them at the sheriff's office—if not, there ought to be." His voice lowered warningly, "Don't take those hombres lightly, Nicholas, they are dangerous men."

"Appreciate you telling me. Work has slowed down, so Ralph can cut loose long enough to take them in. It might be a few days before he can strike out though. All of the signs indicate a cold spell moving in. We'll just have to see what the weather looks like in the morning. I would do it, but the wife's time is getting close and I wouldn't want to leave her now, especially if there's a chance of getting snowed in for a week or two at Silverlode."

"Can't say that I blame you. Speaking of your wife, there is a man with me she will be eager to see."

"Clint?" A wide smile spread across Nicholas's face.

"Yeah, he's riding one of the hombre's horses and leading the other."

"You're right. Susan will be glad to see him. She has been expecting him for the past few months now." With an inquiring grin, he asked. "Is he alone?"

"Alone? What do you mean?"

"He's been gone for so long, I sort of figured he'd be bringing back an English bride."

"No, he's alone, and he never said anything about having a wife."

While talking, they moved around to the stagecoach door. Witherspoon had already climbed out of the coach and was stretching. Nicholas glanced inside and was startled momentarily by the woman's presence. He quickly extended his hand to help her from the coach.

32

He could feel her trembling from the cold. "Ma'am, you look like you're 'bout half froze . . ."

At that moment, Clint walked up, leading the horses. One was favoring his foreleg.

Nicholas whirled about and grasped Clint's hand in a hearty shake. "Glad to see you! It is about time you showed your ugly mug!"

Their greeting was so amicable, it was obvious to Angela that Clint and the rancher were friends. She felt as though she were intruding on something personal, but she did not know what else to do but to wait until they had finished.

A flash of humor crossed Clint's face. "Surely I'm not that late, am I? The horse I was riding threw a shoe, and the stirrups were too short on the other one, so I decided just to walk on in instead of switching gear."

Nicholas threw back his head and laughed heartily. "I was referring to you going to England and staying there for so long."

Clint shrugged his shoulders. "Dad had too many unpleasant memories of crossing the Atlantic when he was a child, so he wanted me to go for him. I never intended to stay a year though. It just took longer to settle the estate than we figured. I found out whenever a wealthy relative dies—even if he is distantly related—all sorts of poor relations come out of the woodwork." He chuckled. "I imagine they said the same thing about my dad, but he was *mentioned* in the will. Anyway, after the business was all settled and since I was that close, I decided I might never have the opportunity to see other countries again, so I took a few months and visited Ireland, Scotland, and France. If you all are interested, I'll tell you about it at supper. And, by the way, I brought a few things back for Susan."

"Uh-huh," Nicholas said knowingly, "a peace offering is a smart move. I know one thing, if Susan had any idea you would be coming through, you could have bet your bottom dollar we'd be having hot apple pie after supper. As it is though, you'll have to eat what we common folks do."

Clint guffawed and pointed to the paunch protruding over Nicholas's belt. "I see how badly you've been suffering."

Angela felt increasingly uncomfortable. She had no idea how long their good-natured banter would last. It was obvious the rancher had forgotten about her, and it was just as noticeable that Clint was intentionally ignoring her, for he had not once glanced her way or acknowledged her presence. But that came as no great surprise. He had been very cold toward her ever since the hold-up.

"Excuse me, Mr. Meyer, if you will tell me where to go . . ."

Nicholas reeled about and looked at Angela shamefaced. "I'm sorry I forgot about you, Ma'am! Go on in the house. There is a good hot fire in the fireplace. And if you don't mind, tell my wife to set the table for five extras and fill two plates for those men. They might be thieves, but they get hungry too." Then he spoke in a louder voice, "Folks, the wife will be putting supper on the table shortly. You men wash up on the porch, then go on inside. Jonesy, my gun is out in the barn. If I can use your shotgun, I'll escort those two owlhoots to the bunkhouse and have a look at that wound while Ralph takes care of the horses."

Clint glanced questioningly at Bill and Jonesy, and seeing them nod, he said, "We'll help you with those men." He knew without someone standing guard, either man—even though one would still be tied—might try to get the jump on Nicholas while he was cleaning and dressing the wound.

Angela hurried toward the house, eager for the promised warmth of a roaring fire. For the past two hours it had become increasingly colder, but she knew the weather was not altogether responsible for the icy feeling that had settled in the pit of her stomach. The harder she tried to ignore the truth, the more it persisted. *It was Clint Rutledge!* The man disturbed her more than she cared to acknowledge, and for reasons she did not understand.

After all, what he had done was unforgivable. How could she possibly be attracted to anyone who placed a higher value on money than four innocent lives! *But she was attracted to him!*

The admission was dredged from a place that defied logic and reason, for she had only known him a few hours. For so long she kept such a tight reign on her emotions, it was unlike her to be so reckless, and that was disturbing too.

Reaching the door, Angela knocked, then waited until a voice told her to come in. She entered and quickly scanned the room until her gaze rested on a woman about the same age as herself. She said shyly, "Mrs. Meyer? Your husband sent me in. He said to tell you to set the table for five extras and to fill two plates for the men in the bunkhouse." Subconsciously Angela's brow furrowed when she noticed the startled expression that had momentarily shaded the woman's face, then disappeared just as quickly. Nicholas Meyer had had the same expression. What was it about her that caused this reaction?

The woman smoothed her hands over her apron and

smiled. "Please call me Susan. Mrs. Meyer sounds so—stuffy. Come on in and warm yourself by the fire. I imagine you are about to freeze. This time of the year the mountain air is terribly cold at night. Then too, the stage is later than usual. I was beginning to worry."

"My name is Angela—and we ran into a little trouble. That's why the stage is late." Angela briskly rubbed her hands together, then held them close to the fire. She was impressed with the young woman's friendliness, which made her initial reaction even more puzzling.

"Trouble? I hope it wasn't serious."

"Well, I suppose it could have been. Two men attempted to rob the stage, but they were stopped." Again, fury raged through Angela at the thought that they could have all been killed, thanks to Clint Rutledge!

"Was anyone hurt?"

"One of the bandits received a flesh wound, and the other felt the sting of the driver's whip. The men are putting them in the bunkhouse and attending to their wounds."

Susan hurried toward Angela with a surprisingly lithe gait considering her advanced pregnancy. "Let me take your shawl." She hung it on a cloak rack that stood beside the door, frowning when she saw how thin it was. It was far too flimsy for the harsh Colorado winters. "You will have to forgive me if I appeared to be startled when you came in. We seldom receive female passengers except when the stage is on its way back to Silverlode. This is the second year that we've served as a way station, and you are the first woman to go to Clear Creek after late July. It is so isolated up there, most women spend the winter in Silverlode."

"Oh, I see," Angela murmured, relieved by her expla-

nation. "I was beginning to wonder if I had grown another head, especially since your husband . . ."

Susan chuckled. "No, it was just your presence." Her
huge brown eyes became soft and knowing. "Do you
have a young man up there, or by chance are you answering an advertisement?

"An advertisement?"

As Susan walked back to the table and began setting
it, she explained, "By your reaction, I suppose not. This
past summer twelve women came through who were answering advertisements that had been placed in the eastern newspapers by men seeking wives. Only one has
returned thus far, so evidently, most women found suitable matches."

"Oh, no," Angela hastened to say. Being from New
Orleans, she knew about mail order brides—the legend-
ary *casket girls* had helped settle the Crescent City. "I
am not answering an advertisement and there is no
young man. I am going to my father. He lives in Clear
Creek."

"I see." A pretty smile spread across Susan's face.
"Then perhaps I should give you fair warning."

"A warning?"

"Yes, last I heard, you'll probably be the only unattached female in Clear Creek besides Sadie, and she's a
lovable tyrant who runs the boardinghouse. Of course,
there are the . . . other women who . . . who . . . well,
the women who work in the saloons." Susan blushed
at the thought of how women could degrade themselves
that way. Not wanting to dwell on that particular subject, she added quickly, "I imagine the young men will
soon be beating a path to your father's front door."

Angela was stunned. She had never thought that
Clear Creek would be so isolated and that she would be

the only unattached woman. Men had never played a part in her past and she did not want to be bothered with such things until she had the opportunity to get reacquainted with her father. Immediately, the image of Clint filled her mind, but she quickly pushed it aside.

Susan sighed and made a clicking sound with her tongue. "Here I am, rattling on and on. You and the other passengers are probably starved half to death. Excuse me while I put supper on the table."

"Can I help you?" Angela offered. She felt ill at ease not helping, especially since Susan was so obviously pregnant.

"Oh, no, just stand there by the fire and warm. It will only take me a few minutes."

When Susan disappeared into the kitchen, Angela glanced about the room with an appraising eye. It was rustic and very clean. Two doors apparently leading to bedrooms were on the far side of the room. Four comfortable chairs sat around an oval braided rug near the fireplace, and a bookshelf held many volumes of leather-bound books. Tiny porcelain figurines filled a huge shadowbox, and a few paintings hung on the walls.

Toward the doorway that led to the kitchen was a huge table covered with a red and white checkered tablecloth. The table had bench-type seats on both sides and a captain's chair at each end. It appeared that all of the furniture had been meticulously handcrafted. Clearly, this house had been built and cared for with love.

For a moment Angela was envious, she remembered how the atmosphere of Julia's house had always been so cold and without feeling. Love had existed there, but it

38

had existed between Julia and her daughter, with never a scrap left over for her.

"Are you getting warm?" Susan asked, setting a platter of roast beef on the table.

Angela glanced about sharply as she was pulled from her unpleasant reverie. "Yes, thank you. The fire does feel good." She breathed deeply. "And supper smells delicious!" The mouth watering aromas that wafted from the kitchen made her stomach rumble from hunger.

"And I thank you for saying that! Most times the passengers just sit down and shovel the food in without a word of appreciation. Sometimes, I think I could cook a pine board and they would eat it and never know the difference." Susan paused, her pretty features turned red. "I didn't mean it was my cooking . . ."

Angela laughed. "I know what you meant. I've cooked at a boardinghouse before. And I often had that very same feeling."

The front door suddenly flew open. Clint stood in the doorway and bellowed, "Where's my brown eyes?"

Susan, who had disappeared into the kitchen, rushed back out. With a squeal, she ran toward Clint's outstretched arms. "It's about time you decided to come home!"

Clint hurried to meet her and swept her up in his arms, swinging her around. Then, he blanched and set her down even though she was smothering him with kisses. "Careful there, little mama." He patted her protruding stomach. "We don't want to hurt Junior."

Pretending indignation, Susan tossed her head and waved her arms. "And how do you know it's a boy?"

"Because that's what I ordered!"

Angela was taken aback by their intimacy.

"You men are all alike. It so happens that I want a

39

girl!" She reached out and tugged none too gently on his earlobe. "You could have written, and you didn't have to stay gone for so long either."

"Oh, I got detained."

Raising her finely arched eyebrows, she replied, "Yes, I'll bet I know the reason why. Was she a redhead, blonde, or brunette?"

Clint chuckled devilishly and fingered his mustache. "Perhaps all three."

Susan giggled. *"That's* more likely." Then, her voice softened and she hugged him close. "I've missed you so much."

"And I've missed you too, brown eyes."

Clint's gaze caught and held Angela's. His mouth tightened and his eyes glinted coldly. Then, seemingly, he dismissed her presence without a flicker of emotion. He glanced down at Susan and sniffed. "Do I smell biscuits burning?"

Susan's eyes widened, and with a yelp of consternation, she hurried to the kitchen.

Wordlessly, Clint removed his coat and sidled up beside Angela. He thrust his hands out to warm them.

Angela was infuriated by Clint's callous behavior toward her. He acted as though she didn't exist! Still, she felt she should say something to try and soothe the trouble between them.

"Are you related to Susan?" she asked softly.

He glanced at her. "Yes."

Angela waited for him to tell her in what manner they were related, but he said nothing else. "Are you her brother?"

"I suppose you could call it that," he replied crisply. "My dad raised her after her parents were killed."

The silence between them became increasingly pronounced.

"Did you get the prisoners settled?"

"Yes." Clint stared up at the ceiling, placed his hands behind his back, and teetered on his feet.

Angela took a deep but silent breath and tried again. "The man that you shot, was he injured seriously?" She knew he wasn't, it was just an attempt to make conversation."

"Nope," Clint said abruptly.

Her mood veered sharply to unbridled anger. *"Mr. Rutledge,"* she ground out between clenched teeth, "I'm sure you feel that I had no right to voice my opinion after the attempted hold-up, but there is absolutely no need for you to behave like a spoiled child!"

Clint's face looked as though it had been carved from stone as he turned to her. "You have every right to voice your opinion, *Miss Langford,* but in the future do yourself a favor and consider the facts before you form such a stupid one!"

Susan returned from the kitchen and when she saw Clint and Angela standing so close to each other, an impish gleam suddenly appeared in her eyes. They made a very handsome couple. "Well, I see the two of you have met." She gave an exaggerated sigh and pursed her lips. "How silly of me. Of course you have already met. After all, you're both riding the same stagecoach, and I have never known Clint not to introduce himself to such a pretty lady."

Clint, knowing how much Susan liked to play the role of matchmaker, turned and scowled darkly at her; but she merely jutted her chin and smiled sweetly at him.

Nonchalantly, Susan started toward the window to

peer outside. "I wonder what's keeping them? Supper is going to get cold."

As if on cue, the front door opened and the men came traipsing inside, with Nicholas leading the way. The next few minutes were hectic as Susan instructed the people where to sit. Nicholas took his usual place at the head of the table, and Clint sat next to him. Susan placed Angela next to Clint and she sat directly across from him. The other men took their assigned places on the benches.

Not much was said as they all attacked the food ravenously. It was only after the sharp pangs of hunger had been satisfied that the conversation became more animated.

Susan refilled their coffee cups and sank back down. "Clint, tell me about the attempted robbery. Angela mentioned it but she didn't go into any of the details."

He shrugged. "There really wasn't much to it."

Bill butted in, "Like heck there wasn't! Those hombres had us dead to rights. We had just reached the top of Cedar Top pass and the passengers were out in the ... well, to put it politely, they were taking a necessity break. Me and Jonesy had just climbed back up on the box when those owlhoots came out of nowhere. They weren't wearing masks, so you know what *that* meant. I'm not a religious man, but I found myself praying that Clint and Witherspoon would realize what was going on and would try to do something about it. So, I didn't go for my gun, but I had my hand on my whip just in case. Ol' Hiram came out of the woods making so much noise a body would have thought a whole passel of grizzlys were chasing him. It fooled those owlhoots too. They thought two passengers were all we were carrying. Then all hell ... uh ... excuse me ladies, all heck broke loose and Clint read 'em their rights with those pistols he carries." Just thinking about it brought a smile to his face. "Yep, nicest piece of reading I've seen in a long spell."

Susan raised her brows and slowly shook her head. "It sounds like it was too close a call for comfort."

Angela had been listening closely to Bill's version of what had happened. It seemed strange to her that he made Clint out to be a hero. Even Susan approved of his actions. Had they all taken leave of their senses?

"Excuse me," Angela said. "What did you mean about them not wearing masks? Is that important?"

Bill seized the opportunity to set her straight. It had perturbed him to no end when she gave Clint that tongue lashing. "Yes, Ma'am, it is very important. When a robber doesn't wear a mask, it gives a strong indication that he has no intention of leaving any live witnesses. In all likelihood, we'd all be dead now if it wasn't for Clint."

She sat there, visibly shaken, as all color drained from her face. "I-I see," she finally stammered, feeling Clint grow tense beside her. She wanted to look at him, to apologize for judging him so unfairly. But, she was so unnerved, a smirk or one cross word from him would sent her into tears, even though she very seldom cried.

Nicholas, unaware of what had happened, directed a question to Bill. "How is the road between here and Silverlode? Should Ralph take the buckboard when he delivers the prisoners, or do you think he should go by horseback?"

"The road is in pretty good shape. Either way should be fine. It's the road from here to Clear Creek that troubles me." Lines of worry deepened Bill's brow. During his last trip there were places that had scared him to cross, yet he could not voice his concerns here for fear of frightening the passengers. "Without immediate work on it, that road ain't going to hold up much longer. 'Course, can't blame the stage company for not wanting to repair it, not with the railroad going through to Clear Creek next spring. Just a word of advice, I wouldn't trust it at all after winter. Whenever you folks decide to go up there visiting, I suggest you travel by horseback."

Hiram Witherspoon spoke up. "If it is that dangerous, what about our safety?"

Never blinking an eye, Bill replied, "If I have cause for worry, you folks can get out and walk and I'll drive the stage over the bad stretches."

Later, after supper, Angela insisted that Susan allow her to help with the dishes. They opened the kitchen door so that they could hear Clint's tales about his distant travels. Angela still felt ill at ease because of her wrongful accusation, and she desperately wished for an opportunity to apologize to him. It came sooner than she expected.

They had just finished the dishes and entered the dining area when Clint suddenly remembered the keepsakes he had purchased for Susan during his travels. Using the excuse that he needed clean clothes, he went outside to the stagecoach to get them.

Susan, seizing the chance to throw the two together, said to Angela, "Whenever we have female guests, Ralph sleeps in the bunkhouse with the other men, so you can have his room tonight. I know you must be exhausted and ready to go to bed. Why don't you go outside and get your traveling bag while Clint is out there? I personally guarantee that he will protect you from any bears roaming about."

Nicholas started to rise. "I'll go get it for her."

"Nonsense, keep your seat. Since Angela is from the city, a short walk in the fresh mountain air will make her sleep well."

Puzzled, Nicholas looked at his wife, saw the determined expression on her face, and shrugging his shoulders in defeat, sat back down.

Suddenly realizing this was the opportunity she had hoped for, Angela hurried to get her shawl. "That is an excellent idea, Susan. I do think a breath of fresh air would help me to sleep better."

Seeing Clint holding the lantern overhead as he peered inside the boot, Angela walked softly toward him. She was unaware that he had seen her leave the house and was merely pretending to be engrossed in his search.

"Clint," she said hesitantly when she reached him.

Turning his head sharply about, he mumbled, "Oh, it's you. What do you want?"

Her mouth was dry and she tried to swallow, making several attempts before succeeding. "I came for my portmanteau. Also, I want to apologize. I am sorry for what I said. I didn't realize . . ."

"That's right, you didn't!" he retorted more sharply than he intended, as he pushed the bag into her hands.

Her mouth opened, but no words came. She lowered her eyes, grateful that he could not see the sudden tears that had filled them. Blinking them away, she lifted her head proudly and with stiff dignity started back toward the house.

His brows drew together in an agonized expression as he watched her retreating form. He raked his hand through his hair, then swore underneath his breath. He felt as though he was about to lose something very important in his life, something that could never be replaced. Suddenly, taking long purposeful strides behind her, he called, "Angela, wait!"

She stopped and turned slowly to face him.

His large hands cupped her face and held it gently. "At times I am a stubborn, obnoxious man. You were right," he whispered softly. "I have been behaving like a spoiled child. I realize now that you, being from the city, had no idea why I did what I did. Hell, I realized it then, but I was too stubborn to admit it. I should have explained it to you this afternoon." He pushed aside a stray wisp of hair that had fallen over her forehead. Then gently, he brushed his lips against her brow.

Angela's heart slammed against her chest as a rush of emotions surged through her. How could she have such feelings when they had only just met? What was even more astonishing, she wanted to feel his lips press against hers!

Clint was speechless. He'd had no idea he was going to kiss her. Yet he had, and now he wanted more. He had known other women, too many in fact, but at this moment he could not recall their names or faces, nor did he want to. There was something about Angela that was sensuously stimulating, yet he felt so protective.

Finally getting a grip on his emotions, he murmured huskily, "It's getting late and we'll be leaving early in the morning. You had better go inside."

She backed away, not wanting to take her eyes off him. "Yes, it's—late. Good night, Clint."

"Good night, sweet lady," he whispered after she had turned and walked slowly away.

Chapter Four

Angela awoke to the aroma of coffee brewing. Although it was still dark outside, frost had covered the window. It had turned bitterly cold during the night and only a tiny bit of heat had made its way into the bedroom. She snuggled deeper into the feather mattress and buried her mouth and nose under the heavy blankets for added warmth.

Then, her eyes flew open as she remembered the events of the previous night. Something marvelous had passed between her and Clint. Just the memory of his gentle touch, the expression in his eyes, his words falling softly against her ears, made her feel as though she was wrapped in an invisible warmth. And with that feeling came a sense of security, a sense of well-being. Was it love? No—at least not yet. It took time for that strong an emotion to grow, to develop. But without a doubt what had happened between them was a beginning of something, at least for her.

It was strange how quickly circumstances and feelings could change. Yesterday morning she had been lonely, frightened, and so terribly unsure even though she had pretended differently. Today, she was one step closer to her father, she had met a man who was exciting, who made her pulse race just to think about him. For the first time in her life it seemed as though everything was falling into place and that nothing, absolutely nothing could go wrong.

"Angela, Angela, are you awake?" Susan asked as she rapped lightly on the door, then opened it slightly and peered inside.

Not wanting to admit that she had just been lying in bed wool-gathering, Angela raised up, squinted her eyes, and stifled a yawn, acting as though she had just awakened. "What time is it?" she asked sleepily.

"It's time to get up. The stage will leave at dawn and I know how we girls like to have a little extra time in the morning. If we hurry, we can have a cup of coffee together before the men start stirring."

Throwing back the covers, Angela quickly dressed. She liked Susan and wanted to visit with her. It was too cold to comb her hair and twist it into a bun, so she decided to leave the single night-braid to hang down her back. Later, when the room warmed a bit, she would give her hair more attention.

"Hot water's on the stove," Susan told Angela when she came to the table. "And there is a small room on the other side of the kitchen. It's warm. You can wash up there. I'll pour you a cup of coffee."

A few minutes later, Angela joined her.

"You will have to forgive my selfishness for waking you so early," Susan said, a bit sheepishly. "I could have let you sleep for an hour longer, but I get so lonesome for another woman's company, at times I could almost scream. Don't misunderstand though," she hastened to say, "I love my husband and my home dearly. But I sure wish we had neighbors who lived

48

close by. It might be months before I see another female face."

Angela carefully chose her words before she spoke. "I realize it could very easily be lonesome here, but one can be just as secluded in the midst of a crowded city, or in a household full of other women. I think even if one is basically happy and content with her life, a touch of loneliness here and there is normal. I suppose it's included in the overall scheme of things."

"You have a point there."

Not wishing to seem too obvious, Susan studied her closely. She realized Angela had spoken from experience, not from opinion. What had happened to make her so sad? She was too young to be so pensive and solemn. There seemed to be an aura of heartbreak surrounding Angela. Yet she exuded confidence. Susan mentally wagered that Angela was not the type of person to be easily defeated.

Aware of Susan's contemplation, Angela took a sip of her coffee and commented on how good it was. That simple little remark seemed to clear the air between them.

Susan leaned forward, her eyes dancing eagerly. "I recall someone mentioning that you are from New Orleans. I have heard fabulous tales about that city. Will you tell me about it? And tell me about all of the new fashions women are wearing."

In her soft, easy drawl, Angela explained that New Orleans was a veritable melting pot of every type of humanity. She told of the crowded streets in the French Quarter, the open markets, how at one house the pattern of ears of corn were scrolled into the wrought iron fence that surrounded it.

She spoke of the tall ships and steamers coming into

the harbor from the Gulf, and of the huge stern-wheelers still navigating the Mississippi. How so many items could be purchased from colorfully dressed street vendors. The restaurants and their exotic foods. The ladies dressed in the newest fashions direct from France and New York.

She told Susan of the legend of the Spanish moss; how a young woman had cut her hair and flung it on the trees when her love had died, and how it had become gray with age and spread from tree to tree over the years.

How the people buried their dead in crypts above the ground because of the seepage in the soil. And how the first time she had passed by a cemetery at night, she'd imagined that the crypts looked like tiny houses, and how she had always thought of cemeteries since then as being cities of the dead.

Then there were the fabulous plantations, some falling into ruin, but many standing elegant with their massive white pillars, meticulously tended lawns and flowers, and oak-lined drive ways.

"Have you ever been inside such a grand house?" Susan asked breathlessly, her face exuberant with excitement.

For a fleeting moment, Angela stiffened, then laughed a bit too harshly. "No, neither Aunt Julia nor her daughter fit into that social circle—although I do believe either one would have made a pact with the devil himself for an invitation to just one grand ball. And knowing them, one invitation was all they would have needed."

Realizing she had divulged too much, Angela quickly changed the subject. "I think I recall Clint mentioning that his dad raised you. Is that so, or did I imagine it?"

"Yes. He did raise me—and I called him Dad too."

50

Susan leaned back in the chair and rested her hands on her rounded stomach, occasionally stroking and patting it. "Clint's father and my father were childhood friends. When they grew older though, Dad came west and Father stayed in Missouri. Not long afterward, my real father married a woman and they had two sons, but his wife and children died during a cholera epidemic. Then, a few years later, he married my mother and they had me. I well remember the farm we lived on. It was very prosperous for a while, but a two-year drought ended that prosperity. He and Dad had kept in touch through the years and when he learned that the farm had failed, he offered my parents a home on his ranch. My parents accepted his offer, packed our belongings, and we started west." Her voice quivered slightly, "We were attacked by Indians in Kansas. My father hid me and, luckily, my life was spared. Later, soldiers came and took me to the fort. When Dad learned what had taken place he sent for me immediately. That happened when I was ten years old, and he's been my Dad ever since."

"I'm so terribly sorry. I had no idea. . . . I hope my prying did not bring back too many unpleasant memories." Angela thought it was strange that in some instances, their lives had so closely paralleled, yet they were actually miles and miles apart and had veered in such different directions.

Susan shook her head and placed her hand over Angela's. "It's all right. And, if I had thought you were prying, I would not have answered. I suppose I shall always miss my real parents in one way or another. Especially now that I am expecting a child, I wish my mother could be with me. But I feel really fortunate that I had Dad." She took a deep, steadying breath. "Three years ago I met and married Nicholas. I have never re-

51

gretted it and I doubt I ever will. Now, tell me about yourself."

Hesitantly, Angela lowered her eyes. Even though she had no secrets to hide, she did not want to discuss her past. Her past included too much of Julia. To talk and think about what that woman had done to her and her father rekindled bitterness and—as reluctant as she was to admit it—hatred. The passing of time had made it easier to bear, but the hurt was still so raw and painful. For some unknown reason Julia had hated her and her father enough to destroy years of their lives. And if she allowed herself to be consumed with hatred, who would she destroy in return? Herself? If so, then Julia would succeed in what she had originally set out to do. And Angela refused to allow that to happen.

Even though Angela was reluctant to talk about the past, Susan was waiting. She felt she had to say something! But what?

Uneasily, Angela squirmed on the bench. "There's not really much to tell. When I was a small child, my mother . . . became very ill and my father sent us to New Orleans so that she could receive proper medical attention. We were to live with one of Mother's relatives, but mother died shortly after we arrived. I lived with Aunt Julia until . . . until a few months ago. Then I decided to try and find my father. And, that's about all there is," Angela said, attempting to shrug her shoulders indifferently, but the gesture was not quite successful.

"I see." Susan felt there was much more to her story and she was curious. But it was obvious Angela did not want to discuss it further. In all likelihood, cross words had passed between her and her aunt when she decided to search for her father. Susan could not help but wonder why he had never come for his daughter. How could a man abandon his child like that? Perhaps that was the reason she looked so sad. Susan had to suppress the sudden urge to try and comfort Angela.

Instead, she smiled pleasantly. "Is there anything you would like to know . . . perhaps about Clint?"

"No . . . not really."

That was not true. There were numerous questions, but she was suddenly too leery to ask them. From his and Susan's conversation, it was obvious he liked women and they were drawn to him. It was a disturbing thought, but it was quite possible she had read too much into his kiss and the gentle way he had held her. If that was so, she did not want to make a fool out of herself by appearing overly interested in him.

Suddenly, Susan giggled. "Oh, my, this is funny. I can almost see the questions clicking through your mind. Some you are discarding as being too personal, some are going into the *maybe* stack, and some you are about to ask. Of course, in all likelihood, you have the same impression about me."

Angela laughed. "That's true." Wrinkling her brow, she peered at the ceiling as if deep in thought, then she looked at Susan. The last information she'd learned about her father was that he lived in Clear Creek. The man who had told her this had been unable—or unwilling—to tell her anything else. "I think Clear Creek will be safe grounds for discussion. I admit that I am very curious about the town."

"In what way?"

"Well, it is my impression that Clear Creek and Silverlode are about the same age."

"Yes, they are."

"Please bear in mind that I've seen Silverlode and have only heard about Clear Creek, so my questions may sound silly. If they are, I ask your forgiveness now. Why has Silverlode grown into a thriving city, and Clear Creek is still just a small town?"

"Considering that you are not accustomed to such a spacious country, your question isn't silly at all, although the answer is quite simple. To be precise, silver, the terrain, and the railroad are the reasons why. When silver was discovered in what is now known as Silverlode City, the strike was rich and the location was easily accessible, so the railroad came in. And there were so many rich strikes in the surrounding area, it didn't pay the railroad to expand their rails to the higher country where small towns like Clear Creek exist. It wasn't profitable."

"Why is the railroad laying tracks to Clear Creek now?"

"Because some prospectors hit strikes big and rich enough to make it worthwhile for the railroad to extend its services. There has been mining up there for years now, but it has always been small scale operations. Then, about a year ago, two men sunk several shafts and hit a fantastically rich vein. It is rumored that there is no end to it, that it runs all the way to China!

"So, the tracks should be laid and trains in operation by the middle of spring. Of course, that timetable depends on how harsh the winter is this year," Susan added.

"Everybody keeps talking about how isolated it is. How do they get supplies in and out?" Angela asked.

"Pack mules mostly, but they don't use the road that passed through the ranch, they use two different ones.

Remembering the terribly rough ride from Silverlode, Angela asked, "Why? Are they better roads?"

"No, they are extremely rough and even more difficult to traverse. If you haven't already, it will be better for you to set aside your preconceived ideas about the roads and trails here in the west." She pointed in the direction of the road. "A couple of years ago, that road out there was little more than a game trail. Then, when news leaked out about the rich strikes, men came through here like swarms of locust. They came in wagons, they walked, rode horses, mules." Susan laughed. "One old geezer even rode a camel! And I do believe some would have crawled if necessary.

"Finally, the owner of the stagecoach line decided it was worthwhile to start a regular run to Clear Creek, but they received too many complaints about the other roads being so rough. Also, the stagecoaches were always breaking axles and wheels which made them run far behind schedule. Although this road takes longer, is steeper, and more dangerous because it runs along so many canyon walls, it has been used almost exclusively by the stage line because it's a more comfortable ride. In the meantime, the heavy freight wagons have almost ruined the other two roads. I seriously doubt if a stagecoach could now make it through on either one."

"Tell me, how many people live up there?" Angela thought that question very important. The answer should give her some indication of how difficult it would be to find her father when she arrived.

Susan thought about it for a moment. "Not counting the people who have ranches, I would say about seven, maybe even eight hundred."

"And the freight lines are actually bringing in enough food to feed that many people through the winter?" Just the thought was staggering.

"Yes. Even though the population will soon decline,

55

the people remaining will need every barrel of flour and other food staples that can be hauled in."

Apprehension still nagged at Angela, but she couldn't put her finger on what bothered her. "Why is the population declining if the silver strikes are so rich? Is it because of the weather?"

"No, the weather doesn't affect underground mining. It seems that the mine owners are laying off men and scaling back their operations this winter because they won't be able to send the ore to the smelters in Silverlode. No ore to the smelters means no money to meet the huge payrolls. However, it's my understanding that some men have agreed to stay on and work through the winter without pay—of course they will be paid in the spring," she added.

Angela felt terror clutch her heart. Her eyes widened in alarm as all color drained from her face. "Oh, no!" she gasped. "It has been years since I have seen my father. He doesn't even know that I am coming. What if he isn't there? What if he is one of the miners who gets laid-off?"

Then another distressing thought struck her. She was almost penniless and she knew no one there. What if no jobs were available? How could she survive in such an isolated place?

Instantly, Susan understood some of Angela's apprehension. She tried to offer reassurance. "If he isn't, he'll probably return in the spring when the mines fully reopen." Then, suddenly aware of Angela's worn clothing, her pitifully thin shawl, she realized her father was not her only concern.

Without even stopping to reconsider, she graciously offered a solution to Angela's dilemma. "Nevertheless, I doubt if you will want to spend the winter there, so if he has already left, you just climb back on board the stagecoach and come back here. You are welcome to stay the winter with us."

"Oh, no, I couldn't do that. I-I couldn't pay . . ."

Susan gave an indifferent wave of her hand. "I never said a word about pay. Your company would be pay enough. Besides, with the baby coming soon, I might need some help." She rolled her eyes. "If you ever saw my husband *attacking* a kitchen, or attempting to sweep a floor, you would know how inept he is in the house. Why, he is all thumbs!"

Angela's eyes flickered to the beautifully carved furniture, and she seriously doubted Susan's statement. Susan had only said those things so that she would agree to stay.

"Good morning, ladies! When I first awoke, there was so much noise, it sounded like birds chattering in here!" Nicholas teased, adjusting his suspenders as he stepped from the bedroom.

"Just hush! You know I seldom get to talk with another woman. And I am thoroughly enjoying Angela's company."

As Nicholas placed his hands affectionately on Susan's shoulders, the simple gesture made Angela envious of the love they shared. Perhaps someday she would know such love and contentment. Again, the image of Clint crept into her mind. Only this time, she did not push it away because the front door flew open and he came stalking inside.

Seeing the three of them, Clint walked toward the table with a mock scowl on his face. He stopped and stood behind Angela. A powerful, inexplicable breathlessness seized her. She had the strangest feeling that he was about to gently put *his* hands on *her* shoulders. Or, could it be that *she wanted him to?*

Clint tried to make his deep, resonant voice sound angry, but the teasing lilt was unmistakable, "I could have sworn I smelled breakfast cooking, but there is nothing, absolutely nothing on the table! Nicholas, I see right now that you haven't been strict enough with your wife."

"I know it!" Nicholas grumbled emphatically while giving Angela an exaggerated wink. "I came in the other night, the house was filthy, dishes were in the dish pan, dirty clothes were piled up on the back porch, no sign of supper cooking, and she was lying in bed eating chocolates and reading a dime novel."

Good naturedly, Susan glared at him, then looked at Angela. "Don't believe a word of it."

"I don't," she said, smiling.

Susan wagged a finger at Nicholas and swatted a dish towel at him. "You are going to tell that story one time too many and I will deliberately let you find the house in that condition."

"Don't believe a word of that threat," Clint remarked dryly. "If she finds one speck of dust, or a doily out of place, the woman becomes a cleaning tyrant!" He nudged Angela's arm and peered down at her. "You know how some men gain reputations with guns? Why, her reputation with a dust cloth and broom has reached all the way to England!"

Still joking, Susan retorted, "So now I'm a tyrant! If the two of you keep it up, you'll both go hungry this morning!"

Clint stuck out his hand and made it quiver. "Scares me to death. How about you, Nicholas?"

Wide-eyed, Nicholas shook his head. "I'm not about

to push my luck. You can get by with that, but I can't. You'll have me sleeping in the barn!" He stepped into the kitchen and picked up a couple of milk pails. "Speaking of the barn, I'd better go milk while I am still able."

"Are you milking two cows?"

"Yeah."

"Then I'll lend you a hand." Clint moved behind Susan, bent over and brushed her forehead with a light kiss. Straightening, his eyes fastened on Angela and lingered approvingly.

Color stained Angela's cheeks before she found the strength to pull her gaze from Clint's.

Finally, he said to Susan, "Brown eyes, could I persuade you to cook my favorite breakfast?"

"Buttermilk biscuits with crispy crusts, milk gravy, and a side of bacon?"

"Um huh!"

"Well, I don't know why, but I suppose so."

The spell broken, Angela excused herself and hurried to her room to straighten it. Then she packed her nightgown and combed her hair back into a bun before going to help Susan with breakfast.

Slightly after dawn, the passengers all boarded the stage.

Susan and Nicholas stood on the porch and watched as the horses pulled the stagecoach up the small rise. Suddenly Susan had such a feeling of foreboding, an icy shiver raced through her.

"Are you cold?" Nicholas asked, tightening his arm around her.

"Yes, but that wasn't why I shivered. I have such a bad feeling, it's—it's disturbing."

"Maybe it's because you know what Clint will find when he reaches their ranch."

Abruptly, Susan looked at him. "You mean you didn't tell him about Dad having to destroy all but fifty head of their cattle?"

Nicholas shook his head. "I figured he would learn about it soon enough. The way I see it, there was no sense in him worrying until he has to."

"I suppose that's why I feel this way. Everybody says that pregnant women become notional at times."

Susan followed Nicholas into the house. But, before she closed the door, she watched the stagecoach disappear over the rise. Deep inside she knew the chill had nothing to do with cattle.

Chapter Five

As the day progressed, the weather turned increasingly cold. Slowly, the stagecoach worked its way up the steep, winding road. Each time they topped a peak, another was there to greet them, looming taller than the one they had just crossed. The wind whipped through the coach, its icy breath invading every nook and cranny.

The passengers welcomed the brief reprieves from the penetrating cold the few times the coach dipped into low mountain meadows. However, the temperature had dropped so rapidly even the low lands were white with frost and fringes of ice could be seen along the edges of slow running streams.

Feeling the coach shift, Angela knew they were climbing again. Shivering, she drew her shawl tightly around her neck. Her hands had started to turn blue and her breath came in frosty daggers. She was miserable.

Staring hard at her, Clint clamped his lips together and sighed from frustration. He held out his heavy, wool-lined coat to her. "Angela, you are freezing. Put this on. I know it's too large, but it will keep you warm." This was the third time he had offered her his coat. Each time, though, she stubbornly refused.

"No, Clint," she replied adamantly. "Honestly, I am not too cold."

He shook his head in utter disbelief. Women! Why were they so hardheaded? He smiled and decided to change his tactic.

"You know as well as I do, if I decide to put it on, the stage driver will just stop and make us walk again. And it would be far too bulky then." She had lost count of the times they had been forced to walk behind the stage since leaving the ranch. Not actually *forced*, but the steep mountains had made it necessary for them to lighten the heavily loaded stagecoach.

She smiled wanly. "Even though it is warmer to walk, I for one would rather ride for a while. This mountain air is so different from what I'm used to. There just doesn't seem to be as much of it."

She hoped by changing the subject Clint would forget about wanting her to wear his coat and he would put it on instead. He had to be cold too. It did not seem right to make him suffer simply because she had come so ill-prepared.

Witherspoon, overhearing only fragments of the conversation, poked his nose out from beneath the blanket he had covering him and grumbled, "You all can do what you want, but I'm damned sure not walking another step. I paid good money for a *ride* to Clear Creek, and I intend to demand every dime of it back the minute we get there!"

Clint glanced at him in disgust, looked away, then swung his head back around and glared at him angrily. "Where did you get that blanket?"

His mouth took on a belligerent twist and his eyes

62

narrowed slightly. "Out from under that seat she's sitting on."

"Are there any more?"

"Yeah, two or three more, I think."

"Then why didn't you say something?" he demanded. "Can't you see that she is freezing?"

Witherspoon took great pleasure in saying, "If I remember right, you ordered me not to talk to her, remember?"

Clint rubbed his hand across his mouth. It was a gesture meant to keep his right hand busy, for his first instinct had been to backhand the poor excuse for a man.

Witherspoon saw the angry gleam flare in Clint's eyes and he knew he had almost pushed the big man too far. Yet, he doubted if Clint would start anything in the narrow confines of the coach, not with the woman present.

He puffed out his chest and blustered, "If you had not stood out beside the coach twiddling your thumbs the last time we had to walk, you would have seen me getting the blanket from the storage compartment underneath the seat. Besides, I should think the blanket is rather conspicuous. If you'd stop gawking at her," he jerked his thumb in Angela's direction, "maybe you'd have eyes for something else!"

"Please, don't argue because of me," Angela said quickly. She had seen Clint's hands tighten into fists, and she did not want to be the cause of a fight.

Standing as best she could in such a small space, Angela raised the cushioned seat, removed one of the blankets, and wrapped it around her shoulders. Then she sat glaring at Hiram, becoming angrier by the minute.

Finally, she spoke, her voice laced with hostility, "Mr. Witherspoon, I do not understand your behavior. I've done nothing to make you so spiteful toward me. When we got back on board the stage, I noticed that you had a blanket wrapped around you, but I thought it was your own. I'm sure you noticed I only have a thin shawl to wear. You could have told us that there were more blankets stored under the seat."

She seethed with mounting rage. "I will also say this; I think you are the most selfish man I have ever met. You care only about your own comfort. It does not matter if someone else is suffering, Hiram T. Witherspoon comes first! If you are married, I pity the poor woman."

Hiram shrugged his shoulders and turned to Clint. "Do I have your permission to speak to the little lady?" he sneered.

Clint had laced his fingers together, and from the fascinated expression on his face, he had thoroughly enjoyed the tongue lashing Angela had given Hiram. He also figured if the man was foolish enough to come back for more, he was welcome to it. He made a grand, sweeping gesture with one arm. "Be my guest. It sounds like she can take care of herself."

Hiram scowled at Angela. "I guess you are entitled to your own opinion—even if it is wrong. You are just a woman and I never had much regard for a female's opinion. I always figured it wasn't that important."

Her gray eyes darkened like the clouds in the sky. Her nostrils thinned, and her nails bit deeply into the palms of her hands. "You are quite right about one thing, Mr. Witherspoon. I am a woman. I am also very tired of your rudeness. I am tired of your complaints. And I am tired of the way you look at me when you think Clint is not paying attention. So, let this *mere woman* give you fair warning right now. If I hear one more complaint about your having to walk—if I see you give me one more dirty look, I will voice a few complaints of my own!"

"What will you do?" he muttered darkly. A tiny voice inside his head cautioned him that he was pressing the issue too far, but he disregarded the warning. "Have him pistol-whip me?" He laughed. "Think I ought to tell you now, he hires his guns out. You might not have enough money to pay him." A nasty smirk spread slowly across his lips. "But then, you probably wouldn't need any money. I'm sure the two of you could work something out."

Clint started to reach for Hiram but Angela grabbed his hands. Never had she been so angry, but she refused to involve Clint. This was her own battle.

"No, Clint, please. That won't be necessary." Setting her chin in a determined line, she managed to suppress her anger under the guise of self-confidence. She moistened her lips before speaking to Witherspoon, "I'll tell you what I will do. I will demand that the driver stop the stage and then I'll tell him how badly you have been annoying me. From what I have heard, western men will not tolerate a woman being mistreated. The driver seems to be honorable. I'm sure he would make room for you up on the box, or perhaps he would even insist you walk the rest of the way to Clear Creek!"

Clint gave her a look of admiration. He found himself completely mesmerized. He would never have thought she could display so much tenacity, city women seldom did. They preferred to use their feminine wiles. But Angela was nothing like the city women he had known. Unless he was badly mistaken, she would pull with a man instead of against him. Without a doubt, she had a fire in her that would make a man feel needed without being smothered.

It suddenly occurred to Clint that he might be treading on dangerous ground. His thoughts had been those of a man looking for a lifetime partner. Maybe the thin mountain air was affecting his mind. The last thing he wanted or needed was a wife!

Witherspoon started to say something else to Angela, but when the stagecoach halted once again, he rolled his eyes and muttered a curse. "Damn! Stopping again?"

Determined to show Hiram she had not been making idle threats, Angela flung open the door and quickly placed her foot on the rung as she backed out of the coach. Stepping down, she turned her head slightly, then seemed to freeze in midair. Giving a sharp cry of alarm, she scrambled back into the stage, almost knocking Clint over since he was about to disembark.

She gasped in unequivocal terror, "There's no ground out there!"

"What?" Clint asked.

She placed her hand over her thudding heart. "There isn't any ground. I almost stepped off into a canyon!"

Clint gently moved her aside and peered out the open door. His eyes also widened, and his stomach reeled uneasily. There was approximately a foot of ground between the stagecoach and a black canyon, so deep and dark with shadows, he could hardly see the bottom. He knew this spot. The canyon was at least two thousand feet deep and the walls were almost straight up.

If the ground gave away. . . . He shook his head at that macabre thought.

Getting a secure grip on the window post, he leaned

out the door and called up to Bill, "Looks like we've hit a bad stretch."

Bill had tied his hat down with a wool scarf and wore his heavy flannel coat buttoned all the way to his throat. "You damn sure got that right! A fair portion of the road has caved off into the canyon."

A huge gust of wind forced Clint to cup one hand around his mouth to enable Bill to hear him. "Is there enough room for the coach to make it across?" He hoped so. There was an elbow curve right behind them so they could not back up, yet if the road were gone, they wouldn't be able to go forward. They were caught in one hell of a predicament.

Worriedly, Bill shook his head. "I don't know. It will be cutting it mighty close. Even then the road might not be safe enough to cross. It don't hurt to be extra cautious so I think you ought to get the other passengers out of the stage and stand clear."

Clint turned about and his heart twisted when he saw marked terror on Angela's ashen features. "Did you hear what Bill said?"

Sheer fright swept through Angela. She swallowed hard. "Yes. . . . I heard most of it . . . unfortunately."

Hiram panicked. "We've got to get out of here!" His hands shook visibly as he tried to open the door on the opposite side of the coach, but it wouldn't budge. He raised the canvas that covered the window, then swore frantically, "Damn it all to hell! We're butted right up against the mountain! There's no way we can get the door open."

"Just stay calm! Don't panic!" Clint rubbed his chin, studying the problem. They would have to abandon the coach on the most dangerous side. One wrong move and they would all be dead. Their lives rested in the hands of fate, yet if he kept his wits about him, perhaps he could nudge their luck in the right direction. He was the strongest and had the longest reach, so it was up to him to get them out safely.

His tone was calm and matter of fact. "This is what we will have to do. Angela, you have the pleasure of going first. And, Witherspoon, listen up because you will follow her. Just climb out the way you regularly would, only make sure you have a good grip on either side of the door. When you step down to the ground, I'll hold on to your arm while you work your way back to the wheel. I want you to grab it. Once you clear the wheel, keep working your way back until you reach the rear of the stage. Then, get as close as you can to the side of the mountain and put at least twenty feet between you and the coach. Now, Angela, repeat my instructions back to me so that I know you understand."

In a faltering voice, she did as he said.

"Remember this, too; if the ground crumbles underneath your feet, don't panic. I'll have a good hold on you, and I won't let you fall."

A heart-stopping dread ran the entire length of her spine. "W-what if the horses s-suddenly move forward?"

"That won't happen," he reassured her. "Bill knows his business. He'll have the brake set and Jonesy will be up front holding the lead horses to help keep them calm."

She took a deep, shuddering breath, then blew it out. "All right, I'm ready."

Clint stuck his head out the doorway and called out to Bill, "We're coming out now."

"Okay, you folks take it slow and easy. I'll help Jonesy keep a tight rein on the horses."

Clint turned back to Angela. "There's one more thing. Let me take your shawl and that blanket. If you try to keep them wrapped around you, you might lose your balance." Knowing how frightened she had to be, he suddenly reached out and caressed her cheek with his knuckles. "I promise we'll be all right. Trust me," he murmured.

Without saying another word, she handed the shawl and blanket to Clint and moved toward the door.

Angela did exactly as Clint had instructed. As she worked her way alongside the coach, his strong grip on her arm gave her the courage to continue as the ground crumbled beneath one of her feet. She gave a startled cry, but he uttered words of encouragement, and soon, she was safe behind the stage.

Clint quickly knotted the blanket and shawl together. He held one end and swung the other toward Angela. She caught it on the first attempt.

Even though Clint had told her to stand clear of the stage, she had no intention of doing that. Either he or Witherspoon might need her. She wanted to be in a position to grab either man if one lost his hold; her being there might make the difference of one of them living or falling into the canyon below.

Once Angela was safe, Clint slipped on his heavy coat and said to Witherspoon. "Come on, you're next."

Hesitantly, Hiram slid across the seat, but when he saw the dangerously narrow footing and the steep incline of the canyon, he recoiled.

Vigorously shaking his head, he scooted backwards. "No, I'm not leaving! I'll fall!"

"No, you won't, I'll help you."

He stared at Clint, his eyes wide from fear. "You have no reason to help me . . . not after the way . . ."

Sensing that the man was about to become hysterical, Clint shrugged indifferently and said, "That was just petty bickering. As far as I'm concerned, it never happened."

"No ... I can't ..." his voice broke and his eyes slowly trailed down to the dark wet splotch that had suddenly stained his trousers. "I'm ... too scared," he muttered.

Clint saw the stained trousers, but pretended he had not noticed. It would have disgusted him if the situation had been different. But Witherspoon was so afraid, he could not control himself.

Keeping his voice smooth, Clint coaxed him, "Come on, man. It isn't safe in here. The weight of the stage alone could easily cause the road to collapse even further."

Hiram's chin trembled and tears ran freely down his flaccid cheeks. *"I can't! I just can't!"*

"Clint, what's keeping you?" Bill shouted urgently. "I can't hold these horses still much longer. They're getting awfully edgy."

Clint stuck his head out the door. "Witherspoon has balked." He glanced at the man cowering in his seat. "I don't know if I can make him budge." His tone of voice held no condemnation.

"Then leave the damn fool where he's at. These horses are gonna shy if we don't get on with it."

Clint tried one last time to persuade Hiram to leave. He told him that his added weight in the coach was putting Bill's life in jeopardy, but Hiram just sat there shaking his head, too frightened to move.

Sighing with frustration, Clint swung down from the coach and within moments, he and Angela were running clear of the stage. Sticking his little fingers in each corner of his mouth, he gave a shrill whistle, a signal for Bill to start the stagecoach forward.

Jonesy held each of the front horses's bridle bits and tugged when Bill released the brake and gently wiggled the reins. They did not dare try to cross the bad stretch in a hurry; the horses were edgy enough, and there was the ever present danger of the animals bolting and running away. The steep mountainside was no place to lose control of a team of horses.

Each time the rear wheels made a single revolution, Angela came closer to breathing a sigh of relief. Once, the outside wheel was a scant two inches from the crumbling edge, and the other wheel scraped the mountain wall.

The stagecoach was less than thirty feet from safety, when suddenly, the entire road collapsed. Later, Angela realized the disaster had occurred within a matter of seconds, but at the time it seemed to stretch into infinity because she saw each man's last desperate attempt to live.

It seemed that the coach and horses all hung suspended in midair before the stage slowly careened on its side and started plummeting into the deep chasm below.

From inside the coach, Angela saw a hand clawing at the window covering. Then, came a shriek of terror that bore no resemblance to human speech.

Bill tried desperately to jump clear, but the stage upended and he missed the rock outcropping he had leaped toward. He made a desperate lunge for a stunted bush, but more of the road caved in on top of him. His hand was only inches from the bush, then he started to fall. After ricocheting off three huge boulders, he fell, arms and legs outstretched, to the base of the canyon.

His screams, piercing at first, diminished on the way down until they could no longer be heard.

The horses' legs flailed the air and whinnies of terror echoed throughout the canyon.

Jonesy hung precariously over the side, his hands grasping a small rock that jutted just a few feet below where the road had been. He looked toward Clint and Angela. He made one futile plea for help, then as the rock started to give way, his face reflected the terror of facing such a horrifying death. Then, he seemed to reconcile himself to his fate, and strangely, a peaceful expression flickered across his features before he fell.

Angela kept hearing screams, but how could that be? All of the men were dead! Were the cries coming from their tormented souls?

Suddenly, she felt hands on her shoulders, roughly shaking her, then she felt the stinging blow of a large hand across her face.

"Angela, stop it! You have to stop screaming!"

Confused, yet still terror-stricken, she glanced up and saw Clint. He had shaken her. He had slapped her. *She had been the one screaming!* Yet, in her mind, she could still hear the men's death cries.

Her tortured mind in chaos, she finally realized Clint had scooped her into his arms and was running, getting her as far away from the danger as possible.

Clint stopped when he reached a point he figured to be a safe distance from the unstable stretch of road. He knelt and placed Angela on the ground, then wrenched the shawl and blanket from her grasp and wrapped them around her. Gently, he cradled her in his arms and smoothed her hair from her face.

When he finally found his voice, he murmured, "Go

ahead Angela and cry—scream, hit me—do anything you want, but don't keep it damned up inside you."

Then, slowly, he looked up at the sky and sadly shook his head.

Chapter Six

For a moment, all that could be heard was the moan of the wind as it rushed over the mountain peaks and through the valleys.

Angela slowly raised her eyes to meet Clint's concerned gaze. Her gray eyes showed the tortured dullness of disbelief. "I—I can't cry. Oh, God, how I wish I could." She took a deep shuddering breath. "I have never seen men die before. . . . May God have mercy on their souls."

Clint felt he could not allow her to see how the accident had affected him. To do so might shatter her resolve. Quickly forcing his expression into a mask of stone, he carefully observed her. Her lovely eyes were shadowed, haunted. He could see the anguish in them and briefly wondered if what he was seeing was a mirror image of the tragedy that kept flashing before his mind's eyes.

"Are you all right?" he asked, realizing as he spoke how ridiculous the words must have sounded after what had just happened. But it was a question he felt he had to ask, for her behavior was not at all what he expected. Most women would have been hysterical. But, other than being shocked and appalled, she now seemed to have a good grip on her emotions.

"I suppose I am," she whispered slowly. "But I don't know what to think, I don't know what to do—I keep hearing their screams. I think I shall always hear their screams." Her bottom lip trembled and tears misted her eyes. She clutched at his broad chest. "Clint . . . I feel so sorry for them, yet, may God forgive me, I am so relieved that they died instead of us! When I think how easily we could have been in that coach too . . ." her voice broke as she closed her eyes and shuddered. "It makes me feel so guilty!" A look of remorse passed over her features and she had to clench her jaw to kill the sob in her throat.

Clint was amazed by her honesty. It had taken courage to confess her true feelings. Tilting her chin upwards, he murmured softly, "Before you condemn yourself, I want you to know that I understand what you are saying, and I feel the same as you. I think it's natural for us to feel guilty for not ending up in the bottom of that canyon the same as they did. Yet, I'm grateful that we are alive. And I don't believe that makes us cruel-hearted, or any less human."

"I am grateful too, but . . ." Angela looked at him hopefully as she tried weighing the whole structure of events. "Clint, do you think there is the slightest possibility that any of them survived?"

Sadly, he shook his head. "No."

"Shouldn't we try to climb down into the canyon and make sure?"

Clint's jaw clenched, his eyes narrowed slightly. "Angela, no one could survive a fall like that." His voice held a sorrowful tone as he added, "I'm usually the last one to admit defeat, but there is nothing we or anyone can do."

Her face blanched and her brows drew together in an agonized expression as still yet another horrifying thought occurred to her. "Oh, no! What about their bodies? Won't wild animals get to them?"

He stiffened. "Damn it, Angela, I've already told you, there's nothing I can do!" His shoulder muscles flexed as he tore his gaze from what suddenly seemed to be her accusing eyes. He then came to his feet and moved away, staring blindly into the distance.

Did she have no idea how that thought tore at him? Did she believe he had no conscience? Two of those men had been his friends. No man, not even a coward like Witherspoon, deserved to be left like that!

From behind him, Angela touched his arm. "Clint, please, look at me—please don't do this again."

Pivoting around, he asked bluntly, "Do what again?"

Her eyes searched his face, trying to reach into his thoughts. "You avoided me yesterday after the attempted robbery instead of explaining that I was wrong to accuse you. Now, I can see that you are angry with me again, and I have no idea what I said to warrant such anger."

His tone was filled with remorse, "I'm not angry with you, Angela, and I shouldn't have snapped at you the way I did. I suppose I feel frustrated—so powerless . . ." He sighed and shook his head dejectedly. "God as my witness, I wish there was something I could do for them."

Angela cringed at her thoughtlessness. Where was her mind? What had she been thinking to ask such callous questions? No wonder he had snapped at her the way he did. Clint must have known Bill and

Jonesy quite well, and he probably considered them to be his friends.

Still, even after realizing what she had done, there was a persistent nagging in the back of her mind that refused to be stilled. *What if she were the reason he felt he had to abandon his friends?*

"Clint, please be honest with me. I have to know. Would you attempt to reach the wreckage and take care of their bodies if you did not have to worry about me?" She held her breath, waiting for his reply.

He smiled but there was too much sadness about him for it to reach his eyes. However, the smile took the sting from his words. "Angela, even if I could find a way down, I'd never be able to make it back here before dark, and you would never survive through the night up here on this ledge on your own. Look at the sky. Those are snow clouds. It could start snowing within the next five minutes or five hours. We are out in the open without shelter from the wind or the snow, and you are not dressed for this kind of harsh weather."

"I see," she said slowly. "Then it is my fault."

"No, I'm afraid you don't see, so you can stop blaming yourself before you start. The way I feel right now has nothing to do with you. The cold facts are: Bill and Jonesy had a job to do and they did it. They knew the risks involved. And you had better believe they were not the sort of men who would want us to risk our lives just to give them a proper burial. Somehow, it would make their sacrifice seem pointless."

It surprised Clint that he could be so open with her, to tell her his innermost feelings. He raked one hand through his hair and looked at her. "Now that all of that is settled, I suggest we get started. We have a long walk ahead of us."

"Are we going back to the ranch?"

"No, it's too far. Our best bet is to head for the way station."

She gestured toward the gaping hole in the road and took a step backwards, reluctant to approach it—and for good reason. "How are we going to cross that?" she asked, fear edging into her voice.

He looked at the mountain wall as though estimating how difficult it would be to climb. "We're not, the road is too unstable. We'll have to walk back down the mountainside a ways, then cut across country."

Angela stared up at the threatening sky. "Do you think we can reach the way station before dark or before the storm hits?"

He stared at her for a moment, his dark eyebrows slanting in a frown. It was quite obvious that the girl had no idea how serious their predicament was.

After taking a deep breath, he said, "I might as well be blunt with you, so that you will know exactly what we are facing. We are not taking an afternoon excursion to a city park. Our lives are at stake. It so happens that the way station is about thirty miles from here. Walking across country, we might be able to shave five—maybe even ten miles off of that, but don't count on it. We could get lucky and stumble onto a prospector's cabin, but we can't count on that either. We might as well set our minds right now to the fact that it will take us three to four days to reach the way station—that is, if the storm that's blowing in cooperates." He continued harshly, "And, to make it even worse, you are not dressed for this type of cold weather. On top of all that, not a soul knows where we are, and there won't be any cries of alarm when the stage fails to arrive on schedule. If we survive, we will do it by our wits alone. Now," he

78

sighed heavily, his dark eyes prolonging the moment, "do you have any more questions?"

Angela was stunned. There was a lump in her throat so big, she thought it would choke her. She'd had no idea what perils they faced, and for a moment she wished she had never pressed him with her silly questions. Now, she fully understood why he had been so distraught. It wasn't just the death of his friends; he knew the undeniable and dreadful facts of what lay ahead for them. The obstacles seemed to be unsurmountable. Angela longed to just sit down and quit.

Then suddenly, a fiery resolve washed over her. Only cowards quit without trying. That was why Witherspoon had died. She reached down inside of herself and gathered a vast amount of inner strength and courage. Even though her insides still quaked with fear, the expression she presented to Clint was calm and collected, and her gray eyes were filled with confidence and determination. She jutted her chin in defiance. "Yes, I do have one more question."

"What?"

"Do you have a jackknife?"

"Why?"

"Do you have one?" she persisted.

Confused by her illogical request, he merely nodded.

"May I see it please?" She extended her hand and waited until he removed it from his pocket and handed it to her. While opening it, she explained, "I may be *from the city,* but I seldom took *afternoon excursions!* I realize I know practically nothing about surviving in the wilderness. But I have always been an avid reader and I recall reading that quite a bit of a person's body heat is lost if their head is uncovered. Since you lost your hat, you will need some protection."

Touching his head, he looked dumbfounded. "I never noticed it was missing."

Quickly, she cut a long strip from the blanket, then tied it around Clint's head and wound the ends around his neck like a scarf.

Standing back to observe her handiwork, she smiled tentatively and said, "It isn't the most masculine apparel, but I suppose it will do under these circumstances."

He weighed Angela with a baffled squint. Her reactions had not been what he had expected, especially not after what he had just told her. Maybe he should stop underestimating her. Angela was a very complex woman, not at all like the other city women he had known. He could see now that it was a mistake to expect her to behave like them.

Her eyes widened mischievously. "Apparently I have confused you. If you promise never to tell anyone, I will admit to you that quite a lot of my reading material were gaudy dime novels—left behind by male boarders. I never purchased one myself," she hastened to add. "But, I loved reading them. And, if I remember correctly, one of the favorite expressions used by western men is this one." She squinted one eye and drawled in what she figured to be the speech pattern of a crusty old cowboy. "Well, partner, guess we had better git a move on. We're burning good daylight!"

She was so comical, Clint threw back his head and laughed. "Yep, I reckon we are at that. C'mon Slim, follow me. Best that we git off this mountainside 'fore it commences to snow. Need to go as far as we can 'fore we have to find shelter. Then, we'll have to jump us a critter if we plan on eatin' supper." He looked at Angela dubiously. "You can cook . . . can't you?"

"Why, I should smile!" she replied teasingly. Then, an inexplicable sensation swept through her as Clint suddenly reached out and trailed his large hand along the line of her cheek, then cupped her chin. Her emotions whirled and skidded beyond control as blood pounded through her veins. She was so aware of the invisible web of attraction building between them, and it left her feeling invigorated.

Admiration for her shone from his eyes. "Atta-girl, *Slim*" he muttered huskily. "With that kind of attitude and courage, we'll make it fine."

Not trusting her voice, she breathed lightly between parted lips until she was finally able to murmur, "I know we will, but please do not rely on my courage, there's not that much of it."

Clint's expression stilled and became extremely serious, the muscles in his cheeks flexing. His mouth lowered until it was but mere inches from hers. She was surprised and confused by her own eagerness for the touch of his lips. She had never been kissed before and somehow it seemed so important that he should be the first.

Brusquely stepping back, Clint swallowed hard, clearing away the lump that had suddenly formed in his throat. "We're wasting time. We'd better get started." He abruptly turned and walked away.

Angela was astonished at the sense of fulfillment she felt, even though he had not kissed her. *He had wanted to kiss her, though!* And, somehow that was just as important as the actual act.

Squaring her shoulders, she covered her head with the blanket, tucked it around her neck, then fell in behind Clint.

* * *

Clint paused and looked about the rugged terrain. His expression was tight from strain. Even though only a light, dusting snow had begun to fall less than an hour earlier, the snowflakes had already started to cling to the branches of the trees, and the temperature was steadily dropping. He looked up at the sky and estimated there was slightly more than an hour of daylight left. If he did not find suitable shelter soon, not only would they be forced to spend the night in the open, they would go hungry as well.

He turned around to face Angela. She wore the blanket over the top of her head and pulled across her mouth and nose so that only her eyes and forehead could be seen. "Are you all right?"

Angela's feet and legs had become so numb she could barely feel them. Her body felt heavy, as if she had spent a long day under a blistering sun. She had gone just about as far as she could go, but she could not stop now, Clint had not been able to find shelter. Several places had looked suitable to her, but his experienced eye had detected pitfalls she had not noticed. She had to rely solely on his judgement.

She stamped her feet to keep the blood circulating through her body. "Yes ... but I am ... getting tired."

Her tone was not complaining. She was merely following Clint's strict orders. He had cautioned her at the beginning of the trek that exhaustion was as dangerous as the cold, and to be sure and tell him before she pushed herself beyond the limits of her endurance. He had explained that most people who froze when caught out in harsh weather did so because they burned up their stores of energy before stopping to rest, and then they had nothing left to fight the cold. She had reached that point. To continue would be foolhardy.

His expression was grim and he did not attempt to conceal the fact that he was worried. "I don't see any place here where we can hole up. Do you think you can make it for another ten minutes or so? I believe I spotted a likely place when we came down that last ridge."

She slowly bobbed her head as hope sank deeply within her soul. "Yes . . . I think so."

Wordlessly, Clint turned and continued along the edge of the forest, with Angela trailing further behind.

With the rising wind in their faces, they worked their way north until they reached the small stream Clint had glimpsed earlier.

Relief spurted through him when he finally found what he had been searching for. Several blown-down trees had lodged in the branches of the surrounding trees. One, a huge spruce, had heavy branches that reached the ground. Under it were many smaller spruces with skirts of branches that touched the ground.

"Stay here, I'll be right back."

Angela was so tired she sagged onto a large rock, oblivious to the cold, the wind, the snow. She had thought her body was well-conditioned, considering all of the hours she had worked at Julia's boardinghouse, and the menial jobs she had been forced to accept in order to further her search. Apparently, though, she had been mistaken. Nothing could have prepared her for this ordeal.

Clint made his way through the tangle of boughs and discovered that the trees and branches had formed a small but almost solid ring of protection from the wind and snow. The ground was dry and was heavily carpeted with pine needles. There were also dead branches lying about that could be used for firewood. It was perfect! If the snowstorm became a full-scale blizzard, they could hole up in this place until it blew itself out.

Being careful not to dislodge the snow from the branches, he made his way back out to where Angela stood. When she saw the smile on his face, a great wave of relief washed over her.

Although his voice sounded tired, his words were uplifting. "It doesn't have the comforts of home, but it's by far the best place I've seen." He reached out his hand for hers. "Come on, I'll get a fire built."

The instant he heard Angela's ragged breathing, he pulled the blanket from her face. When she looked up at him with unprotesting, yet glazed eyes, he realized she had not fared as well as she had led him to believe. *Damn little fool! She had pushed herself past the point of exhaustion!*

He had questioned her numerous times, and each time she had assured him that she was able to continue. But he never should have listened to her!

He bit back an angry reprimand, realizing she was in no condition to listen, and besides, he was as much to blame as she.

Inside the shelter, Clint guided her to a trunk of a tree, and helped her to the ground. Still furious, he quickly unbuttoned his coat, removed it and wrapped it around her shoulders. He cursed himself for not insisting she take his coat earlier. He had offered it several times, but she had doggedly refused.

Why was she so damned stubborn?

He hurriedly raked pine straw into a large pile, then with his foot, cleared the immediate area so that sparks would not ignite the other debris. After searching for and adding a few twigs and small branches, he lit the

84

fire. It smoldered for only a few moments before the flames caught and burst into a warm blaze. Making a basin by bending together the corners of a sheet of bark, Clint took it outside, filled it with snow then returned and placed it on the fire to melt. He knew the basin would not burn as long as the flames did not reach past the moisture inside. When the snow melted and started to steam, he removed the basin from the fire and held it to Angela's lips.

"Here, drink this. It will help to warm you," he said softly.

Angela sipped at it hesitantly, then as the warmth coursed down her throat, she gulped greedily.

Noting that Angela was now capable of holding the basin on her own, Clint added larger chunks of wood to the fire. Then, placing his hands on his hips, he turned to face her. "Why in the hell didn't you tell me you were that cold and nearing exhaustion?"

"But, I . . ."

Clint continued to rail, "We could have stopped to rest, there were several places out of the wind where I could have built a fire!" He threw up his hands in disgust. "But hell no! You were too damned stubborn to pay attention to what I told you earlier! Didn't I warn you how dangerous it was to push yourself too hard?"

"I-I didn't know I was that tired," she said listlessly, too weary to protest his tongue lashing.

She recognized the fact that Clint was angry, but all she wanted to do was lie down and sleep. She felt as though she would never be warm again, and even though she was hungry, what she longed for the most was clothing—warm, soft, wonderful clothing.

Suddenly, she felt herself drifting effortlessly, as

though on a fleecy cloud, only briefly aware of the strong arms that held her tightly, protecting her from the cold.

Chapter Seven

The campfire had burned itself down to a heap of smoldering coals, and it cast an eerie light on the absorbing darkness. Overhead, the cold wind whispered through the pines, causing an occasional snowflake to fall through the thick boughs and sporadically sift to the earth below.

Being careful not to disturb the natural windbreaks, Clint crawled through a small opening until he reached a spot where he could stand without having to stoop over. He glanced at Angela, noting that she was still asleep in the makeshift bed he prepared for her after she had dropped from exhaustion.

Putting the deer he had killed aside, Clint brushed away the snow clinging to his coat, then quickly added more wood to the fire before he took the time to warm his hands and hang the scarf on a branch to dry.

After sharpening two sticks and cutting small pieces of meat from one of the haunches, he skewered them on the sticks and held them over the fire, turning them slowly so that they would cook evenly.

He knew it had been an uncanny stroke of luck to find an injured deer trapped in a deadfall. The deer was scarcely more than a yearling, but it would provide enough food to last them for several days if the storm forced them to hole up until it blew itself out. He did not think it was a major storm—not this early in the season, but he had learned not to speculate on Colorado's weather. Their lives depended on his judgment and wrong assumptions could prove to be fatal.

While cooking the meat, his troubled gaze strayed to Angela's sleeping form, as though sizing her up. He shifted uncomfortably. What was it about her that had such a disrupting effect on him?

There was no doubt she was attractive, but he usually preferred women who were the exact opposite. He had always fancied petite blondes instead of willowy black-haired women. Strangely enough, he found her uncommonly appealing.

Why?

Clint pulled his gaze away. Perhaps he had forgotten how to appreciate a woman like Angela, one that was not brazen or coquettish. The women he'd had to associate with while he was in England had soured him. Most had been the wives or daughters of titled gentry, and they had been either too haughty or too sniveling, and too bored with their pompous husbands, fiances, and their aristocratic social circles. It had seemed that most of their greatest concerns involved clothing, elegant balls, who was in favor at court, and who was involved in a tryst with what man. He shook his head with disgust. Life there had been shallow, almost without purpose.

He supposed it was possible that was why he found Angela so intriguing. Then too, it could be the simple fact that she was an attractive woman and he was a man who had been without the pleasure of a loving female

88

for months now. If that was the basis for his attraction, then he would have to ignore it. She was not the sort of woman a man could make love to, then walk away from without leaving part of himself behind.

Angela struggled against the stirrings of wakefulness. Her subconscious preferred to remain in the warm oblivion where there were no painful memories. Yet, something kept beckoning her until she finally raised her heavy eyelids partway and let the golden glow of the campfire fill her vision until it was blocked by Clint's masculine form.

She sniffed deeply and the aroma of meat roasting over an open flame filled her nostrils. The juices popped and hissed as they hit the fire, and the food smelled delicious.

Opening her eyes further, she noted that she was lying on a thick bed of pine straw with the shawl and blanket tucked tightly around her, and more pine straw had been heaped on top of the covers for added warmth.

"Is it morning already?" she asked, still disoriented from sleep.

Clint glanced at her as she propped up on an elbow. Dark tresses had come unpinned and hung in tousled curls over her shoulders. He quickly stifled the urge to tangle his hands in her thick mane while tasting the sweetness of her lips. Instead, he cleared away the knot that had formed in his throat and said, "No, you've only been asleep for a couple of hours. I've been hunting and gathering firewood."

"You should have woke me."

He shook his head. "You needed the nap more than I needed help." Smiling, he brandished a stick of food in a tantalizing manner. "I figured you would wake up though, when you caught the smell of food cooking."

"I suppose I did," she responded enthusiastically, brushing away the pine straw and rising. Wrapping the blanket around her shoulders, she hurried closer to the fire, knelt down beside Clint, and sniffed again. "Mm, it smells delicious! What is it?" Her mouth watered from hunger.

"Venison," he replied, handing her a stick of the skewered meat.

She frowned. "Venison? But I thought you needed a rifle to shoot a deer. How were you able to . . .?"

"Not necessarily. I'm just grateful I was lucky enough to get a good shot or we would be spending the night with our bellies growling." Somehow the insinuation that he had brought the deer down with a pistol seemed more heroic than telling her that he had found the animal trapped in a deadfall. Killing it had been just as easy as shooting fish in a barrel. He doubted she would have been very impressed.

Angela stared at the haunch from which he had cut the pieces of meat and her stomach knotted. "I thought . . . deer were larger animals." She wanted to add that the haunch looked so small, it appeared to have come from a baby deer, but she swallowed the remark, afraid that Clint would misunderstand and think she was criticizing him.

"It was a yearling," he explained, not fully understanding her reluctance. "But it will be enough to see us through if the storm forces us to hole up for a few days. Go ahead and eat, you'll need the strength it will give."

In her mind's eye, Angela could see the beautiful, spirited animals grazing in the meadows, then bounding gracefully into the safety of the trees when the coach passed by. Having lived most of her life in the city, she'd never thought about where the meat she ate had come from. Purchasing food from the butcher was so different from seeing a recently killed animal. Nevertheless, she supposed it was the natural order of things, and the food meant their survival.

Holding the stick on both ends, she hesitantly bit into the meat. The outside was charred from the fire, but beneath the darkened crust the meat was juicy, tender, and had a vague sweet taste. "Why, it's delicious!"

"I agree! I'm so hungry I won't even complain about the lack of salt."

They ate heartily and in silence. After Clint had finished, he retrieved his scarf and wrapped it around his head.

Angela quickly crammed the last bite into her mouth and started to put out the fire, but Clint stopped her.

"What are you doing?"

"Why, putting out the fire. Surely you don't intend for us to leave it burning."

"Of course not, but we're not going anywhere tonight. I was just going after some more firewood. There's a deadfall not too far away and I think I should gather as much as I can in case we're forced to stay here for a few days. While I'm gone, you can collect the pinecones and start cooking the rest of the meat." He handed her his knife. "It's too cold for the meat to ruin, but I don't want any animals to catch the scent of a fresh kill. Think you can manage?"

"Of course I can."

"You don't have to cook it thoroughly, just enough to knock the edge off the raw smell."

Color stained Angela's cheeks while she prepared the meat to cook and gathered fuel for the fire. "Clint must think I am a complete dolt!" she finally grumbled aloud. "And he would certainly be within his rights. Only an idiot would think we would leave a shelter during a snowstorm, especially in the middle of the night."

She was still mumbling to herself when Clint crawled back into the shelter, dragging a small tree behind him.

He glanced about expectantly, cocked his ear, and said, "Listen."

Angela turned her head and listened carefully. Recalling Clint's earlier warning about the meat, she began to shake as fearful images of hungry animals stalking their shelter rose in her mind. Wolves? Or maybe even a wild bear! She edged closer to him for protection. If it was a bear she doubted if a pistol could stop it. She might not know much about surviving in the wilderness, but she knew that Clint—even as skillful as he was with a gun—had little chance of challenging a bear with a mere pistol.

A few moments later, Clint shrugged and shook his head. "My mind must be playing tricks on me, or, I guess it could have been the wind," he mumbled. "But I could have sworn I heard . . ."

"Wha . . . what did you hear?"

He grinned sheepishly. "I thought I heard voices, but there's nobody here but us."

Angela stood motionless as she realized that Clint had overheard her talking to herself. She was not about to admit such a character weakness. "I thought I heard something too. But, you're right, it was probably the wind." She quickly turned her attention to the meat.

"Were you scared?" Clint asked, remembering how she had sidled close to him.

"Me?" she queried innocently. "Oh, no, I never gave it a second thought."

Clint didn't believe her for a minute, but he saw no need in pressing the issue. After warming his hands by the fire, he tucked them into his coat pockets. "I'll be back in a little while."

"Where are you going?"

"After wood. Remember?"

"Don't we have enough?"

"Yeah, probably enough for tonight and tomorrow too. But it's snowing harder and like I told you, we might be snowed in for several days. I'd rather have more on hand than not enough. I've already wrestled more trees out of that deadfall, so I won't be gone as long this time." He looked at her dubiously. "Do you want me to leave one of my guns for protection?"

Angela considered his offer. She didn't know anything about guns. If her imagination ran away with her again, why, she might accidentally shoot Clint when he returned. "No, I'll be just fine. I'm not frightened."

She saw Clint breathe an inward sigh of relief. Apparently the same thought had occurred to him.

Clint left quickly before she had a chance to change her mind. If he had felt there was danger present, he would have instructed her on how to shoot, but leaving a city woman alone in the woods with a loaded gun was just asking for trouble. More than likely one or the other would have ended up with a gunshot wound, or even worse!

Pushing such thoughts from his mind, Clint busied himself with the matters at hand.

Less than an hour later, he was sitting by the campfire warming himself while Angela placed the last of the seared meat in a mound of clean snow she had gotten from outside the shelter.

Clint had been dreading this moment, but he couldn't

delay it any longer. When he spoke, his tone was tinged with reluctance, yet it was firm and filled with authority, "Angela, we need to clear the air about a certain matter before something else happens. . . . Something that could be very serious."

Angela's brow furrowed, she wondered what she had done wrong. "My goodness, you sound so solemn," she said, wiping her hands on her skirt.

"This is serious. I have to make sure that you completely understand what I have to say." He waited until she had joined him beside the fire. "Earlier today, I warned you what could happen if you pushed yourself past the point of exhaustion. Then you deliberately disregarded my warning. That was dangerous, Angela. Not only dangerous, but it was a damned fool thing to do," he added bluntly.

Clint's sharp words took her by surprise. "But . . . I didn't want to complain. I thought you had enough to worry about without having to listen to me whine and snivel."

"Complain? Whine and snivel? Damn, Angela, there's a big difference between doing those and voicing a reasonable request! This is high country. The air is thinner here than what you've been used to, and it makes it more difficult to breathe. I've only been away for about a year and I've found myself getting short-winded. When you combine that with the cold, the accident, also the fact that you look as though you haven't been eating regularly . . ." He shook his head vigorously. "So, the way I see it, your telling me that you are tired doesn't tally up to be a complaint."

Moistening her lips, Angela looked away. "You don't understand." How could she explain Julia's hateful personality to him when she had never understood herself why the woman had always been so heartless and cruel?

Clint gestured helplessly, palms raised. "What am I not supposed to understand?

Angela sighed heavily as she searched for the right words. "The woman who raised me never tolerated complaints or excuses of any kind. She claimed they were signs of weakness."

"Then she was a damned fool! She didn't know what she was talking about!" Immediately, Clint's features softened. He raked a hand through his thick hair. "I'm sorry. I shouldn't have said anything like that about your relative."

She shot him a withering look, but there was undeniable pain in her eyes. Her voice grated harshly. "She's not a relative, and you can say anything you want about her—I don't care!"

"I hope you never get that riled against me," Clint said softly.

"Riled? Oh," she murmured, "you mean angry. My feelings toward her have gone far past anger."

Clint realized he had hit upon a sore spot. His dad had taught him never to pry into anyone's personal business. He always said, if a person wanted to discuss his past, he would in his own due time. Clint agreed with his father up to a point. But it seemed to him that Angela was carrying a heavy burden, and she might need a little prodding to get rid of it.

"It sounds as though you two had words when you decided to come to your father."

Angela toed the ground with her shoe. "I suppose that is an appropriate way to describe it."

"Want to talk about it?"

"Not really."

"Why?"

"Because—because I don't want to!" she snapped.

"Doesn't sound like it to me."

Angela had been forced to hold her temper and tongue in check all of the years she had lived with Julia, and she was determined never to let that happen again. "Will you please stop harassing me? My relationship with Julia is not any of your business. Even if I live to be a hundred years old, I never want to discuss that woman! Now ... the matter is closed!" Her annoyance increased when she found her hands were shaking. She wished for a room to stalk out of and a door to slam.

Clint knew that whenever Susan had been so adamant about anything, she would say the opposite of what she meant. Now that his curiosity was fully aroused, he decided to try the same approach with Angela.

"That's true," he agreed, "it isn't any of my business." He waited a moment, then feigned a heavy sigh. "Poor old thing," he murmured with a pitying tone, "I can imagine how it must have broke her heart when the young girl she sacrificed so much for, ran off the first chance she got."

Angela shook her head in utter disbelief. "Surely you are not referring to me and Julia? That *poor old thing* could best be described as ... as ... Lucifer's Angel! Why, I'd wager if they met face to face, he would give her the keys to Hell, then run from her as fast as he could! Why, I could tell you things about that woman that ..."

"Why don't you," he said softly.

"Because ... because ... I'm afraid that if I allow my thoughts to dwell on her ... I'll become so full of hatred ... I'll end up just as mean and spiteful as she is." Her voice floundered, but the sincerity of her words made her sound adamant and determined when she added, "And I think I would rather die before I let that happen."

Clint realized her admission was dredged from a place far beyond logic and reason. It was evident by the intensity of her feelings that if she continued to hold in her bitterness, she would never be able to put whatever happened to rest.

"Perhaps you're right, but then, maybe you're wrong. I have always believed harboring a grudge tends to make it worse. It's like ignoring a tiny sore. It soon grows and festers until it becomes untreatable. Maybe if you talk about what happened, you'll purge yourself of those hard feelings."

She jerked her head about and glared at him. "Are you suggesting that I forgive her?"

"No, but I'm suggesting that you might be able to put it behind you." He stared back at her without blinking an eye. "My dad taught me an excellent philosophy concerning life. I try to apply it to my own problems when I have them."

"Here comes a *profound* statement, I'm sure!" she remarked caustically, rolling her eyes.

Clint ignored her sarcasm. "When faced with a problem, it is all right to worry about it, *if* doing so will help solve it. But if there is no solution, no way for you to *fix* it, then leave it alone. Put it behind you. The same theory can easily be applied to grievances and grudges."

Doubt reflected from her eyes like smoke from a fire. She flung her hands in the air. "You mean I am going to wipe away the memory of all those miserable years just by talking about it? I'm supposed to forget how she destroyed my life, and what she did to my father too? Just like that?" she asked, snapping her fingers.

"No, that's not what I said." He was beginning to get an inkling of how miserable that woman had made Angela. He put his arm around her shoulder and drew her close to him. It was not a gesture of love or passion, but of one human comforting another during a time of need. "Come on, Slim, talk it out. If it doesn't make you feel better inside, what have you lost?"

Wrapping her arms around her legs, she pulled her knees up and rested her chin on them. She remained silent for a long agonizing minute. When she finally began to speak, it was as though a dam had burst.

"Julia and mother were childhood friends—apparently, the very best of friends. They even kept in touch after mother married my father and they moved west to the mining towns in Nevada. Julia later told me that mother never fully recovered after I was born. As the years passed, her health continued to worsen. Evidently, there were few doctors in the region, so when she became very ill, my father sent us to New Orleans, to live with Julia, but he stayed behind so that he could work. He hoped she would recover with proper medical attention. But, she was too weak, too frail, and her illness was too far advanced. She died about a month after we arrived in New Orleans.

"I was six years old at the time. After mother died, I remember waiting for my father to come and take me back home. But he never came.

"Clint, I adored that man. Before he sent us to New Orleans, I remember when he came home every day from the mines, after he washed and did the chores, he would go out on the front porch of our cabin and sit in the rocking chair. Mother would send me out to keep him company while she put supper on the table. I'd sit on his lap and he'd sing folk songs from the old country

98

until Mother called us in to eat. I realize now that my father was not the sort of man who frittered away time in a rocking chair. He did it to be with me.

"It's . . . so difficult to describe the effect he had on our lives. Even as young as I was, I noticed the difference between him and other fathers. It was like a light shining brightly when he was home, and gloomy darkness when he wasn't. We adored him and he cherished us.

"That's why I couldn't understand why he didn't come for me. I sat on Julia's front steps every single day, waiting, and watching for him." She closed her eyes. The misery of those days still haunted her.

"Then, about three months after Mother died, Julia called me into her sitting room—a room I was never allowed to enter." Tears choked Angela's voice, making her words jagged and painful sounding. "She told me that my father had been killed in a mining accident."

Confused, Clint frowned. How could Angela be going to her father if he had died a long time ago?

Angela took a long, shuddering breath. "I suppose Julia felt she had to put a stop to all of my questions and that was the best way to do it. Although, I have no way of knowing if that was her original intention or not.

"For several years after that, she threatened to send me to an orphanage. That is . . . until the estate her husband left her dwindled and she was forced to convert her home into a boardinghouse. Then I became a convenience she could not afford to lose." She glanced at Clint, her expression tight with strain. "Don't misunderstand, I never objected to the hard work. In fact, I preferred doing the chores myself instead of relying on Dahlia. She always put her duties off until the last minute, then I would have to help her. Then, if they did not suit Julia, *I* was blamed for it—Dahlia always made sure of that!"

"Who is Dahlia?"

"Julia's daughter. She's a year older than I am." Her brow pulled into an affronted frown as she recalled so many unpleasant incidences. "I—I'd rather not discuss her. She was worse than her mother."

"It sounds as though you had ample reason to resent them," he remarked dryly.

"Of course I did. I'm not a saint! I despise the little hussy . . . almost as much as I do her mother." She slammed a fist into her hand. "What irritates me so much is the fact that I could have left their home when I became eighteen—probably even a couple of years earlier. I was capable of taking care of myself. I am an excellent cook, I can clean a house until it shines, and I am a very good seamstress too. I suppose I just never had the courage to strike out on my own."

"Apparently something finally happened to give you that courage. What made you decide to leave?"

"I learned that she had lied to me," Angela said softly. "It was a despicable lie that changed not only my life, but my father's life too.

"One day, I was putting Julia's unmentionables away when a letter fell from the bureau drawer to the floor. I picked it up and noticed my father's name on the return address. When I removed the letter from the envelope, I—saw that it was dated three years ago." She paused for a moment, besieged by an onslaught of memories. "He wrote of his eternal grief over losing his beloved wife and daughter, and from the tone of the letter, he had enclosed a bankdraft to cover the upkeep of the graves."

Clint whistled softly through pursed lips. "So, your

father was alive all the time." Suddenly, he frowned. "Wait a minute, I don't recall you mentioning a sister."

It seemed impossible for Angela to describe the depth of her feelings, so she did not even try, but dispassionate as she tried to be, she could not prevent the bitterness from creeping into her voice. "You are right, I didn't. I was their only child. Not only did Julia lie to me, but she lied to him too. When I confronted her, she refused to explain why she had done those terrible things to us. Needless to say, I refused to stay under her roof one minute longer than necessary. Fortunately, I had a little money saved from my sewing. I left New Orleans the following morning and have been tracking down my father ever since. He moved about quite a bit, but I finally learned he is in Clear Creek, or was a year ago. That's why I am going there."

She looked at Clint expectantly. "So, now that you know all about my past. I'd like to ask you a question. When is this heavy burden supposed to be lifted from my shoulders? When does the hating stop? When does it change the way I feel?"

Sadly shaking his head, Clint replied, "I don't know, Angela, maybe never. But, at least you admit to hating that woman and her daughter now. The way I see it, that's a step in the right direction. It seems to me, you have two choices. You can either put it aside and make the best out of a terrible situation, or you can allow it to destroy any future happiness. But, if you do the latter, Julia will come out of this the clear winner."

"That's why I didn't want to talk about it! It was like reliving it all over again!"

Clint was afraid if he looked at her, she would start to cry. If that happened, she'd probably be embarrassed and it would make him feel even worse than he already did. He never should have pried. He picked up a stick and began poking at the fire. Finally, he said, "This proves my dad was right. He always told me to keep my nose out of other people's business. Now, I know why."

Angela was not fooled by his attempt to smooth over the awkward situation. She found herself studying him with a different sort of awareness. Her thoughts went back to her first impression of him, that he was dangerous and he could strike with a quick, deadly force. Yet, now she could clearly see an extremely sensitive man. While this trait might have seemed unmanly in other men, it only served to enhance his masculinity in her eyes. Maybe this was part of the reason she had been attracted to him almost immediately.

Clint feigned a yawn. "I suppose we ought to turn in. If this storm blows over, tomorrow will be a long day. Uh . . . it's going to get colder tonight. The temperature will drop at least another twenty, maybe even thirty degrees before morning."

He raked his hand through his hair, a habit that he had, Angela noted, whenever he was reluctant or had something pressing on his mind.

"Well, hell!" he swore. "I'm not noble enough to risk freezing to death, so I might as well be blunt. Both of us need as much sleep as we can get. We will have to huddle together tonight and share the cover we have."

Angela had dreaded this moment, but common sense had told her it would come. She struggled to keep her features deceptively composed. "Clint, we have ridden and walked at least forty miles today. We have survived a terrible tragedy and seen men die. Our survival hinges on your ability and experience. I'll be the first to admit that I am no expert on judging people, but I doubt that you are the sort of man who would mistreat a woman, or take unfair advantage of her. I figure if you were so inclined, it would make no difference if we were laying side by side, or sitting across from each other. So, if you expect me to be shocked at the idea of us sleeping together, or to create a scene, then you are badly mistaken."

Clint looked at her and a grin tugged at his lips. "You know what, Slim? You're one hell of a gal!"

Chapter Eight

It never occurred to Clint to think of the cabin as *quaint* or *rustic* when he topped a small rise and first saw it nestled in the frozen wonderland of snow–laden evergreens. Snow reflected like dazzling jewels and prisms from the steep pitched roof. A magnificent palace straight from the tales of *1001 Arabian Nights* could not have been a more welcome sight.

For the past four days, he had been leading the way, breaking the path through the heavy drifts of snow so that Angela could follow more easily. Fatigue was deeply etched on his face. His eyes were red-rimmed, and icy needles clung to his mustache from his vapored breath. He looked as though he walked hand in hand with death, but looks were deceiving. At that precise moment, he was the happiest man alive.

He wheeled about and shouted to Angela who waited hopefully at the bottom of the ravine. "We made it! We've reached the way station!"

Angela stared at him in disbelief. "Are you sure the cabin is really there?" she questioned, needing to be re-assured what Clint said was true. He had been telling her all morning that they were getting close. She had just about given up hope of them ever finding it.

Using her last reserve of strength, she crammed the long stick she carried for balance deep into the snow and began scrambling up the hill, slipping and sliding in her eagerness.

Loose particles of snow whirled in a flurry as Clint charged down the incline to help her.

A jagged sigh escaped his lips. He felt as though a tremendous weight had been removed from his shoulders. "Yes, I'm sure. It's there!"

Happy tears welled in her eyes when she saw the cabin. It had been a week since the stagecoach had plunged to its doom. From that point on, their horrendous nightmare had only worsened until it had become almost unbearable.

The first night, the storm had increased its fury until it became a white, blinding tempest raging with a ruthless force around them. Angela had been convinced that night that *one* of them—if not both—was bound to die. Their firewood and food had disappeared at an alarming rate until they were forced to constantly huddle together just to survive the cold.

Then, on the fourth day, they awoke to an eerie silence. The storm had abated, but it left in its wake a numbing cold that pierced and spread through their bones like a deadly cancer feeding on itself. They were almost out of food, and to have stayed at that makeshift shelter would have meant certain death, for the cold had sent the wildlife deep into their burrows.

They'd had no choice but to leave the shelter, and strike out for the cabin that lay ahead. The distance was not so great, but combined with their lack of food and warm clothing, it had seemed insurmountable.

The days that followed seemed to be without end. It was as though they were caught in a swirling vortex of deep snow, feeling bitter cold, hungry, and left with the most desolate feeling that they would never survive. At times, Angela had even wondered if they were alive. She considered it a distinct possibility that they had died when the stagecoach plummeted off the mountain and were doomed to spend eternity wandering through the frigid purgatory.

All that suffering is behind us now, Angela thought. A vision of a table covered with bowls of steaming food, positioned close to a warm, glowing fire, filled her mind.

They were about twenty yards from the cabin when Clint stopped abruptly. "That's why I couldn't find it," he muttered. His thoughtful glance quickly took in the cabin, barn, corral, a small out building, and outhouse. The snow around each structure was unscarred by tracks or footprints.

"What did you say?"

"Look at the cabin. There's no smoke coming from the chimney. As cold as it is, there should be a plume of smoke that could be seen two miles away." He cupped his hands around his mouth and shouted, "Hello." But no answer came in reply.

Glancing toward the barn, he noticed the doors were standing wide open and that it was obviously empty, which was not so much out of the ordinary considering the time of the year. In all likelihood, the stageline had already moved the livestock quartered at the station. Clearly, the way station had been deserted.

Why? Neither Nicholas nor Susan had mentioned anything about it. In fact, he distinctly remembered

Nicholas referring to the station during the course of general conversation.

"What's wrong, Clint?" Angela asked, sensing his growing apprehension.

"Maybe nothing," he said, shrugging off his uneasiness. "It just seems to me that someone should be here." His eyes narrowed. Perhaps the place wasn't deserted. With his mind's eye he could visualize a man lying inside, injured or sick, too weak to keep the fire going. He quickly strode toward the cabin.

Angela placed her hand on Clint's just as he was about to open the door. "Clint, wait . . ."

Puzzled by her sudden reluctance and hesitant tone, he looked at her expectantly.

Under his questioning eyes, Angela felt herself wilting. "Never mind . . . it's . . . it's . . ." Then, she squared her shoulders and raised her chin. "Considering our circumstances, I know it is ridiculous for me to feel this way . . . but it seems wrong to barge into someone's home as though we . . ." her voice trailed off and she lowered her gaze, but not before she saw the aggravated expression on Clint's face.

Rankled by her unexpected burst of idiocy, Clint rolled his eyes. Just about the time he thought Angela possessed a little common sense, she spouted this sort of gibberish. They were half frozen, nearly starved, yet she was reluctant to enter what appeared to be an abandoned cabin. *God, save me from city women!* he muttered under his breath as he shoved open the door.

Inside, the large, one room cabin was reasonably neat, but a sweeping glance was all it took to tell them it was empty of human life and that whoever had lived there had not bothered to take many of his possessions—if any. A thick, frayed Bible had been left

107

open beside an oil lamp that sat in the center of the table. A stack of dime novels and newspapers were also there. In the corner was an open trunk filled with clothing. A rain slicker and a lightweight jacket hung on pegs beside the door, and underneath them was a pair of worn-out boots.

There were two rifles in the gun rack on the other side of the door, and when Clint saw an empty slot, part of his uneasiness left him.

"Maybe he rode into Clear Creek and decided to wait out the storm," he mused aloud. "That would certainly explain why there's no livestock in the barn and why his belongings are still here." The notion that something was wrong, something was out of place still nagged at him, but there was nothing tangible he could put his finger on.

Angela forgot about her reluctance when she saw a thick blanket folded over the back of a rocking chair. Flinging the wet blanket and shawl off of her shoulders, she wrapped the dry blanket around her. Her breath came in frosty puffs and she shivered. "Ooh, it's cold as a tomb in here!"

Clint glanced sharply at her, wondering at her choice of words whether she had experienced the same feelings he'd had.

He hurried toward the fireplace. "The first thing on the agenda is a roaring fire and something to eat."

Kneeling in front of the hearth, he quickly raked the ashes into an ash pan and handed the blackened coffee pot to Angela. "Here, wipe this out and fill it with clean snow, then look in the pantry to see if you can find some coffee to go in it."

While Angela cleaned the pot and filled it with snow from the porch, Clint built a fire and added small pieces of kindling until it blazed high enough for him to add heavier chunks of wood. Finally satisfied that the fire was drawing properly, he walked over to the trunk and began searching through it.

"Clint, you shouldn't . . ." Already chastised once for speaking before she thought, Angela clamped her mouth closed, then, when curiosity got the best of her, defiantly asked, "What are you looking for?"

"Socks," he stated matter-of-factly.

Their cold, wet feet had been a primary concern all along. His boots had been more skillfully crafted than Angela's high-buttoned shoes, preventing less moisture to seep inside. Nevertheless, they'd had to stop several times just to build a fire so that their stockings and shoes could dry.

Angela grimaced. During the excitement over finding the cabin, she'd forgotten how cold her feet were.

"I struck paydirt!" Clint announced, holding up two pair of woolen socks and throwing one pair to Angela.

Angela avoided looking at Clint while they removed their wet footwear and slipped on the dry socks. She was still embarrassed by her foolish reluctance to enter the cabin. After wiggling her toes, relishing the warmth of the woolen socks, she went inside the pantry to look for coffee.

A few moments later, she shrieked wondrously, "Look what I found!" She burst through the doorway, brandishing two large shiny apples. "There's a burlap bag of them!" She handed one to Clint, then sank her teeth into the delicious crispness. The sweet tartness exploded in her mouth and small droplets of juice gathered in the corners of her lips as she ravenously bit into the apple again and again.

Clint tore into his apple, taking large voracious bites,

chomping and savoring every morsel. Suddenly, he began to laugh. Angela smiled, then she too began laughing. Their laughter stemmed from a combination of giddiness and relief that they had overcome formidable odds by refusing to let death claim two unwilling victims. They had won. They had proved victorious.

Clint put an arm around her shoulders and pulled her close to him. She looked up at him, and suddenly they both sobered. She sat rigid and unyielding as he leaned closer. Though she tried to fight it, every feminine desire she possessed came alive in her. Their eyes held, then his lips were lightly touching her own. He parted her lips, his tongue sliding along the outer edges as he grasped her hair with one hand and held it tightly. He kissed her gently again and drew back, letting out a long strange sigh as though disgusted with himself.

For more nights than he cared to remember, he'd held her in his arms, molding his body close to hers, protecting her, sharing his body warmth. More than once lustful thoughts and desires had filled his mind, but through sheer willpower his body had not betrayed his honor or Angela's trust.

They had grown close during their ordeal. What began as an attraction soon became a friendship. Now that they were safe, it seemed his feelings had come full cycle. It was no longer just a mere attraction. It was no longer due to the fact that it had been a long time since he'd had a woman. He wanted *her!* He desired *her!* He wanted to fully explore the heady sweetness of her lips. He wanted to taste her swelling breasts, to nudge and suckle them, to tease them with is tongue. He wanted the core of her femininity wrapped around him, snug and warm until their passion heated into white hot flames.

Instead, Clint's shoulders slumped. He felt as though someone had knocked every breath of air from his lungs. Heaven help him, he could not do any of those things, even though he wanted her more than he had ever desired another woman. Angela was too innocent, too naive, and she had been hurt too badly by those she had trusted.

Angela stared at him in astonishment, her mouth slightly parted, color scorching her cheeks. She had often wondered what it would feel like for him to crush his lips against hers in a passionate kiss. During their ordeal, she had even fantasized about it. But never in her wildest dreams did she think it possible for him to be attracted to her. He was such a handsome man, he could have his pick of any beautiful woman, so why on earth would he choose her? Her features were too plain, her hair too thick and lackluster. She could not even lay claim to having an abundance of feminine curves. Instead, she was slender as a marsh reed and just as unappealing. *Then why did he kiss me the way he did?*

When Clint finally trusted himself to speak, he shook his head slowly and said, "I'm sorry. I don't know what came over me."

Angela's heart sank to the pit of her stomach and formed a hard knot. She lowered her lashes, not wanting him to see the gamut of emotions that she knew had to be raging over her features. "That's all right. I—I think we are both a little out of sorts."

So, the kiss had only been his way of expressing relief. But, that's really for the best, she quickly reminded herself, remembering her earlier determination not to become involved with a man until after she had the chance to become reacquainted with her father. Still, she felt a vague sense of disappointment.

111

Clint declared a little too loudly, "That apple only whetted my appetite." He strode to the pantry and searched for something more substantial.

Dejected, Angela huddled by the fire, waiting for the snow to melt and begin boiling so that she could add the coffee grounds to it.

Clint came from the pantry carrying two jars of canned beans: "I think we're hungry enough to eat 'em cold, but they'll be more filling if we wait until they heat a bit."

Angela nodded, firmly pushing the memory of his wondrous kiss from her mind.

She watched while Clint opened the jars of food and dumped the contents into a pot. It occurred to her how extremely fortunate they were. She doubted if they could have lasted another day without food and warmth. All morning long, she had been tasting a bitter sweetness in her mouth that she knew signified the onset of starvation. Under normal circumstances, she knew that people could go without food for a much longer period of time than they had experienced. But, they were so ill-prepared for the cold, their bodies had used up their reserve energies at a much faster rate. She did not know the scientific terms for this phenomenon, it was merely something she had picked up while reading.

When the storm first hit with such fierceness, it had not taken her long to realize she could not have survived without Clint, even though he had placed his own life in jeopardy. Not many men would have been willing to risk such an ultimate sacrifice for someone they scarcely knew. Again, her heart swelled with feelings that went far beyond those of mere gratitude.

Clint scooped a heaping spoonful of beans and sniffed deeply. He looked at Angela and grinned. "See

112

if you can find us a couple of plates and spoons." He put the expression on his face that he'd seen on English butlers, and bowing stiffly, he announced in an arrogant, haughty voice, "Dinner is served, Madam."

The tension Angela experienced evaporated like wispy steam. Joining his frivolity, she peered down her nose. Having lived most of her life in New Orleans, French rolled easily from her tongue. *"Oui, Monsieur, immediat."* She hurried to the cupboard and returned with the plates and spoons. *"J'ai faim."*

He sniffed disdainfully. "I beg your pardon, Madam, this is an *English* feast, not *French.*"

She stamped her foot. *"Non, non, Monsieur, ce n'est pas exactement ce que je cherche. J'insist* upon French cuisine!"

He puffed out his chest and spoke precisely enunciated words. "The menu for dinner is: cucumber sandwiches, steak and kidneys, epping sausages, toad-in-the-hole', watercress, and Windsor pudding."

Angela placed her hands akimbo. *"Pardon à différence! Le menu* is: *bouillabaisse, escargot, asperges etouffered avec creme sauce, coq au vin, chateaubriand, beurred croissants, et cerises jubilee."*

His expression fell. "Damn! Yours sounds better than mine." He looked at the pot and sighed heavily, then he began spooning out the food. "I don't like to argue, so we will have to compromise. The beans on the right are English, and those on the left are French. Agreed?"

"Agreed," she replied. Her mouth watered with anticipation.

For the next few minutes the only sounds that could be heard were sighs of satisfaction and spoons scraping against the plates.

A short while later, Angela paused and looked dubiously at Clint, one eye slightly squinted. It was difficult for her not to laugh. *"Toad-in-the-hole'?* My word! What on earth is that? Frog stuffed inside. . .?"

Clint chortled. "No, it's some sort of a sausage dish. Actually, it's pretty good."

"Sounds terrible."

"Not any worse than *snails.*" He shuddered at the thought.

Angela shook her head with wonder. More in a musing tone, she said, "I've never known anyone like you before."

"How so?"

She shrugged. "It's difficult to put into words."

"You've piqued my curiosity. How am I so different?"

"Well," she chewed on her bottom lip, "I think it's your sense of humor. Most of the people I've known . . . I think their faces would break if they smiled. They were so serious about everything. Whereas you're nothing like that. I doubt if I have ever known anyone who would have joked about the food the way you did."

He shot her a twisted smile. "At times my head is a little too thick. Are you complimenting or scolding me?"

"Definitely a compliment. It's just . . . you are a man with many faces."

He raised his brows and remarked dryly, "Now she calls me two-faced."

"Nooo! I didn't mean it that way either." Angela paused for a moment, then lifted her chin determinedly. She was tired of never being able to express what she thought or felt. "To be completely honest, I think you are arrogant, stubborn, strong and decisive. Yet, on the other hand, you are kind, yielding, compassionate, and at times, you are completely full of nonsense, like pretending to be a butler, setting an elegant feast. It reminded me of something that a mischievous little boy would do."

Dumbfounded, Clint looked at her and let out a whistle of air between his lips. "Do you always analyze people?"

"I never thought about it one way or the other. I do like to watch people, study their habits."

Clint shrugged noncommittally. "I'm not sure if I agree with your evaluation of me, but I will plead guilty to having a sense of humor. I like to laugh and I like to hear other people laugh."

Angela was slightly disconcerted at being so candid, even though it had felt good to say what was on her mind. Deciding to move on to a safer subject, she placed her empty plate on the hearth and filled two mugs with coffee. Handing a mug to Clint, she asked, "Will we be leaving in the morning?"

Clint pretended to give her question serious thought. They could leave the following morning and probably reach Clear Creek by late afternoon, but he was hesitant to leave so soon.

Why? Another hot meal or two and a good night's rest should see them on to Clear Creek without any problems.

The nagging doubts he'd had suddenly exploded in his mind. *He was not ready to be separated from Angela.* When they reached Clear Creek, she would belong to her father, he would go home to the ranch, and by the time he had a chance to return to town, some other man might have staked a claim on her heart.

What am I thinking? Why should I care if she becomes involved with someone else?

Because you do care! his conscience shouted. *You have feelings for her . . . yet, you're not sure how deep they run. If the two of you had the opportunity to spend a couple of days at this cabin, you could probably decide what kind of a commitment you wanted to make . . . if any. You know Angela likes you. Love? Now that is a different matter, but with time, a definite possibility. No, the fair and honorable thing to do is to take her on into Clear Creek, in the morning.*

He took a sip of hot coffee, then cupped the mug in his hands. "I know you are eager to see your father, but I believe we should stay here for a couple of days so we can build up our strength."

"But I thought you said earlier that it was less than a day's walk from here to town."

"It is. But that's under normal conditions." Truth and integrity shone from his face as he told another lie. "As weak as we are, and with the weather so unpredictable . . ."

Color drained from Angela's face. She glanced out the small window at the diffused sunlight. "Y-you mean another storm is threatening? Why, how can that be? The sun is trying to shine!"

"You're right, it is." He shrugged off any feelings of guilt. "But in this climate, another storm could hit just like that." He snapped his fingers to emphasize his statement. "If we were caught out in another blow . . ." He shook his head solemnly. "I doubt if we'd have the strength to press on."

Disappointment swept over Angela. She was so close to seeing her father again, yet it seemed as though fate was trying its level best to prevent their reunion. "I suppose . . . you know what's best. I'd hate to come this far and have something else happen."

116

Relieved that she had bought his bald-faced lie, Clint stood. "There are plenty of supplies in the pantry. Why don't you put a stew on to simmer while I bring in some snow to melt. I think we'll feel a lot better after we wash up, put on some dry clothes, and catch a few hours sleep. And by preparing the stew now, we'll be able to eat when we wake up."

"That sounds like a good idea."

Soon, Angela had the ingredients for the stew spread on the table. She peeled and chopped the vegetables while Clint brought snow into the cabin in a foot tub, then filled a wash pan and placed it on the fire so that the snow could melt and heat. When the stew pot was filled, Clint hung it over the fire by its bale on a metal rod designed for that purpose.

Angela then looked into the trunk and pondered aloud, "I wonder if anything will fit?"

"I don't much care . . . as long as its warm and dry," Clint remarked as he removed his coat and once again tugged off his wet boots.

Clint held a pair of trousers against him and slowly shook his head when the legs fell slightly below his knees. "I don't recall wearing knee britches even when I was a boy," he commented dryly.

Angela held up a gray, knitted wool union suit, named for its union of top and bottom to form a one-piece men's undergarment. "These might fit." Amused, she tugged on the fabric and wrinkled her nose. "They are sort of stretched out though."

Merriment twinkled from Clint's eyes as he pretended to be incensed. Planting his hands on his hips as she had earlier, he raised his voice in a falsetto tone, "Are you suggesting I wear baggy drawers?"

Angela tried to keep her face straight. Clint still had

117

the strip of blanket he had used for a head scarf tied under his chin. A heavy growth of whiskers covered his face, and his mustache was no longer neatly trimmed. His hair had grown during the past week. It hung down the back of his neck, and errant curls peeked around the edge of the scarf. It was difficult to decide if he looked like a sissified man or an extremely ugly woman. She struggled not to laugh but was unsuccessful.

Clint grinned, not realizing how ridiculous he looked. "So, you think I'd look funny in baggy drawers, huh?" Then he chortled as he tossed a faded red union suit to her. "Aha! This lovely creation must have been designed with you exclusively in mind!"

The protest that they were much too large died in her throat. She had to have something to wear while she washed and mended her clothes.

Not wanting Clint to know how much she abhorred the thought of wearing such an atrocity, she raised her elegant nose. "Ah, yes. I could recognize Henri's handiwork anywhere." She ran her hand over the faded fabric. "See how the couturier mingled the colors to give the garment such an exquisite, yet rustic effect." She turned the garment around. "And this opening is . . . is . . ."

Clint took great pleasure at guffawing over her confused expression. "That particular endowment is called a trap door," he informed her.

Angela never batted an eye. ". . . has been enhanced with buttons which completes the homespun image."

"That image can be drafty at times," he teased, devilish lights dancing in his eyes, a mirthful grin tugging at the corners of his lips.

She dismissed his remark with a wave of her hand.

"Nevertheless, one has to make occasional sacrifices for such an exquisite, original creation."

Realizing he could not win, Clint acquiesced graciously. He gestured toward the pantry, the only place in the cabin where there was privacy. "Ladies first."

Angela found a wash cloth and a bar of soap before filling the wash pan with hot water. Looking at the enamel pan with wistful eyes, she sighed heavily. "Oh, how I long for a bath. A real, honest to goodness bath— scented with rose water. I think a steaming bath is the only thing that will make me feel warm again."

"Yeah, a bath would be nice, but we do have soap and water. At least we can wash the surface grime off." He cocked his head thoughtfully. "It could be worse. We could have been stranded in a desert. After a week without a bath, we'd smell strong enough to warn people we were coming two miles away. As for you being cold, it will help after you wash up and get out of those wet clothes. Then too, there's something I might be able to do."

The memory of the past week and snuggling close together for warmth flashed through her mind. "Surely you're not suggesting that we continue . . . I mean . . . it was necessary while we were . . ." She clamped her lips tightly together when Clint pulled one of the cots close to the fireplace. Heat crawled up her neck and her face reddened. She quickly tossed the union suit across one arm and carried the wash pan to the pantry, closing the door firmly behind her.

Clint chuckled to himself as he made up the cots and spread blankets over them. He knew what she'd thought. It was odd—but a predictable human trait— people tended to suppress their inhibitions when faced with a crisis. Then, as soon as the circumstances re-

119

turned to normal, barriers and restraint became the common rule again.

However, Clint did not want Angela to slip back into her role of prim and proper maiden. He preferred the girl with the ready smile, keen wit, and merry eyes. He figured it was up to him to prevent their relationship from lapsing into one of polite acquaintance. She was too special for him to allow that to happen—even if he had to act like a buffoon to do it. Wearing a mischievous smile on his face, Clint dragged a chair near the pantry door and practiced making leers.

A few minutes later, Angela called out in a hesitant voice, "Clint . . . would you please hand me a blanket?"

"They are already on the beds."

"*Clint,* I need one to wrap around me."

He crossed his arms and stretched out his long legs, thoroughly enjoying her predicament. "Nope, you laughed at me a while ago. I seldom get angry over something like that, but I do like to get even. I figure I have a good belly laugh coming."

A long, audible sigh came from behind the door. "If I begged?"

"My heart is made of stone. I can't hear a word you're saying."

The door squeaked slightly when she slowly opened it, and his lecherous grin quickly turned into one of pure amusement. She looked as though she had been swallowed by a strange, faded red monster. She stood clutching the stretched-out neck to her throat, and the sleeve of the other arm dangled at least twelve inches past her hand. It was the crotch that sobered him though. It hung down between her knees.

Her eyes smoldered with indignation as she grumbled emphatically, *"Don't you dare say a single word!"*

Shaking his head, Clint swallowed the laughter that threatened to burst from his throat. He held out his hands palms up. "A single word never occurred to me." He allowed his gaze to slowly travel the length of her, lingering over certain areas that left little to the imagination. "However, you might want to speak to your couturier—what was his name—Henri? I think he made a mistake on your measurements."

Glaring at him, she marched over to the foot tub and crammed her clothes down into the water to soak. Then, she flung back the blankets on the cot, plopped down, and pulled the covers over her head.

Under the privacy of the blankets, Angela smiled to herself when she heard Clint singing in an off-key voice while he prepared his wash water. She wasn't really angry. There had been a few moments when she could have easily strangled him with her bare hands, but that was before she had seen the expression in his eyes. He had made no attempt to mask his amusement; he had expected her to look ridiculous, but she had detected something else. Something quite wonderful, especially after that kiss they had shared. No man had ever looked at her with such genuine appreciation . . . and yes, even admiration. There was no denying, Angela knew she looked a fright, but perhaps she was not as homely as Julia and Dahlia had always claimed. Apparently Clint thought she was pretty, and it was his opinion that was important to her.

Now, how could she extricate herself from the corner she'd painted herself into? She'd behaved like a righteous snob who could not take teasing. It was one thing to pretend to be insulted by his laughing at her, but pouting seemed so dishonest. That had been a favorite ploy of Dahlia's—one that Angela abhorred. The honest thing to do would be to offer an apology for behaving so snappish and petty. And once she had reached that decision, she sat up and waited for Clint to finish washing up and changing.

All thoughts of an apology flew from her mind when Clint stepped out of the pantry. He looked so comical, she could not have hidden her smirk if her life had depended on it. While the union suit fit his torso fairly reasonable, it was much too short. The bottom portion was large around the waist, he'd had to bunch them around his middle to keep them from falling down. By doing this, the suit legs ended on him at mid-calf, revealing his hairy legs. To make matters worse, he still wore the scarf over his head. He had forgotten about it. How he had washed his face and failed to remove the scarf, she would never know.

He looked at her sheepishly, then his eyes narrowed minutely and he thrust out his chin. "I knew you would be sitting out here, waiting, ready to gloat!"

"Who, me?" She touched her chest innocently. "Why, whatever gave you such an idea?"

Pacing beside her cot, he stopped, opened his mouth, closed it, then started pacing again. Halting once more, he started to rake his hand through his hair, but stopped when he realized what he still had on his head. Yanking the scarf off, he glared at her. "You could have told me!"

"Told you what?"

"That I still had that . . . that . . . rag on my head!"

She shrugged guilelessly. "I figured you were wearing it for a reason. I thought maybe your ears were cold . . . or maybe because you had such a good sense of humor?" She raised her eyes questioningly.

"I do! It's just that . . ." He winced visibly. "I'm not acting like I do, though. Am I?"

"Not any worse than I did."

Clint sat down on the cot beside her. His fingers trailed down her temple, then he cupped her face with his large hands. "Think maybe we could call a truce?"

"I'm willing," she replied huskily, her heart hammering wildly against her breast. Their eyes locked as their breathing came in unison.

"Me too."

His hand came up to caress her cheek. His touch was stirring and tantalizing. She traced her finger over his sensual lips. She had the wildest desire to throw her arms around his neck and kiss him. Such bewildering and unfamiliar emotions raged inside her. He was everything a man should be, and at that moment, she knew without a doubt there could be no other man in her future.

"Slim," he whispered hoarsely, "I—I've never felt . . ."

"Clint . . . I think we should . . . get some rest," she stammered, suddenly frightened by the turbulent emotions surging through her.

His entire being seemed to slump with disappointment. "Yes, I suppose you're right. We're both tired." Leaning over, he gently brushed his lips against her cheek.

Chapter Nine

Angela snuggled under the blankets, sighing and stretching languidly. She felt deliciously warmed and relaxed, yet something was tugging her into the realms of wakefulness.

The fire cast a soft, golden glow throughout the room. One quick glance toward the window told her it was dark outside, but she had no idea of the time or how long she'd slept. Clint's breathing was deep and even, although, judging by the fire, he had awakened sometime during the day or night and added more wood.

She groaned inwardly, not wanting to rise, but there was an urgent need to go out-of-doors. That must have been what woke her, she decided, flinging back the covers. Careful not to disturb Clint, she wrapped a blanket around her shoulders, slipped on her shoes and crept outside, closing the door quietly behind her.

She stood on the porch for a moment to allow her eyes to adjust to the peculiar light caused by an overcast sky and snow covered land. The two outbuildings were approximately the same size, one close to a sparse stand of trees and one further behind it on a low mound. She set her sights on the building farthest away.

Afterwards, she positioned the latch—a piece of wood nailed to the outer wall—to prevent the door from swinging back and forth, and hurried toward the cabin.

As she passed by the other outbuilding she heard low, guttural growls and she let out a startled cry. Quickly looking about, she could see yellow eyes glowing in the darkness underneath the trees.

Wolves!

Instinct told her not to run; to do so would surely incite a predator to attack. She immediately flattened herself against the wall of the building, wishing that she could somehow melt into it. The distance between her and the safety of the cabin suddenly seemed to grow father as the yellow eyes came closer and closer. She could see the bodies that belonged to the eyes, five of them, long, lean, and snarling.

She wanted to shout for help, but was afraid her screams would enrage the wolves into an attack. In her mind's eye, she could see them lunging at her, sinking their long fangs into her flesh, tearing her limb from limb.

Attack? What am I thinking? They will attack regardless if I call for help or not!

Her brain finally won the battle over her fear when she realized where she was standing—a building always had a door. Or did it? So many times, small outbuildings were nothing but sheds. But, *if* she could inch along the wall without provoking the wolves, *if* the building was enclosed, she might possibly bolt herself inside until her screams brought Clint to her rescue.

She did not want to think what would happen if the building did not have a door. Then she supposed she would have to make a mad dash for the cabin and hope for the best.

Hugging the wall with her back, she explored the area ahead with her hand. Angela knew in the actual span of time, it had only taken a few moments for her to reach the corner of the building, but it felt like hours had passed.

The yellow eyes glowed brighter, and the growls sounded more menacing. And God help her, they sounded hungry.

Inching around the corner, a sob escaped from Angela's throat when she realized her worst fears had come to pass. The building was nothing but a three-walled structure.

The leader of the wolf pack advanced in a low crouch, then snarling viciously, he lunged, knocking her backwards. Angela flung out her arms, grasping for the wall as she struggled to regain her balance. She knew if the animal ever pinned her to the ground, escape would be impossible.

There was a frenzied melee of savage growls and gnashing teeth as she scrambled for safety, but there was no place to go. It was difficult for her to stay on her feet, the earthen floor was covered with hay and pine straw. Suddenly, long, strong, hairy arms snatched her from harm's way and shoved her aside. She heard ragged breathing and growls of a different sound, then yelping, before she caught a fleeting glimpse of a tremendous giant raising a wolf over its head and flinging the beast toward the wolf pack. She was acutely aware of a rank, dreadful odor before hearing the sharp retorts of a gun firing.

"Clint! she cried. "Help me! Please, help me!" Darkness hovered over her before it slowly lowered its shroud. She could feel herself falling . . . falling . . . falling . . .

"Angela, wake up." the voice urgently insisted. "Snap out of it, Slim! Right now! Come on, sweet lady, wake up."

Angela resisted the fervent voice. She wanted to burrow deeply into the refuge of the murky twilight and remain there in its warmth and safety. She was dead, the wolf had killed her. Why couldn't the voice leave her alone and let her rest in the peace and tranquility she had found in this vast abyss?

Dead? Was she really dead? She trembled and her eyes fluttered, fearing to test this distressing thought.

"Are you cold?" Clint's hoarse whisper barely broke the silence.

Her smoky eyes flew open and she looked into ones as dark as midnight itself. "Thank God! I'm not dead!" she exclaimed weakly. A wave of relief washed over her as she realized she was safely inside the cabin.

Clint leaned forward, his expression tight with strain. "Of course you're not, you've been unconscious. You must have hit your head when you fainted."

Her thoughts were fuzzy and slightly incoherent, seizing upon irrelevant matters. She did not think it was strange to scan his handsome, bold features, and notice immediately that he had shaved. "When did you do that?" she asked, her speech garbled.

"What?"

"When did you shave?"

"While I was waiting . . ." his words broke off and his nostrils flared. His stare drilled a hole through her. The corner of his mouth twisted with exasperation.

127

"Whether I shave or not isn't important. Don't you realize you could have gotten yourself killed! Don't you realize you scared the hell out of me! Why were you traipsing around out there, anyway? I thought you would have better sense than to do something like that by now!"

Wincing from pain, she raised up and gently pressed her hand to her brow. "Please don't shout—the sound—my head hurts."

Concern overtook his worried anger. His tone softened considerably, "Then you'd better lie back down."

"No! I don't want to!" Rankled by his attitude, Angela pushed the pain from her mind, and retorted in cold sarcasm, "For your information, I was not traipsing anywhere! I had to *go* outside! You may not have human needs, but I do!"

In New Orleans she would never have discussed rudimentary necessities with another woman, much less a man, but that had been a lifetime ago. Besides, she had never been so viciously scolded for attending to such needs.

"Oh." Blinking, he paused, then focused his gaze accusingly. "Well, regardless, you should have woke me. When I heard those wolves and realized you were not in the cabin . . ." He looked away, reliving those agonized minutes.

Astonished, the heavy lashes that shadowed her pale cheeks flew up. It was natural for someone to show concern for another person's safety, but Clint's frantic reaction seemed to go much further than that. A tentative smile brought an immediate softening to her features. "Were you worried about me?"

He gave her a sidelong glance of utter disbelief, then threw his hands up with disgust. "Worried? Me? Now what would give you an idea like that? When I heard what was going on out there, I calmly said to myself, 'Self, it sounds like wolves. Hmm, sounds like they are planning to have Angela for supper. Poor things, no more meat than she has on her bones, if there are very many of them, they'll only get a bite or two.' " He folded his arms together and glared at her. "Hell yes, I was worried! Don't you ever go outside at night without me again!"

In spite of her throbbing headache Angela wanted to squeal with glee, fling herself into his arms, and smother his handsome face with kisses. But, considering his mood, she quickly decided that might be the wrong thing to do.

"Clint, you are being completely unreasonable to expect an unmarried woman to ask an unmarried man to escort her to the . . . to the . . . well, you know where."

He thought about it for a moment before conceding. "Maybe so, but a little embarrassment is a small price to pay for your safety. Just do us both a favor and humor me until we get back to civilization." Bewildered, he shook his head. "It is hard to figure. It's rare for wolves to come this close to a cabin. Oh, I've heard of it before, but it was always at the end of a very harsh winter when game had been scarce for a long time." He said pointedly, wagging his finger at her, "Since they were hungry enough to come this close, you can consider yourself lucky those wolves ran off when they heard the gun shots."

"But that wasn't what scared them off."

"Oh?" His expression was dubious.

"There was someone . . . or something out there in that shed." It suddenly occurred to her what Clint had said earlier. "And I didn't faint. He . . . or whatever it was . . . pushed me away at the very moment the wolf attacked. He actually picked the wolf up over his head and threw it at the other wolves."

Clint raised one brow skeptically. "He picked up an attacking wolf and threw him?" He shook his head. "I think you were imagining . . ."

"But he did!" she insisted. "He did it as easily as you could toss a twenty pound bag of flour over your shoulder. Then he charged after the wolves and they were already running away when you fired the gun." Suddenly, realizing how preposterous she must be sounding, her certainty wavered. "At least . . . I think they were running."

By Clint's expression, it was evident he did not believe her explanation.

She sighed heavily and shrugged, shaking her head with dismay. "I'm not really sure . . . everything happened so quickly."

Clint breathed an inward sigh of relief that she had given him an out. He smiled benignly, as if dealing with a highly emotional child. "I realize how a woman might imagine all sorts of things when she's frightened . . ."

She lifted her chin and boldly met his gaze. "Don't you dare be so condescending. The only doubt I have is the sequence of how it happened. It's your choice to believe me or not, but some*one* or some*thing* was out there and he saved my life."

Her eyes widened with wonder and her words came in a rush, "And, Clint, it was huge! I know it was at least seven—maybe eight feet tall, and he had long hairy arms." She wrinkled her nose. "And he smelled terrible! I know you must think I've lost my mind . . ." Realizing again just how ridiculous her story sounded, she faltered. Plopping her elbows on her legs, she

130

dropped her chin on doubled hands and slowly shook her head. "But I could have sworn . . ."

Clint reared back, making a sweeping slap against his forehead. "I should have known who you were talking about! That must have been George!"

She mouthed uncomprehendingly, "George? George who?"

"Just George, and he is not necessarily a who, but a what." He ran the back of his hand across his mouth. "I never considered that it might be him, but the minute you said how tall he was and that he smelled terrible . . ." He paused, smiling at his memories.

She inhaled in irritation. "For heaven's sake, don't leave me dangling like this! Who is the world is George?" There was an arrested expression on her face. "For a while there, I was beginning to think that I had lost my mind!"

"Don't worry, you haven't." He stretched out his legs and took a deep breath. "The legend surrounding George goes back to when I was a baby. My parents had just settled . . ." He paused when he heard Angela's stomach rumble, and chuckled when he saw her face turn apple red. "Don't worry about it, I'm hungry too." He gently brushed her hair away from the lump that had formed on her forehead. "Do you feel up to sitting at the table and eating some stew while I explain about George? If not, I can fill a plate and bring it to you," he offered.

"My head doesn't hurt that much. I've never been the type to take to a sick bed over every little ache and pain."

Angela started to refuse his assistance when Clint stood attentively and helped her to her feet, but she quickly clamped her mouth shut. Why should she be foolish enough to protest when his touch and nearness seemed to turn her insides to jelly? Her heart raced wildly when he gently placed his hand under her arm. It suddenly occurred to her that this was the reason some women wilted and became totally helpless in the presence of a strong, handsome man. Maybe they were not as silly as she had always thought. It was a feminine ploy that she wouldn't want to use often, but if by doing so, he became more aware that she was a woman, what could it hurt? And what would it hurt to pretend to be a little more frail?

She allowed herself to go limp. Clint immediately caught her, and she marveled at the feel of his arms so tightly around her.

She gazed up at him and fluttered her long, thick lashes. "Why, thank you, Clint," she murmured helplessly. "I never realized I was so weak."

His face immediately creased with apprehension and worry. Again, he asked, "Are you sure you feel like sitting? I can bring the stew to your bedside, I don't mind."

"No, I'd rather eat at the table." She batted her eyes. "Honestly."

Clint quickly scooped her up into his arms, carried her to the table, and gently placed her on the chair. Slowly, reluctantly, she uncoiled her arm from around his neck, and sensually trailed her fingertip along the line of his jaw. She heard him take a deep, swift breath, and noticed a dim flush race like a fever over his face.

She gently squeezed his upper arm, feeling his taut muscles. "My, you are so strong. You lifted me so easily."

His reply stumbled over his tongue. "Uh . . . you w-weigh next to nothing."

"But you haven't had a decent meal in a week."

"For that matter, neither have you."

"I didn't lift over half my weight either." She could see his chest swell a bit.

Clint cleared his throat and glanced anxiously about for a way to escape from the spell of her mesmerizing eyes. "Coffee! Do you want some coffee?"

"Yes please, with the stew."

"You need something to cover your shoulders, we can't have you catching a chill." He hurriedly ripped a blanket from his cot and carefully tucked it around her.

Unaccustomed to this sort of pampering, Angela decided to play it for all that it was worth. She pressed a trembling hand against her forehead and moaned.

A strange sound emitted from Clint's throat. "You sit right there and don't you dare move," he ordered. Rushing about the room in a frenzied pace, he wet a rag and gently placed it across her brow. "Would you rather have a warm cloth," he asked worriedly.

"No, this cool, wet one is fine."

"Do you want a drink of water?"

"No, I'm not thirsty."

He whirled about, frantically running his hands through his hair. "Food, she needs food," he mumbled to himself. Rushing over to the cupboard, Clint dropped three plates before he managed to hold on to one, then he raced over to the fireplace and began ladling stew into the dish. His hands shook so badly, he spilled as much as he managed to pour.

Angela stared at him. Her mind acutely analyzed his strange behavior, and she was appalled by what she saw. If she'd had a perverse sense of humor, Clint's bumbling would almost be comical as he rushed about, trying to fulfill her every need. She lowered her eyes with shame.

Apparently this was why some women chose to use unscrupulous feminine wiles and ploys, and some did not. Men like Clint, who were unaccustomed to frailty, could be easily duped into overly solicitous behavior. But if it meant losing her and Clint's integrity just to attract his attention, then she would have to do without such tricks.

She wanted to apologize, but that would call for an explanation. She could not bear for him to think she had tried to manipulate him.

Clint set a heaping plateful of stew in front of her. "Now, I order you to eat every bite."

"Where's your plate?"

"I'll eat after a while."

"You have to be just as hungry as I am."

"I'll wait until I put you back to bed. You might become lightheaded again."

Stubbornly, Angela crossed her arms. "I refuse to eat unless you do. I am not going to faint—I—I just had a little dizzy spell, but I feel fine now."

He saw too much obstinate determination in her for him to refuse. "All right. Let me get a plate and some coffee."

Angela waited until Clint joined her. She continued then as if she had never instigated her silly scheme. "Now, what is so mysterious about George?"

"Well, as I said earlier, I don't know if he's a who or a what. But, I think my dad invented him." Clint's mouth twitched when he saw the skeptical look glinting in Angela's eyes.

"That was certainly no invention I saw out there," she said dryly. "It was a flesh and blood . . . something."

134

He chuckled and explained, "I need to start at the beginning for any of this to make sense."

"Please do."

Between bites, he began, "My parents were the first white people to settle in this immediate area. For the first four or five years, their nearest neighbors were a tribe of Utes. Dad said he met with the chief and they agreed not to bother each other. Their arrangement worked until other whites started moving in. By that time, the chief, along with many of the tribes' elders, had died, and young, hotheaded bucks had taken their place in the council.

"Dad started losing a few head of cattle—the loss of cattle didn't bother him too much because he had always given the Utes cattle during lean times—but he didn't like the idea of them stealing from him. He rode to their village and parlayed with the elders about the situation, but it didn't help. It kept getting worse until finally he realized he would have to do something about it.

"Everything came to a head one day while he and the ranch hand, Amos Kieffer, were out rounding up strays. About ten young warriors came to the ranch and threatened Mother. They didn't hurt us, but they wrecked the place, breaking lamps, turning over furniture, and they looted Mother's root cellar and stole her milk cow.

"When Dad came in late that evening, he got madder than a wet hornet. He knew he had to do something or the Utes would think he was a coward and believe they had free rein to raid the ranch anytime they wanted. If that happened, it would only be a matter of time until there was bloodshed. The problem was, he only had one hired hand, and that meant they were outnumbered about fifty to one.

"His only recourse was to use his wits instead of force. He was aware of an old Ute legend involving a giant man-beast and decided to take advantage of their superstitions." He paused, searching for the right explanation. "I suppose their legend was about the same as our modern day bogey-man. This man-beast had an Ute name, but he never could pronounce it—neither could I, so that's when he invented George.

"He took a stovepipe, and stretched a green fox hide over one end—when I say green, I mean freshly killed and skinned—and made a sort of drum. Then he ran a heavy piece of twine through the center of the hide. He waited until the hide dried a bit—a week or two—then he took that dumbull out of the barn, rosined the twine, and he started talking to those Utes."

"Talking to . . ." Angela shook her head. "I'm sorry, I don't understand."

Clint grinned. "By running the twine through the hole and applying different pressure, you can make the most God-awful sound a human ever heard. He did this for four nights running. Earlier, while the hide was drying, Dad made a pair of moccasins out of an old bear skin, and naturally, he made them about this long." Clint spread his hands apart to indicate an enormous length. "Then during the night, he'd put them on and walk all around the ranch, leaving tracks.

"When he figured the Utes had had time to do some serious thinking, he saddled up and rode into their camp and laid down the law."

"All by himself?" Angela gasped. "Why, they could have killed him!"

"Yeah," Clint said, smiling, "But he figured he was fairly safe when he told them that he had much magic and had called upon the man-beast for help after they

136

raided our ranch. He also warned them what would happen to anyone who harmed him, his family, or his property. From that time on, he never had any trouble out of them . . . to this day."

Angela thought about the story for a minute, then she said, "That explains your father's situation, but I *know* what I saw out there and it wasn't a pair of oversized moccasins and a hide-covered stovepipe!"

"I never said that was all you saw. You probably saw a big bear . . . the same as almost everybody in this area has seen at one time or another. You see, to keep the Indians convinced, Dad had to drag the old dumbull out occasionally and romp on it. The Indians were not the only ones who heard that terrible racket, the whites heard it too. Dad couldn't let anyone else know what he had done, so he sort of expanded on the idea of a man-beast."

"Expanded? As in a tall tale?"

"Exactly. There's no man alive who enjoys a practical joke more than my dad. As the years passed by, though, people began claiming they had actually seen the beast. We had to give it credibility when their descriptions were all the same. But in all probability, what they saw and what you saw tonight was a big ol' bear that somehow has become half-tame."

Angela considered it for a moment. Even after Clint's rationalization, there was still a nagging doubt in her mind. Bears—even giant ones—had fur. The creature she had seen had hair, long, stringy hair. Finally, she decided to just leave it be. She slumped in her chair and exhaled a deep rush of air. "I think I can accept that explanation, at least it's logical." Her eyes widened expressively. "It's certainly better than what I was thinking!"

"And what was that?" Clint pressed.

"That my guardian angel looked like the boge man!"

He lifted an eyebrow as devilment twinkled in h eyes. "When you stop and consider what has happen this past week, some folks might say that I am yo guardian angel."

She looked at him boldly. "You said that, not me.

"Are you implying that I might be the bogey-man'

A slow, sensual smile spread across her lips. "I su pose that remains to be seen."

Chapter Ten

Angela watched the sky turn from black to pink as sunlight weakly filtered through the small window. She lay with her cheek pressed against the pillow, her thoughts on last night.

Why had she listened to the lures and schemes Dahlia and her girlfriends had always boasted about? Guaranteed to tempt any man, they'd claimed. But after trying to entice Clint, all she was left with were feelings of guilt and shame. She had never thought he could be so easily manipulated.

A dreadful thought struck her. Or had he been manipulated? What if he had known all along what she was attempting to do and merely pretended to be captivated by her womanly charms?

Captivated, my foot! she thought. In all likelihood, he had wanted to hoot with laughter at her childishly clumsy attempts at seduction. Shame bit into her as she groaned and pulled the blankets over her head.

Disgraceful! That's how she had behaved and she had no one to blame but herself. What on earth had possessed her to flutter her eyes and priss about like a back alley trollop? Why had she made such risque remarks and provocative innuendos? Why had she behaved so stupidly? Why, why, why?

Finally, weary of chastising herself, she stealthily crept out of bed and put a few logs on the fire, being careful not to wake Clint. She wanted time to summon the courage to face him.

Checking the garments that were hanging close to the fireplace, she was grateful to find that they had finally dried. At least she could do something right!

It's a good thing I relied on my washing, ironing, cooking, and cleaning skills to get me this far, she thought wryly. If I'd had to count on my feminine wiles, I'd probably still be stuck in New Orleans.

Clint awoke to the smell of fresh brewed coffee and the aroma of bacon frying. Swinging his long legs over the side of the narrow bed and sitting up, he groaned painfully. "Damn cots were not made for a man of my size."

Linking his fingers together and turning them inside out, he raised his hands high above his head and stretched with the litheness of a mountain cat. Then he rolled and moved his shoulders to work the kinks out of them.

"Now I know what they must have used for torture racks in those old English dungeons."

He squinted one eye at the brilliant sunlight streaming through the window, then glanced at Angela who stood by the fire cooking breakfast.

His heart thudded in response to her loveliness. She was dressed in her own clothing, her hair had been washed, combed, and braided, and she had wrapped it bun-like on the crown of her head. Her face, chapped by

140

the cold weather, had started to heal and return to its delicate creaminess. Still, the redness left on her cheeks added color, enhancing her beauty. His blood surged with molten heat.

Damn! She looked sexy!

Studying her further, Clint decided Angela's sexiness came from more than a pretty face and a seductive body—slender as it was. He recalled his first impression of her. It was her spirit and strength that had captured his interest and imagination. Her fiery nature begged to be tamed, and any man worth his salt would bend her, but never break her, to his will.

Clint wiped the sweaty palms of his hands on the blanket. The indentation running down the sides of his mouth had deepened considerably. A vein ticked in his temple.

Damn, damn, damn! It might be nice to face each morning like this. Although, her cheeks would be flushed from his vigorous loving and not from . . .

Suddenly, he scowled as he became aware of a throbbing ache deep within his loins. To his consternation, he felt himself grow hard with desire. Stifling a groan, he willed his masculinity to revert to its regular state, but it would not cooperate.

What in the blue blazes! He'd always considered himself to be a well-disciplined man, able to practice self-control whenever necessary. If Angela saw him in this condition . . .

Angela tossed a casual glance at him as she turned the bacon. Her tone was polite but cool. "It's time you got up, I'm about to start the flapjacks. There isn't any butter, but there's plenty of honey and sorghum syrup." She nodded toward a pan of water with steam rising from it. "That's your hot water, and your clean clothes are over there." She indicated the garments draped across the back of the rocking chair. "I'm sorry they're wrinkled—I looked for a flat iron, but I couldn't find one to press them."

"That's all right," he muttered. "I can put up with the wrinkles as long as they fit."

Grabbing his trousers and clean underwear, Clint carried them in front of him to conceal his obvious malady as he hurried to the pantry to dress.

When he came out, Angela was treated to an unrestricted view of his muscular torso. This was the first time she had ever seen a man without a shirt and what she saw could have been the handiwork of a sculptor's fingers. Without a doubt, Clint was a magnificent sight to behold.

He was lean, but every rippling cord was clearly defined. His shoulders were broad and powerful. The muscles of his upper arms curved and cupped into them smoothly. His chest was a chaos of crisp dark hair, thickly curling and twining against the tawny hue of his skin. Almost hidden in the curling mass were flat brown nipples, crinkling from the chill of the pantry.

His chest tapered down to a hard, flat stomach. A sleek line of hair connected the forest on his chest to the thatch that swirled around his navel and disappeared under his waistband.

Her mouth went dry and she pressed her knees tightly together to keep her balance. Any weakness she suffered now was definitely not feigned, nor was it a coquettish attempt to entice him.

Lord, help me not to swoon!

For several moments she stared at the spot that captivated her imagination. Then, as if coming out of a trance, she blinked her eyes and drew a deep ragged breath. Gradually, her muscles relaxed and the tension eased from her limbs. She was amazed to find that a piece of bacon had wastefully been dropped to the floor.

Clint had seen the look that bordered on desire and he stifled a groan as, once again, his body betrayed him. Hastily pulling on his shirt and tugging on his boots, he didn't even stop to get his coat before rushing outside into the frigid cold.

When Clint finally returned, Angela was sitting at the table drinking a cup of coffee. She rose and put the heavy, cast iron skillet on the fire to heat, then vigorously stirred the flapjack batter. There was not a single lump in it, but she had to have something to do.

Noting how busy she pretended to be, Clint decided his best course of action was to act nonchalant, as if it was perfectly natural for a man to bolt into the freezing cold without stopping to get his coat. Although, the way her hips and breasts moved while she stirred the batter, it was not going to be easy.

"Brrr," he said, shivering. "The sun may be shining, but it's still just as cold out there as it was yesterday."

"Yes, I noticed the cold when I first rose this morning. The fire had almost burned itself out."

Clint filled the wash basin with hot water and moved it to a small table near the door. He removed his shirt, then bent down and splashed water on his face and the back of his neck before lathering his hands. Repeating the process, he rinsed and vigorously shook his head to rid it of dripping water. Drops flew out around him like a shower of sparkling jewels, each facet catching and reflecting the sunlight. Angela watched, mesmerized.

"Breakfast sure smells good!" Clint said, drying his face and neck with a towel. Slipping his shirt back on, he hurried to the table and sat down.

"Why, thank you." A different hue stained Angela's cheeks. It was rare for her to hear compliments about her cooking. "How many do you want?"

"Oh, I don't know, ten—twelve. As many as you feel like cooking. I'm hungry." He was determined to keep his mind and their conversation on safe subjects. Food and weather were always harmless topics, weren't they?

Smiling, she placed a steaming cup of coffee in front of him. "You look like the sort of man who likes a cup of coffee the first thing in the morning." Hurrying to the skillet to turn the flapjacks, she scolded without turning to look, "And get your finger out of the honey jar!"

Guiltily, Clint jerked his finger back and quickly licked it. "How did you know what I was doing?"

Turning sideways to see him, she replied smiling, "Would you believe me if I said I had an eye in the back of my head?"

"No. That's what Mother always told me, and she had me convinced for a long time. I finally wised up though, so you will have to come up with a better reason than that." When Angela did not answer, Clint pressed, "I'm waiting."

"Well, if you insist, it's because you remind me of a big ol' bear."

He chortled. "A bear like George, or is it because I've been so grouchy?"

"No . . . it's . . ." She lowered her lashes and blushed. She couldn't tell him it was because he was so handsomely woolly. A dreamy look veiled her eyes and a secretive smile softened her lips as she envisioned tangling her fingers in his heavy mat of chest hair and feeling his hard muscles.

"Are you going to keep me in suspense?" Damna-

144

tion! he thought. Angela had better quit looking at me like that or I'll have to take another walk outside!

Setting the plates on the table, she shrugged and said hesitantly, "You ... just look like a man ... who likes honey."

Clint felt like he was caught in the midst of a whirlwind. Even though he knew he was treading on dangerous ground, he refused to let it lie. "I think you're trying to tell me that I was grouchy last night."

"But you weren't grouchy," she rushed to say as she sat down. Then, she took a deep shuddering breath for courage when she realized this was the perfect opportunity to apologize. "Clint ... I ... it embarrasses me to even think how I acted last night." She shook her head and sighed. "I made a fool out of myself."

"Oh? How did you do that?"

She shot him a grateful look. "Thank you, but you don't have to pretend that you didn't notice. I imagine it was difficult for you to keep a straight face at the way I fluttered my eyes, pretending to be so delicate and weak, then throwing myself at you like a ... a ... bawdy-house wench." Unable to look at him, she kept her eyes riveted on the table. "I'm sorry, I don't know what came over me."

He reached out and gently tilted her chin upwards. The mere feel of her flesh against his fingers sent an arousing tremor through him. He murmured huskily, "Angela, an apology is not necessary. But ... why did you behave that way?"

The time for all pretense had passed. She struggled to maintain an even, tone, and said, "I just wanted you to notice me ... to recognize me as being a woman ... and to have feelings for me." Again, she lowered her gaze, unwilling to look at him, fearful of seeing ridicule and scorn. "I should have known better."

A surge of conflicting emotions charged through Clint. Why had she automatically assumed he was not interested in her?

"What do you mean by that?"

Her bottom lip quivered, but her eyes flashed with prideful defiance. "Please, Clint, let's just drop the subject. I don't want to feel more foolish about it than I already do."

Stubbornly, Clint jutted his jaw. "There's no reason for you to feel foolish. But I do want to know why you think you should have known better." He waited expectantly.

Angela's gaze darted about the cabin, as if searching for means of escape. Finally, she sighed heavily and spoke in a resigned voice. "Clint, I'm not usually this forward, but since you insist upon an answer, I'll give you one . . . and it's blunt." She nervously moistened her lips before proceeding. "A man as nice and as handsome as you could have any woman you wanted. There is no earthly reason for you to be attracted to a woman like me . . . it's silly for me to think otherwise."

If there had been one ounce of truth in what she had said, Clint would have let the matter drop, but she was spouting utter nonsense. There had to be a reason she felt unworthy of his affection, and because of that, he could not leave it alone.

"What in the hell is wrong with a woman like you?" he demanded to know.

Desperately wishing she had never initiated this conversation, Angela rose suddenly from the table and moved to stand in front of the fireplace. "Since you insist that I spell it out for you—all right, I will. Look at

146

me! I am not pretty! My features are too plain and my mouth is much too large! I'm too tall and clumsy. I have no soft curves like most women do. And my hair is unbecoming, it straggles all over my head . . ." Tears choking her voice, she turned on her heel to stare gloomily into the fire.

Suddenly, she felt Clint's hands biting into her upper arms as he spun her around, forcing her to face him. His handsome features were masked by a glowering rage.

"Where in the hell did you ever get hair-brained notions like those?"

"Wha—what do you mean?"

"Who filled you with that nonsense?" he demanded.

"Why, Julia and Dahlia repeatedly . . ."

Clint looked away and cursed under his breath. The misery in her eyes jabbed through his heart. "Sweetheart, did you ever stop to consider that they might have been jealous?"

Stains of scarlet appeared on her cheeks as she tried to pull from his grasp. "Clint, please don't embarrass me further by saying things like that. I never thought you would make fun of me . . ." Her voice trailed off as she tried to pull away.

Clint refused to release her. "Oh no you don't. We are going to settle this now!"

"Clint, please, let me go." She willed herself not to cry.

"Not until I speak my mind. I don't know what that despicable woman and her fiendish whelp did and said all of those years to make you feel this way, but they were malicious lies, more than likely brought on by jealousy! You said you're not pretty—why, that's the most preposterous statement I've ever heard!" His voice softening, his eyes devouring her every feature, he edged closer until he felt the heat emitting from her body. "Your face is lovely. Your cheeks are high and delicately structured. Your nose is exactly right, not too big, not too small. The little dimple in your chin is perfect. And your eyes—God, they're beautiful. The color reminds me of wood smoke on a cold morning. I can see gentleness in them, yet they are filled with fire, desire, and a passion for life." His voice softened into sensual huskiness as he slowly released her hair from its braided knot and ran his fingers through the raven tresses. "And sweetheart, I've seen your hair at its worst, and I never thought it was unbecoming. It's my opinion that it enhances your beauty like a shimmering crown.

"And too tall?" He shook his head and trailed his fingertips sensually along the line of her jaw. "Not for me, I want my woman to fit into my arms exactly like this." He gently drew her to him, circling his arms around her slender body. "Too thin? Perhaps a little—but good food will take care of that. No soft curves?" He ran his hands over the slight swell of her hips. "Some women don't develop too many of them until they've known the love of a man ..."

Clint paused, not wanting to sound crude, but he didn't want her finding something else to be self-critical about either. "And before you say something about having small breasts, most men believe that more than a handful is nothing but a pitiful waste."

He could see her pulse beat a sensual rhythm in the hollow of her throat as he lowered his lips close to hers. "Your lips? I agree, they are just a little wide," he murmured. "But I've always heard that made them perfect for kissing."

Angela closed her eyes as his mouth touched hers in

a gentle caress. A tantalizing brush of lips. An exchange of breath. Again, and again. Then he pressed his mouth over hers, and stayed.

Angela felt cherished, wanted, needed, by a man—a man who made her heart swell with adoration. Her arms went timidly around his neck. The peaks of her breasts pressed against his chest and he almost forgot to go slowly.

He hungrily probed her lips until they parted—and the heated invasion of his tongue inflamed her entire body. Suddenly, she became aware of another fire, an inferno that started in the pit of her stomach and spread like wildfire into her loins.

She reached with a startled cry when an electrifying jolt straightened her body and pulled it up hard and high against his. It was as if a powerful magnet had fused them together.

Clint was lost, irretrievably lost, in her taste, her scent and softness. Breathing raggedly, he stepped back and held her at arm's length. His dark eyes delved into hers, stripping away all pretense between them.

"I want you, Angela. I want to make love to you. I want to make love to you now."

She moistened her dry lips. "Now? But . . ."

"The time for childish games is over, sweetheart. I want you the way a man wants a woman—in every sense of the word. I've never considered myself to be self-sacrificing, but I suppose the noble thing for me to do is to give you the opportunity to say no." He pulled her toward him, then gently caressed her neck with his hands. "So, I'll make the noble gesture, but I warn you now, my virtuous streak won't last long."

All the reasons they shouldn't evaporated like a faint wisp of smoke as she raised her hands and touched his face, acquainting her sense of touch with each rugged contour, each prominent bone. She was lost to his charm and she knew it was useless to fight it.

"Oh, Clint," she murmured huskily, "yes, my love. *Yes!*"

Chapter Eleven

Later, much later, Clint eased from Angela. Lightly, he fingered a loose tendril of hair on her cheek, then smoothed the tousled strands from her face, releasing the tension where the tresses were caught beneath her shoulders. He rolled into a sitting position and sensuously trailed his fingertips along her arm, her long slender neck, and along the edge of her temple. Her lips were swollen from all of the homage he had paid them.

Angela tried her best not to recoil from Clint's gentle ministrations even though his touch made her flesh tingle and crawl. She knew without a doubt that this was one of the worst days of her life. If only Clint had not led her to believe . . . it could have been so different.

So many emotions swelled inside of her until she felt she had been irreversibly altered. She felt as though every hope and dream inside her had been scooped out, jumbled, reconstructed, then carelessly shoved back into the same mold, leaving her only a facsimile of her former self. Her heart still beat beneath her breast, blood flowed through her veins, but inside, she was cold, empty of life.

* * *

How many times had she lain in her bed and gazed out at the moon and stars, and wondered what the future held? Her life during those times had been so bleak, hopes and dreams had been her only release from her pathetic existence. In the privacy of her tiny room, she had often escaped into her imagination and envisioned sitting in a parlor with an adoring husband, surrounded by three or four cherub-faced children. Life with Julia and her spoiled-brat daughter had not been easy. And most times, her dreams and hopes were all she had to cling to.

As she grew older, she gradually realized that fantasies were childish, a waste of time and effort.

All of that had changed, however, when she had learned her father was still alive. Finding him and becoming reacquainted had been her first priority, but those old fantasies had once again taken seed when she met Clint.

He was the epitome of her dreams. So much so, she had suffered no great qualms about making love without the benefit of marriage, because *she thought he loved her.* Instead, he had only wanted a woman to sate his lustful desires. He had murmured all of that nonsense about her being pretty and desirable just to get her into bed with him! She was nothing but a scatter-brained fool!

Clint frowned when he saw tears welling in the corners of her eyes. "Angela?" The name ripped from his throat as he gathered her into his arms and pulled her close. "Don't cry, sweetheart. It was wonderful . . . you were wonderful," he murmured huskily.

Swallowing a strangled cry, Angela flattened her palms against his chest and tried to push away.

Confused by her reaction, Clint's grip on her tightened. "Sweetheart, don't pull away." To him, the gentle loving afterwards was as important as the arousal and actual lovemaking. Without it, a vital part was missing.

Angela balled her hands into fists and struck his chest repeatedly while sobbing, "Leave me alone!"

Catching her hands in a vise-like grip, he spoke again with quiet emphasis. "There's no need for that. You mustn't feel guilty or ashamed over what we did."

Her voice was cold and lashing, "Please, just leave me alone!" She was unwilling to face him, yet unable to turn away.

Clint's mind spun with confusion. He had never realized before how an accusing look and the welling of tears could be so expressive. Her countenance was that of a docile animal trapped by a stalking beast. Why was she so afraid of him?

He *thought* he had made love to her so gently, so tenderly. He *thought* he had fondled her body, caressed her silken flesh, whispered sweet words in her ears, so lovingly. He *thought* he had been so gentle—especially after learning for certain that she had never been intimate with a man before.

"Did I hurt you?" Clint asked slowly. He waited expectantly for an answer, but was met by a wall of silence. Out of frustration, he threaded his fingers through his hair and cursed under his breath. He was not accustomed to this sort of situation, but then, he had never made love to a virgin before, either. If she had been any other woman, he would have put on his clothes and stalked out of the cabin in a rage. But this was Angela and he cared too deeply to let her emotional barricade build into something unsurmountable.

"Damn it, Angela, don't do this to us!" he railed in frustration.

Her bottom lip trembled as she wiped the tears away with the corner of the blanket. "Do what to us?" she asked accusingly. "Y-you got what you wanted. Wasn't that enough?"

Clint was completely bewildered by her spiteful allegations. Then his bafflement suddenly turned to anger. He firmly grasped her by her upper arms and yanked her close to him. The terror in her eyes instantly brought him to his senses. Sighing heavily, he slowly released her.

"I didn't force you, Angela," he responded bitterly. "You came into my arms of your own free will. Now you are acting like . . . I raped you! You act like you're terrified of me . . . or you hate my guts!" His eyes narrowed suspiciously. "Is this another game you're playing? Is that it? Are you trying to manipulate me again? If you are, your scheme isn't working!"

"I never said you forced me! And no, this isn't a game, and I'm not trying to manipulate you!" she shouted, her tone bordering on the edge of hysteria. "You know what you did," she charged viciously.

Clint's nostrils flared, his eyes smoldered with rage. He struggled for self-control as he held his hands out and imagined how good it would feel to wrap them around her lovely neck.

"No, I don't!" he finally bellowed. "And I've never been worth a damn at reading other people's minds! So, you are going to have to tell me what I did . . . or didn't do! Hell, at this point, I have no idea . . ." He clamped his mouth shut before he said something he might regret.

Clutching the blanket close to her, Angela's accusing gaze never left Clint's tormented features.

Suddenly, Angela felt as though a steel rod had been inserted down the full length of her back. She had pulled herself up from the depths of despair before and she could do it again, but not by wallowing in a sea of self-pity.

Raising her chin proudly, she masked her inner turmoil with a deceptive calmness. She spoke in a cold, precise tone. "I suppose I took my anger and frustrations out on you. For that I apologize. I placed all of the blame on you when I should have been blaming myself."

Clint looked at her as if she had lost her mind. Then, he shook his head as though to clear it from fuzzy thoughts. "I have no idea what you're talking about," he said slowly. "If I didn't know better, I would swear I had just walked in on the middle of a conversation you were having with someone else." He then exploded angrily. "I don't know which is worse, your silent accusations, or your talking in circles!"

"Oh, Clint, for Heaven's sake, please quit acting like you're so concerned about me," she snapped, mustering all the pride she could summon. "All you ever said was that you wanted me, that you needed me. You never made any promises." Her voice trembled ever so slightly, "It is my fault that I assumed there was more to our relationship than . . . your need for a woman."

"My need for a woman!" Clint mouthed incredulously.

A wild rose flush glowed on her cheekbones, but her smoky eyes remained steady. "My mistake was assuming you felt the same way about me as I feel about you . . ."

"When did you reach these earth-shattering conclusions?" Clint asked sarcastically.

She raised her chin, meeting his icy gaze straight on. "When you made love to me . . ."

He stopped her with a raised hand. "No, wait a minute. Let me rephrase that question. *Why* did you reach these conclusions?"

Angela swallowed hard and blinked back the tears that threatened to fill her eyes. "You never said you loved me," she replied in a whisper.

"Well, I'll be a son of a . . . !" It finally made sense.

Suddenly, he yanked her roughly to him. She reacted with a startled catch of her breath and something akin to fear in her eyes.

Before she realized what was happening, his arms were around her and her face was buried in the crook between his shoulder and neck. Tears flowed from her eyes. Her hands clenched and unclenched against the muscles of his back. He rubbed his face in her hair. His hands spread wide over the small of her back, drawing her closer, making her as much a part of him as possible.

"I knew I was going to get poleaxed the minute I first saw you," he whispered hoarsely. "I didn't know when or where, but I knew it was coming. I fought it every step of the way. I tried to tell myself that I didn't care, but I knew all along I was lying. I tried to think of other women I've known, but every time I brought them to mind, your face would push theirs out of the way. I met you a little over a week ago . . . but I feel I've known you all of my life. I realize you haven't had it easy, and because of Julia and her cruelty, you're reluctant to trust

156

anyone. But, God as my witness, you can trust me." He paused and guided her chin up so that his eyes could burn into hers.

"I've never told a woman this before. I love you, and I want you to be my wife. I want you to be the mother of my babies."

Angela's whole body shuddered and she drew in a ragged little sigh. She opened her mouth to speak, closed it, and tried again. "You're in love with me?"

"Of course I am." He did not tell her how deeply she had hurt him by her belief that he would have taken her virginity without being in love with her. It was just something he would have to accept. A misunderstanding like this would probably never happen again once she learned to trust and believe in people.

His words had drained all of her doubts and fears. Giving a joyous cry, she wound her arms tightly around him and showered his face and neck with tiny pecking kisses. Sobs of relief mixed with laughter. "I was so afraid. Without your love, I didn't even want to live." She sniffed loudly and swiped her nose with her hand. Her eyes sparkled with a frenzied ecstasy. "I don't know why I'm crying when I'm so happy! Oh, Clint, my love—my love! I'll be the best wife a man ever had!" Her voice rang with an exuberance Clint had never heard before. "Our babies will be so pretty! We'll have all sons. How many do you want? I think half a dozen is a good round number, don't you?"

Clint grinned and cocked one heavy brow. "I wouldn't mind us having a girl or two. And if they're anything like their mama," he feigned a sigh, "I'll have to keep a shotgun loaded with rock salt."

Angela wrinkled her nose and nodded. "You're right, a couple of girls would be nice, but I think we ought to have at least three boys first. Our firstborn will be named after you, and our second will be named after your father or mine . . ." She stopped abruptly. Her eyes widened and her face drained of color. "Clint, what about my father? What if he isn't at Clear Creek?"

Angela's expression was as readable as a book, as doubt after doubt tore through her mind. How could she marry Clint and continue the search for her father? Had fate dangled happiness in front of her only to cruelly yank it away?

Clint was determined not to let anything spoil the magic that existed between them. "Sweetheart, let's not look for trouble until we know it's there. We'll deal with that possibility if and when we have to," he stated firmly.

"But, Clint, what . . .?"

He placed a finger across her mouth to silence her. "Hush. Don't be a worry-wart. Let's just wait and see what happens before we set a specific wedding date. If he's there, I believe you should take the time to get to know him, and during that time, we can have a proper courtship. If he isn't there . . ." He looked at her pointedly. "I know how important it is to you to find him. But, I don't want you to go gallivanting all over the country looking for him either."

"Are you forbidding me to . . ."

Clint laughed. "I have better sense than to do that. I do think a Pinkerton man would have a better chance of finding him, though."

She looked at him wondrously. "You mean you would hire a private detective to find him?"

"Of course I would."

"Aren't they terribly expensive?"

"Probably, but I don't care. I would do anything within my power to make you happy."

Angela felt as though the weight of the world had been lifted from her shoulders. "You really mean that, don't you?"

Clint's heart lurched at the loving expression on her face. He doubted if he could ever comprehend how lonely and miserable her life had been.

Cupping her face with both his hands, he murmured huskily, "If I had the money and if the world was for sale, I'd buy it and lay it at your feet."

Tears of happiness pooled in her eyes. "Oh, my love, I don't want the world . . . I just want you." Shyly, she leaned forward and smothered his lower lip with tiny, nibbling kisses.

Clint swallowed hard and sweat beaded on his brow. His heart beat a staccato rhythm against his chest. His voice croaked, "Do you mean that literally?"

She wound her long arms around him and her fingers trailed sensuously down the back of his neck. Her smile was as intimate as a kiss. Angela was not frightened or reluctant. With his declaration of love, her sexuality had been unlocked as if by a magic key, and now her body stood on the threshold where some great treasure of un-determined wealth was concealed. All that she had to do to obtain the riches was to take that first step forward.

"Would you think I was a shameless hussy if I said yes?"

Mesmerized, Clint moved toward her provocatively inviting lips. "Yes, I would. But I've always wanted to make love to a shameless hussy."

The passionate joining of their lips jolted Angela as nothing ever had before. Fiery sensations raced through her body to every nerve ending.

Clint's mouth caressed hers, savoring the sweetness of her lips. His ardent tongue darted forth to trace the outline of her mouth, then parted her honeyed lips to seek the nectar inside. Lowering her to the cot, he cradled her head against his shoulder, then his hands were on her like a restless wind, tantalizing, stormy, making her moan softly.

Angela eagerly responded to the demanding pressure of his lips, the hungry probing of his tongue, and rapturous feel of his hands exploring her body.

Tugging away the covers, his eyes devoured her loveliness. Her raven hair fanned the pillow like a dark halo, her mouth was red and rosy from his kisses, and her eyes glistened with excitement and anticipation.

His hands moved over the gentle swell of her hips, slender waist, and on to her breasts. Her body trembled as he gently stroked her breasts with his fingertips, then his lips, then his tongue. Softly, titillatingly, wetly, until the rosy nipples hardened with a will of their own.

Tingling sensations raced from the stiff peaks in all directions. His lips were warm, his breath hot as his hungry, searching mouth closed firmly over one rigid peak. He sucked it slowly, deliberately, tongue swirling and teasing, the tickling of his mustache enhancing the delicious sensation.

Then his lips were back on her mouth—searching, teasing, taunting, until her frenzied body responded hotly to his.

A savage, strangled cry came from deep within Clint's throat. Swiftly, his hand traveled the length of her silky body until he found her velvety-soft womanhood, warm and moist to his caressing touch.

The fury of their passion left her limp and pliable. She felt as though she were clay and he the master potter, shaping her into a great piece of art, for suddenly it seemed she had no bones, no will of her own. She soared on rapture's wings—and clung even more tightly, feeling dizzy and faint from hot desire. She whimpered with delight as his fingers searched and gently explored the portal of her womanhood. A ravenous hunger encompassed her, devoured her, until it screamed its need for fulfillment.

The tiny glimmer of sanity that remained within Clint told him that he could not wait much longer, not if he wanted Angela to obtain satisfaction.

He position his knees between her thighs, lowered his body onto hers, and passionately ravished her mouth while his maleness teased the outer folds of her femininity. Clint entered her gently, his unhurried, deliberate movements belying his desperate need for release. He thrust slowly, languidly, moving within her as if she were a delicate rosebud unfolding fragile petals.

Each thrust brought them to a new plateau of pleasure, until Angela was sure they could climb no higher. She grew hotter and hotter, melting beneath him, while molten rivers coursed through her veins as though they had broken through a towering damn.

Yet, higher she did go—and higher—and higher. Torn free of all restraints, her mind and body soared with unimaginable joy. There was only her and Clint and what he was doing to her. Then there was a realization of oneness.

She and Clint were caught in a private whirlwind of passion, set far apart from the rest of the world as they flew together on invisible wings. Then, lips and bodies ignited and joined in a fiery climax that touched the depths of their souls.

Chapter Twelve

Angela leaned against the windowsill and watched as Clint tossed a piece of wood on a huge pile, then positioned another round log on the chopping block, hefted the axe over his shoulder, and split it with one clean fell. He had told her that they should leave the cabin and woodpile the same as they had found it. While they could not replace the food, he could restock the wood bin. But, from the looks of the heaping woodpile, he could have stopped an hour ago, so she knew there was more to it than that. Their lives had changed so drastically in the past twenty-four hours, he had just used that—in part—for an excuse to be by himself for a while without hurting her feelings. Even though she dreaded being apart from him for more than a minute, she understood his need for privacy.

In her opinion, for love to endure, it had to be treated like a fire; if carefully tended and stoked, and drafted properly, it would burn forever. Whereas, if one constantly poked and prodded, or did not let it breathe, it would soon smother and die. A person had to learn when to leave things alone or tend to them.

Turning from the window, she was tempted to pinch

herself to see if she were dreaming. It was difficult to believe that so much happiness could be possible. When Clint had told her that he loved her, it was as though she had been reborn, and her life was now starting anew. There was so much love in her heart, there was no room left for bitterness. Given a little time, all of those miserable years she'd lived with Julia would become fuzzy memories. Perhaps when she saw her father again, she would be able to banish those memories completely.

Angela's thoughts returned to Clint; how he had proposed, the countless number of times he'd told her he loved her, and had *proved* it in such a sensual way. Had it all happened just yesterday? Their bodies had been ravenous for each other. Each time they made love, it seemed to whet their appetites for more.

One thing was certain, she decided. If his sexual prowess was any indication of his virility, they would definitely have more than six children. She blushed and smiled at the pleasant thought.

Angela pulled herself from her reverie and checked the food simmering over the fire. She opened an iron door under the oven and added some wood. Smoke from the fire under the oven was directed around the small iron enclosure through spaces between it and the rocks of the fireplace, pulled by air from the fireplace and sucked up the chimney. The extra iron insert created a very fine oven for baking. Mentally thanking the anonymous man who had built the fireplace for his ingenious idea; she took a towel and removed an apple pie from the oven. Spicy steam escaped through the slitted top. She smiled, knowing Clint would be pleasantly surprised by this delectable treat.

* * *

Clint wiped off the axe head and wedge, then picked up the maul and put the tool away. He sat down in the barn on a sack of grain and rolled a cigarette out of tobacco he had found in the cabin. He lit it and wrinkled his nose at the stale taste. He rarely smoked cigarettes, preferring instead a pipe or an occasional cigar, but he was reluctant to throw the smoke away. It was something to keep his hands busy while he thought.

The icicles hanging from the eaves had started to melt. His and Angela's time at the cabin was coming to an end. They would have to practice more restraint and not make love with such wild abandon. The man who lived here could return at any time, and while he was not ashamed of loving Angela, he did not want to risk putting her in an embarrassing situation. A woman's reputation was a fragile thing and he did not want hers blemished.

He glanced out the back door of the barn at the sky. If the weather continued to hold, they should be able to leave early the following morning and be in Clear Creek by midafternoon. He had mixed emotions about leaving. It would be hard to share Angela with other people without letting on that an intimacy existed between them. Yet, he was almost as anxious as she to learn if her father was still there. Then too, it had been a long time since he had seen his dad.

Thinking about his father made him smile. There was no doubt in his mind that his father would be as smitten by her as he. Clint chuckled. Probably more so when he learned what a good cook she was.

"Halllo, the cabin!" a raspy voice bellowed. "Don't care if you're friend or foe, put the coffeepot on, 'cause you got company!"

At the sound of the voice, Clint quickly ground out

the cigarette with the heel of his boot and hurried through the barn to see who was there. Angela had walked out on the porch, and was staring with open–mouthed astonishment at a wiry little man dressed completely in furs, cradling a buffalo gun in one arm and holding the reins to a cream-colored donkey with the other.

"Ah ha! I knew it! That voice could only belong to an ornery rascal by the name of Amos Kieffer!" Clint shouted as he hurried toward him, a smile stretching from ear to ear.

Amos whirled about, and when he saw Clint, a toothless grin split his face. "Clint? You young snapper, if you're not a sight for sore eyes, I don't know what is!" Cackling with glee, he whipped off his fur cap and slapped it against his leg. Excitedly, he leaned over and yelled in the donkey's ear, "Looky there, June-Bug, it's Clint!"

Angela stood on the porch smiling and shivering while Clint and his old friend pounded each other on their backs and traded a few friendly insults.

Still smiling, Clint glanced at Angela, noting she looked like she was about to freeze, but was apparently too curious to go back inside. "Would you mind making a pot of coffee? I'll introduce the two of you after we take June-Bug to the barn and tend to her."

Bobbing her head, Angela hurried into the cabin and put the pot of coffee on the fire to heat.

Soon, the men came inside, stamping the snow from their feet and hanging their coats on the pegs by the door. Amos stripped off his fur leggings and hung them on the pegs also. Upon remembering he was in the house, he whipped off his cap and tucked it under his arm.

Completely fascinated, Angela stared at the little man. She judged that he stood slightly over five feet tall and weighed one hundred—maybe a hundred and twenty pounds at the most. He was of an undeterminable age, but he was old. She would guess anywhere from sixty to eighty. He had a full white beard, long, thin white hair tied back with a leather thong, and skin that looked the texture of leather. When he smiled, not a single tooth could be seen. His legs were so bowed, they looked like he could straddle a pickle barrel without touching either side. His eyes were a deep blue and very friendly. Even before they were introduced, she liked him immediately.

Clint made the introductions. "Angela Langford, I'd like for you to meet Amos Kieffer. He's the man who helped my folks settle our ranch."

"I'm very pleased to meet you, Mr. Kieffer." Angela smiled and extended her hand.

"Pleased to meet you too, ma'am." Amos started to take her hand, but pulled his back when he noticed how dirty and soot stained his hand was compared to hers. He quickly shook his head. "I ain't stuck up none, just don't want to get your hand dirty."

"Well, if you do, it can be washed." Stubbornly, she thrust her hand out farther. She made a mental note not to let him see her wipe it off if by chance he did smudge it.

A trace of surprise flickered in his eyes. Most women avoided him like he carried the plague. Hesitantly, he accepted her hand and was immediately impressed with the strength of her grip. It was not too strong, yet it didn't feel like he was shaking a limp rag either.

"Speaking of such, I think by the time you gentlemen wash up, I can have supper on the table. It's ready, I've been keeping it warm . . ." She blanched. "Oh, my goodness, Mr. Kieffer, you must think I'm terribly rude, coming into your home and . . ."

"Oh, no, ma'am, this ain't my place, it belongs to a friend of mine," Amos rushed to say, "But if it were, you'd be most welcome to anything you wanted. And if I know Zebulan, he won't mind none either." Appreciatively, he sniffed the delicious aroma that filled the cabin. "Fact is, he'll be right sorry he missed you."

Her mood buoyant, she exclaimed, "At last! The mystery about the man who lives here is about to be solved. We were surprised to find no one here. It was obvious the cabin had not been abandoned. I think we were both worried that the man had been caught out in the storm when it hit."

Amos grimaced in good humor. "He got caught alright, but not by the storm. Old Zeb had a sudden hankering to see that Indian wife of his. Dad-blamed fool wasn't watching where he was going and he got his foot caught in a bear trap—tore it up real bad too—his foot that is." His gaze strayed to the fireplace where the food was simmering. "Lucky for him I came along when I did or he would have lost it for sure. I carried him on in to the Ute village. That old coot was more worried 'bout the stage coming through and him not being here to tend to it than he was 'bout his foot, so I told him I'd come back and take care of things. I would have done it too, if I hadn't had to hole up when that storm came."

At the mention of the stagecoach, Angela jerked her head about and she looked solemnly at Clint.

"While we were in the barn, I told Amos what happened to the stage," he explained, noting the immediate look of relief flash through her eyes.

Clint, knowing Amos had too much pride to admit to

167

being hungry, clasped the old man on the back of his shoulder. "I don't know about you, Amos, but I'm starved." He motioned at Angela. "And she's a tyrant, she won't let us eat until we wash up." He gave Angela a conspiratorial wink as he poured warm water into the wash basin.

Amos swatted at Clint with his cap. "Boy, your ma taught you bettern' that! Carry that wash pan outside where it belongs. Ain't proper to wash up in a woman's kitchen."

"It's too cold to wash outside," Angela protested, although she wanted to laugh at the stunned expression on Clint's face.

Amos's eyes glinted with stubbornness. "Might be cold, ma'am, but it's still the proper thing to do."

"Don't waste your breath, sweetheart. It's useless to argue with him." Trying not to grin, Clint sighed heavily and shook his head. "I've never won one."

"It's 'cause you pick the wrong things to argue about, young'un," Amos said adamantly as he opened the door and carried the basin outside.

Clint shrugged, threw a towel across his shoulder and followed meekly behind.

Amos shoved his plate back and rubbed his stomach. "If I didn't know better, I'd swear I had done died and went to Heaven. That was the best grub I've had in . . . Lordy, I don't know how long. And that pie, Miss Angel . . ."

Angela drew in a ragged breath of air. *That name!* Her mind reeled from long-forgotten memories. Her father had affectionately called her his little angel, and she had forgotten all about it until now.

168

". . . I swear, it melted in my mouth!" There was a slight tinge of wonder in his voice. "And you're only the second woman I've ever known to make a decent cup of coffee that's fit'n for a man to drink. The first was Clint's ma."

Stalling for time, Angela coughed to regain control over her emotions. "W-why, t-thank you," she stammered. "Mr. Kieffer, if you don't mind I would like to ask . . ."

"All my friends call me Amos," he said firmly.

"All right . . . Amos." She smiled, realizing he was not the sort of man who usually offered his friendship so readily.

"Now, what was it you wanted to ask me?"

Glancing at Clint for reassurance, she gained courage when he nodded encouragingly. She was not afraid to ask her questions, but she feared what his reply might be. "Have you been in Clear Creek recently?"

"No, cain't say that I have. It's been a long spell since I've been in these parts."

"Oh, I see." She clenched her jaw as a dismal look passed over her features.

Clint spoke up quickly, "Amos, I figure you must know half the people in this part of the country. Have you ever met or heard of a man by the name of Samuel Langford?"

Amos stroked his chin thoughtfully. "No, cain't say that I do. Might know him by sight though. What does he look like?"

Sadly, Angela shook her head. The image of her father was so vague, and so many years had passed, she realized she could not give an accurate description of him. "It's been so long, I'm really not sure."

169

"You have the same last name, I take it that he kin?"

Wanting to protect Angela from having to delve into her painful past, Clint spoke up, "He's her father, Amos. They were separated years ago, and Angela has been trying to find him. She heard he was in Clear Creek, and I guess we both hoped you knew of him."

"I see. Is he a miner?" Amos directed the question to Angela.

"Yes, I remember him referring to himself as 'Cousin Jack.' "

"Oh, a Cornishman is he? I'll say one thing, they are first-class hard-rock miners." Still stroking his beard, he nodded thoughtfully. "It might very well be that he's at Clear Creek. Rumor has it that they've hit a big bonanza there. It's big enough that a good man who knows ground, how to sink a shaft and get the ore out, can just about name his price. That's one reason why I came back to these parts." He chuckled. " 'Course, my hard rock mining days are over—have been for more years than I like to remember. I imagine the good claims are already taken, but I thought I might be able to scratch around and luck on to something the others have overlooked."

Angela was aware that the old man had skillfully changed the subject from her father's possible whereabouts to his personal plans. For that, she was grateful.

Clint looked at Amos, affection for the old man apparent in his eyes, but concern for him was evident too. "I wish you would take Dad up on his offer and move out to the ranch. You know you have a home there any time you want it."

"I know I do. Fact is, might just sit the winter out with you and Tom. Not at the ranch though," he has-

170

tened to add, "I was thinking about putting the line shack to use. Having to hole up like I did when that cold spell hit, reminded me how old I'm getting. But don't go digging a hole and covering me up yet. There are a few things I still want to do."

Angela regarded him with avid curiosity. "I hope you don't think I'm prying, Mr Kief ... Amos," she corrected herself, then grinned sheepishly. "Well, I suppose it would be prying."

"You just go right ahead and ask any question you want to, Miss Angel. It's been quite a spell since I've talked to anybody other'n June-Bug, and half the time she pays me no attention." He propped his hand on his leg and grumbled more to himself than to Clint or Angela. "Cantankerous old bag o' bones, she acts like she's deaf, but I ain't fooled. She's so mule-headed, she only pretends she cain't hear. She does it on purpose 'cause she knows it makes me mad."

Angela tried her level best to keep a straight face. Why, he spoke as though that donkey was human. Then, she felt ashamed for wanting to laugh. The old man was just lonesome, and more than likely the donkey was the only company he had for months at a time.

Amos waited for a minute. "Well, what in tarnation did you want to ask me?"

"I'm just curious. . . . I noticed there were quite a few furs on June-Bug's pack, so I assumed you were a trapper, but you mentioned that you're a miner, and Clint said that you worked on the ranch. So ... what all do you do?"

Thinking about her question, Amos scratched his beard. "I reckon a body could say I've done a little bit of everything. I was a tinker by trade, but I've always been a wandering man by heart. Oh, I would take root

171

in a spot for a while, then 'fore too long, I'd start to wonder what was over the next mountain. If I didn' have a pack, I'd stuff my belongings in a flour sack and off I'd go.

"I've hunted buffalo, been an Indian scout for the Cavalry, was a Texas Ranger for a while, busted broncs, drove cattle, did some sheriffing in some two by twice towns, and back in '52, I even sailed the China seas for a spell." He chuckled, but his laughter held no humor. "It wasn't by choice though. Some Frisco wharf rats caught me not paying close enough attention. There were six of 'em and it took every man-jack *and* their clubs to get that burlap bag over my head and put me on that slow boat to hell. Took me five years to escape and let me tell you, I swore right then that I'd stay away from oceans and boats. Why, to this day when I come to a river or a creek that runs over ankle deep, I get leery."

She gasped. "You mean they kidnapped you! How could men be so ruthless?"

"Weren't no kidnapping to it. They shanghaied the hell out of me!" He immediately ducked his head. "Excuse me, Miss Angel, shouldn't have cussed."

She brushed it off with a wave of her hand. "Think nothing of it. Sounds like you have every reason to be angry. It's just hard to imagine that men could be so cruel."

Amos studied her for a moment, then said, "Miss Angel, I can tell by your voice you're from the south, and more'n likely a port city. Where 'bouts?"

"New Orleans," she replied, amazed at his perception.

"You familiar with the docks at all?"

"Not too much, but I have occasionally witnessed ships being loaded and unloaded. Why do you ask?"

He wagged his finger at her. "Just be patient. I'll get to the gist of the matter in a minute or two. Now, let's mosey back to my questions. Were the docks and the area around them busy?"

"Yes, indeed they were," she replied with a significant lifting of her brows.

"Would you call the dock area civilized?"

Angela recalled the congested narrow streets leading to the docks, the hustle and bustle of teeming humanity all pressed together, the rise and fall of voices flavored with foreign tongues. Yet, there had been a semblance of order about it all.

"Yes, I suppose so, but I'm sure the police had a lot to do with it being civilized."

"You asked how men could be so ruthless. Just imagine New Orleans without any law and order, and overrun with the dregs of mankind. Now, keep all of that in mind only add a hundredfold to it and you'll have an idea of San Francisco back in the early fifties.

"You probably ain't never seen cattle or buffalo stampede, but that's what comes to mind how men behaved when the cry went out that gold had been found in California. They came by any means they could—and I imagine some of 'em even crawled part of the way. There for a while, whenever a ship sailed in with a load of passengers, the crews would jump ship until there were hundreds of them abandoned in the harbor. Men from every walk of life poured in by the thousands, each one lusting for easy riches. They'd heard that there was so much gold there, that all a body had to do was bend over and pick up a nugget. But it dang sure weren't that easy. Then, when some men learned there was backbreaking work involved, they took to stealing and even worse—it was easier and quicker than trying to earn an honest dollar. Even virtuous men were sometimes tempted to do things they wouldn't have done back in the states."

He sighed heavily and shook his head. "The point I want to make is this; I reckon the lure of easy money is what makes some men ruthless and cruel enough to destroy another man's life. Miss Angel, you watch out for yourself now. Clint, you keep an eye out for this little lady too, 'cause mining towns are all the same. Where silver, gold, and easy money is concerned, all towns become just like San Francisco was back then. I've known many good men to turn bad when money—and a pretty woman is involved."

Clint covered Angela's hand with his and gently squeezed it. "I intend to, Amos. I intend to do more than keep an eye on her."

Amos flashed a toothless grin. "That's 'bout what I figured. Not even a blind fool could miss how smitten you are with each other." He chortled at their expressions. "Did you young'uns think you were hiding something from me?"

Clint remarked sheepishly, "No, but I didn't think we were that obvious."

"I saw the same look in your ma and pa's eyes." Amos rose slowly, his knees and joints popping. "And you tend to forget that I've knowed you since you piddled in your diapers, and your face is just like an open book. Least-wise it is to me." He ignored the red flush that began on Clint's forehead and swept downwards, and Angela's muffled laughter.

Amos glanced about the room, noticing there were only two cots. "I had planned to sleep in the barn, but

174

I reckon I cain't now. Dang-blast-it, never did like to be an old mother hen, but to keep Miss Angel's reputation above board, guess I have to act as a chaperone. Where's the spare blankets? We need to get bedded down if we plan to get an early start in the morning. A pallet right here in front of the fireplace will do just fine."

Clint brought a stack of folded blankets over near the fire and started spreading them out on the floor. "I'll sleep on the pallet, Amos, and you take the cot over there."

Amos eyed him defiantly. "Are you saying I'm too old to sleep on the floor? Why, young'un, you ain't seen the day . . ."

"No, I don't think you're too old. It's just that . . . those cots are so blasted short and I'm so tall. I figured I could rest better on the pallet."

Amos waited what he considered a respectable passage of time before reluctantly agreeing to sleep on the cot. "Well, since you put it that way, guess I can oblige you." He walked over to the door and slipped on his coat. "I have to go say good night to June-Bug, or she'll get her feelings hurt and sulk all day tomorrow."

"Wait a moment, Amos," Angela said, pushing a bowl of apple peelings and cores into his hands. "Do you think June-Bug would like these?"

"I imagine she'd find them right tasty."

As soon as Amos closed the door behind him, Angela rushed into Clint's waiting arms. "Has anyone ever told you that you have a soft heart? I'll have to admit, you were very clever the way you got him to agree to sleep on the cot."

Clint shrugged. "I doubt if I could have slept very good knowing he was on the floor. But, I had to say

175

what I did to make him think he was doing me a favor. That old man has too much stubborn pride."

"You're very fond of him, aren't you?"

Clint chuckled. "What do you think?"

Angela wound her arms around his neck. "I think you had better hurry and kiss me before he comes back inside." Clint willingly obliged.

Amos stroked the ancient donkey with a gentle hand as he held the bowl of apple peelings to her muzzle. "Clint has finally found himself a pretty gal and looks like he's ready to settle down. Sure takes a powerful load off my mind. There for a while I had my doubts about that boy. He sowed a heap of wild oats—probably several fields if the truth be known. But, I should have knowed better than to worry. Only thing is, I noticed he still has those guns. Sure wish he'd hang 'em up and forget about 'em. Maybe that little gal will make him want to do it though. Maybe she will."

Chapter Thirteen

Clear Creek was not what Angela had expected. It was located in an extremely narrow valley surrounded by tall, craggy mountains. On the outskirts, scattered stone shacks, some ramshackle huts of dirty canvas and planks, log cabins, and a few frame houses had been erected and spaced haphazardly with no apparent forethought for future growth or properly planned city blocks.

The actual town itself was not much better, although stakes with tiny red flags atop them lined the major street in a somewhat well-ordered fashion where businesses and residential dwellings had not yet been constructed. Heavily loaded wagons, pack animals, and the melting snow had turned the streets and alleys into muddy quagmires.

Wide, rough planks had been placed in front of the business establishments so patrons could walk without sinking knee deep into the mud. Planks had also been laid across the street, enabling people to cross.

Gaping dark holes dotted the surrounding mountainsides indicating individual efforts apart from the one rich strike that had caused such a stir. A large tin building had been erected midway up one mountain, and Angela assumed from all of the heavy machinery, and so many men bustling around, that was the famous mine she'd heard so much about.

As they made their way through the business section of town, Angela could see that Clear Creek consisted of two general stores, a blacksmith shop and livery stable, a barber shop with a huge, hand-painted sign advertising medicinal products and hot baths. There was a sheriff's office with a twelve by twelve stone structure behind it with bars covering the windows, four barrack-type buildings, a restaurant, eight saloons with raucous voices and boisterous laughter coming from them, a boardinghouse, a cobblers-shop, and several other buildings having no signs by which to identify them.

There were signs in front of structures under construction indicating the future homes of two hotels, another restaurant, and the Denver and Rio Grande Railroad Depot.

The trio's tattered appearance did nothing to draw much curiosity from men passing by. To them, the tall man was probably a gambler, and his companions were an old mountain man and his Indian squaw with her blanket pulled over her head for warmth. Those who looked twice wondered if they had seen a lovely young woman, or if they had just imagined her. Unbeknownst to Angela, one man tossed his whiskey bottle away after passing by. He decided when an Indian woman started looking that good to him, he'd had too much to drink.

Clint's countenance had become somber by the time they stopped near a false-fronted general store. He had not spoken since arriving in town. With hands shoved in his coat pockets, his broad shoulders slightly hunched forward, he looked slowly about, scowling.

Amos shook his head in disbelief. "Lordy, would you look at this! Never thought I'd live to see the day that Clear Creek turned into another two by twice town!" His mouth was tight with strain as he looked at Clint. "I'll tell you one thing, this place is too crowded for me to stay longer than I have to. I'm going into the store and buy my supplies, then I'm heading for the line shack. Be sure and tell your pa that I said howdy, and I'll mosey down to the ranch in a week or two." Having stated his intentions, he tied June-Bug's reins to a hitching post and disappeared into the mercantile.

"This is certainly not the sleepy little town I envisioned," Angela said slowly as she turned her gaze to Clint.

The muscles in his jaw tensed as he watched a husky bartender hustling two miners out of a saloon by the backs of their necks and toss them into the street. What was even worse, the people passing by acted as though such behavior was a normal, everyday occurrence. In all likelihood, it happened all too frequently to create a furor.

"I knew it had to have changed," Clint muttered solemnly. "I only hoped it wouldn't be this much, though." He smiled at Angela, but it was without humor. "Standing around with a long face isn't going to change it back to the way it used to be, so I guess we ought to take care of business." He gently gripped her arms with his hands. "Sweetheart, I know you're eager to start inquiring about your father, but first, we need to go over to the stagecoach office and let them know what happened."

There was a faint tremor in her voice. "Do I have to go?" She moistened her dry lips as a shudder passed

179

over her. "They will want a detailed report and I would rather not have to relive that horrible . . ."

Clint quickly soothed her trepidation. "No, you don't. I will take care of it myself." He glanced about at all of the new stores and shops. "I guess the best place for you to wait is at the restaurant."

"The restaurant?" She shook her head in dismay. "I cannot go in there looking like this." She gestured at her clothing. "My dress is soiled, the hem is wet and filthy, and I'm not about to go into a place like that wearing a blanket over my head."

Aggravated, he drove his fingers through wind-blown hair, then laced them together. "You can't wait outside, and that's all there is to it," he stated firmly.

Immediately realizing he had spoken too harshly, his tone softened, "Folks out here seldom pay attention to what other people are wearing unless they are at a Saturday night social." He grinned and gently trailed his fingertips down her arm. "That's when the ladies all buzz like bees."

"If you think you can tease me into agreeing . . ."

Clint interrupted. "You have to wait inside somewhere and it might as well be the restaurant where it's warm. It's too chilly to stand out here, and . . . well, a lady should not be on a street alone in a town like this." Not giving her a chance to protest, he slipped his hand around her arm and escorted her to the door of the restaurant.

Withdrawing some money from his pocket, he thrust it into her hands. "I don't want to go inside with you. If I run into someone I know, there's no telling how long I'd be detained. You go on in and order something to eat, and I'll be back as soon as I can."

"I'm not very hungry, I'll just wait on you." Angela

180

knew she was being unreasonable by stalling, but she was scared. Not of the town, or of Clint leaving her alone; she was afraid of what lay ahead during the next few hours.

Clint strived to control his temper. Sighing raggedly, he said, "Slim it isn't like you to be so difficult. I don't blame you for not wanting to go to the stage office, but you have two choices. Either you come with me, or you go in there, and if you do that, you will have to order a meal. Restaurant seats in a mining town usually come at a premium. Most of them have a rule, 'If you don't eat, you don't sit.' " He spoke in a voice that forbade any further argument. "Now, will you do as I say?"

Having no other recourse, Angela nodded. "Yes, but . . . will you please take the blanket? I feel foolish enough wearing it out here." She quickly removed it from her head and shoulders, thrust it at him, then clutched her tattered shawl tightly about her neck.

Without saying a word, Clint crammed the wadded blanket under his arm and waited until she had entered the restaurant before he turned and walked with long, angry stride toward the stagecoach office.

Angela stood just inside the doorway and looked for a place to sit. Long tables covered with blue and white checked oil cloths filled most of the room, with only small spaces between them for waitresses to walk. There were mostly benches and very few chairs on which to sit. On the far side of the building, two tables and part of another were filled with men. The three women present were carrying trays heavily loaded with food.

Angela was acutely aware that the din of noise had gradually diminished until all conversation had ceased. Men gaped, then poked and prodded each other until the

181

men sitting with their backs to her turned around to stare also. Her first impulse was to turn on her heel and flee. Instead, she held her head proudly and walked to the first table. Deliberately, she faced the door to avoid having to look at the men who continued to gawk at her.

"Hey, Mabel," a deep voice called out, "is *that* on today's menu? I'll take a piece of it for dessert. And I like it sliced right down the middle."

"Shut your foul mouth, Obie," someone said. "If you want to talk that way to women, go down the street to Crockett's place."

"You gonna make me?"

"If he don't, I will," someone else threatened. A chorus of voices joined in agreement.

Angela, not wanting any trouble, bolted from the restaurant and hurried in the direction that Clint had gone. Then, her steps slowed. He had already disappeared.

She clenched her hands in frustration. How she wished for a rolling pin or a heavy iron skillet; she was angry enough to clobber that dirty-mouthed man over the head. Until her journey west, she had seldom come in contact with men other than the ones who attended their church, or merchants, or those who stayed at the boardinghouse, and they had never been so rude, at least not like the man in the restaurant. No wonder Clint had shown so much concern over her safety.

Looking anxiously about, Angela did not know what to do. She could not go back inside, yet she could not stand out here for an indefinite length of time either.

Angela shook her head to clear it. What was wrong with her? Had her courage disappeared? She had traveled across half the country using only her wits and determination. Now, she was cringing like a timid child frightened by its own shadow. Could she not do anything on her own without Clint? It felt so good to depend on him, but there were some things she had to do for herself.

Squaring her shoulders, she approached the first man who walked by. "Excuse me, sir. Could you please direct me to the main mining office?"

The man whipped off his hat and stared at her. When he finally discovered he could speak, he asked, "Which mine are you needing?"

Startled, Angela blinked. "There's more than one?"

He replied with a nervous chuckle, "Yes, ma'am. Probably fifty or more, but only five or six that's any size a'tall. There's the Angel, the Holy Moses, the Kentucky Belle . . ."

She chewed on her bottom lip while thinking about what he had said. Then, she decided she might as well inquire about the only one she had heard of. "Which one of them was the first big discovery?"

"That would be the Angel. You can find all of the mine offices down that street there." He pointed toward what seemed to be an alley running between two false-fronted buildings.

"Thank you." Warily, she peered at the narrow street.

"Ma'am, I hope you don't think I'm being forward, but I'd be proud to escort you across the street and wait and see that you made it all right. Most men here wouldn't dream of gettin' out of the way with a lady, but there's always a few who . . ."

"You were in the restaurant, weren't you?"

"Yes, ma'am." He grinned sheepishly, then clenched and unclenched a hand that had started to swell. "I think Obie will be eating soup for the next few days."

Smiling her appreciation, Angela extended her elbow. "I would be honored to have you escort me."

183

"Oh, no, ma'am, believe me, the pleasure is all mine."

Upon reaching the other side of the street, the man stopped and folded his arms and braced his legs. "I would escort you further, but don't want it bandied about town that you were seen going down an alley with a man."

Angela started to protest, then she realized there must be a reason why he said what he did. "Why, thank you, Mr . . ."

"Eubanks, Jeremiah Eubanks."

Although reluctant to impose further, Angela felt she had to let Clint know where she was. "May I ask another favor of you?"

"Why, yes, ma'am."

"Would you go to the stagecoach office and tell Clint Rutledge what happened at the restaurant and where I am?"

"I sure will."

She smiled her gratitude. "Maybe someday I can repay you for your kindness."

Jeremiah blushed and toed the sidewalk with his boot. "Shucks, ma'am, you already did that when you let me walk you across the street."

Angela waved when she reached the door of the mine office. Then, she took a deep breath and went inside.

A man sat at a massive oak desk working diligently on a thick ledger. Although he faced the door, he did not glance up when Angela entered. "Take a seat, I shall be with you presently," he said, tallying a long column of numbers.

It had been a long time since she had heard an Englishman speak, and found the crisp, precisely spoken words very pleasing to the ear. It helped to put her more at ease.

"Yes, sir," she murmured.

Startled by the sound of a female voice, Richard Grissom jerked his head up, dropping his pencil in the process. "I beg your pardon. I thought you were . . ." Rising, he pushed his chair back and started around the side of the desk, then stopped abruptly. In an attempt to regain his composure, he cleared his throat and asked politely, "How may I help you?"

He was a short man—slender, but thickening through the waist. He was meticulously groomed: his slightly graying dark hair had been parted and combed to the side in an effort to conceal a bald spot, but not a single lock was out of place; his pencil-thin mustache was trimmed to perfection, and his carriage was ramrod straight. He posed a formidable figure even though his face looked harried and weary. He could have been the proper English gentleman except for his hands. They were large, heavily-veined, and callused.

Angela's voice was calm, her gaze steady, but her insides felt like a quivering mass of jelly. "I would like to speak to the owner or manager."

He indicated by a motion of his head that he was the man she sought. "I am Richard Grissom."

Angela clenched her hands in an effort to keep them from trembling. "I am searching for my father. He is a Cornishman—a Cousin Jack. I have reason to believe he may be employed by you."

A flash of sympathy glinted from his eyes. How many times had he received letters from children, wives, mothers, inquiring about their lost loved ones? Multitudes of young men came west with the lust for riches and adventures pulsating through their veins only to disappear and never be heard from again. Numerous men did so by choice, but all too frequently it was by chance. No one would ever know how many men lost their footing while crossing a river, counted on a water hole in the desert only to find it dry, were murdered by a thief in the night or severely injured too far from civilization. There were so many different ways a man could die or disappear in the west, it was too difficult to count.

"Ma'am, I do not want to sound discouraging, but there are several thousand Cornishmen—Cousin Jacks—within the boundaries of Colorado, and hundreds within fifty miles of Clear Creek. The odds are astronomical that he is employed by the Angel Mine." He turned, walked back to his desk, and picked up a small ledger. "However, I am sure the impossible does occasionally happen. If you will tell me his name, I will check to see if he is listed in the book. I pride myself on keeping meticulous records. If he works, or has ever worked for us—me, his name will be listed." He opened the ledger and waited expectantly.

Angela crossed her fingers and whispered a silent prayer before speaking, "Samuel Langford."

Jerking up his head, he stared hard at her. "I beg your pardon. Will you repeat that name?"

"Samuel Langford." She studied the gamut of expressions sweeping across his round face and was puzzled by the abrupt changes.

Grissom slammed the ledger shut and threw it on his desk. The contempt in his voice cut like a finely honed blade. "How long has Sam been your father? Two weeks—three?"

"You know him?" A portion of her was ecstatic, yet the other part warned that something was dreadfully wrong. Then it occurred to her what he had actually said. "Why, he has always been my father."

His face was a mask of loathing as he removed his pocket watch from his vest and glanced at it. "I will give you precisely two minutes to leave my office. And, if you have not left Clear Creek by the top of the hour—which occurs in twenty more minutes—I will summon the sheriff and prefer charges."

"Prefer charges? For merely asking about my father?" she asked incredulously. She crossed her arms and thrust out her chin defiantly. "Evidently you know him and you can summon the sheriff, his deputies, the entire town if you'd like, but I refuse to leave until you tell me where he is!"

Grissom returned to his desk and sat down. He applauded mockingly. "I must say, your performance is brilliant. You are wasting your talent on this incredible scheme." He glanced at his watch again and gave a flippant wave of his hand. "Please continue if you would like, it is your time that you are wasting."

Angela did not come this far, or suffer through months of hardships, to turn aside like a docile lamb. She stalked over to the desk and pounded her fist against the top. "What scheme? And don't you dare tell me I am wasting my time! You know my father and I demand that you tell me where he is immediately!" she shouted.

The door opened abruptly and Clint walked inside. Anxiously, he looked at Angela, then at Grissom. "What's wrong? What's all the shouting about? I could hear you all the way down the street."

In a lightning fast motion, Angela ran to him. "Clint, he knows my father, in fact, I think he works for him.

187

But—but he refuses to tell me anything about him!" she cried.

"Ah ha!" Grissom exclaimed with feigned gaiety. "Her partner in crime has arrived! But of course, she had to be in cahoots with someone!"

Clint inhaled a deep breath, his brows drawn together in a frown. "I don't know what I walked in on here, but I damn sure don't like the tone of your voice. I think we should start at the beginning. If you know her father or his whereabouts, I suggest you tell her where he is, or how we can find him."

Grissom's eyes became hard and his voice threw down the gauntlet. "No, I shall be the one who makes suggestions here," he said, suddenly leveling his pistol at Clint.

Clint stood perfectly still, making sure his hands were well away from the guns strapped to his hips. He wanted to do nothing to make Grissom think he was going for them.

"Evidently, the two of you have devised this wretched scheme in an attempt to swindle me. Did you actually think I would hand over Sam's share of the mine on the basis of your claim that you were his daughter?" He rolled his eyes superciliously when Angela gasped.

"Sam's share? You mean he *owns part of the mine?*" Clint was beginning to understand the Englishman's attitude. "So you think she is . . . we are . . ."

"I think the two of you should have checked your facts before you wasted your time and mine! If you had, you would have learned that Sam and I formed our partnership years ago. He was not only my partner, he was my friend, and I knew his personal business as well as I know my own." Grissom puffed with rage as he glared at Angela. "You are nothing but a fraudulent little charlatan with a scheme to get your slimy little hands . . ."

"No, no, you're wrong!"

"And for you to come in here claiming to be his daughter right after . . ."

"But I am his daughter!"

"Like bloody hell you are!" His voice was venomous. "I was with him the day he received the letter informing him of his wife and daughter's death!"

Tears of frustration welled in Angela's eyes. "But I didn't die! I can prove it if you will just tell me where he is. I don't have the papers with me . . . they are at the bottom of the canyon, but I can tell him things that I remember . . ."

Grissom pounded on his desk, his face mottled with rage. He shouted, "I would like nothing better, but you know as well as I, that is impossible!"

"Why, for Heaven's sake?" she implored.

"Because he died a month ago."

Chapter Fourteen

Angela's chest rose and fell. Excruciating agony tore through her heart. Her body spasmed from the pain. She clutched at Clint frantically when he reached out to hold her steady. Her face crumbled and terrible sobs choked her throat, strangling her. She stared at Richard Grissom in horror.

"Please tell me it is not true!" Then, her voice rose piercingly. "You are just making that up because you do not believe I am his daughter. But I am! I swear I am! Please, I will do anything—just tell me he is not dead!"

His eyes glazed, and his voice rang hollow and empty. "Much to my regret, I am afraid it is true."

Angela, sobbing bitterly, buried her head against Clint's strong shoulder.

Taut muscles stood out along Grissom's jaw. He forgot his anger at the girl, he forgot everything except the painful memory of his friend's death. "It happened while we were eating dinner one night. One moment we were laughing and conversing, and the next . . . he suddenly clutched his chest and keeled over. By the time I came around the table and knelt down beside him . . . he was already gone." Grissom shook his head. He still found the loss difficult to accept. "That wretched day I lost the best friend a man could ever have."

Angela sank into a chair, her mind and body numb. She was unaware of speaking her thoughts. "It isn't fair! It isn't fair! How could fate be so cruel to him as well as to me? All of those wasted years, we could have known each other—loved each other, instead of . . ." Her voice trailed off as she began to weep softly.

Clint knelt beside her, wanting so desperately to comfort her, but knowing there was nothing he could say or do to ease her pain. He felt so helpless. He wanted to be angry at Richard Grissom, but for the life of him, he could not summon a bitter rage, not if he looked at the situation objectively. Under the circumstances, the man had every right to be suspicious.

Grissom shot Clint a baffled look. The girl sounded so sincere. If he did not know differently. . . . He quickly pushed those thoughts from his head. He had always been an easy mark for virtually any man or woman with a hard luck story. But this was more than a hard luck story, it was an outright scheme to defraud him, and he was not about to be duped.

Clint straightened and met Grissom's eyes. "Don't you think you were a little rough on her?"

He raised one brow and allowed his gaze to sweep scathingly over Clint from head to toe. "Out of curiosity, who are you supposed to be? Samuel's son?" he added caustically.

Clint scowled. "No, not hardly. The name is Clint Rutledge." He did not offer him his hand.

"Rutledge?" The name was very familiar to Grissom. If he had not been so distraught, he would probably have recognize the striking resemblance immediately. "Are you Tom Rutledge's son?"

Clint nodded. "You know my dad?"

This entire situation was becoming more perplexing by the minute. "Yes, I know him quite well. I have found him to be an honest and trustworthy man. We purchased several steers from him. That is, until . . ." Realizing he might have said too much, a veiled look quickly descended over his face. "Haven't you been abroad?"

"Yes." Much to Clint's relief, Grissom had lowered the gun.

"Have you just arrived home?"

"To Clear Creek. I haven't been to the ranch yet."

"I see. Have you been in contact with your father?"

Clint's opinion of the man rose several notices. By his words and actions, it was clear Grissom was aware of the misfortune his father had suffered with the ranch. "No, I haven't, and you don't have to mince words with me. I've just come from the stage office. They told me what happened to the herd."

Grissom's face reflected no trace of his former animosity. "It is a relief to know that you have returned. Tom was so excited about the spring calves. Then, when he had to destroy his life's work," Grissom shook his head sadly, "it devastated him."

Clint's stomach balled into a hard knot. His dad had taken so much pride in the cattle he had spent years cross breeding. "Yes, I imagine so. Just the mention of the word anthrax is enough to send a cattleman . . ." He quickly clamped his mouth shut and protectively placed his hand on Angela's shoulder. "I didn't come here to discuss my dad's run of bad luck with the ranch. Under the circumstances, I can't fault you for being skeptical about Miss Langford's claim. But you could at least listen to her side of the story."

Grissom's next glance at Angela was sharp and assessing. "I will admit that her distress seems to be genuine. But, her story has to be a fabrication. There is no denying the fact; I was there the day Samuel received word that his family had succumbed during a terrible epidemic."

"What if that letter was a fabrication?" Clint countered. You have already stated that you and Samuel were more than partners—you were friends. What would you do if you found out later that she is his daughter, and that you had refused to even listen to her story with an open mind?"

Grissom started to speak, but Clint stopped him. "No, before you say something you might regret, I suggest you think about it for a while. She's too upset to discuss it further anyway."

Clint helped Angela to her feet and made their way to the door. He paused and looked over his shoulder. "I can't speak for her. I have no idea how she will want to pursue this matter. However, if you decide you want to see her, you can find her at the ranch. I am taking her home with me."

Once outside, Clint cupped Angela's chin tenderly in his warm hand. "I'm so sorry about your father, sweetheart. I know how much you wanted to find him and build a relationship to make up for some of those lost years."

A glint of wonder flashed through her eyes. "Then you do believe me."

"Of course I do."

Regardless of what happened to them in the future, she thought that she could never love him more than at this moment. "That man made so many dreadful accusations, I was afraid that you might . . ."

Clint's gaze burned intensely. "Sh, hush, sweetheart. I love you, remember? And with love comes trust." He smoothed an errant curl from her forehead. "Unless you feel that you have to talk about it, let's put it aside for now."

Nodding gratefully, she sighed. "I doubt if I could muster the strength to discuss what's happened. I'd just like to lie down for a while."

"As soon as we get to the ranch, you can do that. The livery should have carriages for rent." Taking her by the elbow, he led her toward the street, then stopped and turned abruptly. "Let's go the back way. I'd rather avoid meeting any of my old friends and acquaintances right now."

Numbly, Angela placed one foot in front of the other as they made their way to the outskirts of town where the livery stable was located.

The cold mountain wind that cut deeply into her flesh was nothing compared to the frigid state of her heart. Her entire body was engulfed in tides of weariness and despair. Julia had won after all. Her attempts to prevent Angela from knowing her father were more successful than she could ever have imagined.

The livery stable had a pungent scent that was a combination of horses, leather, hay, and grain. There were four stalls on either side of the barn, three filled. Two carriages were side by side at the rear, one covered with canvas.

"Louis?" Clint called. "Where are you?" He looked about for the man who owned the livery stable. A man whom Clint did not know came forward from the shadows of the back of the barn.

"He isn't here," the man said. "I bought him out last

spring." He extended his hand and merely nodded to Angela. "My name is Morgan. What can I do for you?"

Clint walked over to the stalls to look at the horses. "I need to rent a rig for a few days."

Stopping in front of the first stall, Morgan frowned. "A few days you say?" He shook his head. "I usually rent them by the hour—half a day at the most."

Clint ran his hand over the horse's forehead and fore-lock, then patted him on the neck. "All right, but I still need one for a few days. I'll return it day after tomorrow."

"That morning?"

Clint nodded. "If you need it then."

He scratched his head. "In that case, I guess I can cut you a little slack. How does thirty dollars sound to you?"

"Hell, man, I just want to rent him, not buy him!"

Morgan shrugged indifferently. "I usually charge a dollar an hour. Like I said, I'm cutting you some slack, so you can take it or leave it. Makes no difference to me."

Clint's mouth thinned with indignation as he crammed his hand into his pocket and withdrew a money clip. "I assume that price includes a lap robe?"

"Nope. That's five dollars extra. And don't complain, or the price might go up."

Clint slapped thirty dollars into the man's out-stretched hand. "I'm not complaining. But you can keep the robe. If there wasn't a lady present, I'd tell you where you could *put* it." He slipped a lead rope on the horse's bridle and led him toward the carriages. Peeking under the canvas, he decided it was in much better condition than the one with the stuffing coming out of the cushions.

"That one's not for rent. That's my personal carriage."

Ignoring his vehement protests, Cling flung the canvas off the carriage, then turned his attention to the long wooden runners that were propped against the wall.

The ski-shaped runners were equipped with a locking device to clamp them to the wheels, thus converting the carriage into a sleigh which made the mountain trails and passages more accessible.

Selecting the two best runners, Clint placed them aside, then began hitching the horse to the carriage, still ignoring the man's heated protests.

The man blustered. "If you make one move to climb into that carriage, I'll get the sheriff!"

"Go get him, but there's nothing he can do. I paid the price you asked." Clint escorted Angela to the carriage and helped her aboard before he climbed into the seat beside her.

The man knew Clint had bested him at his own game, but he was determined to have the last word. "If you're one minute late, I'll press charges against you for horse stealing."

The steely look in Clint's eyes nailed Morgan to the wall. "Was that a threat or a promise?"

"Call it what you want," the hostler snarled.

"Let me give you a piece of advice, friend, and I won't even charge you for it. I realize prices go up whenever a gold or silver strike is involved, but you are entirely out of line. I have no use for a man who engages in legal robbery—a town has no use for a man like you either. When I return this rig day after tomorrow, I had better see a sign hanging outside with new prices on it . . . reasonable prices. If I don't, you'll close your doors by the end of the month."

Morgan bristled angrily. "You threatening to burn me out or something?"

"No. I'll just buy one of those town plots, put up a barn and open a livery of my own." Clint flicked the reins and drove the carriage out of the barn.

This was a side of Clint Angela had never seen, and she admired it. She knew the man at the livery stable had made him furious. But instead of ranting and blustering like the hostler, he had held his temper in check, and methodically thought of a way to restrain him.

That observation had barely crossed her mind before another followed. She regarded Clint with somber apprehension. Could his reaction to the hostler's legal thievery be a not-too-subtle warning that he would not tolerate an opportunist? Regardless of his denial, did he have doubts about her claim that she was Samuel Langford's daughter? Quickly, she banished the thought. She had enough on her mind without creating more anxiety.

Instead of heading for the ranch, Clint turned the rig back towards town and within a few minutes, pulled to a stop in front of a general store. Stepping down from the carriage, he held his hand out for Angela. "There are a few things we will need. The selection may not be as good as that larger mercantile across the street, but I know the owner of this one and he is an honest man." Grinning sheepishly, he gestured toward the other store. "If their prices are outrageous, I doubt if I could afford to open a mercantile. Besides, I've never had a desire to be a salesclerk." Angela managed to smile at his remark. but her expression was sad.

"I remember what you said a while ago about it not being safe out here, but I'd rather not go inside." Her eyes, slightly red and swollen from crying, were tacitly pleading with him not to object.

He regarded her for a few moments, then slowly nodded. "All right, but if anybody bothers you, or if you see the man from the livery heading this way, come inside and get me." He removed his coat and wrapped it around her shoulders. Then he gently squeezed her arm and smiled reassuringly.

The bell hanging over the door tinkled when Clint opened it. Jack Buchanan, the proprietor, looked up from the catalog he was studying, and smiled broadly. Hurrying from behind the counter, he grasped Clint's hand in a hearty shake. "It's good to see you. A fellow told me you were back, but I didn't know if you would have time to stop by. Is it true what I heard about the stagecoach?"

"Unfortunately, it is."

Shaking his head, Jake clicked his tongue. "It's a damn shame. Bill must have driven the stage over that road several hundred times, and on his very last trip something like that happens. Makes a man think how fragile life can be, and how a minute or two can make a difference between living and dying."

"Those same thoughts occurred to me."

Jake moved his hands in a dismissing gesture. "Enough of that. Pull you up a seat and I'll pour a cup of coffee. I'm eager to hear all about your travels." He reached for two mugs on the countertop and headed toward the pot-bellied stove where a coffeepot sat in attendance.

"I'd like to, Jake, but there's a lady waiting for me outside in the carriage. Then too, I'd like to get home before it becomes too dark."

"A lady? I suppose she's the one who was on the

stage?" Jake peered out the window, craning his head for a better look.

"Yes, she is." Clint had known it would not take long for the news of his return and the stagecoach disaster to spread.

"You and the lady were mighty lucky."

"Yes, we certainly were." Clint glanced about. "Is your son here?"

"He should be in the back."

"Would you mind if I sent him over to Sadie's for me? We haven't eaten yet . . ."

"Heck, no, I don't mind, but you're welcome to have supper with us. That little gal of mine has become a good little cook," he boasted.

"I appreciate it, Jake, maybe some other time. I need to get on home."

"Of course." Jake walked to the rear of the store and opened the door leading to the stock room. "Dustin," he yelled, "Come here, boy."

Moments later, a chubby little boy whom Clint knew to be about eight years old, burst through the doorway. "Did you call me, Papa?"

"There's a gent here who needs you to run an errand for him. You remember Clint Rutledge, don't you?"

Dustin's eyes lit up and he grinned broadly. "I sure do! Hello, Mr. Rutledge. It's good to see you again."

"What's with this *Mr. Rutledge?* I thought we were friends, and friends always call each other by their given names."

Casting an anxious glance at his father, he lowered his voice in a conspiratorial tone, "Papa's been telling me and Steffie that just because we live so far up in the mountains don't mean we have to behave like uncivilized heathens. He says that progress is coming in with the railroad and we are gonna have to start showing respect to grown-ups by addressing them properly. Don't know if I like the idea of progress though."

"Oh? Why not?"

"Most all of the grown-ups acted plumb silly when silver was found. They said that Clear Creek would grow and business would get better. Seems to me all it has done so far is to make my papa have to work harder by keeping the store open longer. And if a body has to walk down the street, he has to step around some ol' drunk who has been tossed out of a saloon. If that's progress, don't know if I can tolerate much more of it."

Clint was amazed at the speech coming out of this little boy's mouth. "I know it seems sort of bleak at times, but many good things come with progress too. Churches, schools, a doctor, and families start moving in. And think about this, there will be boys and girls your own age to play with."

Dustin crinkled his nose. "Ugh, girls! Don't know why there's such a big fuss about them! They are nothing but a big ol' pain in the neck if you ask me!" He gazed up at Clint. "What do you need for me to do?"

Relieved that their conversation was over, Clint quickly handed him some money. "Go over to Sadie's place and get four roast beef or ham—some kind of sandwich, it really doesn't matter. Tell her they're for me and that you're in a hurry. And you keep whatever change is left over. Okay?"

His eyes lit up. "Oh, boy! Thanks, Mr. Rutledge."

After the boy had slammed out the door, Jake shook his head, slightly awestruck. "I don't know what to think about that boy. At times, I wonder if an old man wasn't born in a child's body."

His eyes followed Clint as he walked over to the

200

wearing apparel and yard goods, and began looking through the limited assortment. "Need some new clothes?"

"Yes, for myself and the lady. All of our belongings were lost in the accident. I might have a couple pair of trousers and maybe a shirt or two at home, but I'm sure they have seen better days." He selected a few garments for himself and placed them on the counter. "I'll need two blankets. That crook at the livery stable wanted to charge me a small fortune just to rent lap robes."

Jake's face colored. "You might call me a crook once you look at my prices. The freight companies raised their rates, and I had no other choice but to pass it on to my customers."

Clint pitched some socks on the counter along with some underwear. "I have no objection to a man making a decent profit. I've always known you to be fair and honest, and I figure your goods are priced accordingly." He grinned. "Hell, I sound worse than some old skinflint. That man just rankled me. I guess I'm too stubborn for my own good, but it goes against my principles for someone to take advantage over someone else just because he can."

Jake laughed. "Yeah, I know what you mean. Principles usually end up costing a man twice as much in the long run."

"I agree. But when a man's integrity is involved, no price is too high." Clint ran his fingers through his hair and said with an embarrassed grin, "I think your boy must have started something. It sounds like we're getting philosophical in our old age. And by the way, I need a hat! I lost mine and I feel naked without it."

"Those are all I have," Jake said, pointing to a stack.

Clint tried several on before he was satisfied with the

fit of a flat-crowned, tan Stetson. He creased the brim and tilted it back on his head. "Now comes the difficult part."

"Oh, what's that?"

"The lady needs clothes from the skin out." He glanced at a rack where dresses were hanging. "I'll look through those if you can select the other items she will need: undergarments, nightgowns, stockings, a hairbrush, hairpins ... whatever. You know more about women's articles than I do." He measured with his hands. "If it helps, she is about this big around and about this tall."

Clint pulled dresses from the rack and quickly chose three that he thought would fit her, and he also found a heavy woolen cloak. Knowing how pitifully thin her shawl was, he added it to his selections. Then, several bolts of material caught his eye. He piled them on the counter and requested matching thread, needles, buttons, scissors, and a thimble. Jake scurried about the store pulling items from the shelves until he was panting from the effort.

Clint, remembering that she had been crocheting on the stagecoach, said, "Add a crochet needle and thread, and I think that will do it. If she needs anything else, we'll get it later."

Jake looked at all of the items piled on the counter and slowly shook his head with amazement. "Good God Almighty, Clint, I know you said that all of yours and her belongings were lost, but I never expected you to buy her all of this. What do you intend to do, marry the woman?"

Clint teetered back on his heels and could not resist grinning. "That's exactly what I intend to do!"

Jake's mouth dropped open in surprise. He started to

say something, but he clamped his mouth shut when Dustin hurried into the store, carrying the food wrapped in a clean, white napkin.

"Here are your sandwiches, Mr. Rutledge. And Miss Sadie said that you had better come in to see her just as soon as you could."

Clint ruffled the boys hair. He asked Jake, "How long do you think it will take to tally all of that?"

Jake stroked his chin thoughtfully. "About an hour."

Clint frowned. "I really don't want to wait that long. I'll tell you what. Go ahead and total the cloak, blankets, and two complete changes of clothing for each of us, and I'll stop by for the other things when I bring the rig back day after tomorrow. I'll settle up with you then, if it's all right."

"I don't have to total it today." Jake began bundling the items. "I know the prices of my merchandise, and I know what you are taking with you. As for paying me, your credit is good. You can settle up whenever you want to." Purposely, he had not wrapped the blankets or the cloak. He shoved the bundle into Clint's hand. "Now scat, get out of here or it will be midnight before you get home. Dustin, get the door for him."

"Appreciate it, Jake. See you day after tomorrow."

"Your order will be ready and waiting on you."

Impatiently, Jake patted the floor with his shoe. He waited for what seemed liked forever before Clint got settled in the rig and pulled away from the store. Hurrying to the window he peered down the street until the rig disappeared from sight. Whipping off his apron, he slipped on his coat. "Dustin, go fetch your sister. I want the two of you to watch the store. I have to go tell Sadie something!"

"What is it, Papa? Is something wrong?" Dustin asked, his big brown eyes wide with curiosity.

"Mr. Rutledge has him a lady friend. They are going to get married!"

Dustin wrinkled his nose and sighed with disgust. "Golly! I thought Mr. Rutledge was smarter than that!"

Chapter Fifteen

Clint reined the horse to a stop on a small rise overlooking the ranch. A surge of exhilaration raced through him as he relished the sight of his home. Then slowly, a feeling of peace, a sense of belonging, enveloped him like comforting arms. It felt so good to be home again.

The ranch proper was a sprawling log house with a porch that wrapped around the front and either side, a long, narrow bunkhouse, a large barn, chicken coops, and several miscellaneous out buildings. It was all nestled in a mountain meadow surrounded by Ponderosa pines that stood guard like watchful sentinels.

A faint plume of smoke rose from the chimney and hovered low over the snow-covered roof. The single pale light that glowed in the front window seemed as brilliant as the brightest beacon offering its welcome.

The moon, large and perfectly round, hung suspended in the sky, its lower rim just barely kissing the treetops. The light from it cast a waxen sheen over the snow that appeared to be unmarred by human feet. Somewhere in the distance, a mountain lion snarled at its mate, and a lone coyote romanced the moon.

Clint smiled lovingly down at Angela, cuddled in the

crook of his shoulder. She had fallen asleep almost immediately after they left town. Delicately tilting her face upwards, he gently brushed his lips across hers.

"Wake up, sweetheart." He wanted her first glimpse of the ranch to be from this magnificent vantage point.

"I will if you'll kiss me again," she murmured sleepily. When his lips met hers again, more ardent and demanding this time, her heart swelled with love until it overflowed.

"We're almost home, love," he whispered raggedly.

"Home," she mouthed the word solemnly. What a wonderful sound it had to it.

He made a sweeping gesture with his hand. "There it is, the Double R."

Astonishment touched her pale face. The sight before her was so lovely and serene, it could have come directly from an artist's pallet. Awestruck, she gasped, "Clint, why—it's beautiful!"

"It sure is," he agreed, unmistakable pride in his voice. Slipping his arm back around her, he flicked the reins, and within a matter of minutes, they were standing on the front porch.

"Since Dad is not expecting me, I guess I had better knock, or we might be greeted with a loaded shotgun," Clint said, while rapping impatiently on the door. When no one responded to his knock, he turned the knob and pushed, but the door was locked. "Dad! Dad!" he called loudly. "It's me, Clint. Open the door."

Listening carefully, he breathed a sigh of relief when he heard footsteps scuffing against the floor.

There was a glimpse of movement at the front window, then they heard the sound of someone fumbling with a latch. Clint's father flung the door wide open.

"Son?" The word was a cry mixed with uncertainty and jubilation.

Clint grinned from ear to ear. "Do you plan on keeping us standing out here on the porch all night, or can we come inside?"

The man's unabashed laughter was infectious. "Get your ornery hide in here, son!" He grabbed Clint in a bear hug, embracing him affectionately.

After their greeting, Clint's father peered at the feminine figure standing in the shadows. Her hooded cloak masked her features. "Who is that with you? Susan?"

"No, Dad, this is Angela Langford. Angela, this is my dad, Thomas Rutledge."

Angela stepped forward and extended her hand. At her first glimpse of him, she was startled to see an older version of the man she loved. They could have been poured from the same mold, except Clint's father had silver hair and his face was more weathered and lined. Other than that, their resemblance was uncanny. "It is my pleasure, sir. Clint has told me so much about you."

Countless questions about the young woman ran through his mind. Nevertheless, Tom acted as though it was an everyday occurrence for his son to bring a pretty lady home with him. He accepted her offered hand. "Well, you look like an intelligent young lady to me. Maybe after you've known me for a while, you'll be able to shift through all of the lies he told you and decide for yourself what the truth is."

"Oh, but it was all nice—" Her protest was left unfinished as she realized he had been teasing.

Tom chortled, then shook his head when he realized they were standing on the porch with the front door open wide. "Come in here where it's warm." He ush-

207

ered them inside to a spacious living room. "Are you two hungry?"

"I'm not," Clint stated, "but Angela might be." He looked at her questioningly. She had only eaten a few bites of her sandwich before she had nodded off.

"No . . . to be perfectly honest, I'm too tired to be hungry." Usually, Angela was not so forward, but she was too weary not to express her feelings. In all likelihood, if she did not lie down soon, she would faint from exhaustion.

Tom quickly appraised her ashen features, the dark circles under her sad eyes, and his heart lurched with compassion. "We can certainly remedy that! Clint, get the lady's bags and show her to Susan's room."

His request had been unnecessary. Clint had already moved toward the door. "I'll be back in just a minute."

"But . . . I don't have—" Angela's voice trailed off. She wondered why Clint was leaving. He knew all of their belongings had been lost.

Tom suddenly remembered his manners. "Please, be seated. Make yourself at home," he said, escorting Clint's guest toward a huge chair. "I have a secret hunch that whoever invented the stagecoach built it with his worst enemy in mind. They can be mighty uncomfortable. Makes the ride out here to the ranch seem like a pleasure excursion."

It quickly occurred to him that something was askew. At the mention of the stagecoach, the young woman's ashen face had paled even further. Though he seldom went into town anymore, he knew that the stage's last run had been scheduled for sometime last week. Even if the cold spell had delayed the stage, it would have been impossible for the coach to cross those treacherous mountain passes after a heavy snow. In fact, that road would be impassable until spring.

Disconcerted, he crossed his arms and pointedly looked at her. "You and Clint didn't come by stage, did you?"

"If you don't mind, sir—"

"Surely the two of you did not come across country?"

"Yes . . . well, no . . . not really. You see, there was a tragic accident." A look of distress crossed her face. "Please . . . I'd rather for Clint to explain what happened."

Clint returned, carrying the bundle. He stamped the snow from his boots on a rag rug just inside the door.

"What in blue blazes is this about an accident?" Tom asked in an explosive tone.

Clint's dark eyes sharpened, his gaze darting from his father to Angela. One glance at her drawn features told him that she had emotionally and physically reached far beyond the point of her endurance.

"Dad, why don't you make a pot of coffee for us while I get Angela settled in? Then after I tend to the horse and put the rig away, I'll explain everything that's happened."

Tom nodded as he headed toward the kitchen. "All right, you just see to the little lady, though, and I'll tend to the coffee and to the rig."

Clint took hold of her elbow and guided her to a room at the end of a long hallway and pushed open the door. "Susan insisted on having this room for privacy," he said, his voice holding no rancor. "She claimed Dad snored too loud. I'll always believe she only used that as an excuse, though, because this room has the best view in the house. I'll open the shutters tomorrow, then you can see what I mean." Tossing the bundle onto the bed, he walked over to the bureau and quickly lit the lamp that rested there.

Angela scanned the room appreciatively. It looked like Susan, bright and cheerful, feminine, but not audaciously frilly. The dressing screen and the yellow curtains hanging in a swag over the double windows matched the heavy, patchwork comforter that covered the four poster bed. There was an oak bureau, a writing desk, and an overstuffed chair with a small table sitting beside it. The gap between the wall and dressing screen revealed a commode, with a porcelain pitcher and basin sitting atop it. There was also a small stone fireplace in the right corner of the room.

Timidly, she looked at Clint. He made no attempt to hide the fact that he was watching her. Her emotions whirled and skidded. Why didn't he take her into his arms? Why could he not sense her need to be held tightly, to be comforted? Even though he had been kind and attentive since that horrible debacle at the mine office, she had sensed in him a hesitation, a slight withdrawal. It was nothing substantial, just a nagging feeling of something being wrong.

Or was it fear? a tiny voice inside her asked. *Even though he had said he believed her, could he now be having doubts about her claims, about her honesty?*

Feeling uneasy over the perusal of her sad, sorrowful eyes, Clint briskly rubbed his hands together, while sniffing as if to locate an offensive odor. "It's cold and a little musty in here. Knowing Dad, this room has probably been closed up for months. We'll have to air it out tomorrow. In the meanwhile, you'll need a fire tonight." Annoyance flickered over his face when he saw that the wood box was empty. "I'll go get some wood.

210

While I'm gone, if you want to look through the bundle, you can separate your things from mine."

Her things? Angela quickly ripped open the bundle, gasping with surprise when she saw the new clothing. Two dresses, undergarments, stockings, a warm flannel nightgown, a brush and comb, hairpins—everything she could possibly want.

A hot tear rolled down her cheek. New clothes. How many times in her life had she owned new, ready-made clothes? She could count the times on one hand and still have fingers left over. New dresses had always been purchased for Dahlia, while her clothes were either purchased at a second-hand shop or sewn from cheap fabric. Occasionally, Dahlia had grown weary of a gown and had given it to her, but it never fit properly and always had to be altered. Then, there had been the embarrassment of Dahlia pointing out her generosity to her circle of snobbish friends.

A huge lump constricted her throat. She always hated to cry, feeling tears were nothing but a ploy for sympathy, or a display of weakness. And that was all she seemed to be doing lately. Maybe that was the reason Clint was behaving so standoffish. Maybe he had become weary of her sniveling and carrying on.

"Do you think they'll fit?" Clint asked, coming into the room, dropping the firewood into the wood box and walking over to her. His heart swelled with pleasure at the look of gratitude and delight on her face.

"I'm sure they will, but if they don't," she shrugged casually, "a few tucks in the waist will remedy anything." Shyly, she buried her face against the corded muscles of his chest, relishing the feel of his hands exploring the hollow of her back. "Thank you so much. But you didn't have to—"

"Oh, yes, I did!" He pulled reluctantly away and held her at arm's length. "You had to have something to wear."

"But I could have done something else. I could—"

"No, you couldn't. I bought you those things because you needed them, because you did not have anything else to wear . . . and because it made me feel damn good to buy them for you." His features and tone softened. "Here I am, practically shouting at you . . . after what you've gone through today."

"Clint, please don't . . ." She took a deep, steadying breath, and gave him a brave smile. "You go visit with your father. It has been a long time since you've seen him and he is eager to know all about what has happened. Just as I'm sure you want to know what happened to his cattle."

"Do you mean about the anthrax?"

"Yes, I heard what Mr. Grissom said. I may be from the city, but I have heard about anthrax and how devastating it can be to ranchers. Now, go!" She made a backward waving motion with her hand. "I've been putting myself to bed for years and I am still capable of performing that feat all alone."

"Well . . . I'll build the fire first."

"I can do that too." She grinned sheepishly. "Although, I would appreciate it if you positioned the damper so that the fire will draw properly."

He smiled broadly, his dimples two deep slashes in his cheeks. "I think I can manage that little chore." He adjusted the damper, and still smiling, stepped forward and clasped her body tightly to his. He pressed his lips to hers, caressing her mouth more than kissing it.

"I hate to stop at one kiss," he murmured softly, "but

I think that ought to be my limit for tonight. Goodnight, sweetheart."

Angela softly closed the door behind him. Regardless of her earlier determination, she leaned her forehead against the door, and yielded to the compulsive sobs that shook her.

Tom sat silently at the kitchen table and watched while Clint filled a thick mug with steaming coffee. He waited until his son has settled himself in a chair before he asked, "What is this about an accident with the stagecoach?"

Clint blew on the coffee before he took a sip. Starting at the beginning, he told him what happened to their arrival at Clear Creek, but he made no mention of any personal details concerning him and Angela, or her purpose for coming to this area.

Tom made no comments other than to mutter a few curses during Clint's account of what had happened.

"Bill was a good man," he said after Clint finished. "I didn't know the other one, but at least he didn't leave a family behind like Bill did. Do you reckon the stage line will help his widow out any?"

"I doubt it. Bill told me that the company had just about been breaking even for the past two or three years, thanks to the railroad. Jake Buchanan's little boy made a comment today that's been on my mind. He wasn't sure he liked the progress that silver strikes and the railroad brought. And I've a half a mind to agree with him."

Clint stood and refilled their coffee cups. "Oh, by the way, when I saw Susan, she said to tell you that they are doing fine and she sends you her love."

"Yeah, her baby is due before too long." Tom's voice was soft and slightly tinged with sadness. "I sure do miss that little gal." Suddenly, eyeing Clint curiously, he said, "Speaking of little gals ..." He motioned toward the back room with his thumb. "You've never brought one home with you before."

Clint grinned. "That's right, I haven't."

Tom waited expectantly, but when Clint added nothing further, he stroked his chin, then tugged at his earlobe. "Am I going to have to drag it out of you?"

Clint delighted in aggravating his father. "Drag what out of me?"

Tom's eyes narrowed, his teeth worrying with the corner of his mouth. He started to say something, then changed his mind. "For a few minutes there, I thought ..." Then he gestured with his hand as though he'd had an absurd idea. "Naw, it couldn't be. You've always had an eye for yellow-haired gals with a little bit of extra meat on their bones."

"Well, now that you mention it—"

Tom deliberately wrinkled his nose. "This gal here, she sure is a scrawny little thing, isn't she?"

Any trace of a smile disappeared from Clint's face. "She might be a little too thin, but you have to consider what all she's been through recently. Then too, I doubt if she's had enough to eat in the past eight months or so to keep a bird alive!" he stated defensively.

Tom snapped his fingers and pointed at Clint. "That's it! A bird! That's what she reminds me of! That long, tall scrawny body of hers, all of that black hair on her head ... and the gawky way she walks ... why, a good gust of wind and she'd take off like a black bird!"

Clint slammed his cup against the table, sloshing coffee from it. "By damn, it so happens that I think she is very pretty! And her movements are not gawky!" He glared hard at his father. "This isn't like you, Dad. I've never known you to make fun of anyone."

"I've never had to drag information out of my son before about the woman he loves," Tom said dryly.

It took a few moments for his father's words to sink in. Clint sheepishly realized that he had just been paid back for deliberately being so evasive. He laced his fingers together and popped his knuckles. "Dad, you know that I love you, and I have always respected you . . ." Then a wide grin spread across his face. "But has anyone ever told you that you can be a genuine pain in the butt!"

Tom threw his head back and guffawed. "Yep, I reckon they have. Many a times. Only bad thing is, you and I were cut from the same cloth!" Still laughing, he leaned forward. "Now, tell me about your girl. And why in blue blazes hasn't she been eating properly?"

"All right, Dad, but first, how did you know that I was in love with her?"

Grinning, Tom sighed heavily and rolled his eyes. "For one thing, your feet haven't touched the floor, for another, you have a silly grin plastered on your . . ." his voice trailed off, and suddenly became sober. "I shouldn't be teasing you about something as serious as this. You were curious how I knew? It's very simple; a body would have to be deaf and blind not to see or sense the feelings you two have for each other. Now, answer my question."

"I need to start at the beginning in order for it to make sense . . . well, almost at the beginning."

"Go ahead, take all the time you need."

"Does the name Samuel Langford sound familiar to you?"

"It certainly does. Sam was—"

"Samuel Langford was Angela's father."

Tom's eyes widened, his brows raised, and he made a small whistling sound between his teeth. "By all means, start at the beginning."

"When Angela was just a small child, her mother fell into ill health. Samuel sent his wife and child to New Orleans, to live with Julia Stanton. She's either a distant relative or a friend—I'm not really sure. Then, Angela's mother passed away not long after they arrived. Exactly why Julia did what she did, I have no idea and Angela doesn't either. But Julia sent Samuel a letter telling him that his wife *and child* had died. In the meantime, she told Angela that her father had been killed in a mining accident."

"Why all the deception on this woman's part?"

"Like I said, I have no idea. Anyway, years passed, and during those years, Angela was not physically mistreated, but emotionally—that's a different matter entirely. After you've been around Angela for a few days, you'll understand what I'm talking about. She'll remind you of a little pup that's been kicked around—I guess the best way to describe her is cowed down, but she's gradually coming out of it," he added optimistically.

Tom urged him to continue.

"Several months ago, Angela discovered a letter her father had written to Julia Stanton. From the date and gist of the letter, Angela realized Julia had lied to her. When she confronted the old bat, Julia admitted what she had done. That very day Angela took what little money she had stuck back, packed her few belongings, and left. The letter gave a few clues to his whereabouts, so she began tracking him down. Most of the time she hit upon cold trails, but she was determined to find him.

216

She would go as far as her money would take her, then she'd work a while, and take out after him again."

"It doesn't sound like she's too cowed down," Tom remarked. "Sounds to me like she's a mighty brave little gal."

Clint nodded. "She has more courage than she thinks, but she has been browbeat . . . and very thoroughly. She has very little self-confidence. Like I suggested earlier, just watch her for a few days and you will understand what I mean."

"How did she take the news that her father was dead?"

Clint shook his head. "Not very well. Richard Grissom didn't help matters either. In so many words, he called her a liar and a cheat, and accused her of being an impostor out to bilk him out of Langford's estate. And, Dad, to be fair about it, I really can't fault the man. He has apparently known Sam Langford for years, and even claimed he was with Sam when he received the letter informing him about the death of his family. There is no reason to doubt his word about that because his and Angela's stories coincide."

"Surely the girl has something to prove her identity."

"I'm sure she does—but whatever proof she had is lying at the bottom of that canyon with no way to retrieve it until spring. Even then, there are no guarantees that it will still be intact. The elements could destroy it, wild animals could tear into her baggage—anything could happen to it."

Tom worried with his earlobe. "She's in a hell of a shape then, isn't she?"

"Yes, when it comes to proving her identity, she is. The thing about it is, I doubt if the size of his estate has occurred to her—and I have a hunch that when she gets

217

over the initial shock of his death, the money won't be all that important to her."

"You really think so?"

"I do," Clint stated firmly.

Tom's brows drew downward into a speculative frown. "You met Angela on the stagecoach, right?"

"Yes."

"If you don't object to my asking, how far has your relationship gone? And I'm not asking for personal details," he hurried to clarify. "You've stated quite clearly how you feel about her and from all appearances she—"

Clint interrupted, "I have asked her to marry me and she has accepted. Now, quit beating around the bush and get to the point. What is eating at you?"

Tom crossed his arms and stared directly at Clint. "Son, I realize I'm taking a chance on making you mad at me. . . . I just don't want you to get hurt. But, there's something I feel I have to ask." He took a deep breath and plunged ahead. "Are you satisfied that she is telling the truth?"

Clint returned his piercing gaze and without a flicker of doubt, he stated, "Yes, sir, I am."

Tom nodded decisively. "That's good enough for me. Whatever the two of you need, or decide, I'll stand behind you all of the way."

"I appreciate it, Dad." Clint pressed his hands, palms down, on the table. "Now that we have that matter all settled, let's talk about you for a while."

"Do you want to discuss anything in particular?"

His jaw tightened. "We have already played cat and mouse. I heard in Clear Creek that you were hit hard by anthrax and had to destroy the herd."

Tom let out his breath very slowly and lowered his head. Rubbing the back of his neck, he stood, walked over to the kitchen window and stared forlornly into the night. Finally, he turned and faced Clint. "I'd say that pretty well sums it up."

"Nothing was said about the other ranchers being hit."

"Fortunately, in that respect, it was just the Double R. I'm grateful my stupidity didn't wipe out the others in the area." Although it hurt Tom to talk about it, he knew Clint was anxious to learn what had happened. "You know we sold off a good part of our stock before you left for England."

"Yes, but those cattle needed to be sold to carry out our plans on improving the herd."

"I know. The point is, though, we lost quite a few cattle last winter—it was the worst winter I have ever seen in these parts." Pride edged into his voice as he let his thoughts wander. "The cross-breeds made it through the winter just fine though . . . just the way I figured they would. However, some of the smaller outfits were not so lucky. The harsh winter wiped several of them out.

"Knowing we needed enough cattle to take to market this next summer, I bought all that I could find. Also, I bought nearly a thousand head from a small outfit making the rounds of the mining camps. Most all of the man's hands had quit on him when they became struck with gold and silver fever, and he could not handle that many head of cattle. I figured that we had to have a herd, and you know as well as I that we were going to have to wait at least another four or five years before we could even think about selling any of the special breeds, not if we wanted to raise those cattle exclusively."

"There's no argument there, Dad. It takes time to

build up a herd, and the special breeds were worth being patient. And I see nothing wrong in your buying those cattle either. It sounds like it was something you had to do."

"Up to a certain point. I spent almost all of our cash reserve though." Obstinately, he jutted his chin. "If it sounds like I'm trying to make excuses or apologize for what I did, I'm not. I'd probably do the same thing over again if given the same opportunity."

Chagrined, Clint winced slightly. "Did I sound condescending?"

"A little," Tom replied tersely.

"I didn't intend to."

Tom sighed and rubbed his face. "I know. I guess I'm too defensive about it."

"Where did the anthrax come from, or did you ever learn the source?"

"Oh, I found out all right. Now, you have to keep in mind that we had just suffered the worst winter in anybody's memory, and grass wasn't all of that plentiful. When an outfit came through with thirty wagon loads of hay, I jumped at it like it was manna from Heaven. I figured I could supplement the hay with what grass there was until the higher meadows could hold the cattle."

It seemed to Clint that his father was aging right before his eyes while relating the story, but he had pushed the issue, and he had to let Tom continue.

"The hay was infected with the germ. I sent after vaccines, but we needed so much, it didn't arrive in time. Within five days over half of the entire herd was dead, and all of the special breeds were sick." he sighed regretfully. "I had made it a point to feed a good portion of hay to them. We rounded up all of the cattle and drove them into a box canyon. I bought some dynamite from Richard and Sam, sealed the canyon off, then set off charges around the rim. We burned the other carcasses."

Tom's face was bleak from the flood of desolate memories. "The horses, in fact all of the livestock, even my dog and the chickens, had to be destroyed to avoid infecting the other ranches—that is, the ones who made it through the winter." His voice trembled. "I even had to destroy your mother's mare."

A cold, congested expression settled on Clint's face. He knew how badly that must have hurt his father. His mother had raised the mare from a colt, and she had delighted in riding her. He closed his eyes and he could remember how his mother looked when she rode Cleopatra, wind whipping her hair, her cheeks flushed with color. No, it didn't hurt his dad, it probably damn near killed him. Actually, the old mare should have been destroyed several years ago when she lost most of her sight. But, his dad had refused to consider it as long as she wasn't suffering.

"What are your plans now?" Clint asked, wanting to get his dad's mind off all of those unpleasant memories.

"After being wiped out completely, I really haven't made any. I had to let all of the hands go, but I have been taking care of what needed to be repaired." He shook his head. "It has been a long time since I had to think about rebuilding from the ground up, and I don't know if I still have it in me." He shrugged and said offhandedly, "I guess any future plans will largely depend on what you want to do."

Clint did not mince words. "The ranch is my home. I know for a long time there I never showed an appreciation for it, but all of that is behind me now. I'm willing to start from scratch, but I'll need your help."

Tom shook his head. "You're young. You can do it alone if the "want to" is there."

"I imagine I could. You and Mother started out with less than what Angela and I would have. But that's not the point. I want you to be standing beside me. You can retire to the rocking chair after Angela and I have a few sons."

Tom grunted. "What if you have daughters?"

Clint grinned. "Well, I guess we would have to teach them how to ride and rope."

Tom was still not quite convinced. "How do you propose to get a herd together? We're broke."

"You could loan me the money you received from your inheritance in England."

Tom's face brightened and an excited light gleamed in his eyes. "Well, damn! I had forgotten about that."

"Can I have the loan?"

"It's really not enough."

"But it's enough to buy three, maybe even five hundred head of cattle. You started with less than that," Clint reminded him.

Tom stroked his chin, then a broad smile slowly spread across his face. "What do you think about us being equal partners? I'll put up the experience and the money, and you do the work. But, I'll help, of course. It wouldn't be right not to."

"Sounds like I'm getting the best end of the deal!" Clint started to seal their agreement with a handshake, then he stopped abruptly and placed his arms around his dad's shoulders. "I might be a grown man, but to hell with a handshake. That hug felt mighty good a while ago."

Chapter Sixteen

The sun slowly rose over the eastern horizon. The soft yellow glow sent marmots, rock squirrels, and mice scurrying to their burrows. Pine martens scampered deep into the shadows of the Ponderosa pines and when a majestic eagle soared above him, a white-tailed grouse froze and blended his body into the snow.

Angela lay huddled in bed, reluctant to rise and face the day. She had been awake for quite some time, thinking about the path her life had taken. She felt that her heart had been divided into many different pieces—not broken, but methodically sectioned into individual portions. One portion was reserved for her father, one for Clint, another for Julia, and still yet another that contained all of her hopes and dreams.

Then, her thoughts turned in a different direction. Perhaps it was predestined that she would never have the opportunity to know her father. Maybe those years she lived with Julia were part of a higher power's master plan. Perhaps all of those things had to have happened for her to find her rightful place in life—standing at Clint's side, being his helpmate.

Suddenly, instead of being awash in emotional turmoil, a feeling of tranquility swept over her. She knew those suppositions would not take away the pain of her father's untimely death, or the bitterness she felt toward Julia. But, hopefully, this new insight would enable her to put everything in its proper perspective, and help to soothe her soul's open wounds.

"I think I have wallowed in self-pity long enough!" she stated aloud. She threw back the covers, climbed out of bed, and added wood to the embers in the fireplace. She caught a glimpse of herself in the bureau mirror and shook her head in dismay. Her face was streaked with tears and her hair was a snarled mass of tangles. Clint's father had probably thought she was the most unkempt woman he had ever seen. Why, she looked worse than a dirty street urchin.

Not having a dressing gown, she slipped the cloak over her shoulders and opened the door, paused and listened closely for sounds of Clint or his father stirring about. Deciding they were still asleep, she moved quietly down the hallway and searched until she found the kitchen. There, she filled the water kettle that was sitting on the huge kitchen stove and carried it back to the bedroom.

While the water heated, Angela made her bed, then vigorously brushed her hair. Spreading the dresses out across the bed, her eyes glowed with anticipation as she tried to decide which one to wear. One was dark blue with a pale blue trim. It had a small collar attached to the rounded neckline, long, slightly puffed sleeves, a formfitting bodice, and a gathered skirt. It was simple in design, and although practical, it was feminine and very pretty. The other dress was dove gray, trimmed with a white collar and matching cuffs, and although it had been sewn from the same basic pattern, black piping ran

MORE PASSION AND ADVENTURE AWAIT... YOUR TRIP TO A BIG ADVENTUROUS WORLD BEGINS WHEN YOU ACCEPT YOUR FIRST 4 NOVELS ABSOLUTELY *FREE* (AN $18.00 VALUE)

Accept your Free gift and start to experience more of the passion and adventure you like in a historical romance novel. Each Zebra novel is filled with proud men, spirited women and tempestuous love that you'll remember long after you turn the last page.

Zebra Historical Romances are the finest novels of their kind. They are written by authors who really know how to weave tales of romance and adventure in the historical settings you love. You'll feel like you've actually gone back in time with the thrilling stories that each Zebra novel offers.

GET YOUR FREE GIFT WITH THE START OF YOUR HOME SUBSCRIPTION

Our readers tell us that these books sell out very fast in book stores and often they miss the newest titles. So Zebra has made arrangements for you to receive the four newest novels published each month.

You'll be guaranteed that you'll never miss a title, and home delivery is so convenient. And to show you just how easy it is to get Zebra Historical Romances, we'll send you your first 4 books absolutely FREE! Our gift to you just for trying our home subscription service.

BIG SAVINGS AND FREE HOME DELIVERY

Each month, you'll receive the four newest titles as soon as they are published. You'll probably receive them even before the bookstores do. What's more, you may preview these exciting novels free for 10 days. If you like them as much as we think you will, just pay the low preferred subscriber's price of just $3.75 each. *You'll save $3.00 each month off the publisher's price.* AND, your savings are even greater because there are never any shipping, handling or other hidden charges—FREE Home Delivery. Of course you can return any shipment within 10 days for full credit, no questions asked. There is no minimum number of books you must buy.

4 FREE BOOKS

TO GET YOUR 4 FREE BOOKS WORTH $18.00 — MAIL IN THE FREE BOOK CERTIFICATE T O D A Y

Fill in the Free Book Certificate below, and we'll send your FREE BOOKS to you as soon as we receive it.

If the certificate is missing below, write to: Zebra Home Subscription Service, Inc., P.O. Box 5214, 120 Brighton Road, Clifton, New Jersey 07015-5214.

FREE BOOK CERTIFICATE
4 FREE BOOKS

ZEBRA HOME SUBSCRIPTION SERVICE, INC.

YES! Please start my subscription to Zebra Historical Romances and send me my first 4 books absolutely FREE. I understand that each month I may preview four new Zebra Historical Romances free for 10 days. If I'm not satisfied with them, I may return the four books within 10 days and owe nothing. Otherwise, I will pay the low preferred subscriber's price of just $3.75 each; a total of $15.00, *a savings off the publisher's price of $3.00.* I may return any shipment and I may cancel this subscription at any time. There is no obligation to buy any shipment and there are no shipping, handling or other hidden charges. Regardless of what I decide, the four free books are mine to keep.

NAME

ADDRESS _____ APT

CITY _____ STATE ____ ZIP

( )
TELEPHONE

SIGNATURE _____ (if under 18, parent or guardian must sign)

Terms, offer and prices subject to change without notice. Subscription subject to acceptance by Zebra Books. Zebra Books reserves the right to reject any order or cancel any subscription.

ZB1293

lengthwise down the bodice giving it a pleated look. Either dress would enhance her complexion and the color of her eyes and hair.

Unable to decide, she picked up both dresses, closed her eyes and rapidly switched them from one hand to the other until she had lost track of which dress was where. Finally, selecting one, her eyes danced with joy when she opened them and found that she had picked the blue one. Then, she chuckled, knowing she would have been just as pleased if the gray dress had been chosen.

Angela entered the kitchen feeling pretty and full of confidence, but her poise wavered when she saw there were still no signs of Clint or his father. Having no idea what Tom's reaction would be if he found her making herself at home in the kitchen, she was reluctant to try and find the necessary items for breakfast, yet, she was averse to sitting idly by until they arose.

"I'm sure he would not object if I built a fire in the stove and put on a pot of coffee," she muttered under her breath, still feeling ill-at-ease.

The aroma of freshly brewed coffee had just started to waft throughout the kitchen when the back door flew open and Tom entered carrying a pail of milk, still steaming from the frosty morning air, and a basketful of eggs.

"Morning, my that coffee certainly smells good!" he remarked with gusto, setting the milk and eggs on the long kitchen counter.

Angela breathed a sigh of relief that Clint's father did not appear to be upset over her intrusion into his kitchen. Still, she felt awkward. "I didn't know whether to begin cooking breakfast or not. Clint never mentioned anything about you having a housekeeper or a cook, so I really didn't know what to do . . ." her voice trailed off.

Tom sensed the girl's uneasiness at being in a strange kitchen—in a strange house for that matter. He smiled at her. "Rest easy, little lady, and make yourself at home. After what Clint told me last night, I'd like for us to start out being friends."

"What d-did Clint tell you?"

"He told me everything about you; everything from New Orleans up through what happened yesterday. I might add, he couldn't have made a prettier choice for a wife."

Angela blanched as images of their passionate love-making flashed through her mind. "H-he told you everything?"

Tom swallowed a laugh when he noticed the stricken expression on her face. "Well, I'm sure there were a few personal details he kept to himself." As casually as he could manage, he added, "I'm sorry about your father. It's too bad that you never had the opportunity to get to know him. He was a fine man."

Her chin trembled slightly and her eyes suddenly glistened. "Thank you."

Not giving the girl a chance to dwell on unpleasant memories, Tom quickly changed the subject. "I'm glad you took it on yourself to make the coffee. There's nothing I like better first thing in the morning, but Bessy was bawling to be milked, and it had been a couple of days since I had gathered the eggs."

Tom removed his coat and hung it on a rack beside the door, then wiped the mud from his boots on a rag rug. "One bad thing about snow is the mess it makes when it starts to melt," he commented, not expecting a reply.

Angela walked over to the counter and peered into the huge wooden pail. "How many milk cows do you have?"

"Just one."

Her eyes widened with amazement. "One cow gave this much milk!"

"Yep, she's a jim-dandy."

"And you have chickens too?" She tried to remember how long it had been since she had eaten an egg or drank a glass of milk. Her mouth watered at the thought of it.

A pang of sadness stabbed at Tom at the tone of her awefilled voice. Poor little thing, Clint was right. She was half starved! Oh, no doubt that she had received nourishment—just not much there was a big difference in filling one's belly with whatever was available, and eating good, healthy food. It was not just food that came to mind either. She was starved for friendship. Tom took a deep breath. He had a few remedies up his sleeve that would heal almost any kind of ailment. Give him a week or two, and he would make her into a new woman.

Crossing his arms, he peered at her curiously. "Tell me, girl, can you cook?"

Angela was unsure what to say. If she gave an affirmative answer, he might think she was too boastful. Yet, she did not want to lie. Straightening her shoulders, she replied, "Yes, sir, I can."

A shadow flicked across his face. "I'm curious, do you plan on calling me that in front of my grandchildren?"

"I beg your pardon?"

The beginning of a smile tipped the corners of his mouth. "Since you and Clint are getting married, the way I figure it, when the grandchildren start coming along, they will think their mother doesn't like their granddad if she calls him "sir" all of the time. I have no objections to Tom, Thomas, Dad—anything but sir, or Mr. Rutledge." He thrust out his hand. "Deal?"

Angela felt a warm glow flow through her. If she'd had any doubts whether he approved of their impending marriage, he had just dispelled them. She was not aware that her happiness was so noticeable on her face and in her eyes. Smiling, she accepted his hand and said, "Deal."

"You said you can cook. How good?"

Still not wanting to sound arrogant and boastful, Angela momentarily vacillated, then she lifted her chin, placed her hands on her hips, and boldly met his gaze. "When I said that I could cook, I meant that I am a *good* cook."

"I'm a fair cook myself, but I can't make biscuits worth a damn."

She raised her chin a tad bit higher. "I can make biscuits that will melt in your mouth."

Without saying another word, Tom turned on his heel and opened a door. He wiggled his finger, motioning for her to follow him. "I'm not a "doubting Thomas", but I do think a lady should have to prove her brash statements. This is the pantry. If you can cook as good as you say you can, then you need to familiarize yourself with it."

Angela's eyes widened at the sight of the many shelves filled with foodstuff. It contained enough food to feed a small army for a month or better. Why, it

228

could last three people through the entire winter and there would still be food left.

"As you can see, it is well-stocked and you should be able to find anything you need." He pointed to a trap door. "There is also a root cellar down below where you'll find potatoes, onions, all different kinds of vegetables and supplies. I'll show you the smokehouse later. There's also an icehouse, but we seldom use it until late spring and on into summer. You'll just have to use your own judgment about where to keep the eggs and milk. Usually, the pantry is fine, but if the weather is too warm, the root cellar keeps the milk nice and cold."

Taking her by the arm, he led her back into the kitchen and showed her where all of the cooking utensils and tableware were kept. Then he placed his hands on his waist and looked about as though wondering if he had missed anything. "I think that just about covers it all, unless . . ."

"Unless . . . what?"

"It will take you a while to become acquainted with where everything is located, so if you don't mind, I'll be glad to help with breakfast. Besides," his mouth widened in a grin that reminded her so much of Clint, "it will give us a chance to get better acquainted."

She flashed him her most brilliant smile. "I gladly accept your offer."

"I'll strain the milk and slice the bacon and the ham. Or would you rather have sausage? Clint and I like two different kinds of meat for breakfast," he offered in explanation.

"It doesn't matter, just whatever the two of you prefer," she said, clearly surprised that he would ask her. Her preferences or opinions had seldom been considered in the past. But, that was in the past, she reminded herself as she sifted flour into a huge crock bowl. The future will be remarkably different!

Soon, the biscuits were ready to go into the oven. Angela kept busy by setting the table and adding butter, jellies, jams, and honey. Not familiar with the oven and how quickly it cooked, she kept a close eye on the biscuits so the bottoms would not burn. Not wanting to start frying the eggs until the biscuits were closer to being done, she prepared a large skillet of milk gravy from the ham drippings.

Finally, she looked at Tom who was sitting at the table impatiently smelling all the delicious aromas permeating the kitchen, and nursing a cup of coffee. "Do you want to wake Clint? Breakfast is almost ready." She began cracking eggs and dropping them expertly into a skillet of bacon grease.

"Clint!" Tom bellowed. "You had better get your lazy carcass . . ."

"This lazy carcass is already awake and about to starve to death," Clint said from the doorway. He looked at his dad, then at Angela. He had been standing in the dining room for several minutes listening to their light-hearted banter. He was a little confused, but pleasantly surprised, by their relaxed camaraderie. "Breakfast sure smells good. You should have woke me when the two of you got up."

"Truth is, son, we forgot all about you," Tom said solemnly. Then he grinned at the wounded expression on Clint's face. "Now, son, you ought to remember how much I like to josh you. The truth is; we thought you might appreciate getting a few extra winks." Tom did not think it was necessary to admit to Clint that he had not been discussed.

While his dad chattered on, Clint's eyes were fastened on Angela. The blue dress brought out the color in her cheeks and the sparkle in her eyes. Her hair had been brushed until it gleamed with a luster he had not seen before. Instead of a bun, she had pulled the top and sides back, and tied it with a ribbon. The only time he had seen her look more beautiful was right after they had made love. The desire to take her into his arms was overwhelming.

"You certainly look pretty this morning."

"Why, thank you." Laughing, she held out the skirt and whirled around. "Is it me or my new dress?"

"It is definitely you, sweetheart. You put the dress to shame."

She was pleased by his admiring perusal. He had always been attentive and complimentary, but this was the first time she truly felt he meant it. "How many eggs do you want?"

"Oh, four or five, it doesn't matter."

Angela's eyes widened, her mouth gaped from surprise. "Are y-you serious?" Julia had only allowed her to serve each boarder two eggs at the most, and the other boardinghouses she had worked in never served them. They were always too expensive.

Clint did not understand her reaction. "Yes, I said I was starved."

She wet her lips. "Tom, how many would you like?"

"You might as well cook a dozen."

Numbly, she nodded. "A-all right." She wondered how they could possibly hold so many. Why, one or two should be enough to satisfy even the most ravenous appetite, especially with all of the other food available.

Clint poured himself a cup of coffee and sat at his regular place at the table. "Dad, I thought you said last

231

night that you had to destroy all of the livestock? I see that you have fresh milk and eggs, ham . . ."

"I did, but a man still has to eat. I bought the Bakers' laying hens and milk cow. They had three hogs they were fattening up, so I bought them too. I butchered the first one last week when the weather changed."

Clint could hear his dad talking, but the words did not really register as he continued to study Angela. He was quickly becoming more confused by her cheerful behavior. What in the hell had happened to the tired, grief-devastated woman he had put to bed last night? From the way she was laughing and carrying on, no one would guess she'd just been told a few hours earlier that her father had died. He had not expected to see her weeping or flailing her breast, but he had not envisioned such vivacious gaiety either.

Tom broke into Clint's thoughts. "Do you intend to wait until your breakfast is cold before you eat?"

"What?"

"I said, eat!"

Clint plastered a smile on his face and picked up his knife and fork.

Later, Tom shoved back his chair, and rose, clutching his stomach with both hands and moaning. "Ooh, God help me! I ate too much!"

Shaking his head, Clint guffawed. "You're not getting any pity from me. I told you that you were making a pig out of yourself."

"I know, but it tasted too good to resist." He looked at Angela. "Little lady, if you ever see me reaching for a seventh biscuit, will you promise to break my hand?"

Angela knew that he was teasing, and that he was just pretending to be miserable, but she appreciated his indirect compliments.

232

Still clutching his belly, Tom waddled over to the coat rack and slipped on his coat. "I have to go walk some of this off."

Clint playfully poked Angela in her ribs. "If I know my dad, he will have his misery walked off by the time the dishes are washed. At least he always did when we were having to batch it."

"Batch it?"

"It's a saying people use when a man lives alone. I suppose the word comes from bachelor."

Angela could not help herself as she burst out laughing. "And he always stuck you with washing the dishes."

"Yes, he always did."

As soon as they were alone, Clint's expression became somber. He felt helpless and angry with himself, and angry at Angela for making him feel the way he did. There was no doubt that he had fallen hopelessly in love with her. But, what would he do—what *could* he do if he discovered she was not the woman he thought she was? When she asked him yesterday if he believed in her, his faith had not wavered one iota. But now, after witnessing her spirited cheerfulness, he did not know what to think.

Suddenly, he visualized a tiny devil sitting on his shoulder, prodding him with his trident, *"What happened to her, Clint? Tell me, why is she so happy and cheerful this morning? Is this the same girl you saw in Richard Grissom's office weeping bitterly after learning of her father's death? What happened to her grief? Looks to me like that was a short mourning period. Does it make you wonder if she has been telling the truth? Maybe Grissom was right by not accepting her word at face value. If she would lie about one thing,*

233

then she would lie about another." The devil laughed evilly. *"Under the circumstances, I would be having plenty of doubts if I had asked her to marry me."*

"Are you feeling all right, Angela?" Clint asked, a little more harshly than he had intended.

The merriment slowly disappeared from her face when she straightened and saw his dark, clouded features. "Yes, I feel fine. Why do you ask?"

"Oh, I just t-thought. . . . You were so tired last night . . ." His voice sounded unnatural, even to his own ears. "I figured you would want to stay in bed for a few days."

Angela frowned. "Why would I want to do that?"

"Why do you have to answer every damn question I ask with a question of your own?"

Her thin fingers tensed in her lap and she felt the first stirrings of apprehension begin to build. She knew of no reason why Clint should be so annoyed with her. Awkwardly, she cleared her throat and to her dismay, her voice broke slightly. "I was not aware that you had asked a question. If you will tell me why you think I should remain in bed for several days, I might be able to give you a reasonable explanation."

He started to say something, then he waved it aside. "Never mind, just forget I ever mentioned anything about it," he snapped.

"No, something is bothering you. I don't know if you are angry at me, or whether you are merely taking your anger *out* on me. Regardless of what the reason is . . ." She reached out her hand and gently touched his cheek. "I love you. I don't want us to argue, especially over something that is probably a simple misunderstanding."

Angela looked and sounded so sincere, so truthful, Clint mentally kicked himself for allowing doubts to creep into his mind. There has to be a reasonable explanation for her behavior, he thought miserably.

Stifling a groan, he tenderly cupped her face between both hands and smiled at her. It was the tenderest expression she had ever seen on his face, an almost apologetic smile that rid his face of the cold cynicism that had gripped it only moments before.

Then slowly, so slowly, his hands lowered to her neck as his lips found hers. It was a gentle kiss at first but quickly grew more demanding as he traced the inner edges of her lips with his tongue before plunging deeper to explore the sweetness of her mouth. Her tongue timidly fenced with his until she initiated darting attacks of her own.

A deliciously thrilling shiver seemed to take hold of her, making her entire body shake as his chair fell backwards when he moved closer to her. The sound of the chair crashing against the floor brought her back to the world of sanity.

Smothering a groan, she unwillingly pulled from his embrace. Her voice was reluctant, "No, Clint, please, we cannot . . . not here, not now. . . . Your father could come in at any moment."

Breathing raggedly, Clint reached out, not wanting to let her go. "But, sweetheart . . ." Then, his common sense prevailed. He sighed heavily. "You're right. I'm sorry, I lost control of myself. I'm going to have a hell of a time keeping my hands off of you."

"I know. . . . I think we might have opened Pandora's box when we made love the first time. It seems we only whetted our appetites for each other." She was flustered and invented activities for her hands to cover it, patting her hair back into place and smoothing her dress.

Clint wiped his hands on his pants leg. The lines running down the sides of his cheeks had deepened considerably and a vein ticked in his temple. "Next time I start behaving like a jackass, just give me a swift kick in the seat of my pants."

Angela had no idea he was also referring to something other than their moment of stolen passion. Placing her hand over her chest to quell the rapid pounding of her heart, she tried to ease the tension between them by remarking in a forced, lighthearted tone, "Your father wants me to break his arm and now you tell me to kick you in the rear. You two must think I am a terribly violent person."

Still feeling too ashamed for any attempts of levity, he shook his head. "I doubt if you could deliberately hurt anyone. I'm the one who . . ."

Angela quickly placed a trembling finger over his lips. "If you were about to say something insulting about the man I love, please don't." A strange, contemplative look flashed in her eyes. "Why were you angry?" she asked abruptly.

Stalling by running his hand through his hair, Clint's mind clicked at a swift pace. How could he tell her that he'd had doubts about her honesty? Had she not suffered enough without his moment of idiocy adding to her burden?

He shrugged, looked her straight in the eye, and deliberately lied. "I wasn't angry at you," I was mad at myself. I knew that you had been through an exhausting ordeal. You haven't had enough food to eat or enough rest. Then, after what you learned yesterday . . . I guess it just made me mad to see you running yourself ragged waiting on me and Dad when I should have been taking care of you."

"I wasn't running myself ragged."

"But that is how I saw it."

"Then . . . you mean you were angry during breakfast too?"

"Yes, I was," he admitted reluctantly.

Her heart sang with delight, and her smile broadened with wonder. "And you didn't want to say anything then for fear of ruining my appetite. Something must have told you how long it had been since I'd had an egg to eat or a glass of milk to drink." She flung her arms around his neck, her soft curves molding to the contours of his muscular body. "Has anyone ever told you that you are a big, softhearted . . ." she searched her mind for the right word but could not find it. ". . . I don't know what."

Clint's conscience stabbed him hard. He said dryly, "Yes, at times I have a voice inside me that calls me quite a few names." He could imagine how that little devil was jumping up and down with glee over the trouble he had almost caused.

"Well, you tell that little voice that I am not fragile, and I am not an invalid. I really think it would do me more harm than good to stay in bed. It would give me too much time to think, to dwell on unpleasant thoughts and memories."

She moistened her lips and slowly pulled from his embrace. "Clint, this morning . . ." her voice trailed off. She took a deep breath and tried again. "Yesterday, when I learned that my father was dead, I felt so devastated, I didn't know what to do, what to think." Her throat knotted with emotion. "I suppose I just wanted to dig a hole, crawl into it, and pull the world right in on top of me."

"I don't blame you for feeling that way. There is no

telling what I would have done if it had been my father."

"No, please, let me finish. Before I arose this morning, I was trying to sort everything out in my mind. That is when I began to wonder if what I actually felt was grief for my father . . . or pity for myself. The more I thought about it, the more I realized that I have spent most of all my life mourning for him. I am so weary of that. I realize this may sound terribly selfish of me, but I want to start living. I want to enjoy life for a change."

"I think I see what you're getting at," Clint said slowly.

"While doing all of this soul-searching, I came to a few more conclusions. There are several passages in the Bible that I have always found to be comforting, especially in Ecclesiastes, where it speaks of there being 'a time for all things.' If that is true, and I do believe it is, then there has to be a reason for all of the things that have happened in my life. If Julia had not lied, and if I had not discovered her deception, I would not have been on that stagecoach. Just think, Clint, if all of those events had never happened, I never would have met you." Her faint smile held a touch of sadness as she reached out and covered his hands with hers. "I believe it was all meant to be. I believe today, tomorrow, and for years to come, is '*our* time for all things.' "

In one fluid motion, Clint took her into his arms. Angela's breath caught in her throat and tears suddenly filled her eyes. She tried to prevent her bottom lip from trembling by clamping her teeth over it but to no avail.

Clint felt her body tense. "What's wrong, sweetheart?" he asked, caressing her cheek with the knuckle of his hand. At the base of his throat a pulse beat and

238

swelled as though his heart had risen from its usual place.

"Nothing."

"Then why are you crying?"

His nearness was so overwhelming, it made her voice come in hiccuping gasps. "I don't know, unless it's because I love you so much."

"Being in love shouldn't make you cry," he said gently.

She tried to smile. "Then maybe it's because I am so happy."

Women! Clint thought to himself as he took her into his arms and lowered his lips to hers. There was no rhyme nor reason about them. Although, if he had the power to change them, he knew that he could never bring himself to do it.

Chapter Seventeen

"Am I interrupting something?" Tom asked as he slipped out of his coat. His eyes twinkled with amusement when Clint and Angela sprang apart, looking flushed and guilty. "I thought there might be some coffee left." He pretended there was nothing out of the ordinary as he walked over to the stove and shook the pot. "Yep, there's still plenty." He bit his bottom lip to keep from grinning as he reached for his cup. "You two want to join me?"

The color in Angela's face deepened as she turned her back to him and wiped the tears from her eyes. Then, she quickly began clearing the table by stacking one plate on top of another. "No, not me," she finally mumbled when she felt she could trust her voice to speak. "I need to wash the dishes and tidy the kitchen."

Instead of being annoyed at his dad for interrupting them, Clint was amused and a little saddened. Either he sensed their passionate need for each other and was determined not to let them become too tempted, or he was lonesome for company. That had to be it, he thought. And, it was little wonder his dad was so lonesome. There was no telling how long he had been in seclusion at the ranch without seeing another living soul. Then too, since Clint had been abroad for so long, it only seemed reasonable that his dad would want to visit with him and get better acquainted with his soon to be daughter-in-law.

He and Angela would just have to tolerate his interference until he overcame his loneliness. Although, it would certainly put an end to any thoughts he might have about making love to her. Maybe it was for the best, then. He would never want her to start feeling guilty about their lovemaking. And, until they could be married, that was a strong possibility.. Women were much more sensitive about matters like that than men were. The only thing was he did not know how he could handle being in such close daily contact with her without satisfying his desires. That could quite possibly drive him out of his mind. Clint blew out a heavy breath. He saw many long, sleepless nights ahead of him.

"What do you think about that idea, son?" Tom asked.

Jerking his head around to look at him, Clint muttered, "Wha . . . what were you saying, Dad?"

He shrugged offhandedly. "Oh, I was thinking about climbing up on top of the roof, flapping my arms until a good gust of wind caught me, then trying to fly over to Clear Creek."

Clint chuckled as sat down across from his father. When he was a child and his dad caught him not paying attention, his dad would never scold him, but he would make some ridiculous remark so that Clint would know he was aggravated.

Although his words were chiding, his tone held no animosity. "Dad, I am not ten years old anymore."

241

"I know that. It was just . . ." he paused and grinned at Clint. "You looked like you were a hundred miles away, and I guess I was just feeling neglected." He glanced over at Angela who was standing at the sink. "Girl, I realize you and Clint will be wanting to spend time alone. Anytime you think I am meddling too much, just tell me to butt out."

She turned to look at him. "Why, I could never do that. This is your home—"

"No, it is *our* home."

Elation soared through Angela. Home! A solitary word never sounded so reverent! Her hands began to tremble and her heart thumped at such a loud, vigorous pace, she was afraid they could hear it too. She could feel her chin quiver and tears of happiness pooling in her eyes.

Clint knew if he did not do or say something fast, Angela would start crying. If she did, it would embarrass her to no end.

"Uh, Dad, what do you think about turning Shaggy Meadow into a hay field instead of using it as pasture land?"

Tom realized what Clint was trying to do. He quickly replied, "Well, I've never given it much thought before, but it sounds like it might be a good idea. I reckon we could try it for a year and see what happens."

Deliberately ignoring Angela, they fell into a discussion about cattle and grasslands. Then finally, Tom impatiently drummed his fingers on the table. "Girl, why don't you leave some of those to soak and let me and Clint show you around the place?"

"I'm eager to see it, but it will only take a few more minutes for me to finish."

"Do you want some help?"

"No, I don't." Her reply was firmer than she had intended. But she had always preferred to do the kitchen chores by herself. Julia had constantly grumbled and complained, and Dahlia had been so sloppy and careless that her chores always had to be done over. It was always much easier for her to do them in the first place.

Also, even though it was very considerate of Tom to offer, it went against her grain to even think of men doing women's work. Angela decided she might as well get this matter settled once and for all. She moved her head a quarter turn and peered over her shoulder at Tom. "I appreciate your offer to help with the dishes, but . . ."

Tom's eyes glinted mischievously. "Oh, no, girl, you misunderstood, I was offering Clint's help."

"Thanks, Dad," Clint muttered dryly.

Angela turned around completely, tossed her hair across her shoulders in a gesture of defiance, then planted both hands just above her hips. "I believe you implied earlier that the kitchen would be my exclusive territory. Is that not correct?"

Tom replied adamantly, "That's what I said. I'm not going back on my word now, especially after I found out what a good cook you are."

"Then unless I am flat out on my back with some terrible illness, I suggest that the two of you stay out of *my* domain unless you intend to sit at the table or are merely walking through."

Tom raised his brows and puckered his mouth to form a silent Oh. "Is that little girl always so bossy?" he asked Clint with teasing sarcasm.

Before Clint had a chance to reply, Angela's gray eyes flashed a gentle but firm warning. *"Mr Rutledge, sir, I do have a name other than girl."* She wagged a wet spoon at him. "My goodness, what will your grand-children think when they hear you addressing me by that name."

Tom grimaced in good humor. "Ouch! Not only is she bossy, she has a barbed tongue."

Clint knew his father too well to be confused by his bantering. Apparently, *they* knew what they were talking about. He held up both hands in protest when Tom looked at him. "Oh, no you don't. This is between the two of you. You are not getting me involved."

Tom gestured helplessly. "Girl, it's like this; my tongue has a hard time rolling over all the letters in Angela." He thought for a moment. "How does "Angie" appeal to you?"

Even though Clint had just stated that he didn't want to be involved, the teasing was too tempting for him to ignore. He winked at Tom and spoke up before Angela could reply. "Dad, sometimes I call her 'Slim.' "

"Slim? Why, son, that's not a proper name to call a pretty little girl." He stroked his chin thoughtfully while pretending to ignore Angela. In truth, he was rubbing his chin to conceal the twitching of his mouth. By this time, Angela had crossed her arms, and was patting one foot against the floor, glaring at them.

"I know! When I was a boy, one of my best friends had a sister, and she sort of reminds me of her. Let me see—what was her name?" He scratched his head, then snapped his fingers. "I remember now, it was Imogene Gertrude!"

Looking solemn and sincere, Clint agreed, "Why, that's a perfect name."

Angela walked toward them, wagging her finger threateningly. "All right you two! You think you're be-ing clever."

"Who? Us?" they chorused in unison.

She smiled. "I know one thing. If two men—who are behaving like naughty little boys—will stop their tomfoolery long enough to let me wash one more pan, I'll take them up on their offer to show me the ranch."

Hastily, they rose to their feet. "Yes, Ma'am!" Tom said. "Come on, son, let's get out of here so Angie can finish."

"I'll be right behind you."

Clint waited until the back door slammed, then he wrapped his arms around Angela's small waist and pulled her close to him. She wound her arms around his neck and looked up at him with adulation shining from her eyes.

He cocked his head slightly. "I gave you fair warning that Dad had a sense of humor. Sometimes he might carry his joking a little too far. Nevertheless, I have a notion that you'll be able to handle him just fine. I wouldn't be afraid to bet that all you would have to do is crook your little finger and he would be wound around it within a few minutes."

"Well, it so happens that I like him too. I know we just met, but I'm already very fond of him. And don't you dare tell him this, but I enjoy his teasing."

With mock severity, Clint said, "If he wasn't my dad, I might have reason to be jealous."

"Oh, no, you'll never have to worry about that. Another man could never measure up to you."

His mellow voice simmered with barely checked passion, "Hush and give me a kiss."

"It's been so long, I think I've forgotten how," she murmured huskily. "Show me."

So he did.

* * *

245

"Are you two going to start that again?" Tom demanded from the doorway.

"Go away, Dad, you're bothering us," Clint grumbled good naturedly.

Ignoring him, Tom said, "Looks to me like the only way I'm going to get you two outside is to show you the house first." He opened the door leading to the dining room and waited, leaving them no choice in the matter.

At her first glimpse of the house, Angela had known it was large, but she'd had no idea that it was so spacious and well-constructed. Double walls lined the exterior for added warmth during the long, harsh Colorado winters. The logs had been staggered to prevent any cold air from seeping inside. The bark had been peeled from the inner walls, then stained or varnished to seal the wood and make it more attractive, while the outer walls retained their original bark.

All of the rooms with exterior walls had lead-glass windows, clearer and brighter, and much more expensive, than what most people installed in their homes. There were two such windows in the living room, and they were large enough to allow enough light inside to brighten the room on the gloomiest of days. Four huge, comfortable chairs sat in a semicircle around a stone fireplace. It also held a sofa, two arm chairs, various tables, and a piano that belonged to Susan.

There were three bedrooms, a study, a sewing room, and a large dining room that could accommodate at least thirty people. None of the furnishings could have been considered elegant or even stylish, but they were durable, practical, and purchased or built with comfort in mind.

Angela could see Mrs. Rutledge's fine hand in the planning of the house. The spacious kitchen was evidence of that. Although she had no way of knowing if the sink and hand pump had been installed before or after the woman's death. And she did not want to ask.

"There is something I'd like to know," Angela announced after they left the house. "This has been nagging at the back of my mind all morning long. How are you able to keep chickens alive during the winter? It seems to me that they would freeze."

Clint graciously deferred to his father.

"Why, they have their own fireplace!" Seeing the dubious look on Angela's face, Tom burst out laughing. "As ridiculous as it may sound, I have never been more serious."

Angela was not the least bit convinced. "Clint, is he teasing me?"

"No, he's telling the truth."

"My wife's only complaint about living here in the mountains was the fact that it was almost impossible for her to keep up with the laundry during the winter. We lived in a cabin when we first settled here, and after the house was built, she converted the cabin into a washhouse. I figured that she would quit complaining, and she did. Only thing, though, then she started dropping little hints."

Angela listened politely as they walked toward a good-sized outbuilding. Although she had no idea what a washhouse had to do with chickens, she had faith that he would eventually get around to answering her question. It was obvious that he took great pride in his home, and was not the least bit reluctant to talk about it.

"She wanted me to try and figure out a way for us to take baths in the wintertime without messing up her

247

kitchen." He stopped and grinned. "You remind me of her in that respect. That's probably part of the reason why I like—" He cleared his throat and plowed at the ground with the toe of his boot. "Anyway, I had met an old Russian trapper, and I started thinking about the way he had built his fireplace and I wondered if the same principle would work if we applied it a little differently." He pushed open the washhouse door, "Come on in, I'll show you."

Upon entering the old cabin, Angela was immediately impressed by how warm it was inside.

Wash tubs had been set up on one end, and near the other end was a boxed brick structure, about waist high, that ran the entire width of the cabin. Angela's attention immediately fastened on a galvanized bathtub sitting on a wooden platform. The tub was large enough for a person to recline and still have room to extend their legs. Then she realized it was much too large to be a bathtub; instead it was a water trough.

"That old trapper came from somewhere in Siberia, and those folks there had to utilize every means available for heat." He then opened a small metal door in the center of the brick structure. "This is what keeps it so warm in here." He pointed to a very small cast-iron firebox containing ashes and a few glowing embers.

Intrigued, Angela asked, "How can such a small stove keep the building so warm? And besides, the fire's almost out."

"That's all part of the ingenuity. Four stovepipes, having three dampers each, extend from the fire box. It works on the same principle as a chimney flue, only the pipes are vented to allow the heat to sift through. One pipe runs the full length of this room through the ceiling and another runs inside the bricks to heat the water we keep in a cistern. That way, we have hot water for baths and for the washing."

"Why, that is a marvelous idea." Then Angela frowned. "I thought you said there were four pipes. What happened to the other two?"

Smirking, Tom hooked his thumbs under his armpits and teetered back and forth. "When that old man told me how warm this system would keep the building, and how little fuel it would take—never more than a cord for the entire winter—we immediately built an addition on to the cabin, and *there* is where we keep the chickens. They stay snug all winter long, and there's not any danger of anything catching on fire as long as we don't burn pine."

Clint looked at the two of them and merely shook his head. He'd had no way of discreetly warning Angela that she was letting herself in for a long, drawn out explanation when she asked about the chickens. But, she acted as though she enjoyed it, and he knew it delighted his dad to show off this contraption.

Angela looked at the bathtub wistfully. "Do you think I could take advantage of that this afternoon? Washing out of a basin can get one clean, but there's nothing as relaxing as a good hot bath!"

Clint snapped a lecherous grin on his face and jiggled his heavy brows. "Why, sure, sweetheart . . . if you'll let me wash your back."

Clint chuckled, Angela blushed, and Tom rolled his eyes.

"I see right now, I should have taken that boy out behind the woodshed more often than I did!" Tom took Angela by her arm. "Come on, Angie, there's still the chicken coop, the barn, the ice and smokehouse . . ."

249

Angela looked over her shoulder at Clint and gave a shrug.

"Do you mind if I come along?" Clint asked caustically.

"I don't care, do you, Angie?"

Cramming his hands deep into his pockets, Clint fell in behind them, grumbling under his breath.

Late that night, Angela lay in bed unable to sleep. Her mind kept going over everything that had happened that day. Not only had Clint's father accepted her, he seemed to be genuinely fond of her. And then there was Susan; they had immediately liked each other. For the first time in her life she felt that she belonged, that she had a home and people who loved her. She actually had a family!

Maybe this was God's way of easing her pain over losing her father, and her ill-treatment by Julia's hand.

Her happiness would be complete when she and Clint could marry. They had not discussed a date, but she hoped it would be soon. That would probably depend upon when a preacher would be available. She had heard somewhere that traveling preachers made the rounds to mining towns. And if that was so, if he did not arrive soon, they might have to wait until spring before they could marry. She hoped not.

It was shameful to have thoughts like this, but the times they had made love at the cabin only seemed to whet their appetites for more. Her mind told her making love with Clint without being married was wrong, but her heart decreed nothing could be wrong when she was in his arms. She wished he was lying beside her now, kissing her, fondling her . . .

Then why did she feel a dread deep inside of her? That thought was so startling, Angela bolted upright in bed.

Maybe the dread stemmed from her past. Every time she had reached for happiness, she had only been able to hold it for a few moments, then, like sand falling through a sieve, it had slipped right through her fingers. But not this time, surely not this time.

Why did she always have the feeling that there was something sorrowful outside, diligently stalking her, just waiting until she let her guard down to pounce and destroy all that she held dear? Prickles of apprehension caused gooseflesh to pop up on her skin.

"This is ridiculous!" she muttered aloud. "I will not allow my unhappy past to cast shadows over my future. I am not the same frightened person I was when I left New Orleans. If I had stood up to Julia years ago, maybe she wouldn't have treated me so unfairly. No one will ever do that to me again, though; I will not allow it!"

Then, Angela started to laugh. "I cannot believe I am sitting in the middle of the bed talking to myself." She rubbed her face, then combed her fingers through her hair. "Maybe a glass of warm milk would calm my nerves."

Not wanting to disturb Clint or Tom, she tiptoed down the hallway past their rooms. Making her way through the dining room, she stopped suddenly when she heard voices coming from the kitchen.

Angela did not mean to eavesdrop, but she could plainly hear Clint and Tom discussing the ranch and the stock they hoped to purchase in the spring. Since she only had on her nightgown, she turned to go back to her room, but when she heard Clint say something about having to really tighten their belts and that it would be a long, hard struggle, she stopped again and this time she deliberately listened.

A few minutes later, she stole back to her room. So, the ranch wasn't really a ranch. It was just land, this house, and a few outbuildings. Tom had been forced to destroy the entire herd after restocking the ranch. The Double R had been wiped out financially. All of the money they had was what Tom received from an estate settlement, and evidently from the way they talked, it was not a huge sum.

An idea began to form in the back of her mind. She had planned to stay at the ranch tomorrow while Clint and Tom returned the rig to the livery stable in town. But that plan was now changed because there was something she could do about the ranch's financial dilemma. All that she had to do was to stand up for her rights. And by all that was holy, she was woman enough to do it!

Chapter Eighteen

Angela rose early the next morning and had breakfast well under way before Clint and Tom came into the kitchen. Tom grabbed the milk pail and headed for the barn, saying that he would tend to the morning chores and that they needed to leave for Clear Creek as soon as they finished with breakfast.

Angela knew something was bothering Clint when he propped his elbows on the table and gloomily accepted the cup of coffee she placed in front of him without thanking her. Her first thought was that she had done something wrong and was about to ask what it was, then she immediately changed her mind. Why did she always assume that she was to blame when someone seemed to be out of sorts? That was a major fault that she would have to correct.

She lovingly placed her hand on Clint's shoulder and brushed her lips against his cheek. "You look so sad. Are you troubled about something, or are you just pre-occupied this morning?"

He looked up at her. "Is it that obvious?"

Positioning her body between his legs, she sat down on one, slipped her arm around his shoulder and smoothed his hair back from his brow. "I suspect something is wrong."

He wrapped one arm around her waist and sighed heavily. "It's a problem with Dad. I have to have a talk with him, and I dread it. I thought he might have changed or at the very least, mellowed some, but it seems as though he didn't."

Angela was glad she had not allowed herself to jump to conclusions. "Is there anything I can do to help?"

He shrugged. "I don't know—I doubt it. Nothing has helped thus far."

Biting on her lower lip, Angela chose her words carefully. "I don't want to interfere with you and your father, but I am willing to listen if you want to talk about it with me first."

He asked with quiet emphasis, "Use you as a sounding board?"

She nodded and smiled. "If you'd like."

The tense lines on his face relaxed. His words came in a rush, "I think most of our problems stem from the fact that we are too damn much alike. You have to understand, I love my dad, I respect and admire him. He is generous, caring, honest . . ."

His tone hardened, "But he can also be the most stubborn, self-opinionated man who ever existed. I doubt if he ever did it consciously, but he has always made me feel like a clumsy eight-year-old schoolboy. Regardless of what I did or didn't do when I was a kid, I always felt like I fell short of his expectations, that I was a disappointment to him."

"Clint, I will be the first one to acknowledge that I do not know very much about men and their relationships with their sons, but I would be willing to wager many sons feel this way about their fathers."

254

"I'm sure you're right. That doesn't make it any easier for me to live with, though."

Angela regretted having volunteered to listen. She wished she had just kept her mouth shut, but it was too late for that now. Being as tactful as possible, she asked, "Can you be more specific about why you feel the way you do?"

"Yes, I can. It never bothered me one way or the other until I was about fourteen years old. Then, kid-like, I decided I was a man just because I was suddenly an inch taller than my dad, my shoulders became wider than my waistline, and I had to shave twice a week—maybe three times if I just wanted to waste the time. I guess Dad saw that I was getting too big for my britches and he figured he had to take me down a notch or two." He shook his head and chuckled at the memory. "I don't blame him a bit, either. If our roles had been reversed, I would have escorted him out behind the woodshed. But, boys do eventually grow up and start getting a little common sense. Only thing, Dad never saw it. To him, I was still the same smart-mouthed, know-it-all kid. Re-gardless of which horse I selected from the herd, it was a poor choice. If I told him that a certain meadow was ready for grazing, he would always say, 'No, it couldn't be ready yet. Boy, you don't know what you're talking about.' But if he looked at the meadow two days later, then all of a sudden, it was just right for grazing. I re-alize that this might sound petty, but over the years, it has built to a festering point. Last night, for instance, I mentioned that we should get an early start this morn-ing, but you heard what he said when he went out to milk the cow." He drew his lips in thoughtfully. "I just don't want the same old thing to start over again."

"Why haven't you told him how you felt?"

255

"I should have a long time ago, but I guess I never built up enough nerve. You see, my father casts a mighty long shadow, and I suppose I became tired of walking in it long before I grew up enough to tell him how I felt. I left home when I was seventeen; defiant, surly, but ready to prove to the world that I was a man. I bought two Colt .45s, and I practiced using them until they felt like they were a part of me. When I strapped them on, I wore them low to prove to the world how tough and fast I was, then I proceeded to build a reputation. But it was a reputation I wish I'd never acquired." He paused and looked at Angela for her reaction. There was a definite tensing of her jaw.

"My imagination conjured up many vivid images when I first saw you."

"If it helps any, I never started a gunfight, and I never provoked one, although a man doesn't build a reputation of being fast with a gun by keeping it holstered. But I am not wanted by the law and there is no price on my head."

She looked at him quickly, hopefully. "What about us, Clint? What about our future together? I thought we were going to live here at the ranch."

"You have no idea how badly I want to settle down here. If I can work out my problems with Dad, I want our children to call the Double R home. Not to sound like a braggart, but I've learned quite a bit about ranching. I didn't spend all of my time trying to prove how tough I was. I've worked for some good outfits, and I have also ridden the grub-line more times than I would like to admit. But regardless, whenever I signed on with an outfit, I always rode for the brand, and I was always willing to learn what they could teach me."

256

"I'm sorry, I don't understand. What do you mean by the 'grub-line,' and 'riding for the brand'?"

Clint explained, "Riding the grub-line means a man is down on his luck, winter is approaching, and he is willing to work for food and a warm place to stay. Riding for the brand means a man is loyal to his boss, to the ranch. If there was trouble, say a range war, a man stood with the other ranch hands, and at times, it meant using guns. But, I never worked for a brand that ran roughshod over small ranchers. Whenever I came across an outfit that did that, I packed my gear and left."

His eyes clung to hers, wanting to see her reaction. "You can rest assured, the gunfighting part of my life is over and it has been over for nearly two years now. I decided to hang up my guns when I came within a hair of drawing down on an unarmed man. He was in the wrong place at the wrong time. I found it hard to live with the fact that I could have easily killed an innocent man."

"But you were wearing your guns when I first saw you." Her tone was not accusing, it was a statement of fact. "And you had them on when Amos first joined us."

Clint wrapped his arms around her tightly as though he was half-afraid she would slip away like some elusive dream. "The day we met was the first time I'd had them on in nearly two years. Up until then, they had been packed away in my trunk. I was carrying a large sum of money, and I knew thieves worked the road between Silverlode and Clear Creek. You have to remember that we live in an uncivilized part of the world. There are no policemen walking beats, and there are a lot of men who are not what you would call law-abiding citizens. I believe those outlaws we ran into on the mountain are proof of that. Sweetheart, I cannot change my past. But I can make you a promise. I give you my word that I will never carry or use a gun unless it is to protect or defend what's mine. You will have to trust my judgment. If you ever start having doubts, just remember that I'm not an arrogant, surly kid anymore. I am a man." He shook his head and laughed ruefully. "Now I have to try and convince my dad of that."

Angela traced her fingertip along the line of his jaw. She felt she had to do more than just say, *she understood.* "Clint, I haven't known your father long enough to recognize his faults. I suppose I have been too overwhelmed to see anything negative about him." She gave him an enticing smile. "There is one thing you said that I agree with wholeheartedly. You two *are* alike, but there are two things that you've done that no other man could ever do, not even your father."

"Oh? What's that?"

"Hang the moon and the stars," she whispered softly.

Clint breathed a sigh of relief that she had accepted his past without showing any reservations or qualms. He lay his head against her breast, then suddenly jerked back as though he had been burnt. An involuntary groan vibrated through his chest and up his throat. At eye level he could see the outline of her nipples beneath the cloth of her dress. He saw them and yearned. He ached to have her.

"Sweetheart . . .?"

"Yes?"

Suddenly, Clint knew he was going to kiss her . . . and if he did, he would not stop there. He would bury his face between those small but perfectly formed mounds. He would take those sweet peaks between his lips and . . . then completely lose his mind. Any form of

258

sanity or reasoning would take flight, and the moment that happened ... his dad would walk in on them. Swearing softly beneath his breath, he placed both his hands firmly around her waist and lifted her from his leg.

"Sweetheart, if you sit on my lap for one moment longer, I cannot be held responsible for what I do." He blew out a ragged breath and said, "If you want me to keep my integrity, maybe you ought to finish cooking breakfast."

"Yes," she murmured huskily, "perhaps I should."

Angela would have never guessed there were so many underlying tensions between Clint and his father. It was obvious that they loved each other, but maybe they were too much alike to ever be able to work together. Clint had made his intentions quite clear. He wanted a ranch. It was possible that they would have to strike out on their own. That made it more imperative than ever for her to talk to Richard Grissom.

Breakfast was almost over before Angela broached the subject. "Clint, I've been thinking ... do you mind if I go with you to Clear Creek today?"

Tom raised his brows with surprise. "I thought you said yesterday evening that you didn't feel up to making a forty mile round trip."

Clint injected quickly, "I don't mind." He gave his father a defiant look. "That is, if Dad has any horses that have been broke to pull a wagon." He knew that Angela did not know how to ride a horse, and that a wagon would be their only means of transportation.

Ignoring Clint, Tom asked, "What about that cake you were going to bake?"

She raised her chin stubbornly. "I will bake it tomorrow. I'd really like to go."

"I think you should," Clint said, pushing back from the table. "I'd like to introduce you to a few friends of mine. I know you'll enjoy meeting Sadie. She's the lady who runs the boardinghouse. I'll go hitch up the buckboard and the rented rig."

"I don't know, Clint," Tom said doubtfully. "Those horses have only been hitched to a wagon once, and they acted awfully contrary."

Angela, seeing a dark scowl rush over Clint's face, thought quickly. "Why, Tom, I'm surprised at you!"

"Why?"

"Clint told me that you're an expert horseman, that you could tame a horse faster and better than any man he had ever seen. He said that you had a special way with them. I could ride with him in the rented rig and you could drive the buckboard, and—if Clint didn't stretch the truth a tad bit—I would wager that those contrary horses would be eating out of your hand by the time we reached Clear Creek." She batted her eyelashes at him and smiled sweetly.

"Well, if you really want to go . . ."

"Oh, I do."

"Since, I'm going to drive the buckboard, I would rather harness the horses myself . . ."

Angrily, Clint interrupted, "Dad, I've been hitching horses for a long time. I know how to do it."

Tom seemed to be puzzled by the sharpness in Clint's voice. "I know you do, son. You must have forgotten my theory that it's best for the man who drives the rig to harness them—until they get use to pulling a wagon; then it doesn't matter." He grinned. "If you've forgotten that, then you might have forgotten that I like to bribe them with apples. Would you mind getting a couple from the pantry?" He paused before he went out the

260

doorway. "No, better make that three. That livery stable nag probably never gets one."

Angela immediately started carrying dishes to the sink. She did not know how Clint would react to their slight confrontation, and to her interference. She could feel his presence behind her.

"You know," Clint said softly, "Dad never told me anything about his theory. But that's the first time I ever remember him explaining why he did something, and it sounded pretty logical." He walked up behind Angela and slipped his arms around her waist. "As for you, you little minx, I don't know whether to kiss you or to strangle you."

Smiling, she turned her head and looked at him over her shoulder. "Do you mind if I tell you my preference?"

He nuzzled at her earlobe. "I can see right now that I don't have the right ammunition to handle Dad."

"Oh? Why not?"

"I don't have big gray eyes, or long black lashes," he murmured.

"I thought it was because you don't know how to bake biscuits," she teased. Forcing a sternness to her voice, she said, "If you don't get out of here, I won't have time to wash the dishes, and I am not about to come back to a dirty kitchen."

"Yes, Ma'am!" he replied with mock sobriety.

Wanting to look presentable after a twenty-mile buggy ride, Angela brushed her hair back and her nimble fingers quickly plaited a long, single braid. Then she put combs on the sides to help hold her hair in place. Stepping back from the mirror, she smoothed the new gray dress over her hips, and surveyed her appearance. The dress was too full through the bosom, and the waist

261

was not as formfitting as she would have liked, but the looseness helped conceal her too thin waistline. Having plenty of food to eat for a change would soon remedy that, though. Her coloring and skin tone was already improving.

She removed the woolen cloak from a hanger, wrapped it around her shoulders, and hurried out to the front porch where the men were waiting. Once outside, she realized that the weather had indeed improved and become much warmer. The heavy cloak would be too warm further in the day. Yet, she would need something to go over her shoulders.

"Wait a minute," she called out. "I need to get my shawl from the washhouse. I left it hanging out there to dry."

Instead of going around the house and making her way over the sodden ground, she quickly went through it and out the kitchen door. Draping the shawl across her arm, Angela closed the door to the washhouse and slipped a heavy cord through a leather strap on the door to secure it. Suddenly, she had the strangest feeling that she was being watched. She thought she could actually feel eyes boring into her. Remember that Clint had mentioned something about Indians living in the area, cold chills ran up and down her back. She was unsure whether to suddenly turn about or to continue as though she did not suspect anything out of the ordinary. There were so many places where they could conceal themselves. Behind the icehouse, smokehouse, the thick stand of trees. Why, they could be hidden anywhere!

"I'm being foolish, she thought, her hands trembling too badly to tie the cord. The Indians respect Tom, they would never attack his ranch . . . would they? She considered bolting into the washhouse and screaming for help at the top of her lungs. Then she immediately dismissed that thought. If she screamed, Clint and Tom would come running to rescue her, then their lives would be in danger. Besides, the stories in those dime novels she liked to read always said never show an Indian that you feared him. They respected bravery.

She had to do something, but what? The one thing that she could not do was stand in this spot forever. They would soon suspect that she knew they were there, or Clint would come to see what was taking her so long.

Angela took a deep, steadying breath and slowly turned about. When she saw a hound dog sitting on its haunches, wagging its tail not ten feet from her, she sagged against the door and clasped her hand over her thudding heart.

"You scared me half to death!" she hissed.

"Angela?"

"Clint!" she exclaimed with a rush of laughter as he came around the corner of the building.

"What's taking you so long?" he asked, concerned.

Angela swallowed hard. She thought about the fearful images that had raced through her mind. Faceless Indians had swooped down on her brandishing tomahawks and scalping knives. They had tied her to a stake and piled wood all around her, then set it afire. She looked at Clint and grinned. She was not about to tell him how her imagination had ran wild.

"Tha ... that dog. I didn't know if it would bite or not."

"Rooster? Why, he wouldn't bite a flea that was crawling on his back. Of course, you didn't know that, did you?" He whistled and called him, "Come here, boy." But the dog yawned, then stood and slowly walked over to the icehouse and hiked his leg.

Clint guffawed. "Sweetheart, I guess that just proves how impressed he is with us. Seriously though, he's so old, he's lost his sense of smell and is half-blind, and I doubt if he has any teeth left in his head. He can't even chew meat anymore. Dad soaks oats in milk and feeds him that."

"Well, I didn't know that he was so harmless," she protested half-heartedly. "When I saw him sitting there . . . I guess I just remembered those wolves."

Clint nodded. "Come on, we'd better hurry. Dad will be wondering what has happened to us. If we don't leave soon, we won't have time to visit in town."

Before Angela fell into step with Clint, she cast one more look into the trees and an involuntary shudder swept over her.

It sat in the shadows of the trees, watching. His brow furrowed as he tried to formulate thoughts, but that was an impossibility. He was only capable of memory and instinct . . . and a tiny fragment of something else that elevated him slightly above other wilderness creatures.

When those with yellow eyes attacked this female, his reaction had been purely instinctive; they had posed a danger to him as well as to her. But, later, he remembered the scent of her terror, the frantic tone of her voice, the fear that had shone from her mist-colored eyes, and it had rekindled a sad memory of the *other*.

There was a need deep inside of him to guard her, to protect her, to prevent what had happened to the *other*. He would follow, and wait . . . and watch . . .

Chapter Nineteen

Clint stopped the rig at the intersection of the street that ran alongside the mining offices. "Are you sure you want to go in there and talk to Grissom alone?" he asked. "I doubt if he has had a change of heart about you."

Angela shook her head adamantly. "No, I would rather face him by myself. And, I don't care if he has changed his mind or not. After all, like I told you earlier, I just want to talk to him. I want to learn more about my father. And, if by chance I can convince him that I am telling the truth, he might give me some of his personal effects."

She had been careful not to mention her plans to inquire about the estate. If her attempt proved unsuccessful, she did not want Clint to be unnecessarily disappointed.

"Then why not wait for a week or two?" His hands tightened on the reins. "You are coping with your father's death so well, I would hate for you to put yourself into a position that might jeopardize that."

A crooked smile tugged at her mouth. "Patience used to be one of my better virtues, but not anymore. Now that I am over the initial shock of my father's death, I am eager to learn as much about him as I possibly can."

Clint shook his head doubtfully. "I still don't think you should face him alone."

Her dark eyebrows slanted into a frown as she turned on the wagon seat and regarded him with a speculative gaze. "Clint, if our situation was reversed, I doubt if Richard Grissom could have blasted you from his office the other day. Even if he had used a ton of dynamite, you would not have budged until you had gleaned every bit of information from him. And, I also doubt if you would have wanted anyone with you. Be honest with me now. Would you?"

He conceded. "Well ... you have a point there. All right, go on and talk to him. I'll wait for you out here."

Angela wanted to be assured of privacy. "No, you need to return this rig by noon, then you said you wanted to stop by the mercantile for a while. I have no idea how long I will be, so you go ahead and take care of your errands."

"You won't know where to find me when you're finished."

"If you are not at the mercantile, I will go to the boardinghouse and wait for you there."

Clint was not willing to admit defeat. He offered one last argument. "But ... you're forgetting what I said about these streets being unsafe for an unescorted female."

She thrust her chin out stubbornly. "Evidently you have forgotten that I managed to survive entirely on my own for several months without having you to protect me. Now, if I was in the habit of conducting myself in an unladylike manner in public, I could understand why your fears might be justified. However, I am not a painted harlot, and I seriously doubt that men with lolling tongues will stampede if they see me walking on the street."

Clint knew he had lost this battle of wills. Deciding to accept defeat graciously, he shrugged and grinned. "If you're wrong, do you promise to run real fast?"

She gave him a playful swat on his arm. "Oh, you!"

Clint's expression grew solemn. "Will you compromise?"

"How?"

"Agree to meet me at the boardinghouse in an hour."

She thought about his suggestion for a moment. "That sounds reasonable."

He helped her from the carriage. "Don't let him get his bluff in on you," he cautioned. "Dad seems to think that he is an honorable man, but—"

"Will you please quit worrying? Now, go!" She shooed him with her hands.

Angela stood in front of the mine office waiting impatiently for Clint to leave, but he made no attempt. Finally, she placed her hands on her hips and glared at him, and after a long pause he flicked the reins to urge the horse to move. Once the rig was out of sight, she opened the door and walked inside.

"Good morning, Mr. Grissom."

At the sound of her voice, Richard Grissom glanced up from the papers he had been working on, his mouth tightening into a thin, white line.

"I would like to talk to you," she said after he refused to acknowledge her greeting.

He tossed his pencil down on the desk, leaned back in his chair, and sighed heavily. "I have nothing to discuss with you. I demand you leave my office immediately," he spat out the words contemptuously.

She met his anger-filled eyes without flinching. "I refuse to leave until you listen to what I have to say."

He quirked one eyebrow. "I could always have you thrown out."

"Yes, I suppose you could, but I don't think you will. From what I have heard, you are an honorable man who has a scrupulous reputation. However, I doubt if that reputation would remain unblemished when word of your deed was bandied around town. Some people might not think too kindly of a man who threw the daughter of his dead partner out of his office. I am quite sure they would want to know why he took such drastic steps."

Grissom's face flushed with rage. Placing both hands flat on the desk, he rose from the chair. "When they learned this so-called daughter was an impostor, they would know why!"

"Would they?" she questioned defiantly. "I'm sure you know human nature much better than I do." She desperately wanted to swallow the dry lump that had formed in her throat, but was afraid that to do so might reveal her fear. Instead, she moistened her lips and hoped her voice would not crack from her throat's dryness. "I am also quite certain that many people would prefer to think the worst. Why, some might even begin to wonder if the partner's demise was from natural causes. Some might think that his death was somehow hastened." Her tone was inflamed and belligerent. "Now, do you still want to have me thrown out?"

Grissom was livid with rage. "I will not tolerate your threats or your insinuations! Samuel Langford was my friend! He was like a brother to me!" He rasped hoarsely, "Why, I was devastated by his death!"

"I don't blame you for being angry," she said softly.

"As for the threats . . . I am not vicious enough to carry them through." Then her tone hardened. "But did I sound unfair? How do you think I feel? I don't blame you for having doubts about me. But the very least you could do is listen to me . . . if for no other reason than Samuel Langford was your friend."

Angela could see a glimmer of doubt in his eyes. Remembering the argument she had used with Clint to convince him that she should talk to Grissom alone, she decided to use it again. "Tell me, sir, do you have a family? A wife and children?"

"No, unfortunately, I never had the pleasure. Although I fail to see why that is any concern of yours."

Ignoring his comment, she continued, "What if you had died and Samuel Langford lived? What if shortly after your death, a woman appeared—quite penniless— claiming to be your daughter? What should Sam do? He knew you'd had a daughter, but she had supposedly died in her childhood. Naturally, he would have doubts. Naturally he would tend to disbelieve her. But what if she could prove her identity if given the time? Would you want Sam to turn this woman away without listening to her story? Would you want him to turn her away without giving her the benefit of a doubt?"

Angela felt herself shrinking from the intensity of his gaze, but she pressed on. "I cannot even pretend to know the terms of your agreement with my father. I assume since there were no apparent heirs, the surviving partner inherited the entire estate. But, would my father have agreed to those terms if he had known his daughter was still alive? Would you have agreed to those terms if you had a daughter somewhere?" She crossed her arms defiantly. "I think not."

Richard Grissom placed his hands behind his back

and paced the floor behind his desk. He pursed his lips thoughtfully while considering the points she had made.

Angela watched him, wondering if she should tell him that she could let the courts decide whether she had a legitimate claim. If all else failed, she would do just that, but legal action could take years to resolve, and Clint needed money in the spring to stock the ranch.

Finally, Grissom walked over and pulled a chair to the front of his desk, and pointed for Angela to sit down before he returned to his seat.

Leaning forward, he said, "You have a rather poignant way of presenting your case, Miss . . . Langford." His eyes narrowed slightly. "I wish to make it perfectly clear that I am not convinced that particular name belongs to you. I shall, however, address you accordingly until I have proof one way or the other of your true identity."

"You forced me to be rather poignant, Mr. Grissom."

He waved her statement aside. "Nevertheless, I have a few things to tell you before *your* discussion continues. I want to make it perfectly clear that my earlier refusal to listen to your ludicrous story had nothing to do with the estate. While I do wish to live comfortably, obtaining great wealth has never been my desire. Instead, the thrill has always been in the search for riches. There is nothing more exhilarating than to scoop up a pan of gravel and find a nugget—" He shrugged, "The size does not matter. Or, deepening a drift, and finding a little more width to the slender vein that you had been following for weeks, wondering if the next time you sink your pick into the quartz you will find a seam of silver so wide . . ."

Realizing he had revealed too much of his inner self, he coughed to cover his embarrassment. When he spoke

270

again, his voice was soft and reflective, "Sam and I were much alike in that respect." Grissom's heartfelt tone gave Angela a better insight into the man who had been her father's best friend.

Clasping his hands behind his head, he rocked in his chair. "As illogical as it may sound to you, I care little about Sam's share of the mine. The money is unimportant. My share will see me through to the end of my days even if I am outrageously frivolous."

His countenance became rigid and cold. "Miss . . . Langford, if some fraudulent impostor attempted to gain the fruits of our endeavors, I would find it most disagreeable—the impostor would find it even more unpleasant. Since you have been forewarned, please feel free to leave without suffering any repercussions from me. If you choose to stay, may Heaven help you if you are lying."

Angela allowed a slight smile to touch her lips. "Mr. Grissom, when I went to the chicken house to gather eggs yesterday evening, I saw two roosters circling each other, their feathers spread and ruffled. Apparently they had been sparring to see who would rule the roost. I have spread my feathers and you have spread yours. I do not care about the roost. I only want what I am entitled to . . . nothing more." She raised her head a little higher. "I am certain that your motives are honorable. I realize that you feel so strongly about this because you were my father's friend. When this is all settled, I hope we can be friends too."

Grissom nodded minutely. The girl certainly had gumption, and that was a trait he greatly admired in anyone, man or woman. "If you are Sam's daughter, I believe we shall be. I do admire your courage," he admitted reluctantly. "In that respect, you are exactly like

Sam . . . but you bear no distinct resemblance to him, or to . . . your mother," he added. "Enough of this dallying. Explain to me how you are Sam's daughter . . . when she supposedly died as a child."

Angela began with the small mountain cabin; her memory of her father singing to her, the journey to New Orleans that seemed to last forever when she was a child. Her memories of New Orleans, Julia, Dahlia, of her mother's death, and how she had waited for her father to come for her. She told Grissom how she learned of her father's passing, and of the years that followed. Though she only touched briefly on how she was treated at Julia's hand, Richard sensed her loneliness, her misery. Then, she told him how she had discovered that her father still lived and what she did afterwards. Finally, when she finished with her story, she slumped against the back of the chair, feeling drained, exhausted.

Grissom remained silent for several minutes, mulling over the incredible story she had told him. The girl had sounded so sincere, it was difficult not to believe her. But, while her tale seemed feasible, it bordered on the edge of absurdity. How could it be possible?

"Tell me, Miss Langford, why did Julia Stanton go to such despicable lengths to deceive you and Sam? A person does not set out to destroy two lives for no reason whatsoever."

"I have no idea," she replied softly. "If I knew the answers to those questions, in all likelihood, I would not be sitting here now. For some unknown reason, she must have hated my mother, my father, or me, with such vehemence that revenge of this sort was worth any price. What makes it more puzzling, the three of them were such good friends. Mother and Julia were even distantly related—cousins twice removed, I think—something like that."

"And all of your identification is at the bottom of a deep canyon?"

"Yes, it is."

He let out a heavy breath and spoke more to himself than to Angela. "In all probability it is lying exposed to the elements, and by spring it will be completely indecipherable." He looked at her through squinted eyes. "How do you propose to prove your identity?"

"I thought perhaps a letter . . ." Her voice trailed off when she realized how foolish her suggestion would sound. How could a reply to a letter prove her identity? Even though it would confirm her story, it would not offer any definite proof.

"A letter to who? Mrs. Stanton?" His voice was indignant. "I should think not!" He pointed his finger at Angela to emphasize his words. "Bear in mind that I am not thoroughly convinced by your story. But, if you are telling the truth, and if the woman went to such lengths to deceive you and Sam, I would be reluctant to ask anything of her. There is nothing to prevent her from continuing with this horrid deception. Is there someone else? Someone who could corroborate when you came to live in that woman's household? Someone you could trust?"

Angela mused aloud, "Not the neighbors, although she did not get along very well with them. I'd still rather not place much trust in them. There is her attorney, or perhaps our minister? Reverend James Smith is a trustworthy man, and he has led the congregation for as long as I can remember."

Richard handed her a writing pad and pencil. "If you

will give me his address, I'm sure you will not object if I pen the letter."

Angela was tired of Grissom's doubting everything thing she said. Little did he know that she seldom strayed from the truth, but under the circumstances, she could not protest. She kept her features deceptively composed. "No objections whatsoever. In fact, I insist upon you writing it. Out of curiosity though, when do you intend to send it?"

"The mail service to Clear Creek depends largely upon the weather. I would like to see this matter come to a fast conclusion, one way or the other. Weather permitting, and as soon as I can release a man from his duties, I shall send him to Silverlode so that he can post it from there. I do want to caution you, though, it may be spring before I receive a reply. I trust you will not be badgering me constantly?"

Angela stood to leave. "No, Mr. Grissom, I will not badger you, because I trust you. I know my father was a mortal just like you and I, but in my mind's eye I see him as an extraordinary man. I seriously doubt that he would have chosen an unscrupulous man to be his best friend." She bobbed her head politely and said, "Good day, Mr. Grissom, and thank you."

Richard remained seated for quite some time after the girl had left. He found himself pondering her incredible story. One thing was certain, if she was not Angela Langford, someone had milked the child's mind before she died and passed the information on to this young woman. Her description of the small cabin, the recounting of how Sam used to sing to his daughter, had to have come from someone somewhere. Richard found himself hoping that the girl was indeed telling the truth.

It would be comforting to know that a part of Sam still lived.

As Angela walked down the narrow side street, she saw Clint waiting in front of a building on the other side of the main street that ran through Clear Creek. His arms were crossed, one foot was propped against the building. He removed a cigarette from his mouth and flicked it away when he saw her coming.

He quickly scanned her features and when he was reassured that she had not been mistreated or expelled from Grissom's office, he offered her a sheepish smile.

"I know I told you that I would meet you at the boardinghouse, but then I got to thinking about all of those men chasing after you with lolling tongues, so I decided to wait here." When she did not immediately say anything, he asked, "Are you angry at me?"

She could not resist smiling. "No. To be honest, it makes me feel good for someone to care about me so much."

Relieved, Clint said, "It feels pretty damn good for me to have someone to care about." He offered her his arm and they fell into step together. "I can tell that you're not upset, but I still have to ask. How did your meeting go?"

"I think it went very well," she said enthusiastically. "At least he listened to me this time. And I doubt if he is as mean and cruel as I first thought."

"He believed you then?"

"No, not exactly. But he did listen, and I think he wanted to believe me."

Clint shook his head. He did not understand why she seemed so optimistic. He wished she could just let the matter drop. Of course, there were her father's personal effects, and a possible claim to his share of the mine. The money was not important, though. He could take care of her just fine without any outside help. The first few years would be financially strenuous, but that would not matter as long as they were together.

"Mr. Grissom did agree to write a letter of inquiry to the minister of the church I attended. Although, it may be spring before he receives a reply."

Angela had deliberately not mentioned that Mr. Grissom seemed agreeable to giving her a share of the mine's receipts if he were satisfied she was who she claimed to be. She did not intend to say anything about it either. It would be for the best if Clint thought she had just inquired about her father's personal items. She could hardly wait to see the look of surprise on Clint's face when she presented him with enough money to completely restock the ranch. Suppressing a sigh, Angela knew it would be a long, long wait until spring.

Chapter Twenty

The streets of Clear Creek were much more crowded than when they had first arrived that morning. Horses strained against their burdens on the muddy street. Two cowhands, spurs a-jingling, rode by on their mounts, and the boardwalks were thronged with miners in their wet, digging clothes, carrying lunch buckets. Gamblers and drunks lazed indolently in front of the saloons and the barbershop. A few women passed by, taking care to avoid the idle loafers. Their quick, inquisitive glances toward Angela revealed their curiosity. Most women smiled a greeting and a few spoke, but all nodded, indicating their friendliness.

"I did not expect to see so many people in town," Angela remarked.

"Warm weather seems to bring everybody out. The locals know that it won't last long, so they usually come in to catch up on new gossip and to purchase any last minute supplies before winter sets in. I suppose the newcomers are just following their lead."

Suddenly, a belligerent voice rang out from behind them, "Well, I'll be damned! Thought I smelled a polecat. Only thing, this one's got a yellow streak running down his back instead of a white one."

Clint stopped short. His head snapped up and his jaw clenched. He would have recognized that voice anywhere. Glancing at Angela, Clint transmitted a silent warning before he slowly turned around to face the mocking voice. "Hello, Dane," he said tersely, employing every ounce of his will to keep from charging Dane like an enraged bull.

A huge man, just as tall as Clint, but broader and heavier by far, pushed on the bat wing doors of the saloon and stepped outside on the boardwalk. "Last I heard, you had hightailed it out of the country—all the way to England. Had no idea you were *that* scared of me."

"I've no reason to be afraid of you."

Dane Tapley stood with his legs splayed in a threatening stance. He had hitched his black coat over his gun for easy access to it. Grinning evilly, he taunted further, "I should have known this is where you would come to hide. Guess you figured it was safe here, guess you didn't figure I would ever show up in these parts."

Clint grabbed Angela's arm and thrust her out of harm's way behind him. "Don't push your luck, Tapley."

"I am disappointed," the burly man sneered, his eyes narrowing into thin slits. "For a minute there, I thought you had started hiding behind a woman's skirts. That is what I expected from a yellow-bellied coward like you."

Clint swore under his breath, struggling to keep control of his temper. Dane was goading him, deliberately trying to provoke a gunfight. For a moment, he fervently wished for his guns. Then, remembering the promise he had made to himself and to Angela, he was almost relieved that they had been packed away once again. He had left unnecessary gunplay in the past, and that's where it belonged.

"Why don't you quit while you're ahead? There's been no damage here today and I'm willing to let it go at that."

Aware of the crowd that had gathered, Dane preened before his audience. He believed Clint to be afraid of him. He splayed his legs further apart and thumbed the rawhide thong from his pistol. "I think we ought to settle this now."

"That's fine with me, but we'll have to do it with our fists. As you can plainly see, I am unarmed. I don't even carry a gun anymore." Carefully, Clint reached up and pulled on the lapels of his denim jacket, and stretched them out so that Dane could see for himself.

"Don't tell me that the famous Clint Rutledge has hung up his guns." Dane scoffed, aware that many of the people had cleared the street.

"That's right, I have. But I have two good fists."

Dane smirked. "You must be a glutton for punishment. I've already proved that I'm the better man on that score. Or don't you remember the whipping I gave you the last time we sparred? I proved to you then that you don't stand a chance against me."

Clint smiled, slow and easy, but Angela had seen the exact same expression on his face when he had faced those stagecoach robbers, and she felt her limbs grow weak.

The line of Clint's mouth tightened a fraction more. "Oh, I remember it, Dane. I remember all of it. I have never forgotten what that woman's face looked like after you finished with her. I also remember when I called you out over it, how you threw sand in my face, then pole-axed me with a two by four; how you sat on my chest with my arms pinioned by your knees while you beat me within an inch of my life. You are mighty handy with your fists when you're beating a man who's already been knocked senseless, or beating on a defenseless woman. Yep, on those points I have to agree, you're about the best man I ever seen."

Dane's expression took on an unpleasant twist. "Don't push your luck, Clint," he warned, "or I'll kill you where you stand."

The challenge of a fight set Clint's blood to leaping, but he reluctantly pushed it from his mind. "I've already told you, I'm unarmed."

Dane's face flushed angrily. He had worked himself up to an unbridled rage. "I'm sure someone'll loan you a gun. We've got an old score to settle."

"Clint, no, please!" Stark terror choked Angela's heart as she placed a restraining hand on his arm. "Don't do it! He might kill you!"

Clint wanted Dane Tapley. Not necessarily lying dead by Clint's gun, but he wanted to drive his fists into the man's face until he begged for mercy. He wanted him! God, how he wanted him!

Clint looked miserably at Angela, then, remembering his promise, exhaled a deep breath of air, and said to Dane, "Go pick your fights elsewhere, I'm through with killing. He took Angela's arm. "Come on, let's go." With that, he turned, deliberately presenting the man his back, and walked down the street, shutting his mind to Dane's uproarious laughter.

From the set of Clint's jaw and his rigid gait, Angela knew he was angry and that he had been deeply shamed. Earlier, when they had talked about him not using his guns, why had he not told her about this man? How much of his past was he keeping from her?

Finding it difficult to keep in step with him, she yanked her arm from his grasp. "Clint, wait, don't walk so fast!"

He stopped abruptly and spun around, causing her to almost run into him. "Don't ever do that to me again!"

"Do what?" she asked, confused.

"Your interference made me look like a fool."

She protested, "Clint, he was spoiling for a fight. He would have killed you if you had been armed!"

"Thanks so much for your vote of confidence," he groused sarcastically, his eyes cold and hard.

Incredulously, she gasped, "You think I should have stood by and not said . . ."

"That's right! You should have kept quiet. I've been taking care of myself for many years and I damn sure don't need you or anyone else to come to my defense! Maybe that's how men behave where you come from, but out here a man is known by his actions. If he is branded a coward, he might as well hang it up and leave the country . . . only thing, that sort of reputation follows him just the same as an honorable one."

Angela felt that his anger at her was unjustified, but he had to lash out at someone. "I never meant to embarrass you, Clint. I . . . I was just so afraid that he would kill you."

Although still angry, Clint's tone softened slightly. "I remembered my promise to you. When I gave you my word, I meant it, and I still do. I'm tired of bloodshed. But I shouldn't have ignored him. I shouldn't have turned and walked away. I shouldn't have let him get away with calling me those names . . ."

She interrupted, "But being called names . . ."

281

Clint rolled his eyes and sighed hard. "Turning the other cheek is all well and good, but there are times when it is impossible. When word spreads that Dane backed me down, every smart aleck kid eager for a reputation will pour into Clear Creek like a swarm of locust, and if I'm caught out alone, they won't care if I'm armed or not. But one thing you can be sure of; when my body is found, I'll have a gun in my hand. I've seen it happen too many times to other men who have tried to quit."

Unmitigated fear gripped her. "Are you saying that you cannot quit, that it is a death sentence to try?"

"No, not necessarily. But after what just happened, there will be many who will have doubts about my courage. Whether I want to or not, I will have to face Dane Tapley. Perhaps we can settle our difference with our fists, but if not . . ." his voice trailed off.

Seeing the unspoken question in her eyes, he squared his shoulders determinedly. "If it means settling it with guns, then so be it. I hope you haven't forgotten that I put stipulations on that promise I made to you."

"No, I haven't forgotten," she murmured softly, but misery was etched on her face. She had lost every person she had loved. How could she continue to live if she lost Clint too?

Clint noted her expression and realized what she must be thinking. He sighed heavily. "I'll do everything within my power to keep my word. But, if push comes to shove, I'll do what I have to do."

Angela swallowed her fears and arguments. "I suppose that is all I can ask. That is, if you will accept my apology for embarrassing you. I never realized how much harm I was causing . . ."

He finally heaved a sigh of momentary surrender as

he realized it was unfair to admonish her so severely when she had never been exposed to men like Dane Tapley. His features relaxed and he gently trailed his finger along her cheek. "Hush, sweetheart. Let's put it aside and not let it spoil our day anymore than it has. Dad's waiting for us at Sadie's. We'll have to leave for the ranch soon, but I want you to meet her. She's a priceless gem—a little rough around the edges, but . . ." he paused and grinned although the smile did not quite reach his eyes. "Sadie is hard to explain. You'll just have to meet her and form your own opinions. But a word of caution, don't be surprised by what you hear or see."

Sadie MacDonald came running with outstretched arms when Clint shoved open the front door of the boardinghouse and bellowed, "Where's my darlin' Sadie?"

She suddenly stopped short and planted her hands on her willowy hips. "'Tis about time ye brought ye rotten carcass to see me!" she scolded belligerently, the words rolling from her Scottish tongue. "The nerve of ye sending that mere snip of a lad after food the other day while claiming ye did not have time to fetch it yeself. Shame be with ye, Clinton Rutledge, I never thought I would live to see the day when ye did not have time for Sadie MacDonald!"

Laughing, Clint wrapped his arms around her in a bear hug, swung her around, then gently set the tiny woman back on the floor. "My darlin', your tongue is still as sharp as ever." He shook his head and feigned a sad sigh. "How do you think you'll ever snare a husband as long as you use vinegar for bait? You have to remember to use sweet talk."

"Balderdash! This Scottish lass has gotten along just fine for forty-three years without having a man to boss me about, and if I have any luck a'tall, I shall make it another forty-three!" She looked over at Angela and smiled pleasantly. "This must be Angie. Thomas has spoken highly of ye, lass. Although when I first heard that ye had agreed to be this scoundrel's bride, I had to wonder if ye was a wee bit daft! Then when I recalled that this scamp could charm the tits from a milk cow, I knew ye had been besotted. Tis nae fault of yours." She grasped Angela's hand and shook it heartily.

Angela knew immediately why Clint had tried to warn her. She had never met anyone like Sadie before and she doubted if she would ever have the same opportunity again.

Sadie stood about five feet tall, her hair was deep auburn, having only a few wisps of gray around her temples, and it ran on her head like a curly mop. Her complexion was flawless, creamy with apple cheeks, and her blue eyes sparkled with devilment. Angela wondered why she had remained single. It seemed to her that any man possessing an ounce of common sense would have crawled to the ends of the earth to make her his wife . . . even if her language was slightly crude.

"I am pleased to meet you, Miss MacDonald."

Sadie stood with her arm on her hips and shook her head adamantly. "Nae, lass, I be Sadie to me friends."

Angela beamed and nodded her head. "Sadie it is, and I am Angela, or Angie, if you prefer."

"Tis a shame for us to stand here in this drafty old parlor while there is a new pot of coffee and a fresh apple cake waitin' for us in the kitchen."

"And Dad's in there by himself?"

"Aye."

Clint put his arms around both their waists. "Then let's step lively, ladies. Leaving Dad alone in a kitchen with an apple cake is the same as leaving a sly old fox to guard a chicken house. If I know him, he won't even save us a crumb."

"Dona fret none. I heard ye would be back in town today. There be three more coolin' in the pantry."

Tom hastily wiped the crumbs from his mustache as they entered the kitchen. He tried to look innocent when Sadie glared at what remained of the cake.

Knowing he could twist Sadie around his finger with teasing instead of the truth, he grinned sheepishly and said, "Would you believe someone came in the back door, hit me over the head, and stole part of it?" he asked, pointing to the small portion of cake that remained.

"Nae."

Tom sighed heavily and winked at Angela. "I didn't think you would."

"Be forgiving ye this time, Thomas, but dona let it happen again." She instructed everybody to sit down while she poured coffee and cut each one a generous piece of cake.

Angela lowered her gaze and smiled when Sadie cut an enormous piece and set it in front of Tom. She also noticed how Sadie's hand had lingered on his shoulder just a tad too long for it to be an innocent gesture.

Ah ha, she thought to herself. Tom was the reason why Sadie was unmarried. Were Tom and Clint blind? Why couldn't they see that Sadie adored Tom? Or did they know? Perhaps Tom was too devoted to his wife's memory. If that was the reason, then it was sad. His loneliness was so unnecessary.

They soon slipped into easy conversation. Clint acted as though nothing out of the ordinary had happened, and Angela also pushed Dane Tapley from her mind. She was determined to do as Clint had suggested and not allow the unpleasant incident to ruin their visit.

Clint talked about his trip to England and the other countries. Sadie was especially eager to hear about Scotland and her relatives who still lived there. He explained that he had brought her some gifts and a packet of letters, but they had been lost in the stagecoach accident. He knew that Sadie had already been informed of that news; scarcely anything happened in or around Clear Creek that she did not hear about.

"Ah, Angie. I just thought of something, and best ye be prepared. We womenfolk have decided to have a big "To-Do" the Saturday before Christmas, that tis, weather permittin'. If a blizzard blows in, then we shall be havin' it the first fittin' Saturday after the Christ Child's birthday. We womenfolk plan to exchange gifts, nothing fancy though. Perhaps an apron, a doily, embroidery work, whatever. Some women be knitting socks or scarfs for the men. It does nae matter what. Just so everybody will have a wee something under the tree. If ye not be handy with needles, then cakes, pies, doughnuts, or cookies will be just fine. The single men not be choosey. You see how Tom scoffed up the cake I baked."

"I'm glad you told me. It sounds like fun."

"Aye, will give all a chance to meet ye." She gazed at Tom, her eyes soft and doe-shaped, then she turned a sweet smile to Angela and Clint. "Tell me, when will the two of ye be getting married?"

Clint's eyes melted into Angela's and he reached across the table for her hand. "We haven't discussed a date yet. I guess we'll have to wait until spring, or until the preacher comes through. I would like for it to be as soon as possible . . . before she has a chance to change her mind," he quickly added.

"There is absolutely no danger of that," Angela said softly.

"Ah, Thomas, tisn't it sweet? Would ye look at the two of them—so much in love," Sadie gushed. "Tis too bad ye young'uns didnae arrive a week or so earlier when we had a justice o' the peace. He would have read the words over ye."

"You mean we actually had an officer of the court here at Clear Creek?" Clint asked, surprised. "I guess that means we're finally becoming civilized," he mused aloud.

"Ye damn right we're civilized. And why are ye surprised about a justice o' the peace being here? Who do ye think married all of those men and women when the mail order brides arrived?"

"Mail order brides? Here? In Clear Creek?" Clint chortled at the thought, then he recalled Susan saying something about it. But he had not paid much attention to what she had said.

"Aye. There were so many men here this past summer all of the soiled doves could nae keep them satisfied, so they had to order wives." She grunted to show her disgust. "Before the lasses arrived, the men reminded me of a flock of crows watching the corn grow the way they lined up in front of Crockett's place." She glanced over at Tom and muttered defiantly, "See there, ye warnings and threats were for nothing! I am behaving meself and watchin' what I say so I won't shock Angie with me vulgar mouth . . . that ye claim I have."

She smiled at Angela. "Every time Tom comes around, he grumbles about the way I talk . . . but he has no right to boss me about the way he tries to do!"

Angela returned Sadie's smile, but it was a pitiful attempt. She had never heard a woman speak so bluntly before—a man either, for that matter. She sensed there was an argument brewing between Tom and Sadie, but was not sure of the reason why.

Tom chided, "Now, Sadie, you know the only time I gripe or complain is when you cuss and use bawdy examples. You know how I feel about a woman speaking with a foul mouth. It isn't dignified or ladylike."

"Balderdash! Tis hard to be dignified when ye cook and clean after eight burly men." She glared at him. "Ye are the only one who ever accuses me of being anythin' less than a lady. And for your information, if I had wanted to speak with a foul mouth, I would have said that those men reminded me of a pack of dogs swarming after bitches in heat, but I dinnae!"

"Sadie! Watch your tongue," Tom scolded.

"Why?"

"It makes you sound as bad as . . . them!"

She wagged a finger at Tom. "Them? Them, who? The soiled doves?" She shook her head adamantly. "Ye men all be cut from the same pious cloth. If a lass drops her drawers for a man, ye men thinks she's a tramp. I say to hell with that notion! She damn sure dinnae bed herself. The man be just as guilty as the lass!" she stated emphatically. "That's why I keep me drawers on and my legs closed, and just for added safety, I keep a coin between me knees. Me maidenhead might have cobwebs all over it—" Sadie reached over and thumped

Angela on her back when she started choking. "But tis mine to lose it and when I want to!"

Tom glowered at her. "Sadie, damn it, this is not the time to talk about such things."

"Why? Does it plague ye for ye son and future daughter to know that if I was willin', ye would be first in line to bed me? If I'm good enough for beddin', I'm good enough for marrying!"

Tom's eyes flashed with outrage. Shoving back his chair, he grabbed his coat, crammed his hat down on his head, and stomped out the back door, slamming it soundly behind him.

Stunned, Angela stared after Tom, then cautiously looked at Clint and Sadie. They were calmly drinking their coffee and acting as though nothing out of the ordinary had happened. She did not know what to do or say. The room was so silent, she expected to hear their heartbeats.

Finally, she cleared her throat, and said in a disconcerted tone, "This cake is delicious, Sadie. You must give me your recipe."

"Aye, that I will."

It was a wild and lonely country between Clear Creek and the Double R. In places, the land looked to have been furrowed and eroded by thousands of years of sun, wind, rain, and snow, while a short distance away, tall mountains reached for the blue sky. It was a country tumbled and broken as if by some insane giant. Miles of slender valleys were bordered by towering peaks, green from the pines. The grass carpeting the valleys had already turned the color of straw from the cold and the killing frosts.

289

There were no sounds except the footfalls of the horses, the jingle of the harness, and the creaking of the wagon. Once, far off, came the cry of an eagle. A rabbit bounded up and away, bouncing like a tufted snowball.

It was easy for Angela to remain silent on the way to the ranch. Tom reminded Angela of a swelled, angry toad, not even protesting when Clint had offered to drive the wagon. Every so often she would steal a look at Clint, but each time she could tell that he was deep in thought.

She knew he was thinking about Dane Tapley; the man crowded her mind, too. But every now and then, the things that Sadie had said nagged at her conscience. Tom apparently had definite ideas about how a lady should behave. Did he think badly of her when she allowed Clint to act so affectionate toward her?

It was even more discomfiting for her to wonder if Clint questioned her morals because of what had happened between them at the cabin.

She definitely wanted to discuss the matter with Clint at the first possible opportunity.

Chapter Twenty-One

Monroe Herbert opened his umbrella against the heavy downpour as soon as he stepped from his carriage. He hurried to the front porch and rapped solidly on the door. Uneasily, he shifted his weight from foot to foot while waiting for someone to answer his knock.

Out of all of his duties as head of the tax collections office for Orleans Parish, this was the task he hated the most. It could have been delegated to one of the clerks, but sometimes they came across situations that proved too difficult to handle discreetly. There were many reputable families in New Orleans that had fallen on hard times, and their homes were on the sheriff's sale list for nonpayment of taxes. Depending on how prominent the family was, and their remaining contacts, political pressures were often placed on his office to "lose" the paperwork until their financial difficulties improved. Julia Stanton came from an old, established family, but that particular lineage had died out and lost its power and wealth a long time ago. But Monroe was a caring man. He figured if an important family could beat the tax man, he should be able to make allowances for a widow raising her child and give her extra time to try to raise the back taxes before seizing her home. It was the only fair thing to do, although it could mean losing his job if someone figured out what he was doing.

He rapped on the door again, only louder. He could hear laughter and violin music coming from the house; in fact, it sounded like a party. A few moments later, the door was opened by a stout, stern-faced woman. They stood for a moment assessing each other. The thought quickly crossed his mind that she must have been handsome in her day, before forty, maybe fifty some-odd years of hard life had creased her face and laced her black hair with fingers of gray. He quickly whipped off his hat and politely nodded his head. "Good afternoon. Are you Mrs. Julia Stanton?"

"Yes, I am she," the woman said coolly, her eyes raking the man with disdain.

"I am Monroe Herbert . . ."

She interrupted sharply, "I am not in the habit of introducing myself to every deliveryman who comes to my door. In the future, I suggest that you remember to make your deliveries at the back door, and not blunder *uninvited* into the midst of a social event! Did your employer not explain the proper procedures to you?"

Glaring at the man, she gave an irritable tug of her sleeve, aware of the young ladies tittering behind her. While the girls were far from being the elite of New Orleans society, they did come from good families and it was extremely important for them to know she knew how to handle stupid delivery men. Their mothers would question them at length about the tea, and if Julia and Dahlia strayed one inch from protocol, *they* would be the topic of the next ladies social. Julia could not allow that to happen. One tiny little incident or wrong impression could tarnish her daughter's reputation.

The man glanced anxiously about, noticing the younger women's attention directed at them. By the expressions on their faces, he suddenly understood how a wounded mouse would feel if surrounded by many hungry cats. He ran his finger around the neck of his collar, then he discreetly lowered his voice, "Mrs. Stanton, I am afraid you do not understand. I must speak to you in private. I am from . . ."

Julia's voice was stern. "No, quite the contrary, you are the one who does not understand." A taunting smile touched her lips as she made sure the girls behind her could overhear every word she said. "Evidently, you do not possess the intelligence to comprehend perfectly good English. Either go to the rear entrance immediately or take your goods back to the market. And you may rest assured that I *will* speak to your employer about your impertinence!"

That should make a lasting impression on Dahlia's friends, she thought smugly. She started to close the door but the man planted his foot firmly on the threshold.

Stony resolve shone in Monroe's eyes before they narrowed in understanding. In his line of work, he had seen all sorts of people and had to rely on snap judgments. Some were just mean natured—like this woman. She obviously gave no thought to people less fortunate than her, even if her station in life was nothing but a delusion of self-importance. He'd given her a chance, now she would have to bear the consequences for her waspish tongue and arrogant manners.

"Mrs. Stanton, I try to avoid embarrassing situations like this whenever necessary, but you have left me no choice whatsoever." He handed her an official document. "I have been empowered by the District Court of

Orleans Parish, New Orleans, Louisiana, to inform you that you have thirty days in which to pay the taxes that are in arrears on 1243 Briarwood. If the tax office has not received full payment by that time, this premise is to be vacated. If you do not do so voluntarily, the sheriff and his deputies will forcibly eject you and your possessions." His lips twisted into a cynical smile as he gestured toward the girls who stood about in shocked silence. He allowed his voice to drop into a belligerent drawl. "Now, if you don't have the intelligence to understand what I have just said, I'm sure if you ask real nice and polite, one of those young ladies will be kind enough to explain it to you."

Julia placed her pen aside and propped her elbows on the writing desk. She rubbed her temples and her brow, hoping to make the terrible pain disappear, but she knew nothing short of a miracle would help. And she had stopped believing in miracles years ago.

Only one week remained. Then, the sheriff would arrive with deputies to dispossess them of their home; the home she had struggled so long and hard to pay for.

Julia slumped back against her chair and sighed dejectedly. How could she have overlooked paying those burdensome taxes? She had known they had to be paid every year, but without tax statements to remind her, it had been too easy, too convenient to forget, especially with all the added expenses that came with properly introducing Dahlia to society.

Anger suddenly raced through her. She slammed her fist against the desktop. Damn that Oscar Culpepper! The tax statements had gone to him all of those years he'd held the mortgage on Briarwood. But, they were supposed to be mailed to her after the mortgage had finally been paid in full. Now she had expensive back taxes and penalties to pay, and no money with which to pay them. Even though the tax assessor had sworn the statements had been mailed directly to her, he was either lying or ignorant of what had really happened. Regardless, it was impossible to prove her suspicions. Perhaps Mr. Herbert was innocent of any wrongdoing, but she'd wager her last dollar that Oscar had bribed someone in the tax office to conveniently misplace her statements.

It was ironic; not only had Oscar found a way to deprive them of their home, he had ruined Dahlia's chance of ever being accepted by New Orleans's elite society by making sure their predicament was placed on every gossip's tongue. Even though he had vehemently denied it, she knew without a doubt he was responsible for all of this trouble. He had to be!

That despicable weasel had held Dahlia responsible for his gator-faced daughter's disgraceful behavior. But why on earth should he blame her daughter for Constance's disgrace, when she was the silly ninny who ran off with that gambler? He claimed Constance only did it to get away from the embarrassment of being jilted. That drivel he had spouted about Dahlia deliberately coming between Constance and her beau, Claude Bodine, was utter nonsense! Dahlia could not help being so pretty, just as it was not Constance's fault that she so strongly resembled her mother. Constance should have been relieved to learn that her beau was attracted to someone else before their marriage, but evidently neither she nor her father had seen it in that particular light.

And to think, until Oscar had initiated this despicable deed, she had actually felt pity for him when he received word that Constance had taken ill and died in some squalid little cabin up in Natchez after the gambler had deserted her.

Dahlia had done nothing to deserve any of this misery. Her chances for making a *good* marriage had disappeared that day the tax man came. No young man with any breeding at all would tie himself to a woman who would not improve his prestige. Sadly, Julia shook her head. All of her hopes and dreams for her daughter were for naught.

Until the day of disgrace, Dahlia was still naive enough to think in terms of love and living happily ever after. Bless her heart, she was too young to know that love only destroyed one's life. The only real happiness was through security, and the status that came with a good marriage.

Julia never wanted Dahlia to know how it felt to worry about food, fuel for the fires on cold nights, wearing patched petticoats, holes in the soles of her shoes, and trying to remake old clothing into stylish gowns—all of the hardships of poverty. And usually, all of those miseries stemmed from falling in love. Julia felt that she was an expert on that particular subject. All love had ever done for her was to break her heart, condemn her to a loveless, poverty-filled marriage, and a bleak widowhood.

Julia closed her eyes and remembered a time long ago—a lifetime ago. She had not always been so bitter, so caustic. There had been a time of innocence when she too had believed in the possibility of love and happiness.

Tears pooled in her closed eyes as memories of long ago engulfed her. How tall and handsome he had stood the day he came calling. The thrill that swept through her when her mother gave them permission to go on a picnic. A distant cousin accompanied them, but they had taken her to a friend's house to visit so that they could be alone. She could still hear the birds chirping their love songs and smell the overwhelming sweetness of flowers and the musky, cloying scent of the river as it flowed by. She once again felt the terrific pounding of her heart when her love gently stroked her cheeks before he lovingly captured her lips. His gaze spoke of his adoration for her as he lowered her onto a carpet of flower petals and made her his completely. Unbeknownst to Julia, her features had softened from the memories until she appeared almost pretty.

Suddenly, she scowled and pushed the memory of his face from her mind as she brushed the tears from her eyes. "If only I could tell her the truth, I doubt if Dahlia would still be naive enough to believe in love!" she spat angrily. She flung open her address book to see if there was anyone she had overlooked. Surely there was someone who could loan her the money!

She had already gone begging to all of her old friends for a loan, but not one had offered any help. Some of them even had the gall to smugly lecture her about the dangers of living above her means. One woman in particular had told her that she had gotten what she deserved. To make matters worse, once the merchants and storekeepers learned of her plight, they started to demand payment. Evidently, it mattered little to them that she had been a valued customer for years and had always paid her bills. They had even carried her during the times that she had financial troubles and could not pay promptly. Apparently, the past was a closed book, because some of the merchants had started to make serious threats. One even had the audacity to threaten to repossess the gowns she had purchased for Dahlia.

Why couldn't they understand that she had been forced to do what she had done? It had been so very painful to turn her back on them, but Dahlia's future had been at stake, not hers. Through necessity, all old ties had been severed when she had put her plan into action. Three years had been removed from Dahlia's age—even if she was beautiful, who would want to marry a spinster?—and they were only seen in all of the right places—the theater, the opera, the finest restaurants—and they had been handsomely rewarded. Jacques Broussard, the most sought after bachelor in New Orleans, had been on the verge of proposing, but after his sister had witnessed the fiasco with that dreadful tax man, not one word had been heard from him.

She had even gone to the local banks and businessmen and attempted to secure a loan. But either Oscar Culpepper had issued warnings not to help her, or else they were all waiting like circling vultures for the tax seizure, each hoping to obtain a valuable property for a mere pittance.

Julia shook her head sadly. Poor little Dahlia. She had been so mortified by the entire affair, she had locked herself in her room and not ventured out until three days ago. Naturally the poor child was angry at her mother ... only a saint would not feel bitter. If only there was something she could do ...

"Mother, are you going to answer the door or not?"

Julia spun about on her chair and looked at Dahlia who was standing in the doorway. "What? I'm sorry, I was not ..."

"There is someone at the door and I am not about to open it looking this dreadful!" She sniffed loudly and dabbed at her tear-swollen eyes with a lace handkerchief. "Besides, it may be someone else demanding payment. How could you do this to me, Mother," she whimpered accusingly, "how could you?" Whirling around, Dahlia raced up the stairs.

Julia hurried to follow her daughter, but when she reached the bottom of the staircase, she heard Dahlia slam her door soundly, and she knew the child had once again locked herself in her room.

Frustrated by Dahlia's tantrum and the incessant pounding at the door, Julia decided to answer it instead of chasing hopelessly after Dahlia. If it was another merchant—and who else would be calling?—why give the neighbors more fuel for their gossip? From past experiences, she knew the merchant would pound on the door until it was opened.

"Why, Reverend Smith! This is a surprise!" Julia gasped when she opened the door and saw the minister about to walk down the steps. It had been almost a year since she'd been to church; why was he calling on her now? Surely a man of the cloth would not come to gloat over her misfortunes.

Turning, he said with a nervous smile, "Good afternoon, Sister Stanton." He waited for a moment, then asked, "May I please come in?"

"W-why, yes, of course." She opened the door wider and stepped aside. "Please forgive my lapse of manners," she stammered, ushering him into the parlor.

"Think nothing of it."

"Could I offer you a cup of tea, or coffee perhaps?"

"Either one would be fine, whatever you were about to have," he said, with a wave of his hand.

Julia wanted to scream that tea and coffee were luxuries she could no longer afford on a daily basis, that she had only offered him refreshments to be polite. Instead, she smiled courteously and excused herself.

A few minutes later, Julia returned carrying a tray laden with her porcelain coffee service, a cherished heirloom that had belonged to her mother. Her lips compressed into a thin white line when the Reverend added three heaping teaspoons of her carefully hoarded white sugar to his coffee.

He bobbed his head and muttered appreciatively, "Ah, delicious, simply delicious. But then, you always made the best cup of coffee out of the entire congregation."

"Thank you, Reverend Smith." *You miserly old reprobate! Will you please say what you came to say and then leave! Leave me in peace!*

He clicked his tongue in a scolding manner. "We have been missing you at services, Sister Stanton. Whenever a lamb strays from the flock, it tends to disappoint the Shepherd. But, I have not come to scold you. Instead, I bring good tidings."

"Oh?" Julia's interest piqued slightly. *Good tidings? That would certainly be a change.*

"As you are aware, our congregation is small and not too prosperous. And while we are aware of your plight, at this time we are unable to come to your assistance."

Julia stiffened visibly. "I have not asked for financial help from the church, Reverend Smith. I have never accepted charity, nor do I intend to in the foreseeable future."

He wagged a scolding finger and clicked his tongue, something he did often. "Now, Sister Stanton, you know 'pride goeth before a fall.' "

"Yes, Reverend, but I haven't fallen yet. I still have certain avenues to explore before I admit defeat."

The reverend studied her for a moment before he reached inside his coat pocket, removed an envelope, and exhibited it with a flourish. "I think perhaps this might be an avenue you did not know existed. I have here in my hand a letter from a Mister Richard Grissom, of Clear Creek, Colorado . . ."

Julia frowned when she noticed his secretive, yet eager expression. "To my knowledge I know no one . . ."

"Oh, but you do! Mr. Grissom is inquiring about Angela."

Julia gripped the arm of the settee and spoke, trying desperately to keep a venomous tone from her voice. "Reverend, I am afraid I can offer no information whatsoever about her. Why, Dahlia and I have not heard a word from that ungrateful child since the day she left." She fumbled in her apron pocket for a handkerchief and dabbed at her eyes. "I declare, I do believe that child somehow holds me responsible . . ." her voice trailed off. She took a tremendous breath. "I had no way of knowing the information we received about her father was false." She raised her eyes heavenward and gave a long, pitiful sigh. "Young people nowadays have no sense of gratitude. When I think how I took that poor little orphan into my home, fed her, clothed her, and gave her my love . . . and now she has repaid me by not even letting us know if she is alive or dead."

"You may rest assured that she is very much alive and has even come into extremely good fortune. Well, perhaps not all good," he said slowly, remembering that Angela's father had passed on to his reward before they were reunited, and that the letter he held contained information that indicated legal problems, but he was positive those could be resolved. "But when one considers what might befall a young woman traveling in such un-

301

civilized country alone, I would say that the All Mighty has smiled upon her rather handsomely."

Julia's eyes had narrowed slightly at the reverend's mention of Angela's good fortune. She refilled his coffee cup and added sugar to the dark-roasted chicory brew.

He took a sip and smacked his lips appreciatively before continuing, "This letter from Mr. Grissom . . ." Pausing, he reached into his coat pocket for his spectacles. "It seems that Angela was involved in an accident—now, do not fret, she wasn't injured, but all of her personal belongings were lost."

Julia knew the reverend well enough to let him continue without prodding him. He would relate the story in his own due time.

"Personal belongings can be replaced, but all of her identification was among those lost belongings. That presents a dilemma since she is laying claim to her father's estate—a rather sizable one, I might add."

"Her father's estate?" The implication of his words stunned her beyond belief. "You mean Samuel Langford is dead!" her voice trembled.

"Yes, unfortunately, he passed on just a few weeks before Angela arrived in Clear Creek."

Frowning, Julia realized she was sitting on the very edge of the settee. Forcing herself to lean back and relax, she struggled to keep her voice steady. "I am very sorry to hear about Samuel, but I don't quite understand Angela's dilemma. Except to feel sympathy that she did not have the opportunity to get to know her father," she quickly added. "I recall Samuel being an extremely kind and considerate man. How does his death and the letter . . .?"

"Ah, but Sister Stanton, this Richard Grissom was

Langford's partner. Together, they owned a very rich silver mine. Being men of wealth, and believing neither had any legitimate heirs, each man's estate went to the survivor. One can imagine Grissom's surprise and possible dismay when Angela arrived claiming to be Langford's daughter, and her having no documents to substantiate her claim raised further doubts in his mind. You see, he and Langford had been friends for years. He was there when Langford received word that his wife had died. And, he even claims that Langford received a letter stating that the child died too. Which, as you well know, is utter nonsense."

"So, Angela will probably lose her rightful inheritance," Julia mused aloud. *Maybe there is a degree of justice in this world after all,* she thought as a surge of satisfaction washed through her.

"Yes, unless we can send enough evidence for Angela's claim to stand in court. I intend to write a letter and get all of the congregation to sign it. Then, I shall go to the merchants and everybody who knew Angela and obtain their signatures." He eyed Julia speculatively. "It goes without saying, Sister Stanton, that perhaps the best way to convince this blackguard that we will not allow him to defraud Angela of what is rightfully hers is for the woman who raised that child to write a personal letter on her behalf."

Julia could not show her reluctance to help that ungrateful hussy. Instead, she nodded her head. "Reverend Smith, you do not even have to ask. Consider it already done."

He spread his fingers wide and studied his fingernails carefully. "I am positive Angela will be extremely appreciative. Although it will come too late to be of any immediate financial help to you, she will probably be

303

very generous to . . . the woman who came to her aid, and who knows," he added, shrugging his shoulders. "When she learns how the church helped her secure her rightful inheritance, perhaps she will be generous to our small church as well . . . especially if our endeavors are brought to her attention."

Although Julia struggled to keep her expression calm and devoid of her true emotions, she inwardly seethed with rage and indignation. Why should that ungrateful whelp fall into a substantial inheritance when she and Dahlia were facing such terrible hardships in the near future. It was not fair!

Suddenly a plan began to form in the secret drawers of her mind. Even if she could somehow raise the money enabling them to keep Briarwood and remain in New Orleans, socially, they were ruined. They would always be mistrusted and the source of idle chatter for every gossip in the city. No, they could never rebuild their lives here. It was useless to even consider the idea. However, if she took Dahlia to a different part of the country, perhaps . . . just perhaps . . . she would have to readjust her thinking about society, but if there were enough money involved, it shouldn't be too difficult.

She looked the reverend squarely in the eye and said, "Reverend Smith, I realize that I have tried your patience at times because of what you claim to be a rebellious nature, but I am sure that you would agree that I am a truthful and trustworthy person, wouldn't you? That my present circumstances are due to honest mistakes, and not an attempt to defraud or cheat anyone."

"I completely agree. I have known you for at least fifteen years and have never known you to beat anyone out of a single dime. My only concern has been that you have too much pride and that you have blind vision when it comes to your daughter. You know what the Good Book says about 'spare the rod and spoil the child.' I am afraid you have done that."

Julia swallowed her anger at his callous mention of Dahlia. "The point I am attempting to make is this; if I gave you my word about something, you would be inclined to believe me . . . wouldn't you?"

"Of course I would."

"Then I have a proposition to make. Would you be willing to call the elders of the church together and present them an offer?"

"What offer?" he asked, his eyes narrowing thoughtfully.

"I do not care to live here in New Orleans a day longer than necessary. If you could persuade the elders to loan me enough money to satisfy my tax obligations, I will sell Briarwood, repay the loan, and go to Colorado. I feel that a personal testimony would be more beneficial to Angela than a letter, but of course I would take your letter with me. You know as well as I, that I have a certain amount of influence over Angela, and I am sure she would be extremely generous to the church for any help in establishing her claim to her inheritance. In fact, I will see to it that she is generous. I know the roof is badly in need of repairs, and that you have been wanting to purchase a new organ, refinish the pews, and maybe even enlarge the parsonage. Your quarters are so cramped, I don't see how you and Mrs. Smith have tolerated them through the years."

The reverend stroked his chin thoughtfully. He had hoped and prayed for this very offer, but it was something he could not ask of the woman, it was something she had to offer herself. "You mean you would repay the loan *and* see that Angela made a contribution?"

305

"Most definitely."

"I shall see what I can do." The reverend picked up his hat, eager to be on his way. "I will call the elders together immediately."

Julia leaned against the door, a scheming smile on her face.

She would testify at Angela's legal hearing all right. The main thing was to be flexible. Once she arrived in Clear Creek, she could finalize her plans and decide on a course of action. Then, if all went well, she could lay the world at Dahlia's feet. Paris, New York, any exotic city they fancied. She laughed aloud. And to think she would owe it all to Samuel, the man who had callously walked away and left her to face the humiliating consequences of her love, and live with a broken heart. Perhaps there was truth in the old adage that all good things come to people who wait. One thing was certain, she had patience, and she had been waiting for a long, long time.

Chapter Twenty-Two

The morning was heralded by a pleasurable combination of dazzling sunshine and the melodious singing and cries of jays, rosy finches, and mountain bluebirds perched high within the trees about the clearing.

Clint had gathered wood to build a small, smokeless fire so they could make coffee with their basket lunch and to help ward off the chill in the air.

Once the small animals had overcome their fears of both man and the fire—perhaps sensing they were in no real danger from either—they scampered aimlessly about, darting in and out of the forest's edge.

One fearless porcupine waddled by, looked at Clint and Angela curiously, then proceeded unerringly on its way.

Several large tree squirrels with tassels on their ears, chattered noisily in the midst of the ponderosas.

After they had eaten, Clint reclined against the base of a large tree, and Angela lay with her back resting against his chest. She placed her arm on his thigh and trailed small circles on his kneecap with her fingertip.

His arms were wrapped firmly around her waist, and he occasionally lowered his head and inhaled the delicate fragrance of her raven-colored hair. It was a gentle, loving time that reached far beyond burning passion and fervent desire into something that seemed almost sacred. It was nourishment for their souls.

"It is so beautiful and peaceful up here," Angela murmured, gazing about wondrously. "I believe I could stay here forever. No, I *know* I could if you were here with me."

Clint looked at the carpet of brown and tan grass scattered with fallen pine needles and leaves. His keen gaze detected a deer grazing on the far side of them. "You have no idea how beautiful this is in the late spring and early summer when the grass is green and blanketed with every color of wild flower imaginable. I'm not surprised that you find it so peaceful up here. This was my favorite place to come when I was a boy."

He smiled sheepishly at her. "You have no idea how many wars were won and lost here. How many dragons were slain in this meadow." He pointed across the way. "And over there are the remains of a stone fort where I held off hordes of savage Indians."

He chuckled. "One winter I read Daniel Defoe's *Robinson Crusoe* . . . I think about five times. The following summer I pretended the pines were an ocean and the meadow was a deserted island. I suppose it stuck in my mind that goats were a factor in his survival." He chuckled again. "Needless to say, that was also the year I tangled with a Bighorn sheep and lost. Darn thing almost killed me!"

"You make it sound amusing, but I have an idea that it wasn't all that funny at the time."

"No, it wasn't. Scared me more than I'd like to admit. In fact, I take great pleasure when I wear my fleece-lined coat now." He snuggled his arms around her. "Are you warm enough?"

"I sure am." She raised one of his hands to her mouth and lightly brushed her lips across his palm while she watched two squirrels chasing each other on a far limb. "It's strange, I never knew there would be so much animal life this high in the mountains, especially this time of year. I guess I thought they all migrated to the lowlands at the first sign of winter."

"I guess that's the natural assumption someone from a southern climate would make. You've only seen a few animals. There are countless numbers of others that don't let themselves be seen, but you can rest assured that they are out there watching us right now. When we leave and the wind blows our scents away, they'll venture out of hiding and this meadow will be like it was before . . . maybe even for the last hundred years or so. It's odd how time seems to stand still up here. One day stretches into another and into another . . ."

Clint placed his fingers under her chin and tilted her face upward. "Speaking of animals, I think that you are a little minx disguised as a woman."

She turned about to face him and asked laughingly, "What do you mean?"

"What were you trying to do to me at the breakfast table this morning when you trailed your foot up and down my leg and made all those suggestive remarks?"

She demurely lowered her gaze. "I was only trying to spark your memory of a more *pleasurable* time."

He raised her chin with a gentle touch. "You sparked more than just my memory. Haven't I been tortured enough lately?"

Her eyes widened innocently. "Torture never entered

my mind. I was contemplating something entirely different."

Clint grinned at her. "All right. You've excited my interest, what exactly did you have on your devious little mind?"

Her cheeks colored under the heat of his gaze, but her voice was smooth and silky. "Actually, I had intended to ask you to give me a more extensive tour of the ranch. But I have to admit; it would have been because I had an ulterior motive. Touring the ranch would not have been my true purpose."

Clint devoured Angela's beauty. Her hair had been combed back into a classic chignon, but around her hairline, tiny wispy curls had formed. He thought no woman had ever been more beautiful. Her wide, silvery gray eyes darkened while he gazed at her. Was it a stray shadow or the subtle stirring of passion? Her lips, rosier than usual, were full and moist. It seemed as though they were demanding to be kissed.

Squinting, his voice lowered huskily, "That sounds crafty and underhanded to me."

"No, desperate would be a better word to describe it."

At the expression on her face, he threw back his head and chortled heartily. "What would have compelled a sweet, angelic woman like you to commit an act of such devious, crafty, underhanded desperation?"

Imitating one of Clint's favorite facial gestures, she jiggled her brows and grinned lecherously. "You."

"Me?"

"Yes. You."

"Why?"

"Seduction."

A naughty smile spread across his lips. His brows

arched mischievously. "Oooh, seduction, you say? Sounds interesting. Tell me more."

Her gray eyes shone like silver lightning as she studied his face unhurriedly, feature by feature. "I was trying to think of a way to get you alone so that I could proceed to seduce you. But your dad solved that dilemma when he suddenly suggested we go for an outing." She dramatically pressed the back of her hand against her brow. "But now that the problem of getting you alone was so easily resolved by your father, I suppose all that devious scheming was for naught."

"How do you figure that?"

"It seems to me that seducing you away from the house and into my arms is unnecessary now that your dad has decided to let us have time alone together."

Clint chewed on his bottom lip while pretending to ponder her statement. Finally, he feigned a regretful sigh. "Well, darn, the thought of being seduced was rather exciting there for a few minutes. Tell me, how were you planning on going about it?"

"Going about what?" she teased.

"Seducing me. Just how would you go about it?"

"Well, let me think. First, I'd have you lie down."

Clint immediately scooted down on the blanket until he was lying prone, causing her to fall temporarily off balance. "Like this?"

"Why yes!" she replied with mock surprise as she quickly righted herself.

Angela's senses were already aflame with the nearness of him, her head reeled from their dizzying onslaught. Slowly, she bent forward and unfastened the buttons on his shirt. "Then I planned to flutter my eyelashes at you like this—" Rapidly fluttering her lashes, she parted his shirt. "And touch you like this—" She

311

trailed her fingertips over the dark fur of his chest. "Then kiss you like this—" She nibbled teasingly at his lower lip, then gently pressed her lips to his.

Instinctively, he reached out to encircle her with his arms, but she withdrew from his embrace. "Oh, no, you're not supposed to do that. I'm seducing you, remember? All that you're supposed to do is lie back and enjoy being seduced."

Instantly, he dropped his hands to his side. "Sweetheart, if I start enjoying this any more, I don't know if I can stand it."

"Now, let's see, where was I?" she asked in a soft, sensual voice.

"You were kissing me," he quickly reminded her. "And doing a very good job of it, I might add."

"Ah, so I was." Angela was surprised by her boldness. But their relationship seemed so right, so honest, so loving; there remained no room for reluctance or shyness.

"May I request a favor?" he asked.

"I suppose."

"Could you remove the pins and combs from your hair?"

Wordlessly, she reached up and removed both, then ruffled her fingers through the midnight-colored tresses until they fluffed into soft curls around her shoulders. "Now, is that better?" she asked coyly.

"It certainly is." His eyes devoured her loveliness.

Slowly, leisurely, she pulled her blouse from the waistband of her skirt, then began to unfasten the buttons. Once the bodice was open and the lacy undergarment beneath revealed, she lowered her upper torso onto his chest. The pressure of his chest against her breasts shaped them into perfect cleavage.

312

His eyes focused on the tantalizing sight, and his tongue darted out to moisten his suddenly dry lips.

"Are your lips dry, sweetheart?" she asked, her tone alluring and provocative.

Clint's throat felt parched. His voice cracked when he replied. "They sure are."

She traced the outline of his generous mouth with the tip of her tongue. "Is that better?" she murmured, trying to sound unaffected although her face was flushed and her body trembled with desire.

"My mouth is dry, too."

"I suppose I could do something about that." Lowering her lips to his, she kissed him, darting her tongue in and out with timid thrusts. She felt his heart beating a staccato rhythm beneath his chest and a quick glance at the incredible bulge in his trousers revealed a need as urgent as hers.

Angela fumbled with the buttons on his trousers, but her hands trembled too badly to unfasten them. She looked at him imploringly. "Clint, I think there has been enough of this foolishness. I want you so badly, I ache inside."

Clint needed no further urging. He deftly kicked off his boots, then squirmed out of his trousers and shirt. He gave Angela one long, questioning look, then shrugged and covered his middle with a blanket before removing his underwear and tossing the garment aside. "Clint, you will freeze," she protested because although the day was warm for so late in the year, there was still a nip in the air.

"Not the way my blood is boiling," he muttered hoarsely. "Now, let me help you."

With a tantalizing slowness, he unbuttoned the waistband of her skirt and tugged it, along with her petticoats, down over her slender hips while she removed her blouse. She started to unlace the ribbons that held her chemise together, but Clint stopped her.

"Let me do it."

Each time he pulled the ribbon from an eyelet, he kissed the silken flesh that he exposed. She shivered, but he knew it was not from the cold.

In a matter of moments—or was it hours?—she was undressed except for the opened chemise. Her eyes had taken on an unnatural shine, her gleaming black hair was tousled, her cheeks were rosy as were the delicate swells of her breasts. To Clint, she had never looked lovelier.

Slowly, he lowered her to the blanket-swathed ground. Eyes half-closed, she placed her hands at the back of his neck and brought his mouth down to her eager lips. Her blood was like quicksilver as it pounded with the force of a raging river through her veins.

Clint's mouth searched until it found the small, sensitive place on her shoulder he had discovered before and teased the spot relentlessly with teeth and tongue until she made soft mewing sounds of delight.

Trailing kisses down the slender column of her throat, his mouth found her breasts. Lightly, his mustache brushed her nipples and his tongue darted and flicked until they were hard little peaks of excitement, aching for his caresses. His deft fingers slid slowly over the darkened crests; his thumbs flicked at the tiny buds. He took one small button in his mouth and she gasped from the sheer pleasure of it. Languidly, he sucked and tasted until soft moans of delight emitted from Angela's throat. His teeth closed gently around the dark tip, nuzzling and nibbling at it, all the while his tongue swirled around in the most sensual manner. The result sent ripples of ecstasy racing in all directions.

His lips then closed over the other nipple, paying homage to it exactly as he had its mate.

Angela cradled Clint's head, stroking his dark hair with trembling hands as his tongue titillated her breasts until liquid fire coursed through her body, blinding her to everything but her need for him.

His hand traveled slowly down the length of her body, then slid down to her legs, his fingers teasing like silky feathers while they trailed along the insides of her thighs. They moved up, then down, again and again, tormenting her with rapturous delight.

This his fingers slipped in to stroke the length of her with gentle fluttering movements that made her loins quicken unbearably. He stroked and played her like a master musician caressing a priceless violin. The little flower of her secret place budded beneath the heat of his fingers, its delicate petals unfurling until it blossomed in wild profusion.

A passionate moan escaped Angela's lips, her breath became rapid and uneven. She trembled uncontrollably at the delicious sensations Clint aroused in her until she was wet and warm where he touched her. She yearned for him to fill her completely, to make her his once again.

As Clint sought to bring Angela to the peak of passion, his need for her reached a towering height and was climbing further. His mind was filled with swirling, dizzying thoughts of Angela, which flooded through him like a tidal wave, sweeping all realms of sanity away.

Angela's mouth found his and it grew hot inside, tingling where her tongue pillaged it, devoured it. She could not get enough of him.

She felt as though she was a piece of fragile silk that had been engulfed in the raging flames of passion that he unleashed inside of her. She moaned and writhed with fiery desire.

Wild with need, Clint rose and poised above her, and began the wondrous descent into the beckoning chasm. The walls of her hot, scorching flesh closed around him, searing until a glistening sheen of perspiration beaded over his entire body. His masculinity throbbed, pulsating from the heat.

Then, slowly, when Clint could trust himself to move, he began to thrust in and out of her, in a primitive, yet rhythmic tempo.

Angela clung to him, her arms wrapped around his back so that she could feel the rippling of his tautly corded muscles. Her breasts tingled against his hair-roughened chest. She arched her hips and met each of his thrusts with thrusts of her own. Her womanhood caressed and stroked his maleness until his mind became incapable of thought or rationality.

He moved harder, faster, with longer and deeper thrusts which she strained to meet.

Her head grew light and she flew along the rapturous path, faster and faster, until she was suffused with endless waves of pure ecstasy.

At precisely the same moment, Clint plummeted forward one final time, his essence merging with hers in a blissfully voluptuous climax.

It sat in the shadows, cocking its head from side to side, watching. Somewhere in the dark recesses of its small brain, it tried to reason, tried to formulate thoughts. But that seemed an impossibility.

There was a form of memory though. An instinctive memory that caused a deep sadness, a loneliness to envelop him.

Once, he'd had a mate, but she was gone now, she had left a long time ago and that was when the loneliness had begun.

He saw a shiny stick leaning against the conveyance that the humans sat on and moved across the land. His eyes glinted with rage when he recognized it. Such a stick had made a thundering noise like the clouds when they darkened and rolled ominously in the sky. The sound and acrid scent of that stick had taken his beloved mate from him.

It was the only thing he had ever feared, other than the strange creatures who now mated on the ground.

He was too afraid to move, afraid that the stick would point at him and make a noise. Rage and fear constricted his throat.

Angela fitted her hairpins and combs back into place, then smoothed her skirt over her hips. "Will I pass your father's inspection, my love?" she asked, gently brushing a few blades of dry grass from Clint's shirt.

"You certainly pass mine."

Just when Clint was about to lower his lips to Angela's, a bloodcurdling, horrifying screech wailed through the thin mountain air. Her eyes widened fearfully, but before she could scream, Clint's expression turned dark and thunderous.

"Son-of-a-bitch!" he shouted. "It's Dad and his damned dumbull!"

Chapter Twenty-Three

Angela grasped the planking at the back and right side of the heavy springed seat while the wagon clamored over the rough, overgrown mountain path at a frightening rate. Her heart thudded beneath her breast. Her face was pale and drawn, and her eyes were as wide and bright as newly minted silver coins. While they bounded forward at impossible speeds, fear of a serious accident added to the fear of what Clint might do to his father for having pulled such a childish prank.

"I can't believe he did that," Clint muttered through tight lips, his face granite hard while he slapped the reins harder. "I can't believe he would invade our privacy like that."

Neither could Angela. Just the thought that Tom might have gone out there to spy on them after having been the one to suggest they spend some time alone made her feel both angry and violated. Had he watched the whole time they made love? If so, she wasn't sure she could ever forgive him. And to do something like that just when he and Clint had started to put their petty differences aside—what could have gotten into Tom to make him do such a thing?

318

Angela's grip tightened on the seat when Clint, in a jangle of harnesses and the grinding of the metal brake, brought the buckboard to an abrupt halt in front of the barn.

"Go to the house and pack our belongings," he said as he jumped to the ground and headed immediately for the barn. "I will not sleep under that man's roof another night. Not after what he just did."

Angela's eyes widened further still. "Where are you going?"

"To wait for him inside the barn. I have a few choice words I intend to say to my father and I think they'd best be said without you there."

Although still angry herself, for Tom had spoiled their first moment of intimacy in quite some time, Angela feared what Clint might say to him. "Clint, when he returns, promise that you won't do or say anything rash. Please don't say something you might later regret."

"I doubt I'll ever regret what I have to say. Get on to the house and start packing. I want to be out of here before dark." He turned and headed toward the barn, again muttering angrily to himself. "I still can't believe he would pull something like that."

"And what if he didn't? What if it wasn't him?" Angela said, willing to give the man the benefit of the doubt, at least until they had heard his side. "What if we've made a mistake?"

"The only mistake we made was in trusting him."

"But what if it wasn't him?" She shuddered at an equally disturbing thought. "What if it was someone else?"

"No one else I know has a dumbull hidden away inside a feed bin ready to use if and when cattle rustlers

319

or a pack of renegades cross our land again. And no one else knew where we were headed."

Angela frowned. "Since you know where your father keeps the thing, why don't you go see if that dumbull is still there before condemning him for the rest of his life?"

Clint pressed his lips together, wanting to believe it true. "Wouldn't prove much. Could be he beat us back here and had just enough time to put it back." His eyes then widened. "But that would mean having ridden Champ back at breakneck speed. I'll be able to tell if it was Dad by the condition of his horse. Wait here."

When Clint hurried into the barn, the scent of leather, horses, and hay wafted over him like an invisible cloak. He walked over to the roan's stall and realized at a glance that the horse was not saddled and showed no signs of having been ridden hard. Reaching out to pat the animal's cool neck, he doubted the horse had been ridden at all that day. A quick inspection of the other three saddle horses revealed the same thing, and a quick peek into the feed bin at the back of the barn revealed the dumbull half buried beneath an odd assortment of ropes, bits, and broken harnesses. Obviously, he had sorely misjudged his father.

He returned to the wagon immediately and supplied Angela with the answer before she had time to ask her question. "Unless he sprouted wings and flew, it wasn't Dad."

He looked beyond the wagon and saw his father headed toward them.

"Clint, Angie, what's wrong?" Tom was gasping for breath by the time he reached the buckboard.

Angela felt both guilty and confused, for now she, like Clint, had no idea who had spied on them. She blinked several times while she tried to figure out what to say, then smoothed the tell-tale lines in her forehead and shrugged innocently. "What makes you think something is wrong?"

Tom's took several more breaths, then looked at her with a peculiar expression, as if not sure what to think. "Because a person doesn't come tearing into a barnyard like the devil himself was giving chase without something being wrong." He looked at Clint. "Son, you wouldn't misuse horses that way without a good reason. Now suppose you tell me what happened out there? If there's trouble brewing, I should know about it."

He then turned to look in the direction they had come as if hoping to find the answer out there. "Was it that Dane Tapley? I know I haven't said nothing about it but I was hoping he had left this part of the country. After all, it's been over a month since he made such a big scene in town and you haven't heard another word from him." He looked at Clint again. "Is that it? Has he been holed up in the mountains somewhere waiting for the chance to catch you alone and unarmed?" He slapped his thigh when he thought more about it. "I should have known he'd pull something like that."

"No, it had nothing to do with Dane," Clint said, a little stunned that his father recognized the fact he would never misuse a horse like that. Was it possible he *could* do something right in his father's eyes? "Besides, I heard that Dane hurt his right hand pretty bad in a fight just a couple of days after that little show he put on in town. If that's so, it'll be awhile before I have to worry about him trying to call me out like that again. He isn't going to do anything until he's sure that hand is at its best."

Tom scratched the side of his head. "Then what happened out there? What made you come tearing in here like that?"

Clint did not want to lie to his father, so he tried to avoid the question as Angela sometimes did, by asking one of his own. "And where were you that you could see us return like that? I didn't see you out in the yard."

"I was up under the back porch putting a nail to that board that keeps sinking," he said, but was not about to be so easily manipulated. "I spotted you long before you reached the side pasture. It just took me a minute to wiggle out from under there. So, quit all this jawing and tell me what happened."

Aware he had no other choice for his father was not going to let the matter drop, Clint looked at Angela, then back at his father. "I hate to admit to having lost my temper like this, but the truth was, I was very angry when I came riding in here. So was Angela."

Tom looked at Angela curiously and noticed she did not look all that upset, just baffled. Then he looked at Clint again. "Angry? At who?"

"You. We thought you had followed us—"

Tom's eyebrows dipped with further confusion when he interrupted, "Now why would I go and do a fool thing like that? I have better things to do with my time than to go poking my nose into places where it has no business. What could make you think I'd want to come up there and try to horn in on your picnic? After all, I'm the one who suggested it."

Clint's forehead twisted into a perplexed frown for he now had no explanation for the strange noise they had heard. "Angela and I had just finished our lunch when suddenly we heard the awfullest noise—"

"Well, I don't see what hearing a noise has to do with—" He blinked twice when he remembered he had

322

passed gas about ten minutes earlier, but knew that had not been heard all the way up to the high pasture.

Clint remained patient despite his father's constant interruptions. "Truth is, it sounded exactly like that old dumbull of yours. When I heard it, I just assumed you were out there pulling some sort of prank."

Tom shook his head. "But I haven't had that old thing out in years. Haven't had to."

Clint nodded to indicate he believed him, but his forehead was still notched with uncertainty. "Do you know anybody else around here who has one of those things?"

"No, not that I know of." Tom twisted his face while he thought about it, then he relaxed his shoulders as a peculiar gleam flickered from his eyes. Glancing casually from Clint to Angela, he rocked back and forth on his heels and tried to look extremely serious when he said, "Perhaps it was old George come back to stalk us."

Clint let out an exasperated breath. "The only place that ugly creature stalks is in the back of your muddled brain where you first made him up," he said with a flat expression. "You know as well as I do George never existed." The three glanced off toward the area where Clint and Angela had heard the sound. "No, it had to be someone else with a dumbull."

"But why would they be using the thing on my land?"

"I don't know, but I sure do intend to find out," Clint said, then his dark gaze brightened. "I know who it was. It was Amos. He's gotten so bored living up in that shack that he's come down to cause a little havoc." He narrowed his eyes. "Wait till I get a hold of that scrawny little neck of his. He'll regret the day he ever pulled such a stunt." Although eager for retribution, Clint felt relieved. He knew Amos would enjoy the sport of stirring up trouble but would not have stood there watching them like a lecher. Truth was, the way old Amos's eyesight was lapsing, all he could have seen from that distance was a moving blur.

"Don't know that it could have been Amos," Tom said, sounding doubtful. "I don't think he knows what a dumbull is. I never let him in on what I was doing back then for fear he might get a little too tipsy one night in town and tell off on me."

"Well, he must have found out about them from someone," Clint said, then grinned when he realized the perfect reprisal. "I just hope he realizes, two can play at this game."

Clint waited until an hour before dark before hitching the team back to the wagon. Because Angela wanted to take part in the retaliation and had yet to learn to ride a saddle horse, they had decided to take the wagon as far as a wooded cove above the shack, then walk the last quarter mile.

Due to the unseasonably warm weather they had had for the past few days, there was little snow on the ground and the icy patches of mud that formed each night were confined to the shaded areas beneath the trees. They had little trouble getting to the front of the shack unnoticed.

"Why isn't there a light glowing in the window?" Angela asked with a faint whisper as she knelt beside Clint, who sat behind a wooden wellhouse only a few dozen yards from the shack. She pulled her cloak tighter while waiting for his answer. Now that the sun had gone down the temperature had already dropped to the low forties.

"Because the old reprobate usually goes to bed right after the sun sets," Clint said in a voice so hushed it was hard for Angela to tell if he was still as angry as he had been earlier.

He set the dumbull in front of him and grabbed the thong between his thumb and fingers, and again whispered in a voice so low it could barely be heard. "His having gone to bed will just help us to catch him that much more unaware."

Despite the dim light from the silvery half-moon, Angela could see a malevolent smile cross Clint's face. "Wait'll he hears this."

She looked at the strange drum with some doubt, not certain she believed it could make the horrible noise Clint claimed.

"Arughaurgh!" wailed the dumbull when Clint pulled the thong. "Arughaurgh!"

The noise was so unexpectedly loud and abrasive, Angela gasped and fell back into the dried grass, her hand covering her breast as if hoping to keep her pounding heart from bursting right out of her.

Clint chuckled devilishly then pulled the thong again. "Arughaurghhh!"

Angela spun about when she thought she heard a similar noise come from the woods directly behind them, only it had sounded as if it were some distance away. "Did you hear that?"

"What's more important—" Clint said with another soft chuckle, "—did *Amos* hear that."

"No, I mean that noise behind us," she said in a strained whisper while she scanned the shadows be-

325

yond. "It sounded just like your dumbull only it came from over there somewhere."

Clint shrugged, his gaze fastened on the only door leading into the small shack. "I didn't hear anything. It must have been an echo off the next mountain. Don't worry, there's nothing out there. At least nothing that can make a sound like this thing."

Angela wasn't so sure. "Do echoes wait several seconds before coming back to you?"

But Clint was too interested in what was *not* happening inside the dark cabin to hear the question. "He should have come barreling out of there by now. I guess maybe his hearing is going too. Come on. Let's move closer."

Standing to a crouched position, he hooked the dumbull under his arm then darted toward the house with lightning speed. He knelt again just outside one of the only two windows, then motioned for her to follow.

He waited until she was beside him before pulling the cord again.

"Arughaurghhh!"

Angela listened for another echo, but this time heard none.

"Is the old geezer getting *that* deaf in his old age?" Clint muttered, then stood just to the side of the window. "Wait here."

Angela did as told and watched while he stepped over to the door. With the dumbull held ready under his left arm, he reached to turn the latch. Then, at the same moment he kicked the door open, he screeched the dumbull. She listened for Amos's response, but all she heard was Clint stomping around in the dark, calling the old man by name.

"Amos? Amos Kieffer? Where are you?"

326

By the time she had entered the cabin, Clint had struck a match and was touching the flame to a small lantern just inside the door while he looked around the shack with a baffled expression. Other than a wooden bed with a rolled-up mattress, a small table with one bench and two chairs, and a rough-wood cabinet that stood open against the far wall, the small one-room cabin was empty.

"Where is he?"

"Not here," he stated the obvious, then flattened his mouth to show his disappointment. When he slapped the table in a moment of frustration, it left an imprint of his hand in the dust. "And by the looks of things he moved out weeks ago."

He wiped his dusty hand on the back of his trousers and frowned. "Well, that sure wasn't much fun," he muttered with a shrug, not wanting Angela to know how truly perplexed he was. Now he had two mysteries to solve. He still had no idea who could have pulled the prank on them that afternoon and now he had no idea where Amos Kieffer had gone. It wasn't like him to leave the area without telling them first, and where would he go at this time of year? They still had several months of harsh winter ahead.

Angela worried more with each day's passing. For the past several weeks, Clint had behaved very strangely toward her, as if he suddenly wanted to distance himself from her. Whenever she asked to join him for a ride, whether he was headed out to check on a fenceline or to go into town for supplies, he refused to let her ride along. His excuse was that she had not yet learned to ride a horse and the roads were too bad this time of year to take the wagon; but she knew the roads could be no worse than they had been before, because it had not snowed or rained but once in all that time and then only briefly. If anything the roads were probably in much better shape for traveling with the mud having dried.

So why was Clint so adamant that she stay home whenever he went anywhere? And why did he balk whenever she suggested she be taught to ride so she could have the freedom of going where she wanted when she wanted, even during the winter months?

Obviously Clint had started having second thoughts about her. Perhaps the newness of their relationship had worn off and he now saw her for what little she really was. It was just as possible he had become ashamed of being seen with a woman so plain and wanted to be rid of her, but just didn't know how to go about freeing himself.

If that was the case, there was nothing she could do to change the situation; but if there was another reason why he kept demanding she stay home whenever he went off, she wanted to know that too. She decided the time had come to learn to ride a horse. That way he could no longer use her inability to join him as an excuse to leave her behind.

Later that same afternoon, while Clint was gone to a neighboring ranch to help repair a hay barn that had caught fire the week before, Angela asked Tom if he would show her how to ride.

"Sure thing," he said, nodding that he too thought it a good idea. "But I don't know nothing about riding sidesaddle like most city women do and I don't have one of those twisted up saddles. You'll have to learn to ride astraddle like I do." He frowned, causing deep wrinkles to form at the corners of his eyes. "But you got nothing to wear for that. Tell you what, for now I'll loan you a pair of my britches. You can belt them on real tight and roll up the legs. Should work until you can get into town and buy yourself one of those split riding skirts."

"I won't have to wait until then. I've still got some of that material left that Clint bought our first day back. I'll make my own riding skirt. In fact I'll get started on it tonight so I'll be ready to go the next time Clint tells me he's headed into town," she said, following Tom to his bedroom where he promptly produced a pair of brown trousers and a worn leather belt. Within minutes after he had left to go saddle the horse, she was dressed in the awkward looking trousers along with a dark blue flannel shirt she had found in the top drawer of his dresser.

By the time she entered the barn, Tom had his tamest horse saddled and was ready to give Angela her first lesson. To both their surprise, Angela had a natural sense of the horse's rhythm and took to riding right away.

Tom cackled with glee when she dismounted later that afternoon and handed him the reins. "Won't Clint be surprised when the next time he goes into town, he finds out you can go with him."

"Won't he?" Angela said, hoping that surprised was all he would be, because if he proved to be angry, too, it could mean only one thing. He no longer wanted her with him when he was around other people. And if that was how he felt, she might as well start making other plans for herself. She would not force Clint to marry her out of obligation. She loved him too much for that.

Chapter Twenty-four

Clint had the strangest sensation he was being watched, but a studied search of the woodlands on both sides of the road offered no reason for him to think he was anything but alone. Nothing moved but the tops of the trees high over his head. Still, the hair at the back of his neck stood out as if to warn him of some danger.

Ever since that day at the pond, it had felt to him as if someone was out there, biding his time, waiting for the perfect opportunity to catch him off guard. But why? He'd checked on Dane Tapley and was told he spent most of his time in town talking big about his plans for the notorious Clint Rutledge while he carefully nursed both a broken right hand and an open whiskey bottle.

As far as anyone Clint had talked with knew, there were no other known gunfighters in the area, no one else who might want to get the jump on him just to add another notch to a deadly reputation. Other than Dane, no one known for living by the gun had come into town in the past month, and with winter right on them, very few people were coming in at all.

Still, Clint could not shake the feeling of being followed. While continuing to scrutinize everything within his peripheral vision, he glanced down to make sure his father's rifle was still where he could easily get to it. Although he had not yet pulled his pistols and holster out for fear Angela would notice and want to know why, he knew it would be downright foolish to be out in such wilderness without some form of protection. The forests were full of savage creatures—some animal, some man.

That was why he refused to let Angela join him whenever he left the house. If someone was indeed out there, stalking him again, he did not want her getting caught in the cross fire. Nor did he want her worrying about his safety whenever he had to leave the house, which was why he had yet to tell her of his suspicions. Nor had he mentioned the picnic at the pond again, for fear she too would worry that the sound they'd heard had been something to lure him into the woods where he could more easily be shot. The less she knew of his suspicions, the better—for her own sake.

"I'd like to go with you," Angela said when Clint announced a week later that he was headed into town right after breakfast to see if he could get a new pulley for the hay loft. "I would like to speak with Mr. Grissom again. I want to be sure that letter he promised to write to Reverend Smith got off."

"Then it won't be necessary for you to go. I can stop in and ask him for you," Clint stated matter-of-factly. "But I can't imagine the man not sending that letter off right away. I should think he'd want this matter settled just as quickly as you."

Angela felt her stomach muscles tighten as suddenly

331

it felt like her heart was pumping ice water. The time for truth was upon them. "Still, I'd like to go with you. I have a few things I'd like to buy while in town."

"Make a list. I'll get them for you." Clint said and reached for his coffee cup, unaware of the expectant look Angela and his father had just exchanged.

"You know, son, I think it might be a good idea for Angela to go along with you. It looks to me like it will be another sunny day, and she's been cooped up in this old house for nigh on three weeks."

Clint took a long sip of the dark brew, then set the cup down before stating in a clear, but calm voice, "I don't want to take the wagon. The roads are too rutted right now and it would slow me down too much. I want to get back in time to replace that broken pulley before dark."

"Wouldn't have to take the wagon," Tom said, already rising from his chair. "I'll saddle up Jeannie for her."

Clint shot him a venomous glare. "You know as well as I do Angela doesn't know how to ride a horse. She could get hurt."

"By riding Jeannie?" Tom asked with a notched brow. "I doubt that. Those two get along as if they were meant for each other."

Angela watched Clint's frown deepen and knew right then he had no intention of letting her go, whether in a wagon or on a horse. She tried to swallow back the pain that the realization caused.

Clint glared at his father. Every muscle in his body had gone rigid. "And why would you say those two get along as if they were meant for each other?"

Tom looked at Clint with uncertainty. "Just that

Angela has been riding off and on for a week now and I think she's ready to go as far as town."

Clint cut his angry gaze to Angela whose round eyes made her look as guilty as sin. "Is that true? Have you been learning to ride behind my back?"

"I-I wanted to surprise you," she said, uncertain how to handle such a sudden burst of anger. "Like your father said, I'm tired of sitting home all the time. I'd like to be able to go into town now and again to be with other people."

"So what you are saying is that I'm not good enough company for you." He scraped his chair back and glowered at her, furious with both of them for having complicated matters. "And just how long have you felt that way?"

Angela narrowed her eyes, thinking that was a ridiculous conclusion. "You know I enjoy your company as much as ever, but that doesn't mean I wouldn't like to get out every now and then to talk to other people. I really would like to speak with Mr. Grissom about a few things, and I'd even like the chance to visit with Sadie again."

"Sadie?" Tom said, his gaze softening at the mere mention of her name. "Come to think of it, there are a few things I need in town, too. Maybe I'll go along, too."

"Too?" Clint responded icily. "I haven't agreed that Angela can go with me yet."

Tom shrugged, then looked at Clint with an arched eyebrow as if daring him to argue further. "Then she can ride in with me. That way neither of us will have to put up with your foul mood any more today."

Clint looked at his father, then at Angela, and realized they were both determined to go against him on this.

Curling his hands into fists, he pounded the table with such force his coffee cup jumped two inches. "I hope the two of you enjoy your trip," he ground out. "Just don't bother looking me up while you are in town. I have too many things of my own to do."

Having said that, he stormed out of the room, leaving the back door open in his haste to get his horse saddled and be on his way. If there *was* someone out there waiting to catch him unaware, he wanted to be well ahead of Angela and his father. He'd not risk their lives for something as foolish as a gunfight.

Angela fought the burning rush of tears while she stared disbelieving at the open door. It was clear now that Clint did not want any of his friends seeing them together. He did not want anyone reminded of the mistake he had made by asking her to marry him. A sharp pain pierced her heart when she wondered if one of the many *things* he had to do while in town involved another woman.

"I'll just be a few minutes with Mr. Grissom," Angela told Tom after they had tethered their horses in front of Buchanan's general store.

"Sure you don't want me to walk you over?" Tom asked, looking around at how many of the men already stared at her as if she were the most pleasing sight in all of Clear Creek—which he knew she very well might be.

"No, you go ahead and tell Jake what we need so he can be putting the order together while I go have my talk. I'll meet you at Sadie's in about half an hour."

"Half an hour? I though you said you were only going to be a few minutes."

"I meant at the mining office," Angela explained, wanting Tom and Sadie to have a little extra time alone. Although Tom would never admit it, he was smitten by the brash yet beautiful Scottish lady. "I also plan to walk over to the stage office and see if I can get a letter to Susan. I'm worried that we haven't heard about that baby by now."

"But you shouldn't let that worry you none. The road between here and there is down, remember? A new route won't be cut until sometime next spring. Any messages between their house and here would have to go the long way around. Probably would have to go back down to Silverlode, then up again the north route. It could take weeks before we know if they've got a girl or a boy."

"Still, I want her to know I am thinking of her," she said. And she also wanted her to know that she might yet take her up on that offer of a place to stay if she could not secure other arrangements with Sadie later.

Now that she knew that Clint's feelings toward her had changed, she needed to find somewhere else to live. She also would have to find some way to support herself, though that should not be too hard in a town with so many men and so few wives. Everywhere she looked there was a shirt that needed mending or a pair of trousers in need of washing. If she could just talk Sadie into letting her stay the first week on credit, then she should be able to make a place for herself until spring.

Tom was too eager to be alone with Sadie to argue with Angela. If she wanted to send a letter that could take anywhere from two weeks to five months getting there, so be it. Susan would probably enjoy hearing from her. "I'll tell Sadie to expect you in half an hour then."

"It might be even longer. But I'll try to hurry," Angela said as she stepped off the boardwalk onto what had looked to be firm ground. But the lumpy ground crumbled beneath her feet, making the walk just as awkward as if it were still mud.

Tom waited just long enough to make sure Angela had crossed the street and entered the alley where most of the mining offices stood before hurrying into the mercantile to give Jake his list.

Angela paused outside the door to Grissom's office to brush a few wrinkles out of the split riding skirt she had made, then sucked in a fortifying breath, lifted her chin, and turned the knob.

"Mr. Grissom. I'd like a word with you."

Richard Grissom looked up from a report he was reading. His narrow shoulders stiffened when he saw who had entered. "I've not heard a word from your Reverend Smith. Don't expect to for months yet."

"I know. I just wanted to be sure you got the letter off and I also wanted to ask you a few things about my father." It was time to delve deeper into the enigma that was her father.

"Like what?"

Angela glanced around. "May I sit down first?"

Grissom grimaced and gestured toward the nearest chair. "I'm sorry. Of course. Sit down. But I must warn you, I have only a minute because I have an important meeting at the land office at eleven."

"This should take only a few minutes," she said, sinking into the chair, yet keeping her back stiff and her head high. "But I want to know a few things that I think only you can tell me."

"Such as?" Grissom asked as he took his seat. While sitting forward with his hands neatly folded on top of the desk, he studied the girl's determined expression, admiring both her beauty and her courage. More and more he hoped it turned out this really was Samuel's daughter. He wouldn't mind taking the young lass under his wing and teaching her all there was to know about silver mining.

Angela felt something tug at her heart, but she found the fortitude to ask what she wanted to know most. "I've already told you what I have been through, but you never mentioned to me what my father went through. What was his reaction when he received the letter telling him Mother and I were dead? Did he grieve very long?" She hoped not. She hated the thought of that handsome face with anything but a smile on it.

"Yes," Richard said, wording his response very carefully. "He grieved the loss of *his wife* and his *daughter* until the day he died." When he looked at her then, he noticed a glimmer of tears at the corners of her gray eyes. How he wanted to believe those tears were sincere. "All Samuel's dreams of one day being happy again were shattered by that one letter. For nearly a month, he stayed in his room, refusing to come out even to eat. I had to take food in to him and watch while he ate for fear he would starve."

For the first time, Angela wondered where her father had lived. Was there a house? Could she somehow persuade Mr. Grissom to let her rent that house until her identity could be confirmed? It would certainly solve the problem of not having a place to stay. "You say he stayed in his room for a month? Where did he live?"

"He and I shared a house at the north end of town. That's where I have all his personal belongings stored.

337

In the attic. If it turns out that you *are* his daughter and can prove it, then I'll hand those personal belongings over to you and I'll pay you half what the house is worth. Although we built it together, it does not belong to the mining company. We didn't want to chance losing it should we ever have to sell shares in our mine."

Angela let out the breath she had been holding. There was no private house for her to claim. She would have to continue with her original plan to play on Sadie's sympathies. "I see. And what sort of belongings are in the attic?"

"His personal journal. His clothing. A watch. A few documents. And what money he had on him when he died. Nothing of major importance."

"Nothing of major importance?" Angela felt, as much as heard her voice rising. "His journal? His clothing? His watch? And you say nothing of major importance?"

Grissom's eyes stretched to their limits. He had not expected such an angry response and realized that she might not have her father's flaming red hair, but she sure had his flaming hot temper. "What I meant to say was nothing of great value. Nothing that could be sold or used to get much money."

Angela stared at him, fuming. "Those things happen to be worth far more than money to me. Those things belonged to my papa."

Grissom swallowed, then tucked his finger beneath his collar. If looks could kill then he would surely have one foot in the grave. "I can see that they would be important to a daughter. And they will be given to you just as soon as I have clear proof that you are the daughter you say you are."

"Why can't I have the journal now?" she asked, eager to learn her father's thoughts. "I'd be willing to return it when I'm through—that is until it can be proven I am Angela Langford."

Grissom narrowed his gaze suddenly. "Because letting you have that journal would give you a lot more fuel to feed your little fire. The more insight you have into that man the easier it would be for you to convince some judge you are indeed the man's daughter. No, you have enough information as it is. Why you even knew the name of the songs he used to sing, and just a moment ago you referred to him as your papa, just like his little Angel used to do. That's eerie."

"Yes, *Angel,*" Angela repeated in a reverent voice. "That was his nickname for me. I figure that's why he named his mine the Angel. He was naming it for me."

"As a surprise," Grissom said, blinking, unaware he, too, had started to tear. "That was before he was told what had happened to you." Then, he quickly added, "I meant, before he was told what had happened to *her.*"

"I know what you meant," she said and smiled gratefully, for without meaning to he had given a little insight into what her father had been like in the unadoring eyes of others. Obviously Grissom had loved and respected her father a great deal. "And I won't hold you to that little slip."

Grissom's eyebrows lifted at her unexpected generosity. "Why thank you." He studied her a moment more, then added, "I hope you understand the precautions I have taken are nothing personal. It's just that he was my best friend. I'll not have some charlatan coming in here and taking everything he worked so hard to accomplish. It wouldn't be right."

"I understand. And believe me I don't fault you for it. If anything, I admire your loyalty." She then glanced at the clock and saw that she had been there nearly twenty minutes. "I should go now. You have that meeting to prepare for and I have a letter I'd like to get off."

Grissom rose from his chair just seconds after she had stood to leave. "I'll send word out to the ranch the moment I hear from the Reverend Smith. If the proof is positive, then I'll arrange for you to be given Samuel's half of everything right away. I don't want to keep what is not rightfully mine."

Angela closed her eyes briefly, then tried to mask the pain she had felt when she looked again at Mr. Grissom. "Send word to Sadie MacDonald's boarding house. That's where I hope to be when the letter arrives."

Grissom's forehead furrowed. "But I thought you and—" He then shook his head as if to clear it of clutter. "You just let me know where to send word when the time comes and that's where I'll send it."

Dustin Buchanan pulled his cloth cap off his tousled head and held it in his hands when he entered the back door of the kitchen where Sadie, Tom, and Angela sat nibbling cookies and sipping fresh apple cider.

"Mr. Rutledge, my pa said to come tell you that your order is ready. All except for the cinnamon, which we're flat out of right now. Could be some coming in next week if this weather holds up, but then again—they might not have none in Silverlode either."

Tom glanced at the boy, aware of his dark eyes were on the plate of almond cookies, and quickly handed him one. "That's okay. I guess we can make do without cinnamon for a week or two. Tell your pa I'll be right there to settle up."

He waited until the boy had snatched the cookie and clamored out the door before turning back to Angela.

340

"Guess I'd better get on over there and pay the man before he decides to sell those goods to someone else. You two continue your talk. I'll be right back."

Sadie and Angela nodded in unison, both watching while Tom pushed his chair back and rose to his feet. Angela's heart rate doubled the moment she realized she was finally going to be alone with Sadie.

"I'll be right here waiting for you," she said, keeping her tone casual.

"Aye. And I'll be keeping a careful eye on the lass," Sadie said and smiled as she reached over to pat Angela's hand in a sisterly fashion. "I'll see that no harm comes to her."

Angela waited until Tom had plopped his weathered hat on his head, stuffed his arms into his fur-lined coat, and had crossed the alley before leaning forward and speaking in a low voice. "Sadie, I'm afraid I have a favor to ask of you."

"Ye be wanting to borrow a bit of cinnamon," Sadie surmised, already rising from her chair. "I think I kin spare a mite."

"No. It has nothing to do with the cinnamon. What I need is a place to stay," Angela said, racing to the point, not knowing how much time it would take Tom to settle with Jake. "I'll warn you right off that I have only forty cents to my name right now and I saw that your rates are a full three dollars a week, but I figure I'll be able to earn plenty by taking in sewing and darning. I'm really very good with a needle."

Sadie stared at her dumbfounded. "Why would ye be needing a place to stay? Ye be staying with Tom and Clint at the Double R."

"Until now, that was true," Angela admitted and won-

341

dered just how much she should tell Sadie. "But I can't keep taking advantage of their hospitality like I have."

Sadie's expression turned immediately sympathetic when she settled back into her chair. "There be a wee bit of trouble in paradise," she said, nodding that she understood.

"Very much so," Angela admitted, amazed at Sadie's insight. "I'm afraid Clint has lost some of the feeling he had for me earlier."

"And he has called off the marriage."

"Not yet. But that should come pretty soon. So far, the most he has done is ignore me and refuse to be seen with me. It appears Clint is a compassionate man who has not found an easy way to tell me that he no longer loves me."

"There be no easy way to do such as that," Sadie commented. "Are ye sure he no longer loves ye?"

"A woman can sense these things." Angela nodded. "Even after I went to the trouble to learn to ride a horse so I could come with him into town, he refused to let me. He did not want his friends to be reminded of our engagement."

"No, he wouldna. Not if his true plans are to break off with ye," Sadie agreed, looking at Angela with a woman's understanding. "Ye poor thing. I saw how the stars shone in ye'r eyes whenever he was near. Of course ye can stay here. And dona worry about the rent. Ye can pay me when ye have the money. I trust ye."

"Then you have a room?" Angela was so relieved, she felt weak.

"No. But ye can share my rooms until one comes available. And that way I'll only have to charge ye half rent." Sadie again reached forward and patted Angela's hands lovingly. "When do ye intend to make the move?"

Angela glanced at the clock. It was one-thirty. She had just enough time to ride out to the ranch, gather her things, and be back before dark.

"Tonight." She stood to leave, thinking she might save a few minutes by catching Tom before his return. Her hands trembled when she thought of telling him her new plans. He would be so hurt. "I dare not put this off any longer."

Sadie stood, too. "I'll save ye a place at the supper table. Just make sure ye make it back here safely."

Angela waited until she and Tom were out of town before telling him of her plans. As expected, he was against such a move but understood her reasoning why.

"I don't understand that son of mine. I agree he's been acting mighty peculiar these past few weeks, but I don't think it has anything to do with him having lost any feelings for you. I think it's something else."

"You saw how angry he got when we tried to trick him into taking me into town," Angela pointed out. "Why else would he not want to be seen with me?"

"I don't rightly know. But promise me you won't move out until you talk with Clint. I think he has a right to state his side of this." He studied her expression carefully. "If you will just promise to give Clint the chance to have his say, and if it turns out he's in accordance with this plan of yours, I'll escort you back into town myself."

Angela felt a flicker of hope warm her heart. Perhaps when told of her plans to leave, Clint would deny any change in his feelings toward her and give her a good reason to stay right where she was. "I promise. I won't leave until I've spoken with Clint."

* * *

While Clint led his horse into the barn, his thoughts were on the peculiar sounds he had heard earlier. Twice he'd heard the rustle of leaves and the snap of a twig, just as he was leaving that morning, then again on his way back that afternoon. Although he had not actually seen whoever had made the sounds, he was certain now someone was out there secretly following him.

It frustrated him that whoever was tracking him had refused to come out into the open when he had shouted for a confrontation. Whoever was out there was purposely preying on his nerves, hoping to rattle him enough to want to do something foolish. And the truth was, he was just about ready to accommodate the blackguard.

Tomorrow he would take another ride. Only this time he'd be wearing his guns and he would demand a showdown. He had to find out who was after him before he lost his mind completely—and before any danger fell on Angela or his father. It was obvious that whoever followed him was a coward of the worst kind, letting his presence be known, but refusing to show his face. And it was just such cowards that frightened him the most. Those people had no code of honor. There was no way to gauge just what they would or would not do to get what they wanted without bringing any harm to themselves. Some would even go as far as to kill an innocent woman, if it meant rattling him enough to do something brash.

Clint shuddered at the thought.

Chapter Twenty-Five

"Clint, I think you need to get on into the house," Tom said as soon as he'd entered the barn. "Angela has something important she wants to say to you."

Clint had been so lost in thought he had not heard his father's footsteps. "It'll be just a minute. I have to put this saddle away and pour some fresh oats in the trough."

"Those can wait. Like I said, she has something *important* to tell you and you'd better listen up good to what she has to say."

Clint stared at him, bewildered, then his forehead flattened with realization. Angela was going to have a baby. *His* baby. He was going to be a father. It must have happened back when they were at the cabin. That would make her nearly two months along by now. They would have to find some way to be married right away.

"Okay. I'm coming," he said, slinging the saddle over the nearest partition and barely taking the time to shut the stall gate before heading out the door. He waited until Tom had caught up with him before questioning him about this wonderful news. Suddenly he felt more protective than ever. "I guess I'll have to do something pretty quick to remedy this."

"I was sure hoping you'd say that," Tom said, wondering how Clint knew that Angela planned to leave. "The way you have been behaving here lately, I was afraid we had a problem here."

Clint had no time to explain his behavior to his father for they were already on the porch and headed into the kitchen where Angela stood waiting.

"Angela." He frowned when he noticed how pale she looked. She had none of the rosy glow he had seen in Susan's cheeks. "Dad told me you have something important to tell me."

"I do," Angela said in a calm voice that belied the quivering in her legs, for she was not sure she could handle what she was about to find out by watching Clint's response. "I've decided to move to Clear Creek. I'm going to live with Sadie MacDonald for awhile."

Clint blinked, confused by what she had just said. "But why?"

"Because I truly think it is what's best for me." she said, then paused, waiting to see if he would ask her to stay.

Tom did not like the evasive way she had worded that and had to bite down on his lower lip to keep from blurting out the truth, wishing now he had not promised to stay out of it.

Clint looked at his father, then back at Angela, and realized she meant what she said. She wanted to move into town with Sadie and rightfully so. She probably felt uncomfortable living with two men when she was not yet married to either of them, and was probably still angry with him for having refused to let her go with him into town.

Still, his first thought was to convince her to stay, but he quickly checked the selfish impulse. Until he was able to get whoever was following him off his back, it really might be better for her to stay in town for awhile. He trusted Sadie to watch over her.

"I gather your mind is made up on this."

"Yes, it is."

"Then I may as well help you pack," he said, ignoring his father's strangled yelp when he headed toward the door that led into the main part of the house. He wanted to get ahead of them so he could blink back the tears he felt burning the backs of his eyes. He had never felt such frustration and rage in all his life. If only he could catch whoever was following him and put all this behind him.

"There's no need for you to help me pack," Angela said, her voice choked with misery. Already she ached with loneliness. "I've packed everything I feel is mine. Including the embroidery and sewing items you bought me. I hope you don't mind." She knew she would need them before she could start taking in work.

Clint took a deep breath to east the pain clenching his chest, then turned to face her again. "Of course I don't mind. Those were gifts and you should take them."

"I don't get this," Tom said to Clint, having stayed out of it as long as he could. "Aren't you going to say something to make her stay?"

"Not if she's that determined to go," Clint answered in his ordinary voice, which surprised him as he could hardly swallow for the pain swelling in his throat. "I'll go hitch the team to the wagon. It is obvious that for whatever reason, she plans to leave right away."

"That won't be necessary. Your father has agreed to take me."

Which was even better as far as Clint was concerned. That way he would not have to worry about them being ambushed on the way. He knew that whoever was out there stalking him would have a definite advantage should he catch them together, for Clint would willingly give his life if it meant saving Angela's.

"Then I guess there's nothing else for me to do but wish you a safe trip," he said and bent forward to place a brief kiss on her cheek, which was almost his undoing, because he tasted the familiar sweetness of her skin. He did not want to be apart from her, but at the moment did not dare ask her to stay.

The only thing that kept him from breaking down was the realization that as soon as he had whoever was following him out of the way, he could go to Angela and explain everything. She would be angry that he'd kept her in the dark about all this, but she would eventually understand that it had been for her own good. She would have worried herself sick had she known that someone was out there waiting to catch him in a vulnerable moment and claim his life.

Either that or she would have snatched up a rifle and gone out after the culprit herself. And the thought of her doing something like that scared the living hell out of him.

"To tell you the truth, I'm not very hungry," Angela said when Sadie told her that although everyone was already in the dining room, supper had just been served and there would still be plenty for her to eat.

"But ye have to keep up ye'r strength," Sadie cautioned her. "Besides, there is someone in there who canna wait to set his tired ol' eyes on ye again."

Angela's pretty brow wrinkled while she tried to think who that might be. "Someone I know?"

"Surely enough."

"Who?"

"Amos Kieffer. He be looking forward to having ye at the same table. Had me reserve the seat right next to him," she said, then added in a concerned voice, "He was as upset as I to hear about the problems between ye and Clinton. He had hoped the two of ye would indeed get married as planned so ye would present Thomas with a passel of grandchildren. Dona disappoint the man. He even washed his face and combed what's left of his hair when he heard ye would be here for dinner."

"So that's what happened to Amos. He moved into town," Angela said and felt a tender spot in her heart open as she smiled. "All right. I guess I can put a bite or two down. But I do want to put my things away before bedtime, so I can't stay at the table very long."

Sadie's smile stretched dimple deep. "As long as ye eat enough to stay alive. I won't be having ye lose a lot of weight because of what that young man of yours has done. The Rutledge men aren't worth it. Why, if I lost a pound for every time Thomas did or said something to bring a tear to me eye, I'd be a skeleton by now. Get ye on in there and tell old Lynn Ballard who sits at the head I be bringing him more rolls in just one minute."

When Angela entered the dining room, she singled Amos from the other men in the room right away. And just as Sadie had said, there was a vacant spot on the bench next to him.

"I understand this space has been reserved for me," she said in a voice loud enough to be heard over the din of the others when she came up behind him. There were at least two dozen men and one other woman seated at the large table, and each was engaged in a conversation of some sort.

Amos's eyes were wide with expectation when he turned to face her. "Well, I'll be. It really is you." He patted the worn bench beside him. "Young'un, you sit yourself down and start filling that plate in front of you. You're getting a late start but you've still got your choice of chicken or ham and about a half a dozen vegetables, though I see the carrots are already gone."

After Angela gave the tall man at the head of the table Sadie's message, she stepped over the bench as daintily as she could and settled into place, aware Amos had already started filling her plate for her.

"That's enough," she cautioned when she saw the amount of food he had piled before her. "It would be impossible for me to eat all that and there is no sense wasting food."

"You can't eat all that?" he asked, truly perplexed. He reached up to scratch his shaggy white whiskers while he considered what she'd told him. "Why, that's only half what I put on my own plate."

"Still, that's twice what I normally eat," she said, laughing at his puzzled expression. It was then she noticed that the earlier stir of conversation had come to an abrupt halt. All eyes were upon her, waiting expectantly to be told who she was.

With Sadie still gone, Amos decided it was up to him to do the honors. He stood to his full height of five-foot-four and cleared his throat loudly as if he had something very important to impart. "Gentlemen—and I do admit to using that term loosely—this here lovely young lady seated beside me is Miss Angela Langford of New Orleans. Those of you who work with me at the Angel mine might also be interested to know that she's the daughter of the late Samuel Langford."

The conversation around the table started again immediately. Angela caught only bits and pieces, but was happy to hear that some very nice things were being said about her father.

"Why are you back down here working at the Angel?" Angela asked as she picked up her fork and speared a small potato. "I thought you said Clear Creek had become far too crowded for you."

"I thought so, too," Amos admitted as he reached for one of the freshly baked rolls Sadie had just placed on the table. "But that was before I spent some time up at that shack. Didn't seem to care much for that either."

He tore the roll in half and offered part to Angela. When she shook her head, he plopped both halves into his own plate to sop up the juices. "I saw Clint in town yesterday. He didn't mention to me that you two were breaking off your engagement and I do intend to get on to him for not telling me about that. But he did mention that little visit you two tried to pay on me a few weeks back." He grinned as he plopped a juice–laden piece of roll into the back of his mouth. "Sorry to disappoint you."

Angela felt her heart constrict at the mere mention of Clint's name. She wondered how long it would be before she could talk about him and not feel such overwhelming pain. If only her love had been as temporary as his. "He was worried that something had happened to you."

"No. Just got tired of being alone," Amos said, then twisted his face as if trying to decide how much to tell her. "Naw, that ain't entirely true. The real truth is, I'd

351

been hearing some pretty queer noises late at night sometimes and that got me more'n a little spooked. Got to where I was afraid of going off to sleep for fear of being murdered in my sleep. As for poor ol' June-Bug, she got to be as skittish as a new colt. So skittish that there were times I couldn't get her to come out of the cabin. She's a lot happier now that she's got her own stall over at the Angel Mine."

Angela blinked twice when she realized Amos had just admitted to living with that donkey right in the cabin with him, but she said nothing to interrupt his story while they continued to eat.

"I told Clint how it was bad enough thinking somebody was out in those woods watching us for some reason; but when I saw signs of someone having slept in that cove right within spitting distance of where *I* slept, and then food started to disappear right out of the shack, I figured it was time to clear out. That's when Clint told me about that man that's been following him around lately."

Angela looked at Amos, surprised, and although her mouth was full she did not wait to clear it before asking, "What man?"

"Didn't he tell you? Somebody has been following him off and on for weeks now. He doesn't know who it is because he hasn't got a good look at him yet. Nor does he think the culprit actually follows him into town or right up to his house; but whenever he first leaves the place, especially in the afternoon or late evening, he senses somebody is out there watching his every move."

Angela's eyes widened. She recalled having a similar feeling occasionally and wondered just how much danger there was for Clint.

"But why would anyone want to follow Clint? He hardly ever carries much money on him."

"Clint figures it's somebody out to up his reputation a might."

Angela's face twisted while she tried to make sense of that. "By following him?"

"No. By shooting him. I reckon you might not know it but Clint has a pretty big name for being a fast gun, though he earned it years ago when he was very young and reckless. Everyone around these parts knows he's changed. He's not that same wild-eyed kid out trying to prove to the world he's a growed man. But there are still a few men from other parts who don't care if he's changed or not. They would love to be known for having been the one to take Clint Rutledge down."

Angela's heart plunged to the pit of her stomach with a sickening thud, forcing her to set her fork back down. Suddenly she understood why Clint had been so adamant she not ride with him. He had feared for her safety.

"But he gave up wearing his guns," she argued. "He packed them away in a trunk to prove it."

"Don't matter much. Just because he says he is giving up his guns don't mean they gonna let him do it. All it takes is for one hothead to come in here and find out our Clint Rutledge is *the* Clint Rutledge and, pow, the kid has got it in his head to go after him." Amos looked at her stricken face, then reached over to pat her hand reassuringly. "But don't you worry none. Nobody's going to get the drop on Clint. He's got the instincts of a wild animal. You just wait and see. He'll be rid of whoever is tormenting him in no time. Then things can get back to regular around here."

"Do you think the man following him might be that

Dane Tapley who recently came to town?" she asked, remembering the earlier confrontation.

"No. Because yesterday when Clint came into town, he told me that the culprit had followed him more than halfway and I know for a fact that Dane was right here in town then. I saw him headed into the Golden Briar Saloon with a fistful of money barely an hour before I talked with Clint. Knowing Dane, he spent the entire day drinking and gambling. Seems to be his favorite pastime. Other than running his mouth at speeds higher than his brain can handle."

"Are there any other gunfighters in town?"

"None that I know of, but then I don't know all that much about gunfighters. Only know I'm looking at one when I see a fancy gun strapped low on his hip. Problem with that is not all gunfighters wear their guns all the time.

Angela quietly pushed her plate away. Suddenly she had lost her appetite.

When Clint returned from his trip to the line shack to look for evidence of night prowlers, he slammed the door so hard after entering the house that the dishes in the cupboard rattled and a drinking glass toppled over and fell to the floor.

He was dead certain he had been followed again and was both frustrated and furious that whoever it was still refused to come out and face him.

Even at night.

Evidently the man was a bigger coward than he'd first realized—which explained why he had yet to follow him all the way into town.

Although Clint could not be certain, he believed that

whoever was following him always turned away whenever he rode into town or near a house where there might be a lot of people around. It was just a feeling he had, and if it was true, then this fellow was not after a face–to–face confrontation. What he wanted was to catch him off guard, while his thoughts had strayed or he was otherwise distracted.

Anything that would make him an easy mark.

And it was just as obvious that this person did not intend to shoot him in the back to obtain his glory or else he would have already done so by now. Which had to be why he continued biding his time the way he did. Whoever was out there wanted to be able to prove the kill, but at the same time didn't want to chance being blamed for out and out murder. The only way anyone could accomplish both without endangering himself in return, or without making himself look guilty of manslaughter, was to get the jump on him but make it look like it had been a fair fight. To make the kill look good, the man would somehow have to shoot him square through the chest or the forehead, then place a pistol that had been freshly fired in his hand after he was dead.

Obviously, whoever was following him had thought it out very carefully. But there had to be a way to catch the man and have him put away so things could get back to normal. Angela had been gone only a few hours and already he was beside himself with loneliness.

In the two weeks that had passed since having come to live with Sadie, Angela's reputation with a needle and thread had spread rapidly. Eventually she had to start turning work away. Although the advertisement she had pinned to the community bulletin board had mentioned only taking in mending and darning, she already had two orders to sew party dresses for the upcoming Christmas dance—one for Jake's daughter, Stephanie Buchanan, which she had already finished, and the other for the wife of one of the shift supervisors at the Little Meg Silver Mine. In addition, to repay Sadie for her many kindnesses, she was secretly embroidering a dark green velvet jacket for her friend to wear with the new emerald satin gown she had just bought.

Angela could not remember ever having felt better about herself. Within the first week, she had earned enough to pay Sadie for the first month's rent and had enough left over to buy a large assortment of threads and material to keep on hand. Since then, she had also earned enough to buy the material for the dress she hoped would dazzle Clint at the Christmas party and had even had a little left over to put aside for the purchase of a small sewing machine. She knew she could do twice the work and earn twice the money with mechanical help.

"Aye, but ye be working hard to finish that dress for Mrs. Alsobrook."

"That's because I only have a few days to finish. She wants it ready a full week before the party," Angela said around the straight pins she held in her mouth, not about to admit that she worked as hard and as long as she did because it helped keep her thoughts off Clint. "Just in case it doesn't fit right, she wants to be sure I have plenty of time to alter it."

"Why wouldn't it fit? She stops by here almost every day for a fitting. Truth is, she's been driving me batty with all her visits."

Angela took the pins out of her mouth and stuck them

into the cloth cushion attached to her wrist. "I think it is her first new dress in quite some time and even though I'm not asking that much for my labor, the material she chose was *very* expensive. I'm sure it set her husband back a pretty penny. Probably more so than they can really afford."

"Well, I don't care how expensive her material. Or how fancy ye'r stitches. Her dress won't hold a wax candle to mine," Sadie said with a teasing wag of her head. "And neither will that one ye be sewing for ye'rself, though it is very pretty indeed. Because this year, I've a mail-order dress that is sure to make me the belle of the ball."

"Ball? I thought this *do* of yours was just a potluck supper with a dance that follows."

"Shame on ye for trying to burst an old woman's bubble," Sadie said with a quick pout. "If I want to think of it as a grand ball, then that's what it tis."

Angela couldn't help but laugh. "I apologize for trying to ruin such a gala event for you. I'd forgotten just how *old* you really are. Why you are a full ten years older than I am, maybe even fifteen." She wrinkled her brow with concern. "Just don't forget your cane when you go. You might trip on the way over and break a fragile bone."

Sadie chuckled too as she gave her rounded hip a sound whack. "There's too much cushioning around me bones for me to worry about such as that yet. By the by, I was about to walk over to Jake's to get another tin of black pepper for the five bean soup I be making for supper. Want to get over there before it starts to snow. Do ye need anything while I am out?"

Angela thought a minute. "I could use more green thread. I'm almost out." She then set her sewing aside.

"But I think I'll go with you. I've been sitting all day. My legs could use the exercise."

Within minutes, the two women had donned their woolen gloves and their winter cloaks and were headed across the alley toward the street. Although there were no snowflakes yet, the wind was brisk and the sky a threatening gray, which hurried their steps considerably.

Once inside Buchanan's General Store, they headed for the large wood stove near the back of the building while Jake went about gathering the few items they wanted. When they left the store fifteen minutes later, Angela glanced at the sky and realized it could snow at any moment, which would make getting around town a lot more difficult.

"While I'm out, I think I'll walk on over to the post office and see if I have a letter from Susan," she told Sadie as she held her small package out to her. "Would you mind taking my things on to the house with you?"

"I'll do it, but only if ye'll check to see if I have any mail while ye'r there," Sadie said, taking the package and putting it with her own. "Just don't tarry long. It looks like we're in for a real storm."

"It'll just take a few minutes." Angela pulled the hood of the heavy cloak Sadie had loaned her further over her head before stepping off the boardwalk and heading across the street. Any other time and she would have taken a longer route that would let her avoid crossing in front of the two noisiest saloons in town, but with the wind cutting through her the way it was, she wanted to get in out of the weather as quickly as she could.

It was not until she was on her way back with two letters for Sadie but none for herself tucked away in her inside pocket that she realized what a grave mistake she had made by taking the shorter route.

"My, my, my. What have we here?" she heard a deep voice say barely a half second before she felt someone grab her cloak and pull her sideways. Her heart lurched when she glanced over her shoulder and saw the face of the person who held her. It was Dane Tapley, the man who hated Clint with a passion.

Aware there were very few people on the street because of the approaching storm, she decided not to do anything that might provoke him. "Sir, if you don't mind, I'm in a hurry. I'm expected back at the boarding-house."

"Oh, but I *do* mind," he said, moving closer until the steam from his breath reached out to mix with the steam from her own.

Angela stared at Dane, who was wearing only a ruffled dress shirt that looked a little ridiculous on his meaty frame and formfitting black trousers, and wondered how he could stand it outside in such weather with neither a coat nor a hat, then realized he must have been in some hurry to capture her.

"Please," she said, trying her best to keep a calm voice when the insidious gleam in his eye and the cocky smile on his lips made her stomach twist with fear. "I'm cold. I want to get out of this weather."

"Then come on inside the Golden Briar and let me warm you a little." He snaked the tip of his tongue over his lower lip while he studied her startled expression further. "I understand that nothing works better for keeping warm than rubbing two bodies together." While keeping a firm hold on her cloak, he reached forward with his other hand and captured her by her waist. "To tell you the truth, you've already set me on fire and our bodies haven't even touched yet." He pulled her abruptly to him. "Can't you feel the heat?"

359

Angela tried to pull free of his grasp but found he was much stronger than he looked. "Sir; if you don't release me right now I will scream!" She realized it was an empty threat because a woman's scream coming from the area in front of the saloon was not all that unusual.

"No, you won't," he said with eyes glittering. "Because you are just as attracted to me as I am to you. I've seen the way you watch me when you think I'm not looking."

"That's because you repulse me," she said, lifting her chin proudly. "It has nothing to do with being attracted to you."

Dane chuckled and pulled her closer still. "I had a feeling you'd be the type to play hard to get. I like that in a woman. No wonder Clint was so easily taken. He knew he had hold of a real wild one."

"Sir, this is neither the time nor the place." She swallowed hard, and again wondered if anyone would come to her rescue if she did chance a scream. As cold as it was and as hard as the wind blew, the call for help might not even be heard. Did she dare risking his anger over something that offered so little help?

"You are right," Dane said, solving her problem by suddenly letting go of her. "This is not the time nor the place." He then reached forward to touch his fingertip to her nose as if merely flirting with her. "And I know enough about women to wait until both the time and the place are perfect."

Angela stared at him with a look of pure disgust when he turned and sauntered back into the saloon from where he had come, repulsed to know that the man sincerely believed she was attracted to him.

Knowing Dane Tapley to be a man of little honor

who was used to getting whatever he wanted, especially from a woman, she decided she would have to be very careful of him in the future. She could not let him catch her alone on the streets of Clear Creek again.

Chapter Twenty-Six

"Ye sparkle like a true gem," Sadie said when Angela entered her bedroom wearing the dark gown of burgundy velvet and white lace she had made for herself, with her long hair arranged in a thick mass of black curls. "And ye thought ye would not finish the gown in time."

"It came close. I was up until nearly three this morning tacking the last of the lace," Angela admitted. "Which is why I slept so late this morning."

"Well, it is sure to catch the eye of every man there," Sadie said, then grimaced when she noticed the dark green jacket over Angela's arm. "And the jacket is beautiful too—a true work of art—but I dona think it goes too well with the dress. I fear the colors clash."

Angela's smiled widened. "That's because I made the jacket to go with your dress. Merry Christmas a few days early."

Sadie's eyes stretched as big and round as silver dollars. "Ye mean that beautiful garment is for me?" She wasted no time in taking it from Angela and whisking it over her shoulders. It matched the darker trim of her emerald gown perfectly. "I've never seen anything so

362

beautiful. When did ye ever find the time to make such a thing, what with all the other sewing ye had to do?"

"You remember all those nights I worked until after midnight while you went on to bed?"

"But I thought ye were working on Mrs. Alsobrook's gown all those nights."

"No. I was making this special present for my newest dear friend." Her forehead was wrinkled when she realized Sadie was the *only* dear friend she had ever had—besides possibly Susan. But then she had not been around Susan long enough for a deep friendship to develop. "I wanted you to look your very best tonight since Tom has volunteered to be our escort."

Sadie's dimples sank into her cheeks at the mere mention of Tom. "And I have something for ye," she said and hurried to the top drawer of her dresser. Seconds after rummaging around near the back of the drawer she handed Angela a tiny cloth sack made with black velvet and silver cord. "It's a dainty necklace of pearls that will look lovely on ye'r slender neck and will go with ye'r dress perfectly." She winked. "And it is sure to catch Clinton's eye."

"But why would I want to do that?" Angela asked, wondering if her longing for Clint was that obvious.

"Because ye still love the rogue. And because ye are hoping he will change his mind and come tonight after all so he can be reminded how beautiful ye are and how very much he once loved ye."

Rather than argue against the truth, Angela slipped the delicate strand of pearls from the pouch and held them out to Sadie. "Will you help me put them on?"

"T'would be a pleasure."

* * *

When Tom arrived for Sadie and Angela at precisely six o'clock as promised, he could not help but let out a long, low whistle as he swept his hat off his head and held it in front of him by its wide brim. "I've never seen so much beauty in one room before. I'll be the most envied man there."

Sadie beamed brightly at such an unfettered compliment, but Angela was too disappointed that Clint had not changed his mind about joining them to do more than mutter a polite thank you.

Aware of Angela's sudden solemn mood, Sadie reached out to give her friend's shoulder a short, reassuring squeeze.

"Am I to gather that Clinton won't be taking part in the festivities at all tonight?" Sadie asked, knowing Angela would want to be certain.

"I guess not," Tom answered and pursed his lips into a twisted pout. "But then I don't really know what his plans are. He keeps to himself a lot these days." He shook his head with resentment. "To tell you the truth, I think the boy has lost his fool mind. Don't know what to do about it either."

"Why do ye say that?" Sadie asked while she collected the two gifts she and Angela were taking to the party.

"For one thing, he walks around mumbling to himself all the time. And he takes off at all hours of the day and night for no given reason other than his feeble claim to need some fresh air. Another thing that's been bothering me. He carries that rifle with him everywhere now. Why yesterday, I noticed he even toted it right into the privy with him. Something strange is going on with him. I can see that. But he won't to talk about it. Claims he's just being cautious."

Sadie looked at Angela, as if encouraging her to fill him in with a few facts, which reluctantly Angela did.

After hearing what Amos had told her about someone following Clint whenever he left the house, Tom stood staring at the two women with a wrinkled frown. "Why didn't Amos tell me about that the other day when I saw him out near the edge of town?"

"He probably didn't think about it," Angela said. "Or it's possible he thought you already knew. That's how I found out. Amos blurted it out before realizing I had no idea what was going on."

"Or, knowing our Amos, he had something else holding his thoughts," Sadie said. "Ye know how he is sometimes."

"Still, I wish he would've told me. With both Clint and me working to catch this man, we'd have him toted off to jail in no time."

"I imagine Clint does not want to see you in any danger," Angela pointed out. "I'm sure he views this man as his problem and no one else's."

"Which is why he was so willing to let you move into town," Tom surmised, his eyebrows arching high at the realization. "Well, no wonder he'd been acting the way he has. He's been putting up with being followed for weeks now." Scowling, Tom plopped his hat back on his head. "Well, he won't have to worry about it much longer. I'll see to it we capture this fellow right away."

"Now don't ye go trying something foolish, Thomas Rutledge," Sadie warned with a brisk wag of her finger. "This man might not care who he kills just so long as he takes Clinton down in the process."

Angela felt an icy shiver trickle down her back at the reminder that someone wanted to hurt Clint. "Before you do anything, Tom, you should discuss your plans with Clint," she said, worried she had created yet another problem for Clint when all she had wanted to do was clear Tom's confusion.

"You're right, Angie. Clint and I will need to put our heads together on this one so we can set up some sort of trap," Tom said with a sudden gleam in his eyes. "We need to come up with something that will lure the little lowlife right out into the open."

"Just as long as ye promise to discuss it with Clinton first," Sadie said, not wanting Tom to go off half-cocked on this. "Don't ye do a thing without first asking for his approval."

"I won't," Tom said with a puckered expression that made him look like a little boy who had just been chastised by his mother. He held his hand out to take the two brightly wrapped gifts from her, then bent forward to sniff them. He frowned when there was no smell at all. "No chocolate squares this year, Sadie?"

"No. This year I made a lovely red-checked apron with a fancy red ruffle and sash," she said, then narrowed her gaze. "So there'll be no reason for ye to be keeping ye'r dark eyes on whoever gets my present so ye can go begging for a sample before they're all gone."

"*You* sewed an apron?" Tom asked, clearly doubtful. "All by yourself?"

Sadie's mouth flattened. "Yes, Thomas. I *can* sew. I just don't care for it very much. But with Angie sitting around sewing all of the time, it seemed like a good way to share some time with her."

"And she did a lovely job," Angela put in, then looked at Sadie with a teasing grin. "*Almost* as good as the work I did on the sofa doilies I made."

With the light mood from earlier fully restored and Clint's problem temporarily forgotten, Tom reached forward to open the door, then stepped back to let the ladies pass before closing it again. After he put the two packages in a special hopper in the back, he climbed onto the carriage seat beside Sadie.

"Wish it hadn't snowed last week," he muttered as he adjusted his lap robe. "I hate driving this thing when it's a sleigh. Darn thing always tries to shove the horses forward whenever they first start to slow down."

"We could have walked," Sadie said, knowing the suggestion would irritate him. "The town hall is only three blocks away."

"No we couldn't," he said as he snapped the reins and sent the sleigh forward over the snow with a crunch. "If I had to go to all the trouble of putting the rungs on this thing, then by George, I am going to get full use of them."

"Besides," Angela said in a whisper just loud enough for Sadie to hear, "he wouldn't want to risk having an old woman like you fall and break something—" She paused just long enough for Sadie to deliver a quick jab of her elbow then quickly added, "—like the ice on which you fell." Grinning, she leaned back just in time to avoid the second jab.

"What she say?" Tom asked, glancing at Sadie's pursed mouth with a questioning frown.

"Said ye'r sleigh rides as smooth as if it was on rails," Sadie said and cut Angela a sharp look. "I guess this *is* much better than walking after all."

Angela glanced up from the lovely set of blue and white dishtowels she had unwrapped when she heard someone clapping hands and shouting loudly from atop the small stage that had been erected near the back of

367

the large rectangular room. When she did, she noticed a tall man with glistening white hair dressed in an oversized frock coat cupping his hands to his mouth so everyone could hear his next words.

"Well, now that we've all eaten our fill and the ladies have exchanged their gifts, I think it is time to ask Jim and his brother and their boys to get up here and start the music." He dropped his arms and waited for the sudden burst of applause to die down before cupping his hands over his mouth again. "Keep in mind, if you happen to build up a thirst during the next few hours, the women's punch bowl is over here to my right and the men's punch bowl is over to my left, near the side door."

Angela grinned when she noticed several of the older women's sudden frowns, having already been warned by Sadie that the men's punch bowl usually contained much "livelier" ingredients than the women's.

Tired and having lost interest in the whole affair, Angela quickly took one of the many chairs vacated when the music started a few seconds later. She still felt a little depressed knowing Clint had not come, and she had yet to see anyone else she would care to dance with—except perhaps for Tom or Amos, who were both too busy courting special women of their own to notice anyone else. Tom had not left Sadie's side the entire night and Amos had been busy following a tiny little woman dressed in bright yellow.

Sighing, Angela put her dishcloths and the colorful cloth they had been wrapped in under the chair to get them out of the way, then sat watching the men and women on the dance floor while they stomped their way through a brisk Irish jig. Her forehead drew into a questioning frown when she noticed there were far more men on the floor than women.

It wasn't until the music swept directly into a lively polka that it finally dawned on her why. Undoubtedly because there were so few women in Clear Creek, the men saw no reason not to get out on the floor and dance with each other—just as long as they were having a good time. Why, one old geezer didn't care to dance with either man or woman and pranced about with a straight backed chair for his partner.

Angela became so captivated by the fun and enthusiasm she saw in the people around her, she barely noticed that someone had taken the chair next to hers.

"I'm sorry, but we can't allow any women to sit out any of the dances," she heard before she quite realized the words had been directed at her. "Especially a woman as beautiful as you."

Angela's heart soared when she recognized Clint's voice, and her whole body tingled with sudden anticipation when she turned and saw his smiling face.

"I can't believe not one of these dimwits has asked you to dance." His gaze dipped appreciatively over her fitted gown.

"A few of them have asked. But I've turned them all down," she said, feeling the color rise in her cheek for no apparent reason. "I told them I didn't feel much like dancing tonight."

Clint frowned, though his dark eyes continued to sparkle with amusement. "Then I don't suppose you'd be willing to accept my invitation to dance, either."

"I might be persuaded, if the invitation proved sincere enough."

Clint's dimples twitches as he dropped to one knee

and placed his hand over his heart as if pledging his allegiance to her. "Does this seem sincere enough?"

"Clint don't. Someone might see you," she reprimanded, the color in her cheeks turning darker while she cut her gaze to those standing about, glad to see most of them were watching the dancers. "What would they think?"

"That I was determined to convince the most beautiful woman here to dance with me." He quickly stood and held his hand out to her. "Come on. Let's show them how good we look together."

Angela fought the urge to laugh as she accepted his hand. "Since you did go to all the trouble to put on your Sunday finest and ride all the way into town, I guess I could find it in my heart to dance at least one dance with you."

"No, my dear," he corrected as he led her out onto the dance floor. "We are going to dance this night away. We've been apart for far too long."

Although they stood out on the dance floor with their arms outstretched and hands touching, as if fully prepared to join in the polka, Angela refused to take that first step. Instead, she stood stone still in front of him and stared into his questioning expression with a rigid gaze.

"You expect me to dance *every* dance with you? I guess just because you decided at the very last minute to come to the Christmas dance you think I will forgive all those weeks of not seeing you? Just like that?" She gave a haughty lift of her chin, but the outrage she tried to summon absolutely refused to come forth until finally a smile tugged at her lips. She could not really fault him for wanting to keep her out of danger. "Well, if *that's* what you think ... then you are absolutely right. I've missed you."

"And I've missed you," he said, his gaze dipping again as if determined to memorize every tiny detail about her. "You don't know how very much."

For the next several seconds they stood staring at each other as if starved for the sight of one another. It was not until another couple bumped against them that they realized they had yet to join in the swift movement circling the floor and he quickly whisked her away in a lively whirl of burgundy skirts and renewed hopes.

Unable to believe it was true, Angela closed her eyes so she could better enjoy the familiar warmth of his touch as they pranced around the dance floor.

It was as if there had never been a rift between them.

After one full hour of constant dancing, the two men and four boys who comprised the band stopped their playing and announced they were about to take a short punch and cake break.

"Won't be long, folks. We promise."

Although there were a few disappointed groans and rankled shouts, most people took the announcement good-naturedly and headed for the punch bowls themselves. Because of the heat generated by all the dancing, the side doors were flung open to let some cold air in as were two of the windows. Having forgotten her fan, Angela moved closer to the doors to get a breath of cool air.

"Wait right here," Clint shouted so he could be heard over the boisterous crowed after she paused only a few yards from the door. He then dipped forward to steal a quick kiss off her cheek. "I'll get us both some punch."

Angela ran her tongue over her lips and discovered just how dry her mouth had become.

"And from which bowl do you propose to get our punch?" she called back to him, cocking her head to one side as if pretending she did not trust him.

"From the safe one," he said and laughed. "I am dizzy enough just from having seen you again. I certainly don't need anything to make me any dizzier."

Overwhelmed with joy to know that Clint still cared for her, Angela laughed and watched while he made his way through the crowd toward the punch bowl nearest the food tables. She felt a sudden giddiness while watching his agile movements, enough so she lifted her hand to hide her adoring smile.

"Well, if it isn't my favorite little lady," she heard someone say, but because the loud voice did not register right away, she did not turn to see who had spoken. She assumed the words had been directed at someone else. It wasn't until she felt a hand curl around her arm and forcibly turn her that she glanced to see who wanted her attention.

Her heart plunged into immediate despair when her gaze lifted to find Dane Tapley standing barely two feet away, smiling that cocky, off-centered grin of his.

"You look as if you could use some fresh air," he commented, already pulling her toward the door with his right hand.

"I'm just fine right here," she said and jerked her arm away with such force she freed it from his grasp. Seeing how angry that action had made him, she decided it might be wise to let him know she was not alone. "Besides, I am waiting for Clint Rutledge to return with my punch. He's been my dance partner all night."

"All the more reason to be gone when he returns," Dane said and again grasped her arm, this time with his unbandaged hand. "It's the easiest way I know for you to get rid of him so you can spend some time with me."

"The last thing I would want to do on this lovely night is spend any time with you," she said, glowering at him. "Let go of me!" Again she tried to pull free of his grasp, but this time his grip held firm.

"I believe the little lady just told you to let go to her," Clint said, handing the two punches he carried to Amos, who had followed him back from the punch bowl.

Dane's expression darkened to one of pure hatred. "Well, well, well, if it isn't the great lover of all women pure and unpure."

"Let go of Angela," Clint said again. The muscles in his arms bunched as he curled his hands into tight fists at his sides.

"What is it about you that makes you think you can take whatever woman interests me away?" Dane asked, his green eyes boring directly into Clint's. "First it was Christina Brooks and now Angela."

"Christina was a long time ago. And I didn't take her from you. She came to me asking for help because you had beaten the bloody hell out of her. And as for Angela, she was mine long before she even knew you existed so I couldn't very well be taking her from you, could I? It just so happens she is my fiancée and has been for months now, and I would thank you to take your filthy hands off her."

After that last statement, Angela's eyes widened with an odd combination of bewilderment and sheer joy. She had thought their engagement broken the moment she moved out of their house and into town.

"Come now, Rutledge," Dane scoffed. Although he held her with both hands, the grip of only his left hand tightened around Angela's upper arm, causing her to wince with pain. "The whole town knows the two of you had a falling out just weeks after she came here. Why else would she have moved her things and herself into town? And why else would you have let her? Admit it, she finally realized what a sniveling coward you really are and ditched you."

"Why she moved into town is her business, and why I let her is mine. But I can assure you it had nothing to do with my being a coward and nothing was ever said about breaking our engagement. Come spring, just as soon as the first circuit preacher arrives in town, Angela and I have agreed to be married. So, again, I'd *thank* you to take your hands off her."

Dane studied Clint's angry expression a moment, then with his still bandaged hand he felt for the gun he'd been forced to leave at the door. Slowly, he lessened his grip until Angela was able to pull her arm free.

"A wise decision, Mr. Tapley," she said, still glowering at him. "Now if you don't mind, I'd like to speak with my fiancé *alone.*"

Having said that, she took Clint by the arm and led him away before the resentment still simmering between the two men got out of control.

Dane stood unmoving, the muscles in his jaw pumping rock hard.

"Here, Mr. Tapley," Amos said, stepping forward and holding out one of the two cups of punch to him. He squinted to get a better look at the burly man who stood nearly a foot taller than him. "Looks like you could use a drink about now."

Although his eyes remained on Clint and Angela, Dane accepted the small cup of punch, which he quickly tossed to the back of his throat. Immediately his eyes widened and he sputtered with a look of pure horror and disgust, "What was that?"

"Cherry punch," Amos said with a wry look of amusement, knowing Dane had expected something a bit stronger. "Just hits the spot, don't it?"

"Very funny, old man. Very funny." Rubbing his tongue against his teeth as if to rid himself of the sweet taste, Dane turned and stalked from the room. He paused just long enough to give Clint and Angela one last hateful glare, then marched over to the table where he'd left his holster and revolver.

Chapter Twenty-Seven

Feeling much better now that Clint had made it clear to her and the whole town he still planned to marry her come spring, Angela sang a lively little tune while she slipped on the new woolen gloves Tom had given her for Christmas, then headed for the door. "Sadie, I should be back in about an hour. Are you sure you don't need anything while I'm out?"

"Not that I can think," Sadie answered, then turned to look at her from atop the chair she had climbed on so she could dust the upper shelves of her bookcase. "Just be sure ye keep to the boards. As warm as it is getting to be out there, those streets are sure to be a mess."

"I will, *mother,*" she promised with a grin, then spun around and left the room before Sadie could come back with a proper retort that might cause her to stay and banter.

Five minutes later, Angela entered Richard Grissom's office, eager to try one last time to convince him to let her borrow her father's journal. Having just been through the holidays, which was always a time for families to come together, she longed more than ever to know what sort of things her father had written about his daily life. She also wanted to know if by any chance Mr. Grissom had heard from Reverend Smith. Even though it was unlikely any mail had gotten through since that last snow two weeks ago, there was always the possibility that someone had gotten through on foot with a donkey or a pack mule and had been paid to bring a satchel of mail with him.

"Mr. Grissom?" she called out when she entered the office and did not find him seated at his desk with piles of paper stacked neatly around him.

Wondering where he might be, she glanced about the office and noticed a substantial fire roaring in the fireplace with a metal coffeepot on an iron shelf off to one side, keeping warm. She decided that wherever he was, he would not be gone long and headed toward her usual chair, plucking off her gloves while she walked.

When she opened her handbag to slip her gloves inside, she noticed papers scattered across the floor. That puzzled her, for she knew Mr. Grissom to be meticulous with his papers.

"Mr. Grissom?" she called again when she knelt to gather his papers for him, thinking perhaps they had blown off when she opened the door, though there was only a slight breeze outside that morning.

It was when she leaned forward to gather the papers that had fallen just out of her reach that she glimpsed Mr. Grissom sprawled across the floor behind his desk.

"Mr. Grissom!" she shouted, panicked to see him lying there motionless. Her heart twisted with the fear that he might be dead, but when she found the courage to touch his skin she found that rather than cold from death, he burning hot with fever.

Having dealt with fever before when Dahlia's two cousins, Tony and Andy Stanton, had come down with yellow fever one summer while staying with them, Angela first tugged him out of his coat, then unbuttoned his shirt and rolled his sleeves to his elbows. Spying a pitcher of water that was part of the drinking service over by the window, she rushed across the room, hoping to find it full.

When she did not see a cloth lying about, she yanked down a curtain and wet both halves generously while hurrying back to the desk. Setting the pitcher aside, she wrapped half the wet curtain around Mr. Grissom's head and tucked the other half into his shirt. Knowing she would never be able to lift him without help and not knowing where she would carry him if she could, she hurried to the door and shouted to the first person she saw.

"Mr. Grissom has a fever. Go get Sadie MacDonald."

With the nearest doctor being in Silverlode and unattainable until the first good thaw after winter, and Sadie being the only daughter of a Scottish doctor, she was the closest thing Clear Creek had to medical care.

The man glanced into the office and saw Richard Grissom lying prostrate with the wet cloths tucked around him, then hurried to do as told.

Within minutes Sadie was there and making a quick examination.

"Looks like it might be influenza." She then ordered three men in from the street to move him to her boardinghouse. "Angie, I'll have to go with these men to set up a cot in the kitchen where I'll be able to care for him easier. Take these keys that were in his pocket and lock this place. Then come help. Whether it is influenza or not, I'll need to be getting his fever down as quickly as I can."

Angela was sorely tempted to take advantage of being alone in the office to see if there was anything of her father's lying about, or perhaps tucked away in one of the two desks, but she knew Sadie needed her so she hurried to douse the fire, blow out the lamps, and lock the door.

She stopped on the way back to Sadie's to gather an armload of snow from the shadows and carried it into the house with her. She knew it would help to pack it around Mr. Grissom.

"Good. More snow," Sadie said when she looked up to find Angela coming toward her. She had already packed some around the bulk of his body, directly against his bare skin. "Put it around his legs then pull one of those blankets over them to help hold in the cold."

Angela was neither surprised nor alarmed to discover that Sadie had removed all but Richard Grissom's underdrawers, and went about packing the snow she had brought with her around his legs without protest.

"Where are the men who helped bring him here?" she asked, aware they were alone in the kitchen.

"I sent them off. Now that I have him in better light, I feel certain it is the influenza, which is very contagious, especially during the fever," she said, bending forward to feel Richard's neck with the tips of her fingers. "Which is why I be ordering ye out of here, too."

"Order all you want. But you will need my help," Angela said. "At least until his fever breaks."

Sadie thrust her chin forward and opened her mouth as if planning a staunch protest, but in the end shrugged and said nothing.

"I think we should pack his arms, too," Angela said, her way of letting Sadie know that the matter was closed. She was staying to help. "I'll take a basin and bring in plenty of snow."

For the next few hours, Sadie and Angela worked together to bring Richard Grissom's fever down and were feeling disheartened when suddenly he started to shiver and shake.

"He's developed the chills. 'Tis a good sign," Sadie said. "Mean's he'll soon be coming around. Once he's awake, I can give him a swallow of quinine and calomel. That is, if his stomach is of a mind to keep such as that down."

Half an hour later, Richard Grissom did open his eyes, but was too disoriented to know exactly where he was or why he was there. To Sadie's relief, he stayed awake just long enough to swallow some of the medicine she had prepared before drifting back into a restless sleep.

"I guess ye can go get ye'rself a bit of rest now," Sadie said, with a tired but satisfied sigh. "I think the worst of it is over now."

As if such reassuring words had summoned a contradiction, at that same moment there came a loud knock at her back door.

"I'll answer it," Angela said and forced herself from the chair beside Richard's cot to do just that. When she opened the door that led out onto the back porch, she was startled to find two men standing there with a third man being held up between them.

Without waiting for an invitation from Angela, they brought the staggering man inside. "Sadie, Glen's real sick. Got a high fever and can hardly stand up on his own." They then looked with raised brows at Richard Grissom.

As if finding a whole new source of energy, Sadie

sprang from her chair and hurried toward the basement door. "I was afraid there would be more than one. I'll set up another cot."

By bedtime that night, Sadie and Angela had nine men and two children with various stages of influenza bedding with them. The kitchen, dining room, and parlor all had to be converted into sick wards with two of the mining companies supplying the extra cots and all the quinine and calomel that could be found.

By noon the following day, it was clear they had an epidemic because twelve more were brought in, all weak with raging fevers and chills. Soon, there were too many to be housed at Sadie's. A second medical ward was established at the church just down the street. Because there were fewer women and children, it was decided that they would be kept at Sadie's while the men were taken to the church.

Having watched Sadie care for the original patients throughout that first night, Angela volunteered to go to the church and take care of as many there as she could. When she arrived, she found two other such volunteers and together the three women did what they could.

By the second day, the church, too, was full and the supply of both quinine and calomel was rapidly running short. Forty-six people had been stricken with the sickness, with more coming in almost hourly.

The two other women helping at the church soon fell ill themselves and had to be taken to Sadie's for care, but Angela continued to work, stopping only occasionally to rest so that she would not become so weak, she too would fall prey to the dreaded germ.

By the third day, Richard Grissom and Glen Burt, who had been the first to come down with the illness, had begun to recover, and as soon as they felt strong enough to stand, they were at Angela's side, helping as best they could considering how weak they were.

On the fourth day, Tom and Clint were brought in. A neighbor had stopped in and discovered them both weak with fever.

While Angela hurried to bring their fevers down, she wondered how many others might be stricken in their homes, too weak to seek medical help, and asked several of the men to form a small band of riders to scour the countryside and bring in anyone who might be stricken.

She then pushed aside her exhaustion and turned her attention to Clint and Tom, giving them a minimal dose of the medicines, since she was about out of both and knew they would need to continue the medication for several days. She worried about Clint and Tom more than she had the others, mainly because they both meant so very much to her, but she dared not consider the possibility that either of them could die. No, they were too strong and too stubborn to let a small germ get the best of them.

Of the two, Clint turned out to be the least sick and the first to come around. Although he was too weak at first to do much more than talk about getting up, by nightfall, he was on his feet and helping her with the others.

Angela, afraid he might relapse if he didn't take care of himself, begged him to get back in bed and stay there; but as usual he refused to listen to her pleas and was at her side when Amos Kieffer was brought in.

Three of Amos's fellow workers had found him on the road that led into town from the main shaft of the Angel mine.

"Not Amos," Angela wailed, bursting into tears. She

was too tired to handle even one more emotional let-down and went willingly into Clint's arms where she wept bitterly until she could weep no more. Then, as if by purging herself of her tears she had also purged herself of her exhaustion, she went to work trying to bring Amos's fever down.

In all, only two people died in the influenza outbreak that had so quickly swept Clear Creek, and most people credited the low death rate to Angela and Sadie's tireless efforts. To them, Angela and Sadie were town heroes. Many, like Amos Kieffer, swore they now owed their lives to them. *Especially* Amos, for he was certain he had held a heated conversation first with the devil himself, then with a calling angel, all while lying out on that road half buried in snow.

"The devil, he was a hairy beast," he told anyone who would sit long enough to listen. "He loomed over me for the longest, as if trying to decide if he wanted to waste his time claiming me. But I guess he decided against it when the angel showed up because I didn't see him again after that.

"Now as for the angel, she was dead set on me going with her. Said it was my time. But I looked her right in the eye and told her it warn't. I still had too many things left to do," he said with great enthusiasm. "But that angel was a determined critter and followed me all the way into town. She didn't leave my side until she laid her saintly eyes on Angela and realized she had met her match. That angel was sure reluctant to go on back without me, but with Angela taking such good care of me, she had no choice but to give me up."

Angela was not sure how much of his story was due

to his failing eyesight and the late evening shadows, or how much to his vivid imagination, but she did not question the authenticity, not even after he had started to embellish the story with engrossing new details.

Although everyone had pretty much recovered within the first week, it was a full three weeks before things were back to what might be considered normal in Clear Creek. By the middle of February, the mines were functioning again and most of the shops, stores, offices, restaurants, and saloons were open.

It was also about that same time that Clint decided he was safe enough while in town to start courting Angela properly.

Although he still refused to discuss the fact that he was being followed with Angela, and rarely discussed it with his father, he had willingly admitted to them both that it had been his fear of Angela getting hurt that had allowed him to let her move into town. But when time grew near for the coming of spring, and Angela started to press him for a wedding date, he realized the time had come to tell her the truth. He *still* feared for her life.

"Angie, you know I don't want to hurt you, but I think you should know. You and I cannot get married until I finally catch whoever it is that keeps following me," he said in no uncertain terms. Although Angela had suggested they sit and enjoy the cozy fire burning in Sadie's parlor, he remained standing.

"But why?" Angela asked, having had just about enough of his stonewalling. She stood facing him a few feet away.

"Why? Because I won't allow you to put yourself in any danger," he answered with an annoyed frown. "I'd think you'd know that by now. I've said it often enough."

"Maybe too often. It's starting to sound more like an excuse than a logical reason for us not to marry." She met his defiant glare with one of her own.

"You know that isn't true. I *want* to marry you."

"Then set a date," she said and planted her hands on her hips to let him know she was tired of waiting.

"I can't."

"Then I will. Whether or not you have rid yourself of this man you claim keeps following you, we will be married in the church on May 10. Sadie told me that a Reverend Goodson from Silverlode plans to spend the last week in April and the first two weeks of May in Clear Creek and will perform weddings and baptisms for donations of a dollar a piece. She saw the announcement posted on the community bulletin board herself."

"Angie, I don't think you realize just how serious the danger is," Clint argued, feeling a sense of admiration at the stubborn set of her jaw.

"And I don't think you realize how serious I am about becoming Mrs. Clint Rutledge," she retorted with an angry toss of her head, then dropped her voice to a far more persuasive tone. "Clint, please. I'm not afraid of whoever keeps stalking you and I promise to take special precautions for as long as you think he's still out there. I'll even put off my plans to go see Susan and the new baby in June if you still think that man is out there then. Just please say we can go ahead and get married this spring like you promised."

When Clint did not immediately come back with an argumentative response, she hurried to further her cause. "And the danger might not be quite as bad as you originally thought. After all, you yourself admitted he doesn't seem to be following you as often now that your father has been trying to help you catch him. And it *has* been several months now since you say he first started following you."

She took Clint's large hands in her own to encourage him to consider what she had to say more thoroughly. "Clint, I think if that man meant you any real harm, he would have tried something by now; but he hasn't. To tell you the truth, I'm starting to believe you may have built the noises you've heard and the feelings you've had way out of proportion. I think either the man you claim has been following you exists only in your mind, or else you are being followed by someone who is merely curious about you and happens to live in the area."

"I know everyone who lives within ten miles of the Double R, and none of them would take to secretly following me. None of them would have the time, not even in the winter. No, there's somebody out there, all right, and eventually he will either make his move to try to kill me, or he will finally slip up enough for me to catch him."

He refused to tell her about the strange footprints he'd found in the snow just last week. They'd looked like that of a huge man with an abnormally wide arch and tiny gnarled toes, even larger than those his father had made so many years ago. He didn't want to tell Angela because he knew she would demand to know why a grown man would be walking around in the snow barefoot like that, and he had no idea. Nor could he imagine a man of such an incredible size and bulk having been able to slip about unnoticed for as long as he had. It just didn't make sense, and he wondered if the footprints had been purposely planted to frighten him. The only thing he could figure was that the man following him had made himself a pair of strange looking boots, something like those his father had made, specially constructed to make such improbable prints.

Unaware of Clint's growing concerns, Angela looked at the ceiling for a moment while she tapped her boot on the parlor floor before leveling her determined gaze at him again. "Either you agree to marry me on May 10 or our engagement is off."

"I don't like ultimatums," Clint warned, the muscles in his jaw working double-time.

"And I don't like not having a set date for our marriage," she responded, all the while working her own jaw muscles just as rapidly. She was so angry with Clint at that moment, she was barely aware that Sadie and Amos had entered the room.

"My, my," Amos said as he came forward with a peculiar frown pulling at his weathered face. "They look just like a couple of old wet roosters getting ready to fight, don't they?" He stood between them, looking up at each one, then stroked his long whiskers while he considered the situation further. "You know, Sadie, judging by the determined gleam in each one's eyes, I think I know how this one is going to come out."

"And how is that?" Sadie asked and walked over to join him in his close perusal of the two.

Angela tried to hold on to her angry expression, but for the life of her couldn't. A smile tugged at the corners of her mouth while she waited to hear what preposterous thing Amos had to say.

Amos put his right arm around Sadie and leaned toward her while he continued to stroke his long white whiskers with the other. "I know you heard as much of the argument as I did and heard Clint's excuse as to why they shouldn't get married and a good deal of Angela's reasoning as to why they should."

"I also heard the angry determination in Angela's voice," Sadie said, nodding that she agreed with whatever Amos was about to say. "She means what she says, that one. Either they be wed this coming May or she'll find herself someone else."

"Another thing we should consider, too, is the fact that Clint told the whole town that he fully intends to marry her come spring. She would be humiliated if he backed out on that promise. Why, she could even sue him for breech of promise or some such if he doesn't come through with an 'I do' by early summer."

Clint's dark eyes narrowed while he listened to Amos, aware the old man was clearly on Angela's side. "I never mentioned an exact date."

"But you did say you planned to marry her come spring and I'd say at least thirty people in this here town heard you say it. If you two aren't married by then, I reckon she'd have a good case against you in court."

"And the poor darling is doing everything she can to appease him. I heard her promise to stay out of danger as best she could," Sadie put in, nodding while she continued to agree with Amos. "I don't think Clinton could be asking for more than that."

There was a long silence while Angela and Clint continued to stare blankly at each other before Amos spoke again. "Know what else I think?"

Sadie looked truly interested when she turned to Amos and asked, "No, what else do ye think?"

"I think *I* should be the best man." He reached into his vest pocket and took out a folded mercantile receipt and a two-inch piece of lead pencil and started to scribble something on the back. "Guess I'd better make myself a note of that. Best man at Clint's wedding. May 10. Should be an afternoon wedding so I'll put down two o'clock." He wrinkled his nose when another thought occurred to him. "Clint, am I going to have to go out and get me a new Sunday-go-to-meeting coat for your wedding or will a nice white shirt and a string tie do?"

Clint closed his eyes, aware he was outnumbered three to one. When he reopened them, he looked at Angela. "Do you swear by all that is holy and good that you will stay away from any danger if we go through with our plans to marry this spring?"

Angela grinned, knowing he was about to give in and finally agree to a date. "May I be swept away by a villainous fire and burned to an ash if I don't," she answered with a dramatic toss of her head. Then her girlish grin turned into a genuine smile filled with promise and love. "Yes, Clint. I'll do whatever you say, whenever you say."

"That'll be the day," Sadie muttered under her breath but just loud enough for everyone to hear.

Clint's right eyebrow arched a degree, but he kept his gaze locked with Angela's. "That will mean staying at the house most of the time right after we are married if that man is still out there stalking me. Until that man is caught and behind bars, you won't be able to ride into town, either with me or alone, because whoever it is will know that you are my weak spot. The only time you'll be able to come into town and visit with your friends is when Dad decides to come because I know he'll protect you."

"Which is often enough," Angela agreed.

"And you'll have to put off going to see Susan until Dad has time to go in July."

"Agreed."

"Then I guess Amos had better go out and buy himself a new Sunday-go-to-meeting coat and also get himself a good haircut because I plan for us to have the fanciest wedding Clear Creek ever saw."

Amos's hand flew to the bound hair hanging down to the middle of his back then frowned. "Which hair you planning on me cutting?"

Clint laughed but did not answer. His attention was on Angela while he waited for what he had just said to register completely.

"Oh, Clint," she wailed with tears of joy spilling from her eyes as she flew into his waiting arms. "I love you so very much. I'll be a good wife. The best there ever was. Just you wait and see."

Chapter Twenty-Eight

"Mother, I don't care what the man said. I refuse to climb out of this stage and walk one more time," Dahlia said with a determined sniff. "It was wretched enough that we had to stay three weeks in that squalid little hotel while waiting for the first stage to finally leave. How can they now keep insisting we climb out and walk? I have suffered quite enough abominations since we left New Orleans and I don't intend to put up with any more."

"Please, Dahlia, dearest," Julia begged, wringing her hands with a mother's despair. "It's such a pretty day and we are almost there now. And Mr. Baker did tell me that this is the last time we'll have to climb out and walk. It really is for our own safety."

"I think he just said that about the bridges being unsafe to make us do what he wants."

"No, I believe he's telling the truth. I think the bridges really are too weak. I think the winter ice really has weakened them until it is dangerous to have them bear a full load. Why else would these men go to the trouble to carry our trunks across by hand if it wasn't true?

"To annoy me," Dahlia said with an obstinate wave of her lace handkerchief, then snapped her mouth shut and crossed her arms as if to indicate the matter was now closed to discussion.

Julia worried with her bottom lip while trying to decide some way to convince her daughter to cooperate and was startled when a male voice interrupted her thoughts.

"Miss Langford, it's time for you and your aunt to get out now," a short man, with what he had joshingly referred to as his winter's paunch, said after he stuck his balding head inside the coach. In his hands he politely held the battered hat he had worn just seconds earlier. "The other two passengers are already across and we've already carried all the cargo, mail bags, and baggage across. All we're waitin' on now is for you two to climb on out and get on your way."

"Well, you can just keep waiting," Dahlia said and gave the man the iciest glare her blue eyes could offer. "I'm staying right here where I am."

"Ma'am, I'm don't like arguin' with the passengers, but you ain't stayin' in here. You're gettin' out and walkin' just like the rest. I've got my orders and my orders say that unless a person is injured or ill, he or she is to walk across any and all bridges and land crossings until the company can get a road crew up here to reenforce the underpinnings with fresh lumber."

Dahlia glowered at the man with clear contempt. "I don't think you heard me, sir. I am staying right here."

"Looks like you leave me no choice," Baker muttered then plopped his hat back on his head when he leaned back outside. "Hey, Wilson, give me a hand here. Looks like we're goin' to have to carry the one with the red hair across if we plan to be in Clear Creek before night-fall."

Julia's eyes widened with alarm when she reached out and took her daughter's hand in an aunty fashion. "Oh, Angela, dear, I think the man means what he says."

"I do indeed," Baker responded. "Orders is orders. And it's my job to follow 'em."

Dahlia looked at Baker's determined scowl, then at her mother's blanched face, and realized she was in for a very uncomfortable moment if she did not give in this one time. "Very well. I'll walk. But only because I don't care to be carried across like a sack of potatoes."

"Wise decision," Baker said, then rolled his eyes sky-ward as if he'd just about had his limit of this arrogant young girl. "Never mind, Wilson. Looks like Miss Langford has thought it over and changed her mind. Get on up in the seat there. We might still make Clear Creek in time for a bath before supper."

Dahlia waited until the man had stepped back before leaning close to her mother's ear and whispering be-tween tightly clenched teeth. "You and the good rever-end had better be right about Samuel Langford's money, because if it turns out we've come all this way and have put up with all these inconveniences for nothing, I'll *never* forgive you."

"Don't worry," Julia said with a encouraging smile while she reached forward to touch her daughter's cheek gently. "Not only will it be both our words against Angela's, *we* are the ones carrying all the proof, forged though it may be. Don't worry, dearest. We'll be in Paris by autumn. I promise."

* * *

Richard Grissom stood and smiled the moment he saw Angela enter his office. "Good morning."

Angela looked at him curiously. It was still hard for her to believe this was the same man who had scolded her so caustically just a few months earlier.

"Good morning, Mr. Grissom. Sadie said you wanted to see me," she responded, her expression hopeful when she closed the door then came forward. "Have you heard from Reverend Smith?"

He shook his head and lifted a finger of reproach. "You keep forgetting. You are to call me Richard now. I will not allow anyone who saved my life as well as the lives of many of my friends and employees to continue referring to me as *Mr. Grissom.*"

Angela smiled, still finding his sudden change in behavior a little overwhelming. "Very well, *Richard,* have you received an answer from Reverend Smith yet?"

"I'm sorry but no." He gestured for her to sit, which she promptly did. "Although quite a backlog of mail has gotten through during these past few weeks, I am afraid I've not yet received a response from your Reverend Smith. But don't be too downhearted. I understand the first stage out of Silverlode is due to arrive sometime today. Could be it will carry a letter from the good reverend."

Angela felt her spirits plummet. Having been summoned to his office, she had truly expected to be told that today was the day she could start legal proceedings to claim her inheritance, and she really did need the money now, or rather Tom and Clint did. With the weather warming, the pastures starting to turn green, and the price of cattle still low from winter weight losses, now would be the perfect time to restock. "I don't understand. Then why did you tell Sadie you wanted to see me?"

"Because I have reached a decision. I have decided to let you have a look at your father's journal. If for no other reason than to repay you for your recent kindnesses."

"You have?" she responded eagerly and glanced around for sight of it. "Where is it?"

"It is still at my house. I pulled it down from the attic last night and glanced through it and decided it really is something you should read. Especially the pages he penned right after having been told you and your mother had died."

Angela looked at him gratefully, aware he had just the same as admitted he finally believed her. He finally believed she was the daughter Julia had claimed had died. Tears sprang to her gray eyes. "When can I come by to see it?"

"Tonight. Say about seven o'clock? Although I do plan to let you take it with you because it is probably four-hundred pages thick and all but a few pages have been written on, I'd like to see your face when you read the comments he wrote about you years ago. You and your mother were worth far more to him than all the silver in this mountain."

Angela's lower lips trembled and her gaze took on a distant quality while she tried to remember his smiling face and his gentle voice. "He would have come for me had he known, wouldn't he?"

"On hands and knees, if need be," Richard admitted, blinking hard while he tugged at the front of his collar. "You two were his only true joys."

"Thank you," she responded sincerely, then stood on wobbly legs. She wanted to leave before she started to weep her gratitude uncontrollably. "I'll be at your house at precisely seven."

"I don't doubt that for a minute," he said, watching while she hurried from his office to share her good news. "Not for one precious little minute."

"Here comes the stage!" a man at the far end of town shouted, then turned and waved his hat wildly. "Here comes that first stage."

As always in a community as remote as Clear Creek, the coming of the first stage was an event everyone wanted to see and dozens of people came running from stores and houses to line the streets and cheer while the coach clattered through.

Angela and Sadie had heard the shouts through the open windows of their separate rooms and as soon as Angela had set aside her sewing, they hurried out onto the porch to catch a glimpse for themselves, wondering if there would be any passengers on board that first stage. Or more importantly, if there would be any mailbags carrying letters from as far away as New Orleans.

Because it was late afternoon and most of the male boarders were still inside the mines, no one else joined them on Sadie's front porch, giving them the opportunity to move about for the best possible view of the events happening just one block away.

"Imagine that. There's a woman getting out," Sadie said, straining her neck to see over the people who had rushed into the street to greet the stage. She laughed when she saw the woman's startled expression as she stepped out of the stage. "I don't think she expected such a rousing welcome."

Angela stood on the tips of her toes to see for herself

but at the same moment, Dane Tapley, who stood on the main boardwalk between them, shifted his massive weight from one leg to the other and blocked her view.

"Do you think she'll get back on the stage and demand to be taken back down the mountain?" Angela asked with a laugh, then turned to pull one of the slatted chairs forward so she could stand on it.

"Oh, look, now a young girl is getting off," Sadie said squinting as the afternoon sun broke through the clouds and cast a harsh glare over the valley. "She looks to be about ye'r age."

"Good," Angela responded as she stepped up into the chair then held her hands out for balance. "I'd love to have someone else my age to talk with. I think poor Joanie Boswell has to be about talked out by now."

"Not Joanie," Sadie chuckled. "As long as there's a breath in that young lass, she'll have something to say." She squinted again. "My, my, now two gentlemen are getting off. They are the husbands, I suppose. No, I do take that assumption back. The men both look to be in their thirties. Too young for one woman and too old for the other."

Now that she had her balance, Angela stretched to her full height, but frowned when she noticed both females had turned their backs to her. "I wish the women would turn back around so I could get a good look at them. All I can tell about them is the color of their hair."

"The older one with the silver-streaked dark hair is rather tall and stately looking from the front," Sadie informed Angela without taking her eyes off all the commotion. "Looked to be a little snooty, but that could be because she was so overwhelmed by such a curious crowd. And the young one with all that lovely red hair tucked so primly beneath her feathered hat is also fairly tall and perhaps a tad bit too plump for her age, but pretty all the same." Her eyes then rounded as she threw her hand to her throat. "Oh, but look at the gentleman wearing the dark gray jacket. He's about as handsome a man as I've ever seen. And perhaps he's only a few years younger than I."

Angela looked at the man with a curious frown because although he was nice looking, with his clean clothing and city haircut, he could not compare to Clint. "I'm not interested in the men. What I want to know is what the women are wearing. Did you get a glimpse of their clothing before they stepped down from the stage?"

"Aye, of course I did. They are both finely dressed, especially the younger one. Oh, but ye are about to see that for ye'rself, they are headed toward the stage office. When they step up onto the platform, ye should be able to get a fine look."

An irrational feeling of dread swept over Angela while she watched the two women make their way through the milling crowd. There was just something about them that made her stomach coil with apprehension. Still, it was not until they had stepped up onto the platform and turned to see if their baggage was being unloaded that she understood her concern.

"Julia!" she said in a husky voice, feeling suddenly faint.

"Ye know one of them?" Sadie asked, clearly surprised.

"I've known both of them most of my life. But what I don't know is why they are here."

"Then let's go find out," Sadie said and took a step toward the walk.

"I don't know," Angela responded cautiously. "I'm not sure I want to talk to them right now."

"But if ye know them, why not?"

"Because—," she started to say, but her mind was off in too many directions to produce the right words. "I'll explain it to you later."

"Fine, explain it to me later. But for now, let's go down there and find out why they are here and how long they plan to stay. Perhaps the young one has come to marry one of the locals."

Sadie was already halfway down the steps before she turned to see if Angela had followed. "Well? Are ye be coming or not?"

Aware she would have to face them at some time during their stay in Clear Creek, Angela slowly stepped down from the chair.

What are they doing here? she wondered, already knowing the answer would have something to do with her.

"Well, come on," Sadie encouraged, wanting her to hurry. She bent forward to brush a spot of dust from her dark green skirt and adjusted her sleeves. "Introduce me to ye'r friends."

"I didn't say they were friends," Angela commented as she caught up with her.

Sadie slowed her steps. "Oh. I didna realize. Well, then, perhaps it would be best if we turn back."

"No. I feel sure they are here to see me for some reason. I might as well find out what it is they want."

Sadie walked in silence for a moment, then glanced at Angela with a puzzled expression. "What name is it ye called one of them?" Sadie asked thoughtfully while they elbowed their way through a crowd made up mostly of women, children, storekeepers, and gamblers.

"Julia," Angela answered, the name weighing heavy on her tongue. "Julia Stanton."

Sadie paused to look Angela in the eye. "The same Julia who lied about ye to ye'r father?"

"The same," she answered. Her facial muscles hardened with the thought of all she had gone through at the hands of this vile woman.

"Oh, my. I didna realize." She stared off toward the area where the new arrivals stood, then her expression brightened. "But perhaps this is a good thing your aunt coming here. Perhaps now ye will be able to prove to Richard Grissom that ye are who ye say that ye are."

Angela blinked while Sadie's words sank in. Could Julia's coming here actually be a godsend?

If the woman would just go with her to Richard's office and convince him that she really was Angela Langford, then she would be able to get the money right away. If all went well, Clint and Tom could start rebuilding their stock as early as next week. If Julia would only do that. If she would go with her to Richard's office and tell him the truth, then perhaps Angela could forgive her for some of the terrible deeds she'd done in the past.

Seconds later, when she stepped up on the same platform where Julia and Dahlia stood waiting, she noticed Julia scanning the crowd as if looking for her. Although her first inclination was to turn and hurry away, she pooled her courage and pushed her way through the remainder of the crowd.

Julia spotted Angela just seconds before Angela had a chance to call out to her.

"I told you! There she is," Julia said, pointing at Angela with her usual look of disdain. "There's that ungrateful wretch, Ruby Stillrod."

Angela looked truly perplexed when she realized Julia had meant her. "What are you talking about, Aunt Julia? Who is Ruby Stillrod?"

"Why you are, you ungrateful twit," she said in a very loud voice as if acting out a play, then she pressed her hand over her heart in an extremely melodramatic gesture. "How dare you try to take something that rightfully belongs to my dear niece, Angela Langford."

"But *I* am Angela Langford," she said, still puzzled, then realized her aunt was up to her usual tricks, though she did not yet know what was going on. She glanced at the people surrounding them and realized they were all staring at her with raised brows as if suddenly doubting her identity. "Well, I *am* Angela Langford."

"How dare you use my name like that?" Dahlia said, taking her cue. "And how dare you call your former employer, *Aunt Julia?* She's no more your aunt then I am your cousin."

"But you are my cousin, though I don't readily admit it."

Julia lifted her head regally and glanced at those who stood about. "Does this town have a sheriff? I want this woman arrested."

After a moment of silence, Dane Tapley was the one to answer. "I guess you could call Horace Jones the sheriff. He's the one in charge of the jail until this town can hold another election."

"Then bring him to me. I demand that this woman be put in jail immediately."

Dane turned and smiled at Angela tauntingly. "Be glad to. Just see that she doesn't run away while I'm gone."

"Don't worry," Angela retorted. "I have no reason to run away. I've done nothing wrong."

"Nothing wrong?" Julia wailed. "You try to swindle my dear niece, Angela Langford, out of her rightful inheritance by claiming to be her and you say you have done nothing wrong? How *dare* you, you little ingrate?"

"And after all I and my aunt have done for you," Dahlia put in with a disbelieving shake of her head. "How could you?"

Angela narrowed her eyes in anger. "Dahlia, I don't know what this is all about or why you are here, but I'm not about to let you or Aunt Julia try to convince these people that I am not Angela Langford."

"We don't have to *try* to convince anyone of anything. We have brought the necessary proof with us."

"What proof?" Angela asked, confused. She glanced at Sadie, who had turned as pale as she was speechless, then looked again at Julia.

"Proof that we will show to the sheriff just as soon as he arrives," Dahlia answered. "Proof that will let my father's business partner know *I* am the real heir."

Angela fell silent while she absorbed what Dahlia had just said. Finally it struck her. Dahlia was there to steal her inheritance.

"What proof could you possibly have?"

Julia stepped in front of Dahlia as if wanting to protect her charge from any more angry accusations. "Well, Ruby, we certainly don't have the birth certificate you stole from us, but we do have plenty of letters that will prove what we say."

"Letters? From whom?"

"From Reverend Smith for one. He's the one who informed us of your little scheme. And we also have letters from several neighbors. Plus, we have a photograph that Samuel sent to Angela and her mother just days after they came to live with me. Why would we have that and not you if you are the real Angela?"

"Because you never gave it to me," she said, angry to learn that such a photograph existed and had been kept from her.

Again Julia's voice rose for all to hear. "And why would we give you, a mere housekeeper, a photograph of Angela and her father?"

"Because I *am* Angela." Her heart raced while she tried to think of some way to prove it. "That photograph is rightfully mine. Where is it?"

"Come now. Give up this little farce. Can't you understand that it is over, that you have been caught in the act and are about to go to jail for a very, very long time?"

Angela stared at Julia with her hands curled into fists, unable to believe any of this was happening. "You won't get away with this. No one will believe you."

"I think you should look at the faces around you," Julia said with a dramatic sweep of her hand. "These people are not fools. They know an impostor when they see one."

There was a loud muttering among those watching but then all fell silent again when Dane Tapley and Horace Jones pushed their way through the crowd.

"There she is, Horace," Dane said, pointing to Angela with a defiant expression. "You are the acting sheriff. Arrest her."

Chapter Twenty-Nine

Clint slid off his horse even before it came to a stop and gave his reins only one wrap around the hitching post before heading toward the sheriff's office.

"Horace, what's going on here?" he asked as he entered the office that took up the front portion of the new jail and spotted the interim sheriff behind his desk facing several women, one of whom was Angela. "I just saw Sadie MacDonald and she babbled something about you having put Angela Langford in jail."

"Can't rightly say that I have," Horace said in his Texas twang and scratched the top of his balding head with the back of his thumb while he looked from Angela, to Julia, to Dahlia. "First of all, I haven't rightly figured out just which of these here ladies is the real Angela Langford. They have all three put up some mighty convincing arguments for and against. And second of all, I ain't actually put nobody behind bars yet."

"But *we* have shown you actual proof," Julia said with a haughty huff as if she could not understand why the sheriff had failed to perform his duty. "*We* have given you actual letters explaining what happened. All *she* had given you is some lame story about how she was in a stagecoach accident and lost what little proof she had, which I assure you she stole from us the moment she found out how wealthy Angela's father was reported to be."

Julia twisted in her seat and looked at Clint as if to ask what business it was of his anyway. "And when Mr. Grissom of the Angel Mine gets here, he will most certainly verify that we are telling the truth by confirming he did indeed send a letter to Reverend Smith asking about Angela's existence."

"And what will that prove?" Clint asked, confused as hell by what the woman had just said and wishing Sadie had been able to tell him more. But she had been too upset to make much sense when he had stopped by to take Angela to an early supper.

"It will explain how we found out about Ruby's little ploy," she answered readily, looking insulted that he had questioned her. "It will also explain the significance of the letter we brought with us, which was written by the reverend himself." Frowning, she cut her gaze from Clint to Horace. "Who is this man?"

Horace continued to scratch his head while he considered his answer a few seconds. "Well, ma'am, I'm not rightly sure about that either. He's either Angela Langford's or Ruby Stillrod's intended."

"I've not agreed to marry this man," Dahlia protested, though she looked at him with noted interest.

"I meant the other Angela Langford," he said and nodded toward the original Angela.

"Don't call her that," Julia inserted quickly. "I've already told you. That young woman's name is Ruby Stillrod. She is nothing more than a downstairs housekeeper—and a poor one at that."

Horace frowned while he pressed his fingertips to his

temples as if slowly reaching his limit. "I know what you told me. And I know what she told me. But what I don't know is which of you is telling the truth."

"Angela is," Clint put in abruptly.

Horace squeezed his eyes closed and continued to massage his temples. "And which Angela is that?"

"My Angela, of course. I was there the day she lost her trunk. I can verify that she is telling the truth. That it is not just some story she made up to get by not having any identification."

Angela looked at him, truly grateful, but her expression fell into an immediate frown when she saw Richard Grissom and Dane Tapley enter the room directly behind him.

"Horace, Mr. Tapley here said you wanted to see me." He looked around the room questioningly. "But he wouldn't tell me what it was about. Said that was for you to do."

Horace leaned back in his chair and heaved a hefty sigh before explaining the situation as best he could without sounding like a complete fool. "And what we want to know from you is did you send a letter to a—" he paused to pick up one of the envelopes Julia had given him. "Did you send a letter to a Reverend James Smith in New Orleans trying to find out if Sam's daughter really was still alive?"

"Yes, I did," he said, looking at those about him with a perplexed expression. "It was as much Angela's idea as mine."

Dahlia promptly stood to face Richard. "I am Angela Langford, and I *never* encouraged you to write Reverend Smith, though I am very glad you did," she said, then turned to Angela with an accusing glare. "I shudder when I think of what might have happened had the reverend not come to us with that letter."

By now Clint fully understood what was happening and stepped forward to have his say. "What I don't understand is why he bothered telling you about it at all. What business of yours was that letter?"

Julia puffed out in an exasperated breath, then stood beside Dahlia. "When someone attempts to cheat my niece out of her rightful inheritance by coming here and pretending to be her, I think it is very *much* our business and I am still waiting for the sheriff to do his duty and put her in a jail cell where trash like that belongs."

While Richard looked at Angela, then at Dahlia, with a puzzled expression, Horace glanced at the letters and the small photograph on his desk, then at the pretty young lady who had worked so hard to save his own son's life just a few months earlier and shook his head, "I'm not getting mixed up in this. This is one the judge will have to figure out and until he does, I'm not throwing nobody in jail."

"Then I demand to see the judge," Julia said with a forward thrust of her chin.

"And you will," Horace assured her. "Just as soon as I can send someone down to Silverlode to get him."

"Down to Silverlode?" Julia repeated, looking as if she could not possibly have heard him correctly. "How long will that take?"

"Depends if he has any important cases pending," Horace said. "Could be a month, could be just a few days. Can't rightly say until I've sent someone down there to find out."

"A *month?*" Dahlia wailed, clearly not pleased with the prospect. "Do you mean there's a chance we'll have to stay in this horrible little town a whole month?"

"Or more," Dane said, then took several steps toward her. "But don't let that trouble you. It rarely takes that long to get him up here when something as serious as this comes up. And even if he is too busy with something else right now, he's already set to be here his usual two weeks in May." He then offered her his most winning smile. "But then Clear Creek isn't so bad once you get settled in, and I for one will do all I can to see that your stay here is a comfortable one."

From where Angela sat, all she could see was Dane's broad back, but she could well imagine the provocative smile he had just presented Dahlia and realized by the color rising in her *dear* cousin's cheeks how completely affected Dahlia had been by it. Angela fought the urge to comment aloud that those two certainly deserved each other, while she watched Dahlia bat her long lashes and turn on her coquettish charm.

"Why thank you, Mr.—," Dahlia paused to allow Dane the opportunity to supply his name, for they had not been properly introduced; and if there was one thing Dahlia was a stickler for, it was proper protocol.

"Tapley, Ma'am, Dane Tapley. At your service."

"And my name is Angela Langford," Dahlia then supplied, cutting her gaze at Angela as if daring her to deny it.

"Lovely name," Dane responded, then tilted his head at an angle and turned to look at the sheriff. "Horace, if you're through with our two beautiful newcomers for now, then I'd like to be the one to show them where the hotel is. I'm sure they are tired after the ride in from that last way station."

Horace blinked once, then waved them on.

Julia bent to pick up the handbag she'd left on a chair before standing to face the sheriff again. "I'll be by tomorrow morning to find out if you've heard from the judge."

"Don't bother. The telegraph's still down from the winter and my rider won't be back until day after tomorrow at the earliest."

"But what's to prevent her from escaping?" Julia asked, pointing at Angela.

"Don't worry. She ain't going nowhere. The only transportation out of here besides a horse, which she ain't got, is that same stage you rode in on, and I'll make sure she's not on it when it leaves tomorrow."

"See that you do," Julia said and cast Angela a disdainful glare. "I want her here to face her crimes when that judge arrives."

After what had happened earlier, Angela felt a little awkward about stopping by to see Richard. She had seen the doubt on his face after he had heard Julia's accusations and now she was not sure what he believed. Still, he had promised to let her see her father's journal tonight which would be worth any questions she might have to answer.

"Hello," she said with a congenial smile when a short, middle-aged Oriental woman dressed in some sort of robe opened the door and asked to help her. "My name is Angela Langford. Mr. Grissom is expecting me."

The Oriental woman frowned and shook her head. "Mr. Grissom not say he expecting company."

"Well, he is," Angela explained. "And I am that company. Could you tell him I am here?"

"You wait."

Angela had expected to be invited in while the housekeeper delivered the message and was a little surprised when instead the door was closed abruptly in her face. Several seconds later the door opened again and Richard Grissom stood in the doorway looking very uncomfortable.

"I've come for my father's journal," Angela said as a way of reminding him why she had come.

Richard's mouth flattened into a tight line for a long moment as if suddenly lost in thought, then slowly he shook his head. "I'm sorry. But in light of what happened earlier, I'm afraid I'll have to recant my offer. Until I know for certain which of you young women is the real Angela Langford, if indeed either of you are, I cannot in good conscience let Sam's journal out of my sight."

Angela closed her eyes against the sharp pain that sliced through her heart, then slowly opened them again. "I see that my aunt has raised some doubts."

"If she is indeed your aunt," he said, his accent more clipped than usual. "To tell you the truth, after everything I heard this afternoon, I'm not sure what I believe anymore."

"I understand," Angela said, amazed at how calmly she had spoken, all the while holding her head erect when what she really wanted to do was bury her face in her hands and scream until she could scream no more. "I guess there's not much more for us to say to each other until that judge from Silverlode finally arrives and sorts this all out."

"I guess not." Richard studied her reaction closely. Although the other girl had more traits similar to Samuel's, including a similar color of hair, he still hoped this one proved to be the right one. "I think it would be wise for both you and the other young lady to stay away

410

from me until after the hearing. I don't want it said I gave biased testimony in case I'm asked to speak."

Devastated that apparently Julia was determined to ruin her life yet again, and was getting away with it, Angela did not emerge from her room the following morning when it was time for breakfast. Nor did she come out for lunch. By the time Clint stopped by that following evening, wanting to take her to supper, Sadie was beside herself with worry.

"She refuses to come out and talk with me about it. She says there's nothing I can do to help her. Nothing *anyone* can do to help her because Julia Stanton always gets her way. *Always.*"

"That doesn't sound like Angela," Clint said, frowning while he hooked his hat over a wall peg.

"She hasn't been the same since that aunt of hers stepped off that stage. It's as if she lost all her will to defend herself. I canna understand it. She's stood up to you, she stood up to Dane Tapley, and she stood up to Richard Grissom. Why is it she cowers to that woman?"

"Because that woman raised her to be afraid of her," Clint explained. "Angela doesn't like to talk about it, but her life with 'Aunt Julia' and 'Cousin Dahlia' was a living hell."

"Still, I'd think she'd be willing to fight for what's rightfully hers. What was rightfully her father's."

"And she will. One of the reasons I'm here is to tell her that the sheriff's rider returned early and said the judge has agreed to come right away. The hearing is scheduled for next Monday morning in the sheriff's office at eight-thirty. I also hired a lawyer for her. Dad and I agreed that helping Angela was a better way to spend

411

that inheritance money than heading down to Silverlode to buy new cattle."

Sadie looked truly relieved. "Who did ye hire?"

"Tony Andrews. The best Clear Creek has to offer."

Sadie offered a feeble smile. "That's because there are only two real lawyers in this whole town and Patrick Ray is noted for tipping the bottle a bit too often and snoozing in court."

Clint grinned. "Which means that if Julia and Dahlia Stanton plan to have legal counsel, they will have little choice but to retain Mr. Ray."

Sadie's eyes sparkled with sudden understanding. "Why ye young scoundrel. Ye should be ashamed of ye'rself for such a thing."

"Oh, I am, Sadie," Clint responded, looking dutifully contrite. "I most certainly am." He then headed toward the hallway that led back to Angela's room with long, eager strides, wanting to give her the good news.

For the next two days, Angela and Tony Andrews went over all the points and counterpoints Angela needed to be sure and make during the hearing while Amos decided to do a little investigating of his own. He wanted to find out exactly what was in those letters so Tony could plan a good counterattack.

After Horace Jones refused to let them have a peek at the letters Julia Stanton had left in his safekeeping, Amos set out to discover what the two women had up their sleeve in another way. He waited until Dane had taken the younger Stanton to dinner, something the conniving blackguard had done each evening since the day the two women had arrived, then hiked spritely up to the second floor of the hotel and paused just long enough to make certain his hair was still slicked back out of his face before he knocked lightly at the door.

"Yes?" Julia said, looking down at the curious little man dressed in gray trousers and a dark blue dress coat that looked like it has just come off a store rack. "Is there something I can do for you?"

Aware by the obvious disdain in her voice and her puckered expression that his original plan to woo the information out of her was not exactly headed for success, he quickly rethought his original strategy and came up with something entirely different.

"It's more like what I can do for you," Amos said, holding himself erect while he stared her directly in the eye, which meant looking a might higher than he was used to looking whenever he confronted a woman. "I understand that you are in need of legal counsel."

"*You* are a lawyer?" Julia drew her head back with immediate reservation.

"Attorney Amos P. Kieffer at your service," he responded with what he felt was a lawyerly nod. "I know my way around the local judges better than anyone and I understand you are scheduled to come before Judge Garrison Monday morning. May I come in and discuss your case with you?" he asked, being extremely careful of his grammar, knowing how hoity most of them talked.

"No you may not," Julia said, looking appalled that he had even suggested such a thing. "Sir, I am afraid you have been badly misinformed, for my niece and I have already arranged for a lawyer to represent us."

"You mean Patrick Ray?" Amos asked with a rumpled expression that let his honest opinion of the man come through. "Why that old goat can't stay sober long enough to come up with a complete opening statement much less last through to the closing comments."

Julia's nostrils flared as she cocked her head to one side. "Hardly. Our lawyer's name is Walter Dedbyrd. He is from Silverlode. As I understand it, he'll be arriving Saturday afternoon on the same stage as the judge."

Amos's eyes widened. "Walter Dedbyrd? You mean the judge's *brother-in-law?*"

"Yes, I believe Mr. Tapley did mention the fact that Mr. Dedbyrd and Judge Garrison are related. Why? Do you know Mr. Dedbyrd?"

"I've been up against him a time or two," Amos answered in all honesty for Walter Dedbyrd had represented a man who was always having him arrested for trespassing. He had spent many a day in jail because of that slick-talking reptile.

"Then you'll understand when I decline your offer of counsel," Julia said, already stepping back to close the door.

"But what if Walter Dedbyrd doesn't arrive as planned? Don't you think it would be wise to have backup counsel?"

Julia paused as if giving that question serious thought, then abruptly shook her head. "No. Mr. Tapley assured us that Mr. Dedbyrd will be here in plenty of time to go over our case. Said something about Mr. Dedbyrd owing him a favor. And even if he doesn't come, I think I should be able to represent myself with little problem. After all, I have letters from several respected citizens in New Orleans that clearly reveal the truth."

"But I don't understand, if the young woman who arrived in town with you is the real Angela Langford, why didn't she come forward before now?" Amos was still determined to discover at least part of their defense. "Why did she let her father believe she was dead the way she did?"

"Because she did not want to leave me and come here to live. As most of the people in this town have already heard, my niece does not like the idea of living in this sort of place even for a little while. Even as a child, she preferred her comfort as much as she prefers having people around who love her and who are devoted to taking care of her. Whenever I would mention the possibility of leaving my home to go live with her father, she would cry unceasingly until I promised to let her stay"

"Then you and her are pretty close?" Amos asked in an attempt to keep her talking.

"Of course. I am like a mother to her. And the thought of having to leave my side to come out here and live in the wilderness with a father she hardly knew was too much for her. It was her own suggestion that I tell him that she, too, had died so he would leave her alone."

"But wasn't that kind of a cruel thing to do to Samuel Langford?"

"Not when you consider that we did not plan to carry on the farce forever. Just until Angela was of a legal age to make her own decisions—or as soon as she had married and had a husband to make her decisions. Either way, we fully intended to tell Samuel the truth, just as soon as we could be sure he had no legal say over where she lived and what she did or did not do with her life. But all this will come out at the hearing. If you are truly interested, come and hear for yourself all the reasons why Angela chose to deceive her father. I assure you it was not an easy decision for a child so young."

"I just might do that," Amos said and stepped back to

make it easier for her to close the door. He waited until after the door had clattered shut and all he faced was a badly scarred room number before he added in a voice barely above a whisper. "Truth is, you couldn't keep me away if you beat me within an inch of my life."

"She said *what?*" Angela asked, finding the whole thing preposterous.

Amos repeated what he had just told her about his earlier conversation with Julia Stanton. "She said that the reason her Angela decided to tell your father that she was dead was because she had become so truly devoted to her that she could not bear to leave her," Amos replied, shrugging as if he thought it hard to swallow, too. He then looked at Clint who had not said one word since he had returned from his investigative trip to the hotel. "And she sounded so sincere when she said it. She's going to be one tough lady to beat."

"Especially if she has the judge's own brother-in-law representing her," Clint admitted, his hand curling into a tight fist, angry to know Dane Tapley had interfered like that. "If only there was some way we could prove what an out and out liar that woman is." He sat back in the chair, looking at Angela seated on the edge of the sofa for a long moment. "If only she didn't have those blasted letters."

"But every one of those letters is forged," Angela argued, thinking Clint had not yet grasped that fact. "She had to have written every one of them herself."

"And did she also take that photograph of your father herself?" he asked, thinking at that moment more like a lawyer than a fiancé, unaware how it must have sounded to someone as sensitive as Angela was at that

416

moment. "No, there has to be a way to get around all that evidence. Some way to keep those two from putting their hands on all that money."

Angela felt crushed. Clint did not believe the letters were faked. He believed them to be every bit as authentic as that picture of her father, the one that had torn the heart right out of her when she saw it because he had been looking down at her with such love, such devotion—exactly like she remembered.

"Clint, you make it sound like the only reason you are helping me is because of the money," she said, letting her feelings be known. "Don't you believe I am who I say I am?"

"Of course I do," he answered, but was too lost in thought to sound convincing. "And before this is over, everyone else in this town will believe it, too." He then looked at her questioningly. "But I do find it odd that you never mentioned having asked Richard about the possibility of getting all that money. I thought you told me that the money was not all that important to you."

"I never came right out and asked him for any money," she said, feeling suddenly defensive. "But if it is rightfully mine, then I see no reason not to try to claim it."

Clint studied her a long moment, then asked, "And just what do you plan to do if you do inherit Samuel's estate?"

Angela hesitated to tell him the truth for fear he would see it as some form of charity. But she did not want to lie to him, either, and was relieved when Sadie entered the room at that moment to announce that supper was ready.

"Ye'd better be getting on in there and filling your plates if ye be wanting ye'r fair share."

417

Clint stared after Angela, puzzled that instead of staying to answer his question, she followed Sadie out of the room with Amos right behind them both. For a woman who had eaten barely two bites since Julia Stanton's arrival, she certainly had developed a sudden appetite.

Chapter Thirty

Patiently it waited in the shadows beside the road, knowing the tall mate of the pretty one who smelled so good with her long hair and soft voice would come back the same way he had gone. It had been a season since he had seen her; he longed to look at her again. She reminded him of a happier time. A time of warmth and good feelings. And some day he sensed the pretty one would come again with her mate. So he watched. And waited. So again he could be reminded . . .

Dane waited until *his* Angela had closed the door between them before he dropped his seductive smile and sauntered away. The situation was shaping up much better than he had ever hoped.

It no longer mattered that his hand had not healed as quickly as he wanted, because through the eventual conquest of the latest Angela Langford to arrive in Clear Creek, he might yet be able to exact his revenge.

By helping make sure the second Angela came out the victor, not only would he be robbing Clint Rutledge of the opportunity to marry an extremely wealthy woman, Dane realized that if he played his cards just

419

right while courting the second Angela, *he* might end up the one in control of all that Langford money.

In addition, by having gotten his Angela the perfect lawyer, and by helping in any other way to prove her case against that conniving little housekeeper, he will have had a hand in sending Clint's Angela to jail. Not only would he be robbing Clint of the money he and his father so desperately needed, he'd be robbing the meddling bastard of his woman as well. Just like Clint had robbed him of the woman he loved so many years ago.

While headed across the street to the Golden Briar Saloon, Dane chuckled at the thought of being able to destroy Clint's life in such a clever way, feeling for the first time in ages that life was sweet.

"Why has Clinton not been by today?" Sadie asked, when she glanced at the clock and saw that it was after seven. "And why didna he come by to see ye yesterday? Just where has that young man gotten himself off to?"

"I don't really know," Angela answered, though she had her suspicions. It seemed fairly obvious Clint was avoiding her; she had not seen him since Friday night, right after he first let his doubts about her be known. "I imagine he has a lot to do at the ranch now that the weather has turned so warm."

"But today's a Sunday. Surely he dona intend to work on Sunday."

"Clint is not exactly a church-going man," Angela pointed out.

"Still, he's a man who respects our Maker. Just because he does not show himself in a church house every Sunday dona change that."

"Then I guess we haven't seen him because he just does not care to see me right now," Angela said and lifted her chin proudly. "And I can't really blame him,

420

what with all the controversy my aunt has raised since coming here."

"I dona believe that either," Sadie said and gave Angela a harsh look for having said such a thing. "No, something else is keeping him away." Her eyes widened. "You dona think he has been shot do you? You dona think that the man who has been following him has finally gotten the drop on him?"

A sudden chill curled around Angela's spine at the thought of Clint lying out there somewhere dead or dying, but then she realized that Tom would have gone looking for him by now and would have reported such an incident right away. "No, we'd have heard if he'd been shot. The truth is that Clint can't decide who is telling the truth. He can't decide which of us is really Angela Langford. I imagine the fact that Julia has brought letters and a photograph supporting her claim that Dahlia is the real Angela Langford has started to bother him."

"I canna believe that. Clinton has always been the type to trust his instincts."

"Well, perhaps those instincts are now telling him that I just might not be the person I say I am." She paused to collect her scattering emotions. "We will know for sure tomorrow."

"How's that?"

"If he's not in the courtroom, we'll know it is because he expects me to lose and does not want to face the ridicule."

"He'll be there," Sadie said with a stern frown, clearly not pleased with Angela's assessment. "I'll bet my best lace corset on it."

* * *

By Sunday night, Dane had the second Angela right where he wanted her, sitting in a hired carriage on a lonely mining road, snuggled in his arms.

"You know until you came along, I'd just about given up on ever finding the right woman for me," he said, nuzzling her ear, pleased with the way the gesture forced her eyes to flutter shut. "Who would have guessed that I'd find the perfect woman while visiting a place like Clear Creek?"

"Oh, Dane, I do love you so," Dahlia said, so beguiled by his sugary words and the adoring look on his handsome face she could barely breathe as she wiggled closer against him.

Dane swallowed hard, aware of the ample curves being pressed into his side. If it wasn't for the fear he might frighten her away before getting the revenge and the money he wanted, he would take better advantage of her young, voluptuous body. As it was, he had to control himself. Prove himself worthy of being a husband.

"I just hope you don't plan to leave here too soon after you settle your father's estate. I hate the thought of never seeing you again."

"Oh, but you could always come with us," Dahlia suggested, looking at him hopefully. "You'd like Paris."

"I'd like anywhere as long as you were there," he commented, proud of how quickly the silvery words rolled off his tongue. "I wonder how long it will take to settle matters with Richard Grissom and collect what is rightfully yours."

Dahlia dipped her head. "I-I don't know."

Dane felt the hairs at the back of his neck rise with sudden caution. "Why? What's wrong?"

There was a long silence before Dahlia finally answered. "I can't keep lying to you. My name isn't Angela Langford. It's Dahlia Stanton."

"*What?*" Dane asked, feeling his whole body tense at the thought of everything falling apart on him so suddenly.

"My name is Dahlia Stanton," she confided again. "I'm Angela's cousin. Distant cousin, actually, because my mother is not really her aunt, but her mother's cousin."

"But I don't understand," he said, remaining calm in hopes that this proved to be some sort of test of his affections and not the truth. "You have all those letters that claim you to be Angela Langford."

"My mother and I wrote those letters. It was her idea to come here and claim Angela's inheritance. After all, we deserve something for having taken care of her for all those years."

Dane's forehead notched. "So, if the judge were to decide to wire this Reverend Smith everyone keeps talking about, he'd undoubtedly be told the truth."

"But the telegraph lines are down," Dahlia pointed out, remembering how pleased her mother had been to find that out.

"That doesn't mean he won't send someone back to Silverlode to send a telegram," Dane said and pulled away from her. Leaning forward, he tapped his fingers together while he tried to figure out some way to save the situation. "Those telegraph lines are still in fine shape. And Judge Garrison is just the type to do something like that. He can be disgustingly thorough about such matters."

"Do you think he'd really do that?" Dahlia asked in a strangled voice, aware of what the reverend would have to say about them, especially after they had left owing the church all that money. "Do you think he would actually send a telegram?"

When Dane pressed his eyes closed to reorganize his thoughts, he could see his fortune slipping away as well as his one chance to ruin Clint's life forever. "If that man has any doubts at all about the authenticity of those letters, he will."

Dahlia leaned forward to better see his expression. "It could be he won't have any doubts. My mother can be quite convincing you know. And it will be her word against Angela's."

Not if Angela fails to show up to give her side of it, Dane thought and his body slowly relaxed as the perfect solution to their problem presented itself.

"It's late," he said, reaching immediately for the reins. "I had better get you back before your aunt—I mean before your mother starts to worry about you."

"Oh, but she won't worry about me," Dahlia said in an obvious attempt to stay awhile longer. "Not as long as I'm with you."

Which just goes to show how foolish the old bat really is, Dane thought as he sent the carriage forward with a lurch.

Clint held onto the rope even after he had found secure footing near the bottom of the ravine close to the shattered wreckage of the stagecoach. Angela's trunk had to be around there somewhere.

It had taken him two days to finally locate the wreckage in all that undergrowth. That did not leave him much time to search for those papers. First he checked the hull, but as expected, the inside was empty. He then searched the surrounding area, hoping to catch sight of the trunk, but all he found was a splintered crate and a broken shotgun. Obviously the trunk had fallen out much higher up.

Starting to panic, aware he had less than twenty-four hours to locate Angela's belongings and be back in Clear Creek in time for the hearing, he started the slow climb upward, pausing every few dozen feet to search the incline for other pieces of wreckage.

"Where's Angela?" Amos asked in a hushed voice when he saw Sadie enter the sheriff's office alone. He leaned closer to her so no one else could overhear their conversation. "I figured she'd be coming over with you."

Sadie glanced around the room with a worried frown. "I dona know where she is. She was not in her room when I stopped in to see about her this morning. I had hoped she was already here."

"I've been here for well over an hour and I haven't seen hide nor hair of her," Amos said. His face wrinkled with obvious concern. "Clint neither."

"There's Thomas," Sadie said, noticing Clint's father standing in the far corner talking with Angela's lawyer: a tall, thin man of Italian descent with piercing green eyes and immaculate clothes. "Maybe he knows where they are."

Amos shook his head. "Nope. I already asked him about Clint. He said he hasn't seen his son since Friday night when he came into town to see Angela. He said he figured he'd taken a room at the hotel so he could be near her during these last couple of days. He's just as worried as we are."

Sadie looked next at Julia and Dahlia, who both sat primly in their seats while their lawyers went over some last minute details with them. "Ye dona think they kidnapped the two of them, do ye? They look capable of many foul acts, but surely kidnapping is not among them."

"I don't know what to think, Sadie. It's not like either Clint or Angela to be late to something this important."

They both turned with hopeful expressions when they heard the door open behind them, but their hopes were immediately dashed when they saw Judge Garrison standing in the entrance instead of Angela or Clint.

"Sorry I'm late," Judge Garrison said, taking his hat off his graying head and hooking it over one of the remaining wall pegs. "But I had a hard time getting anyone to serve me breakfast."

"That's all right," Tony Andrews said, stepping away from Tom to greet the judge. "My client seems to be having a problem getting here, too."

Again the door opened, and again Amos and Sadie turned hoping to see either Angela or Clint, and again they were disappointed when instead Dane Tapley strode in, followed almost immediately by Richard Grissom, who was carrying a large book.

"Well, I hope your client gets here pretty soon," Garrison said and pulled his watch out of his vest pocket to have a look. "I was supposed to get this show underway fifteen minutes ago." He glanced at Walter Dedbyrd, a short, stocky man, who was at the moment bent over his clients offering last minute instructions. "I'll give her until nine o'clock. But if she's not here by then, I'll have to assume she has flown the coop and start without her."

Tony's smile was polite but did not quite reach the depths of his green eyes. "Thank you, sir. I'm sure she'll be here by then." He then let out a worried breath and returned to the area where he had left Tom.

"I don't know what to think," he said to Tom in a voice low enough so that no one else could hear. "Miss Langford didn't say anything to me about being late."

"Are you sure she understood she was supposed to be here at eight-thirty?" Tom asked, waving across the room for Amos and Sadie to join them.

"I told her to be here by ten after eight so we'd have time to go over everything we wanted to say one last time," he said and shook his head with concern. "Perhaps Judge Garrison is right. Perhaps she did run away. Maybe I misjudged her."

"No," Tom said firmly. "Something has happened and evidently it involves Clint, too. I'm going out looking for them."

"I'm going with you," Amos said, having caught the last of the conversation. He looked at Tony with a frustrated scowl. "Try to stall them as long as you can."

"I'll do the best I can," Tony promised but lifted his hands in the air to show how little control he had. "But if she's not here soon, I think we very well may have lost this case. Without Angela here to testify, I have nothing to disprove their claims. And my only other witness was Clint and he's not here either."

For the next fifteen minutes, Sadie and Tony stood in the corner with their eyes on the door, getting their hopes up each time it opened only to be disappointed again and again.

Shortly after nine o'clock, Tony approached the judge, who was seated at the sheriff's desk talking with Horace Jones, and asked for another ten minutes, relieved and a little surprised when the judge granted the extra time.

Finally at nine-twenty, Walter Dedbyrd came forward and demanded that the proceedings begin.

"It has been nearly an hour. If Miss Ruby Stillrod truly intended to be a part of these proceedings, she would be here by now," he said and planted his hands on his hips to show how annoyed he was with the delay.

"I object," Tony said, though the hearing had officially not begun. "Until proven otherwise, I would prefer Mr. Dedbyrd refer to my client as the alleged Angela Langford number one."

"Whatever," Walter muttered, rolling his eyes toward the ceiling. "But whoever she is, she has had plenty of time to get here. I think we've waited long enough. Let's get this thing underway."

Judge Garrison glanced from one man to the other, then shrugged. "I agree. We've waited long enough. Walter, let me hear what your clients have to say first, then I'll give Tony plenty of time for a rebuttal. Maybe his client will be here by then."

Aware that time had run out, Tony bit his lower lip and returned to his seat where he listened carefully to everything Julia Stanton had to say, which turned out to be plenty.

After nearly half an hour of explaining the letters and reading excerpts aloud, she finally broke into tears and pleaded with the judge to do what was right and declare her niece the rightful heir to Samuel's estate.

"It is obvious that my Angela is the real Angela," she said, dabbing at her eyes with a twisted handkerchief. "If that other woman was telling the truth, she'd be here. But as you can see, she is not. She is too afraid of being thrown in jail for what she tried to do."

"I object," Tony said, for what had to be the dozenth time during Julia Stanton's testimony. "Although I have

428

no idea why my client is not here, it cannot be assumed that it is because she fears being found guilty of fraud."

"Then why else would she stay away?" Julia snapped, coming out of her tearful mode long enough to let her annoyance be seen. "I'll tell you why. Because she's afraid of all those nasty lies catching up with her. Afraid she'll be arrested and spend the rest of her life in jail."

The judge nodded that he agreed, but did not go as far as to say so aloud. "Do you have anything else to say? Anything else to prove your niece is who she says she is?"

"Just those letters and that photograph of her when she was but a small child," she said and stood to lean forward over the desk to point to the profile of the child in Samuel Langford's arms. "As any man with clear sight can see, that is my precious Angela."

The judge squinted as if attempting to find the similarities, but the child's face was dimmed by Samuel's shadow. "Walter, do you have any other witnesses?"

"Yes. First I'd like for Angela to say something on her own behalf, then I'd like for Richard Grissom to come forward and verify that the man in the photograph is indeed Samuel Langford."

"There'll be no need for that. I can see for myself that it's Sam Langford." He then looked at Dahlia and smiled. "My dear, do you have anything you'd like to add to your aunt's testimony?"

"I object," Tony put in quickly. "It has not been established that this woman is truly an aunt."

Judge Garrison nodded an agreement. "Very well." He again looked at Dahlia. "Do you have anything you'd like to add? And keep in mind that this is a court of law and you must speak the truth."

Dahlia looked to Dane for encouragement, then slowly stepped forward. "Just that I did not intend to let my father believe I was dead forever. Just as soon as I was of a legal age, I planned to write him a letter telling him the truth."

At that moment the door clattered open and to everyone's surprise, in walked Clint. He glanced around for Angela, but when he did not see her, he headed straight toward the judge.

"What was that she was saying?" he asked, nodding toward Dahlia with a condemning glare. "Something about the *truth?*"

"Clint," Tom said, so relieved to see his son it did not occur to him that he was interrupting the proceedings. "Where have you been?"

"Out looking for these," he said and held up a small packet of yellowed papers tied together with a rotting piece of thread and a weather-beaten black Bible with faded gold lettering.

Dahlia gasped when she recognized Angela's Bible and looked at her mother worriedly.

"And what are those?" the judge asked, seemingly unconcerned that someone had just interrupted his court.

Julia immediately rushed to Walter's side and whacked him on the shoulder.

"I object," Walter said, rising immediately, as if suddenly coming awake. "This man has not been introduced to the court."

"Very well," Judge Garrison said, then turned to look at Tony. "Who is he?"

"Clint Rutledge, a friend of my client."

The judge's eyes widened. "That's Clint Rutledge?" He looked at him with renewed interest. "I've heard a lot about you, son."

Clint had no doubt. "I hope you won't hold my past reputation against me."

"That depends. What do you have there?"

"I object!" This time it was Julia herself who spoke. "This man has obviously been sent her here to confuse matters. He should not be allowed to speak."

The judge looked at her with a curiously raised brow. "Madam, it is not up to you to object or concede. That is up to your lawyer."

"Then *he* objects," she snapped, crossing her arms in a show of defiance.

"On what grounds?" Walter said, clearly confused by what was going on.

"I don't know what grounds. *You* are the lawyer."

Walter shook his head. "But I don't see any legal reason why this man should not be able to speak. It's Mr. Andrews turn to call witnesses anyway. Besides, what could *he* possibly have to say that could sway Judge Garrison's opinion in any way? We've already proved our case."

"It's not what I have to say. It's what I have brought to show you," Clint went on, not giving Julia another chance to speak. He waved the papers and the Bible in the air again. "I think these should prove to everyone who is telling the truth."

"And what exactly do you have there?" the judge asked again.

"Angela Langford's birth certificate, the letters she found in Julia Stanton's possession indicating that Mrs. Stanton was receiving money as a result of all the lies she had told, and the family Bible which has a description of Angela written in Samuel's own hand." He met Julia's gaze directly. "Seems the real Angela Langford has raven black hair and laughing gray eyes. Hardly a description fitting that young woman there."

"And I have found a similar description of her in Samuel's private journal," Richard Grissom said, speaking up for the first time since the proceeding started.

"That's not true. Th-they are lying." Julia said as she cut her gaze to Dahlia, but when she looked at the grim expression on the judge's face, she knew he no longer believed her. "Okay. It's true," she said, her whole body suddenly trembling. "This is not Angela Langford. This is my own daughter, Dahlia Stanton." Tears filled her eyes when she then added, "But please, judge, hear me out before making *any* final decisions." She glanced about at the people in the room and saw how they all looked at her. "But can't you please clear the courtroom first? Some of what I have to say is a little—a little— well, personal."

The judge had noticed the look of relief on Clint's face when she had hurried forward to have her say. Curious to find out exactly what was going on, he leaned back in his chair and shook his head. "No, the people in this room have a right to hear what you have to say. Your lies have affected each one of them in some way. Therefore they have a right to hear the truth. Just what *is* that truth?"

Julia dabbed at her eyes with a handkerchief she had seemed to have produced out of nowhere. "The truth is that Dahlia is also Samuel's daughter."

The judge's eyebrows rose a notch but he said nothing to interrupt her tearful confession.

"Back when I was very young and very naive, not much older than my own daughter here, I met and fell in love with Samuel Langford. He was so tall and handsome, and knew all the right things to say to turn a young girl's head. And although I knew it was wrong, I adored him so much that I went into his arms willing, thinking we would eventually be wed."

Feeling the shame behind such a confession, Julia pulled her gaze off the judge and placed it on the far wall. "Problem was, Sam did not feel as strongly about me as I felt about him and about that same time he met my cousin, Virginia, and fell in love with her right off. By the time I discovered I was carrying his child, he and Virginia were already married and as fate would have it she, too, was carrying his child."

Julia turned to look at Dahlia's startled face and lifted a trembling hand to the base of her throat. "I'm so sorry, Dahlia. I know I should have told you. But when Zachariah agreed to marry me and claim you as his own child, I promised him I wouldn't tell the truth to a soul."

Tears filled her eyes as she remembered the noble gesture. "And after he died, God rest his tired old soul, with Sam and Ginny happily married and living in another state, there was no reason to reveal the truth to anyone but Samuel, which I did through a letter." Her nostrils flared at the memory and she returned her attention to the judge. "But a lot of good that did. Sam did not believe he was her father and refused to claim her in any way."

"But I don't understand why you told Samuel that his real daughter was dead, when obviously she was very much alive," the judge said, trying to piece all the facts together as best he could.

Julia's whole body shook but she still managed to hold her head proudly. "Because I was hurt by what he'd done and decided that if he would not claim both his daughters, then he deserved to have neither." She lifted her chin higher. "Let it be known that I am also

433

the one who decided to come here and try to get our hands on some of Samuel's money. Dahlia had nothing to do with it. I realize I'm guilty of fraud and if anyone should go to jail for what has been done, it should be me. But, in truth, I felt Dahlia deserved the inheritance as much as Angela. Perhaps more, since she was his first born."

"Whether or not anyone is arrested for fraud will be left up to the real Angela. If she decides to press charges, then I'm afraid you'll both be subject to arrest. But if she decides to let the matter drop, then you will both be free to go, which I would advise you to do. Go as far away from here as possible."

Julia closed her eyes again. She knew Angela hated them both, and rightfully so.

Dahlia sat staring at her mother with the palest expression, too overwhelmed by what she had just learned to realize that Dane now leaned forward in the chair directly behind her with a revived interest.

"So in truth, Dahlia and Angela are both Samuel Langford's daughters," he said aloud, clearly pleased with the fact. "Then they are both heirs to his money."

"Not exactly," the judge put in, having already realized that part. "Even if what Mrs. Stanton says is true, and even if there is proof to back it, Angela is still the legal offspring and Dahlia is not. The only way Dahlia can claim any of the inheritance is if Angela agrees to share it out of the sheer kindness of her heart, or if Angela should die for some reason, which would mean everything would go to her half-sister. That is unless Angela is married by then or has a will stating otherwise."

Dane smiled. "Then *everything* would go to Dahlia?"

Clint felt an icy chill skitter down his spine and again

434

he scanned those seated about the sheriff's office. "Where *is* Angela?"

"Nobody seems to know," Amos said, and looked at Tom worriedly. "She never showed up in court this morning. Maybe she went out looking for you. She was very concerned when all of a sudden you quit coming by."

"Didn't Dustin Buchanan come by with my message?"

"Not that I know nothing about."

Dane saw a ripe opportunity and quickly stood. "He's right. The last I saw of her, which was right after sun-up, she was headed out of town toward your house," he said, repressing a grin. "I figured she was probably headed out to find you like your friend said. But now that you've told us you were off searching that wreckage, I don't know what to think."

"The gunman's got her," Amos said, his eyes filled with fear.

"What gunman?" Horace Jones asked, coming forward to find out more.

"The gunman that's been following Clint around for months now, just waiting for an opportunity to drop him," Amos said, already headed for the door. "Come on. We got to get out there and find her."

Having heard the panic in Amos's voice, all the men in the room cleared out, each heading immediately for his horse or the livery. Even Dane. And within a very few minutes, they had all set out toward Clint's house, eager to find some clue to Angela's whereabouts.

435

Chapter Thirty-One

Dane waited until all the other riders were well ahead of him before reining his horse and turning in an entirely different direction. He did not have much time. Not if he wanted to keep Dahlia from going to jail and losing her last chance of inheriting all of Samuel Langford's money.

He knew that if he didn't kill Angela now, someone would eventually figure out where she was and rescue her, and that simply would not do. Not only would she tell everyone that he was the one who had kidnapped her to keep her from testifying, she would go right ahead and marry Clint Rutledge, which would make him the next in line to inherit all that money.

Unless he hurried and did a clean job of killing her, he knew Clint would end up with everything and he and Dahlia would end up with nothing.

Clint had rushed ahead of the others so he could pull off the road without being noticed. He waited until everyone had passed, including Dane, then followed him at a safe distance.

Although there was no way to be sure, he felt that Dane was somehow involved with Angela's sudden disappearance. And when he saw Dane suddenly take off in a new direction as if the hounds of hell were snapping at his heels, he felt for certain that Dane was involved. But because he knew Dane would never lead him to her if for any reason he sensed he was being followed, Clint waited a full two minutes before starting to trail him.

Although his stomach was clenched with apprehension, he did not sense true fear until Dane's trail led him to a small, swift moving creek where horse tracks were prominent on one side but nowhere to be found on the other.

Not knowing which direction Dane might have taken, Clint had to choose. Either north or south. Unfortunately, he chose south.

Angela heard the sound of a horse approaching from the south and knew Dane had returned. Although she had worked and worked with the ropes, hoping to free herself before he could return, she had been unable to break loose and was still tied to the chair.

Frustrated to the point of tears, she tried one last time to force out the gag and break the bonds, but all she succeeded in doing was to cause her wrists to bleed.

"Stop that," Dane said when he entered the front door of the otherwise deserted shack and found her wriggling like a bound animal. "I don't have time to go chasing you down."

Angela tried to offer a biting retort, but found it impossible with the foul-tasting rag stuffed deep into her mouth.

"Too bad you weren't in court this morning," Dane said, as if holding a casual conversation with her while he hurriedly gathered anything that might prove he had ever been in the small cabin. "You'd be amazed at how everything turned out."

Again Angela tried to answer, but the words did not get passed the filthy rag.

Curious to hear what she had to say, he stepped over and loosened the gag just enough that she could push the cloth out of her mouth with her tongue.

"You won't get away with this," she said, her voice trembling with anger. "I don't care what the verdict was. I'll demand a new trial."

"Oddly enough, the verdict was in your favor," Dane said with a perverse laugh. "Julia Stanton finally broke down and told the truth."

"She did?" Angela found that hard to believe.

"That's because Clint had her dead to rights and she knew it."

"Clint did?" Despite the danger she was in, she felt a glimmer of warmth. "Clint was there?"

"Brandishing your father's Bible like a fired-up preacher at a revival. That fool went to all the trouble to climb down into that ravine and find all the proof he needed to get that aunt of yours started on telling the truth. Too bad for you the truth turned out to be that you and her daughter just happened to have had the same father. What that means is that just as soon as I get you out of the way for good, Dahlia will inherit everything anyway. As your half-sister."

"You are lying," Angela said, not about to believe anything this deranged man had to say.

"Have it your way," Dane said, sounding awfully

438

cheerful for someone who had just been called a liar. "It doesn't matter to me what you believe."

Having said that, he disappeared outside. When he returned, he carried several pieces of firewood.

"What are you doing?" She asked, wondering at his peculiar behavior, though nothing he could answer would surprise her.

"You look a little chilled," Dane said, chuckling at his own cleverness. "Being the kind person that I am, I thought I'd start a fire for you." He then dropped the firewood into the small fireplace and arranged it carefully. "Unfortunately, I could not find any kindling so I guess I'll have to use the kerosene from that lantern over there to help get this thing started."

He hurried to the lantern someone had left on the table and quickly unscrewed the cap. Turning the lantern on its side, he allowed the kerosene to pour out the side spout onto the floor, creating a long, wet trail from the table to the fireplace, making sure to cross directly in front of Angela.

"There, now, that should do it, don't you think?" he asked, and smiled proudly at his own handiwork. "As old and as weather-beaten as this place is, it'll go up like a tinderbox."

"You can't do this," Angela cried. Her heart hammered wildly when she saw him reach into his shirt pocket and come out with a small box of sulphur matches.

"Oh, but I can," he said then threw back his head and laughed.

"You are insane," she gasped, then started screaming at the top of her lungs.

"Go ahead and scream. No one can hear you."

Although she knew he was right, it was her last and

only hope so she screamed louder still, so loud and so hard she barely heard him when he struck the match and tossed it at the trail of kerosene. "Goodbye, Angela dear. It has been nice knowing you."

He waited to make sure the kerosene had caught before closing the door and hurrying away from the cabin. He did not want to be anywhere nearby when the smoke was finally spotted.

Unable to believe what had just happened, Angela watched the flames with morbid fascination, aware of how quickly the flooring itself had caught fire. A thick, black smoke filled the room almost immediately, making it hard for her to breathe, but it was not until the flames trailed up the side of the table where Dane had tossed the lantern and caused it to explode into a blue ball that she started to struggle again.

Pulling her arms with renewed vigor, she tried again to break free of her bonds and surprised herself when she suddenly pulled one arm loose. Not taking time to access the damage done to her wrist, she started working with the other ropes, hoping yet to free herself before the flames consumed her.

Sweating profusely as much from the fear that gripped her as from the heat, she concentrated on the rope that still held her other hand captive behind her back, aware she had started to make progress. As a result of all the smoke, she coughed spasmodically, but did not let that hamper her. She knew she had a very few minutes before either the smoke or the flames overtook her, ending her last chance at freedom.

Aware that the fire was eating away at the oxygen she needed to stay alive, she felt a great sense of relief when suddenly she was able to pull her other hand free. Still coughing from the black smoke that was now so thick she could no longer see her way to the door, she bent forward and worked with the ropes that held her legs together, glad to discover they had not been as carefully tied. Within seconds, she was completely free.

Unable to see the door, but knowing the general direction, Angela reached for her skirt so she could pull part of it up over her nose and filter out some of the smoke that caused her to cough so much. But she barely had it halfway to her face when suddenly she coughed especially hard, and then her lungs refused to take in another breath.

Filled with panic, she pounded on her chest in an effort to force herself to breathe, but her body refused to draw in another ounce of the foul air. The last thing she remembered before the curling smoke turned into total darkness was stumbling toward the door, thinking that maybe she could make it before she passed out completely. Just before she lost all consciousness, she had the strange sensation of strong, warm arms encircling her. Her last conscious thought was that Amos's angel had come to claim her in place of him.

"Angela? What happened? Wake up."

The familiar voice came from far away.

"Angela? Are you all right? Where's Dane?"

The questions came from somewhere in the foggy distance and pulled at her from the roaring darkness that surrounded her. Although she could not focus enough to understand what had happened, she felt someone holding her.

"Angela. Please. Try to open your eyes."

Angela did as the concerned voice ordered and forced her eyelids apart. At first all she saw was a wall of gray, but slowly the gray separated and the shape of a man came through. "Clint? My darling. Is it really you? I thought—"

He held her close. "Yes. It's really me. You're safe now, sweetheart. But tell me what happened. Are you all right?"

Angela thought about that last question while she slowly focused on Clint's frightened face. She knew she was in pain, but could not pinpoint exactly where she hurt. It was as if her mind wanted no part of the rest of her, but slowly, her wits gathered about her and she remembered the fire. Her heart exploded with a renewed burst of terror. *"Dane! Where's Dane?"*

She looked about her quickly and immediately noticed the burning cabin several dozen yards away. The whole structure was ablaze.

"I was hoping you could tell me where he was," Clint said, his gaze scanning the dense woods that surrounded them on three sides.

"I don't know. I don't remember. I-I think he rode off right after he started the fire."

Clint glanced at her briefly, but gave most of his attention to their surroundings, aware that Dane could be out there anywhere. "Do you think you can ride?"

"I don't know. I think I can," she said, but grimaced when she tried to sit up. Suddenly she knew exactly where her pain was. It was in her chest and in the dead center of her forehead.

"Wait. I'll help you," Clint said and moved first to a kneeling position, then slowly pulled her to her feet as he stood.

"I'm so glad you came along when you did," Angela

said and again looked at the burning cabin while she allowed Clint to guide her toward his horse. "I'd be dead by now if you hadn't found me."

Clint looked at her, baffled by her last comment, but decided she was still talking out of her head. "I'm just glad you were able to get out. I hate to think what I would have found if you hadn't.'

Angela's forehead notched. "But I didn't get out. I remember that much. I couldn't breathe. I collapsed on the floor. You pulled me out."

"No I didn't. When I got here the shack was completely encased in fire and you were already lying right there where I found you. Just as pretty as you please, with your hands folded over you as if you had simply lain down and gone to sleep."

"But that's impossible," she said, coming to an abrupt halt to try to figure out what had really happened. "I never made it to the door. It was still closed when I collapsed."

"Well, that proves you are wrong. Look at that cabin for yourself. The door is open."

Angela was amazed to see he was right. Even through all the fire and smoke, she could tell the door stood wide open.

"But I don't understand."

Clint shrugged, believing she still was not thinking clearly and that it would eventually all come to her again. "Come on. We have to get out of here before Dane returns."

Angela agreed. Their first consideration should be for their safety. "Help me up. I don't think I have the strength to climb into the saddle by myself."

Clint slid his hands around her waist and lifted her high enough to swing her leg over and reach for the saddle horn. He had bent forward to capture the reins when suddenly he heard her scream his name.

"Clint!"

Knowing instinctively that she had spotted Dane, he reached for his rifle at the same time he dropped to his knees so he could see in all directions.

"Where is he?"

"Over there!"

He glanced up at her hand then looked off in the direction she had indicated and felt his whole body go limp with relief. It was Dane all right. But he was lying face down on the ground near the edge of the woods. Evidently after having fallen from his horse during his attempt to get away.

"Stay put," he ordered, then made the long walk to where Dane lay, not certain he believed such good fortune possible. He kept his eyes trained on Dane's hands, watching for any sign of movement.

Angela watched while Clint cautiously knelt beside Dane's body, felt for a pulse, then rolled him over.

"Is he still alive?"

Clint stood again and slowly turned to look at her, his face drained of all blood. "Not hardly."

Feeling it safe now, she took hold of the reins and started the horse in that direction. "What did he do, break his neck?"

"Not just his neck," Clint said, then held his hand up to stop her from coming any closer. "No. Don't come over here. You don't need to see this. His body is mangled something awful. It's like a pack of wild animals got a hold of him." He then glanced down and noticed the same strange footprints he'd seen at the other line shack.

"Mangled? How could he be mangled?"

Rather than tell her his honest suspicion, knowing how preposterous it would sound even to her, he shook his head to clear his thoughts, then headed towards her. "My guess is that when he fell from his horse, he got his boot caught in the stirrup and was dragged."

"Oh how awful," Angela said, and meant it. Even as cruel and conniving as Dane had been, it was a horrible way for him to die.

"I think we'd better ride out and see if we can find Horace. He's going to want to see this."

Angela waited until Clint had settled in behind her and they were on their way before saying anything else. "I want to thank you for what you did." She closed her eyes and leaned back against him, relieved to feel his strong arms around her.

"I told you. I didn't do anything. You were already out of that house when I first rode up."

"No, I mean for going to all the trouble of finding my father's Bible. Before Dane left, he told me all about what happened at the hearing."

"Oh, *that*," Clint said and chuckled. "You know I'd sure like to see your aunt's face when she finds out there was nothing in that Bible to hurt her case."

"What do you mean there was nothing? I already told you, there was a description of me when I was a young girl in the back."

"That description was gone. The rain and snow had streaked the ink so badly those pages written by your father were just one big messy blotch."

"I don't understand. Then why did Julia confess?"

"Well, I guess I sort of failed to mention the fact that the ink had smeared. Besides, Richard Grissom had found similar descriptions of you in that journal your father kept, so either way, we had her."

445

"Then it's official?" she asked, turning in the saddle so she could face him. "I'm Angela Langford again?"

"For now," he said and bent forward to kiss her smoke smudged nose. "Until we can get back to town and convince that judge to change your name to Mrs. Clint Rutledge."

Angela's face lit with joy. "Can he do that?" she asked with tears already in her eyes. "Well, of course he can! He's a judge."

"I know you were hoping for a big church wedding with lots of flowers and lots of lace, but I don't want to take any more chances of losing you. I want to marry you right away."

"But I thought you wanted to wait because of that man you said has been following you."

Clint thought about that. "Don't ask me why, but I think I've figured out who's been following me and it wasn't a gunman after all."

"Didn't I tell you?" she said, smiling to know so many of their troubles were suddenly over. "It was all in your head."

He paused for a moment while he recalled the rest of that conversation. "The part I remember is when you promised me that if I'd just agree to marry you come May, you would stay away from any danger."

"I think my actual words were that if I didn't, may I be swept away by a villainous fire and be burned to an ash."

Clint's dark eyes widened just before he turned to take one last look at the smoke billowing into the blue sky above them. "Make me one more promise."

"And what's that?"

"Promise that in the future you will pick your words just a little more carefully."

Assured now that there *was* to be a future for them, Angela laughed as she leaned her cheek against Clint's strong shoulder. "I promise that the next words you will hear from me will be *I do.*"

Acknowledgments

This book is dedicated in part to an unknown young man and his family who gave me the "gift of life."

I would also like to thank the following people who played such a large role in my modern day miracle:

Doctor Michale Carnahan and the staff at Memorial Hospital of Southern Oklahoma;

Doctor Larry Pennington; the transplant coordinator, Beverly Bahr, and her dedicated staff; Mr. Brewster, Mr. Sadler, and Mr. Ross. Ruth Tatryk, Chaplin Dennis, Mr. Shortz, and Oklahoma Memorial Hospital.

Also, to my dear husband and family for giving me so much love and support. To my brother Jerry Eubanks, who refused to take "No" for an answer. To my dear friend, Rosalyn Alsobrook, who gave more than a helping hand. To my sister-in-law, Gloria "George" Haught, who gave so unselfishly of her time. To all of the readers and writers who so generously helped.

I owe all of you my life—and I am forever grateful.

And, a special plea to "you," if you have not signed a donor card, please consider it. Someone's life is depending on your gift. To learn more about giving the gift of life, please call the United Network for Organ Sharing (UNOS) at their national hotline number. 1-800-24DONOR.

Thank you
Jean Haught